A SPACE WITCH NOVEL

A SPARK IN SPACE

JANINA FRANCK

A SPARK IN SPACE: A Space Witch Novel

First Edition

Copyright @ 2021 by Janina Franck
www.janinafranck.com

Published by Snowy Wings Publishing,
PO Box 1035, Turner, OR 97392, USA
www.SnowyWingsPublishing.com

Cover design: KimGDesign
https://www.kimg-design.com
Stock images: Bigstock

Art: Alex van Gore
https://alex-van-gore.wixsite.com/portfolio

ISBN (e-book): 978-1-952667-10-7
ISBN (paperback): 978-1-952667-12-1
ISBN (hardback): 978-1-952667-11-4

To Orion

&

To Zerah

Part 1

Chapter 1

"*TABEA.*"

Calliope's tendrils of energy carefully poked at Tabea's mind, and, when she didn't react, moved farther, weaving together with her synapses, joining the electricity pulsing to and from her brain.

Tabea awoke with a start, gasping for air. Her heart beat at the speed of sound and every one of her muscles was tensed, ready to jump up and run.

After a few moments of her eyes flitting around the room, frantically scanning her surroundings, her breathing finally slowed, and her shoulders relaxed a little.

"I wish you wouldn't do that," she growled and scowled at the room in general. Ruffling through her short, brown hair with one hand, she swung her legs out of bed and got ready for the day, starting by washing her face.

"*I wouldn't have to, if you could get up on your own,*" Calliope said snippily, her voice directly broadcast into Tabea's mind as usual.

Tabea was too busy suppressing a yawn to respond.

"*You're overdoing it,*" Calliope continued, although

more sympathetically, and concern was tinting her words. *"You're taking on more than you can handle."*

Tabea watched herself buttoning up her uniform in the mirror, making sure to leave her tags underneath the jacket but over her gray T-shirt. "I have to. I want to make officer, and I can't rely on my powers alone."

The baggy, dark green uniform didn't suit her at all. It made her look pale and even smaller than she already was. Nevertheless, she couldn't be prouder to wear it. After all, it symbolized that she was truly and undeniably a member of Earth's star fleet.

"I don't understand why you need to take that exam anyway," Calliope complained. *"You can single-handedly do more than all of Humanity put together."*

Tabea raised an eyebrow.

"Will *be able to do more, anyway,"* Calliope added, correcting herself. *"When you've learned the full extent of your powers."*

"Which we have to keep secret," Tabea reminded her friend. "So they don't lock me up. And therefore, I have to take that exam."

Ready to go, Tabea finally left her quarters and made her way to the bridge, where the commanding officers were already gathered, covering the controls.

"Tabea!" Callaghan, their captain and Tabea's mentor during her time at the Academy, waved her over. As per usual, he stood tall and proud, his own uniform fitting as if it had been designed specifically for him. His skin tone was not much darker than her own, a dark brown tone, and his sharp blue eyes created a striking contrast to his black, yet silver-lined hair. A small scar just above his lip completed his imposing appearance.

As she made her way to his side, the head engineer, Hammond, winked at her conspiratorially. She returned the smile.

"Captain." She saluted Callaghan upon arriving by his side.

Both he and Hammond snorted out in laughter. Chuckles could be heard from other officers as well, though none of them took their eyes from their screens.

"Two years aboard the ship, and *now* you start? Give me a break!" Callaghan chuckled.

Tabea broke into a grin and shrugged.

"I figured I'd give it a try. Guess I should stick to old habits."

"And you were hoping to see him blush," Calliope chimed in.

"Would you be quiet?" Tabea chided her silently, speaking only in her head. *"I'm trying to talk to my da-captain here."*

"Out of curiosity, how often have you called him your father to his face?"

"None of your beeswax," Tabea retorted. After a moment, she added, *"Twice. But he only noticed once."*

"That's what you think."

Suddenly, Tabea became aware of Callaghan closely scanning her face. His brows were furrowed with concern.

"What is she saying?" he asked, referring to Calliope.

Tabea sighed inwardly. It was both a blessing and a curse that she was the only member of the crew with a voice in her head. A voice belonging to their starship, the *Calliope,* a unique feat of terrestrial engineering that incorporated an alien energy source — the only ship of its kind. And, as far as Tabea knew, the only ship with consciousness.

"She's being annoying," she said, intending for Calliope to hear as well. "No need for alarm."

She'd hoped he would leave things at that, but his concerned expression remained.

"Have you been sleeping well?" he asked. "Are you feeling all right?"

Startled, Tabea nodded. "Yes, why?"

"You're awfully pale."

Tabea sighed. "I slept fine," she said. "But apparently not very much."

"*Tell him what I said,*" Calliope pressed.

Tabea rolled her eyes.

"And Callie thinks I'm overdoing it, studying for the exam and training my powers. She thinks I should only focus on one of them and save my energy."

A small smirk appeared on Callaghan's lips.

"I don't think I need to guess which one she thinks is more important."

Tabea pursed her lips and nodded.

"I can't say I entirely disagree, though," he continued. "You have clearly been overdoing it a bit."

More to himself than her, he added, "Maybe some sort of scheduling, a timetable…"

Tabea grimaced. He made it sound like she was back at the Academy!

"Oh, let the lass decide for herself, Jim!" Hammond interjected. "She's old enough to look after herself and make her own choices."

The gray-haired, full-bearded man gave her a thumbs-up.

Valeria Shinay, the navigator, swiveled around in

her chair, her long, blonde hair tied in her usual side-braid.

"Agreed," she said, smiling at Tabea with glittering brown eyes. "Besides, her astronomy lessons are going exceedingly well."

Grateful for their support, Tabea beamed at them both.

Unconvinced, Callaghan looked from one to the other but gave in with a sigh.

"Fine," he grumbled as he glanced at his screen. "Ah, perfect timing." He smirked up at Tabea. "Care to take the wheel?"

One glance at the radar told her all she needed to know. Returning his grin, she nodded and proceeded to the center of the room, her favorite place for exercises of this nature. Maneuvering through a small asteroid field like this should be a simple task.

Kneeling down, she placed both palms on the ground and closed her eyes, letting her energy, her essence, merge with the ship.

"*Ready?*" she asked Calliope.

"*Always,*" was the prompt response.

Tabea concentrated on the prickling sensation in her fingers, ignoring the static that was making her hair stand up, and focused on reaching into the ship, into the mundane wiring and electric currents, moving with them and spreading to the different controls, and then farther, weaving in and out to move toward the ship's core, the alien technology that was giving the ship its energy, and incidentally, Calliope's mind. Without hesitation, Tabea let her own consciousness merge with it so she felt and saw the same as Calliope.

Using the ship's radars, she detected every one of the

rocks hurtling through space and the relative distance between them. They were quite far apart from each other and even with the velocity they were at, maneuvering through them should be a simple feat.

Keeping in mind safety precautions, she raised the shields anyway and made the ship lunge forward. First a slight left, then a roll to the upper right, a quick bounce over another asteroid and then a dip and a side swivel. Dancing through the metallic rocks like a celestial ballerina, the *Calliope* was swiftly brought to the other side of the shower.

"*Well done*," Calliope said. "*You're getting better at this every day. I didn't even need to help this time.*"

Tabea smiled to herself, proud of her accomplishment.

"*Thanks.*"

She was about to disconnect when she noticed something strange. There were abnormal energy signals in the distance, flashing and sparking, and not rhythmically, either.

"*What's that?*" she asked Calliope, but the ship could give no answer. "*Move us closer to it so the monitors can show something conclusive,*" Tabea requested. "*I'll talk to Callaghan.*"

She severed her bond with Calliope, trusting the ship would do exactly as she had asked.

As she returned to the senses belonging to her body, she rose up quickly and swirled around to Callaghan, a sudden spell of dizziness almost making her fall over in the process. At least she didn't faint anymore after every merge with Calliope. When she had first discovered her abilities, that had been a real concern. Every action had required an enormous amount of mental energy from a quickly draining pool. However, like a muscle, she'd been able to train and increase her endurance with diligent practice.

Callaghan was smiling brightly at her, clearly satisfied with her results.

"That was splendid!" he called out, but Tabea shook her head.

"There's something out there." She gasped, her breathing and heartbeat rapid.

Callaghan's demeanor immediately became serious.

"What is it?" he asked, scanning his screens.

Tabea shook her head again.

"We... We don't know. There are strange energy signals coming from it, irregular and varying in power. Callie is bringing us closer to it so we can make it out better."

Callaghan's frown deepened.

"Anything on the screens?" he bellowed at the officers.

Maya Glaucia, the arms and defense officer, was the first to respond.

"I see something, I think. There is an energy focus ahead of us. It's inconsistent, but... But it does look like it's getting stronger."

Hammond rushed over to her side.

"Let me see that!"

He glanced over the information on the screen and grew pale.

"We have to get out of here — and fast!" he yelled.

Callaghan was quick to react and turned to the pilot, Kyoko Akari, a short woman with straight, black, chin-length hair and dark eyes, who was waiting for his orders.

"Get ready for hyper speed backward!"

She nodded and busied herself at the controls.

"*It's a ship,*" Calliope informed Tabea. "*And it looks like its core was damaged. It'll blow up!*"

"A ship?" Tabea asked out loud. "Where is it from?"

"*See for yourself.*"

Calliope pulled Tabea into her systems, facilitating and speeding up the entry. Using her powers, Tabea shot energy out through the weapon's dock, doing her best not to get in the way of whatever the commanding officers were doing, and streamed across the empty space, crossing the distance easily to reach the dying ship.

Connecting with it was easy.

Energy was surging through all its systems, overpowering them. Tabea was swept along with it. Even though the energy was almost overwhelming her senses, Tabea was still able to recognize the engineering. She'd studied plenty of designs of ships like this back at the Academy after she'd changed from the pilot to the engineering track.

She checked the ship's mainframe. According to the data log, there'd been a fight recently, a fight that had left the ship badly damaged and killed all of its crew. The arms and defense systems had been used excessively, and the crew had attempted at least two hyper jumps to escape whatever peril had been coming for them. They hadn't even had enough time for a final captain's log entry before they'd all perished.

Except not *all* had perished.

While the ship's systems couldn't detect any life left aboard, Tabea could sense the fine traces of energy. It was weak, but even so, Tabea recognized the signature as one belonging to a living being.

Something was tugging at her. The energy pull of the ship was strong and like a magnet. It tried to draw her close, absorb her into the quickly growing hub.

She fought against the ship's suction, releasing herself, leaving behind only an order: *Use every ounce of power you have left to contain the energy leaks.*

She had to get back to the *Calliope*. She needed to let Callaghan know. Someone was still alive. Someone who could be saved and tell them what had happened here.

At the speed of light, she raced back into Calliope, and from there into her own body.

"We've received an SOS message!" Andrej Szkarisov, the coms officer, yelled out, his prosthetic hand moving even faster across his controls than the other one.

Callaghan's head whipped around. "An SOS? From where?"

"It's from the ship," Tabea chimed in, her heart racing. "It's the Sonata, from the Martian Colony, and there's still one survivor. I've told the ship to contain the energy leak for as long as possible."

Hammond rubbed his chin, his blue eyes flicking from one screen to another.

"That doesn't give us a lot of time," he mumbled.

"How long?" Callaghan asked.

The engineer shrugged. "Maybe two hours or so, probably less. That's not enough time to cross this distance, find a person, get them out, *and* get to a safe distance."

Callaghan grinded his teeth.

"We can't turn our backs on this. There is someone

we can save, and we *have* to find out what happened."

"According to the ship's log, they were attacked," Tabea added.

He nodded. "All the more reason for us to go."

"*Tabea.*" Calliope poked at her.

"*I know.*"

She whirled around to her mentor and saluted.

"Sir! Permission to do something reckless and dangerous, sir!"

Callaghan hesitated for a moment and gave her a long, serious look. She met his gaze steadily. She wasn't going to back down on this, and he knew it. After a moment of mental battling, his shoulders slackened, and he broke his eye contact.

"Don't you dare die," he growled.

"Yessir!"

As she ran to the nearest escape pod, she explained her plan to Calliope.

"*Make sure to give me an energy boost as soon as I've undocked. And start moving to a safer distance. I'll catch up.*"

"*Sure thing.*"

Tabea had just thrust herself into the pod when Shinay plopped down next to her.

"You didn't think we'd let you go on your own, did you?" she asked when she saw Tabea's confused expression. "Someone will need to pilot this thing while you're out cold."

Tabea realized there was no time to argue and even if there had been, this was a commanding officer. What argument could she possibly bring forth to change the woman's mind?

The pod undocked, and, as Tabea had requested,

Calliope used their main weapon's system to blast out exhaust energy to push them forward into the direction of the dying ship.

"I'll be relying on you," Tabea said to Shinay before closing her eyes. She let her energy stream into the pod and then blast through space to the other ship, connecting with it in a heartbeat.

Blast excess energy behind you, she ordered. *Steer toward us.*

The ship obeyed her order, creaking and unwilling. It was falling apart more with every second. Alarms were ringing out. Tabea disabled them. They weren't doing anyone any good anymore.

More and more areas of the ship were compromised with each second as leaks let out the breathable air and sections of the ship were collapsing in on themselves with the change in pressure.

Cursing in her mind, Tabea worked as fast as she could to locate the exact location of the survivor, hoping fervently that they were far enough away from the collapse that they would be able to get to them in time.

There.

The pod was fast approaching the ship. Reversing the polarization of her power, Tabea turned the ship into a magnet and then only used a small blast of energy to serve as cushioning for the docking of the pod.

Returning to her own body swiftly, she noticed that Shinay had already put on her spacesuit. While she busied herself with opening the latch, Tabea followed her example.

They pushed themselves through the halls with

speed, the gravity field having been deactivated. Tabea tried to ignore the sights all around her—the droplets of blood wafting through the spaces, the lifeless bodies of humans... The scratches, claw marks, and firearm impacts on everything she laid her eyes on. Even though she'd known that the *Sonata* had been attacked, she hadn't fully realized what that meant. It was only the pressure of limited time and her sense of purpose—knowing that she needed to save this one last remaining person—that carried her through.

Jumping straight ahead, they made it to the right area quickly: the entrance to the ship's busted escape pods. The survivor had clearly attempted to flee the ship before something must have happened to them. It was the only thing giving Tabea hope that they would already be wearing protective gear as she disabled the pressure lock and entered the room.

Her hopes were answered. A person in a spacesuit was floating limply in a corner, one leg tangled in some loose wiring.

The escape pods weren't only busted, their wirings had entirely burnt out, and one of them looked like it had already exploded, based on the scorch marks by the walls and the debris floating around.

They didn't waste time talking.

Shinay took the lead. She pushed herself off the doorframe and to the survivor, cutting them from the wiring and pulling them with her as she pushed herself off the ceiling back to where Tabea was waiting.

The loose connection that Tabea was maintaining with the ship told her that time was running out. Fast. A low tremble could already be felt in the walls as the ship struggled to keep the energy detained. She helped

Shinay bring the survivor back to their pod, closed the hatch, and reconnected fully with the dying ship. She created an electromagnetic field to push them apart while telling the ship to use its remaining resources to move as far in the opposite direction as was possible. Meanwhile, Shinay busied herself with the controls to maneuver the ship back toward the *Calliope*. Then they both stripped their suits to ease movement.

"Check his vital signs and injuries," Shinay ordered while she kept an eye on the pod's navigation system. Tabea didn't have to be told twice.

She took off the stranger's helmet, careful not to pull on their head too much. It revealed a freckled young man, only a few years older than her, with tousled, singed, ginger hair. She didn't contemplate his youth and luck to have survived whatever had destroyed his ship for more than an instant before she opened the rest of the suit.

The pulse on his neck felt normal, and when she moved him into a more stable position, he moaned slightly, and his eyelids fluttered.

Decisively, she cut open his suit with the army knife she kept in her pocket—engineering on a ship of the *Calliope*'s size meant often needing to cut and mend wires—and pulled it off him.

Shinay's yelling and the frantic beeping accompanied by bright red flashing made her stop in her tracks and whirl around to the controls before she had a chance to inspect the young man's wounds.

"It's happening!" Shinay shouted, yet her movements across the controls remained steady and methodical. "We're too close!"

Tabea, checking the screens giving her the rear

view, had her breath stuck in her throat.

Where the shipwreck had floated in the distance mere moments ago, a white, hot fireball was forming now. Forming and growing fast, extending out like a tumor, along with a rapidly approaching shockwave.

Her connection with the pod was instant.

Get us out of here – NOW!

Then the shockwave reached them.

Chapter 2

When Tabea came to, the other two were still knocked out.

There was no movement in her pod and barely any sounds aside from her own labored breathing. Every part of her body was screaming at her in agony as she pushed herself upright. Her forehead was throbbing with heat and pain, and a quick dab with her fingers made them come away red and sticky with blood. While she was aching all over, she didn't seem to have broken anything. She must have just been knocked about, although the nausea she was feeling might have also been indicative of a concussion.

She took a moment to just stand there, clutching the back of a chair for support.

The room was spinning around her, and she found it difficult to find her bearings. A glance out the window screens proved that they really were hurtling through space, tumbling over and over again. The constant spinning of far-off stars made her feel ill, so she quickly looked at something more stable—the floor just in front of her.

She took a deep breath to collect her scattered thoughts and ran her hand through her short, messy hair. It was a wonder they had made it out of the explosion alive in the first place, never mind racing through space uncontrollably without having sustained major life-threatening damage by some loose debris.

How long had they been traveling this way?

But first things first.

Tabea climbed into the pilot's seat and looked over the controls. She didn't have the energy to connect with the ship. There wasn't enough spark left in her right now.

Her vision was still blurry, but focusing her eyes so hard it burned, helped. A little. At the very least enough to tell that it had been about three hours since the explosion, and Calliope was nowhere near them. There was, however, a record of the final transmission from her crew, sent just before the wreck had blown up. Tabea figured they must have been too busy and concerned with their survival at the time to notice.

Listening to it could wait. Based on their coordinates, they weren't in danger of entering enemy territory in the near future, and the radar didn't show any sign of debris about to hit them.

She handled a lever and pressed a series of buttons to enable the thrusters to stop them from throwing themselves farther through space. Until they had a better idea of their own situation and Calliope's location, it was best to move about less.

Satisfied that the more immediate issues were dealt with, Tabea turned back to the other two, who were still sprawled across the floor.

Taking the first aid kit from one of the

compartments, she knelt next to Shinay and turned her onto her back, giving a little mental note of thanks for Shinay's thin frame, which considerably eased the act. She was breathing normally, but she had sustained a black eye and what seemed to Tabea like a broken wrist, based on the unnatural, sharp angle the hand pointed.

A surge of nausea made her turn away for a moment. Forcing herself to take deep, steady breaths, her eyes fell on the young man they had dragged from the *Sonata*. His clothes were torn, partly ripped and partly cut. Some gashes stretched along his forearms, as though he had tried to protect himself against an attack from a wild beast, and smears of grease lined his face, though from what, Tabea couldn't tell. His messy ginger hair was partly singed, only topped by the burn marks on his hands.

Focusing on the little details helped her calm down and she turned back to Shinay. Her lashes were flittering and Tabea could see the eyeballs move underneath. It was probably best to stabilize the wrist while Shinay was unconscious and wouldn't feel the pain as acutely. She grabbed one of the metal plates from the first aid kit and placed it on top of the wrist. Holding it in place with one hand, she grabbed Shinay's hand with the other and pulled sharply.

Shinay gasped awake with a yelp and jerked up. Her brown eyes were wide, and she was panting, her long, blonde hair come loose, now sticking to the sides of her face. Tabea acted quickly. She grabbed the bandage from the kit and wrapped it around Shinay's wrist and the metal plate, fastening it before the woman fully realized what was going on.

"We're okay," Tabea told her, trying to sound as calm and collected as possible. "The capsule is fine, and we still have enough fuel to make it a few days. We're in a stable position for the moment."

Shinay only made a non-comital sound approaching a whimper. Disoriented, she looked about her surroundings, eventually locking her gaze on Tabea.

She was awfully pale, even more so since she had woken up.

As she propped herself up and got to her feet slowly, Tabea steadied her as much as she could, leading her over to one of the chairs.

"Water?" Shinay croaked, barely audible. Her head was falling to the side, as though her neck were too weak to hold it up. Tabea looked around helplessly. They hadn't taken any extra provisions with them, and while she had been shown where the emergency rations were kept once during her initiation, that had been two years ago, and she'd never needed to think about that information again after that. Well, until now.

Her eyes fell on the young man, still lying unconscious on the floor. There was something more important to deal with first.

Kneeling down beside him, she checked his breathing and pulse. Both appeared normal. She quickly applied some bandages to his arms and spread some soothing cream across the burn marks on his hands. Then she rolled him onto his back and taking off her jacket, placed it underneath his head.

Now, back to water. She briefly closed her eyes and checked if she had recovered enough energy to attempt connecting with the pod. The answer was no. She would need to do this the old-fashioned way.

She considered asking Shinay, but she didn't seem in any state to give coherent answers. Instead, Tabea scanned the walls of the capsule. Somewhere there was sure to be a lever or a handle of some sort. She found it quicker than expected.

After a first failed attempt of opening the door to some basic toilet facilities, her second was met by success and she found the vacuum sealed bags of food and water. She grabbed three of the water pouches and opened one while returning to Shinay's side. Lifting it to Shinay's lips, she was careful not to force the water down her throat, only dripping in a little until she was able to suck on it herself.

Once Shinay seemed to have a hold on the water pouch, Tabea opened a second one for herself.

The first sip was magic. It seemed to flow across her parched tongue like a wild, sudden rain pouring down on a desert—by far not enough, but a wonderfully delicious taste of what might be to come. The second sip created longing, and the need for more was strong. The third sip was not so much as a sip as it was a gulp, washing new energy down her throat and into her arteries.

Far too soon, the pouch was empty and Tabea regretfully put it down. She could have gotten another one out of the reserves, of course, but she didn't want to waste it. After all, they might be stable for the moment, but there was no telling how long their current predicament would last.

At the very least, it had returned some of her energy to her. Enough that she found herself able to inspect her own wounds, which she had neglected up till this point.

Her body was aching, but she certainly didn't have any broken bones, well, except for her pinkie toe, perhaps. That one hurt especially every time she trusted it with any weight, but it was still a dull enough pain to ignore in the grand scheme of things. Bruises covered her body, and she was loath to think how those blue and green marks would look in a day or two. She grimaced at the mental image.

Then, finally, her head. The blood was beginning to thin and dry. As she tapped the skin around her forehead, trying to identify the size and depth of the wound, she determined that it must have been a laceration, potentially caused by getting knocked against one of the chairs or the controls. It wasn't very deep or wide, but it did hurt like a doozy.

Clenching her teeth, she disinfected the wound, ignoring the burning stinging sensation to the best of her ability before bandaging it. There wasn't anything better she could do for the moment.

By the time she was finished, Shinay seemed to be more receptible to conversation. She had turned to watch Tabea, her eyes carrying more strength in them than before.

The young man remained unconscious, though the steady rising and falling of his chest reassured Tabea.

Shinay gave a deep outlet of breath before straightening herself.

"Any pain-killers in there?" she asked, croaking and nodding toward the first aid kit.

Relieved that someone else was finally doing the thinking for her, Tabea reached out and rummaged through it lazily until she was holding the packaged tablets in her hand. She popped one out for herself and handed the package to Shinay. Regretting that she hadn't kept some water for this, Tabea swallowed the tablet dry while Shinay washed them down with a gulp of her water.

"I wish they worked instantly," she groaned and Tabea could only agree.

They sat silently, staring out the front screens for a while. Tabea kept a half eye on the radar and another half eye on the unconscious man. She imagined that Shinay could handle any potentially incoming transmissions.

"We should listen to this," Shinay said after staring at the blinking red light that indicated the message waiting for them.

Tabea nodded. Shinay pressed some buttons, and Andrej Szkarisov's voice echoed throughout the capsule.

"Get out of there! It's about to blow! Don't come straight back; you'll be in the blast zone — we'll wait at the meeting point for forty-eight hours." A set of coordinates followed, which Shinay dutifully noted down. Then the submission cut out.

The memory of fear surged through Tabea's body and put her on high alert. Her breathing rapidly increased and she found herself clenching to the chair and pressing her teeth together, as though she were bracing for impact. She expected the explosion to repeat, to grow out of the empty space ahead of them. Her limbs began to tremble uncontrollably.

They could have died — they had been so close to getting caught in the explosion and being turned to smithereens. Even if they had only been hit by some of the *Sonata*'s debris, their capsule could have been severely damaged. They could have lost their air supply and been sucked out into space to perish instantly from the cold and the lack of pressure. They could have been hurled into the gravitational field of a planet and burnt on entering its atmosphere or crushed when hitting the ground. They could have been thrown into a sun and painfully turned into ashes.

Her eyes closed, millions of different scenarios that left them dying painful deaths playing in her mind. Soon she was gasping for air as her lungs took in too little oxygen.

"It's okay." Shinay's voice reached her. Tabea felt her hand on her arm, a gentle, comforting touch. "We're alive and we'll be getting back to the *Calliope* in no time."

Tabea nodded, and though her eyes were still closed, and she wasn't entirely appeased, she did feel much calmer. She wasn't on her own and her horrible thoughts hadn't magically become reality.

They were alive.

The pod was functional.

They knew where to go.

She opened her eyes again and glanced once again at the boy they had rescued. Then she looked to Shinay, who was beginning to look more awake and together.

"I'm going to need you to fly." Shinay smiled apologetically, holding up her makeshift bandaged wrist. "Can you tell it to just go to the coordinates?" she added hopefully.

Regretfully, Tabea shook her head.

"I don't have nearly enough energy to talk to anything right now. I'm not even sure I could connect with Calliope."

Shinay seemed disappointed for only a moment, but her features brightened again quickly.

"Then you know what to do," she said. "You've been training hard, after all."

Tabea nodded. During her time at the Academy — before she had gained her powers — she had worked harder than anyone to learn everything about flying air and spacecrafts, never mind about star charts, navigation, engineering, and communications. While she hadn't exactly excelled at all of them, she'd always been amongst the top students. Otherwise, she never would have been able to secure the scholarship that had carried her through. The only thing that she had ever failed, and failed consistently at that, had been simulation exercises.

Simulation exercises that were designed to mimic exactly this kind of situation: a small spacecraft, the size of an escape or retrieval pod, piloting without contact to the mothership to a specific set of coordinates.

Tabea had familiarized herself thoroughly with the controls in preparation for her examinations, and in aircrafts she had always been the Academy's star pupil, but when it came to spacecraft simulations.... Well, there was something about them that made her nervous. It didn't *feel* right. And it led to her forgetting about everything she had ever learned.

This being the first time she actually had to fly the darned thing herself for real, and that on top of being in a similar situation to her failed exams, her mouth instantly dried up and her heartbeat quickened.

She knew she could do this. She had piloted the *Calliope* before as well, after all. Although admittedly, that had been with the aid of her technomancy powers… Plus, connecting with a ship, she could feel and sense everything, move about everything as if it were her own body; she didn't have to pay so close attention to the controls in front of her.

But it needed to be done. Someone had to fly them out of here and she was the only person in a capable state.

Besides, there was no way she would allow herself to remain stranded in space and let *Nerissa* take her place as top junior engineer.

Filled with renewed determination, she grabbed the controls and forced herself to focus on piloting the pod and nothing else. She knew how to do this. She could feel the right commands in her very core—even without her powers. She recognized the feelings from before when she'd only been flying in atmosphere.

She suffocated any thought unconnected to her task at hand, concentrating with all her might.

As soon as she started up the engines, everything went as smoothly as could be. The pod followed her commands instantly and obediently, and the radars detected nothing in their way. When they were on a steady course, Tabea double-checked the coordinates to make sure they were on as straight a line as possible toward the meeting point. When this was done, she set up the auto pilot under the condition that, should the radar pick up anything unexpected, it would alert her with a shrill squeal.

Shinay had watched her closely but without getting involved. Now that Tabea was leaning back in her seat and had allowed herself to relax, she caught the little smile and nod of acknowledgement. Feeling as though she had just passed a test, Tabea returned the smile.

A groan from behind her made her turn. The young man was finally stirring, though it seemed as though pain was getting to him more directly than consciousness.

She abandoned the controls to drop by his side.

He stirred as she took his hand and his blue eyes fluttered open as he gripped her hand. Tabea tried to smile soothingly at him, even though she was feeling nervous, as their gazes met.

"It's okay, you're safe. I'm Tabea and we're on our way back to our ship."

The movement was so weak, she could barely detect it, but Tabea thought she could just about make out a nod before his eyes shut again and his grip slackened.

She glanced at Shinay, who nodded. Even though it had only been for a moment, he had regained consciousness. It was a good sign.

Traveling for several hours, Tabea drifted into sleep multiple times. Shinay did the same. They both tried to stay awake while the other slept, but they were too exhausted and in pain to really keep up with that.

As far as Tabea was aware, the young man didn't stir again.

Space drifted past them; stars performed a strange dance—soft and flowing, creating patterns in the void that called forth longing, fear, and comfortableness, all at the same time. Asteroids occasionally crossed their path, but without ever presenting a danger to them, like strangers crossing the street in a lonely night. A song peeled itself from Tabea's mind, accompanying the universe's performance. It was overflowing with discords, chaotic and seemingly random, but all together, they created a melody, one that felt familiar, as though it was knotting together the fibers of the universe, the same way her powers did. The powers that made her a space witch.

Tabea watched the outside passively, barely blinking, almost transcending into a consciousness untied from her mortal shell. There were no questions, only understanding.

Slowly, almost unnoticeably, her powers returned. She only realized that she was sensing the world outside the pod, and the pod itself, when she connected with the *Calliope*'s consciousness, which was in turn reaching out to her.

"I'm so glad you're safe," Calliope whispered, her voice more a feeling in Tabea's mind.

Tabea smiled. *"I'm glad you're safe, too."* She glanced at the young man. *"We were able to save him."*

She commanded the pod to stop its course to the official data point, and instead connected Calliope with the command center, leaving it up to her to pull them back in.

Tabea had long ago ceased to be surprised at the power Calliope had, even though she was only a spaceship commanded by humans. She had a mind of her own, and therefore, abilities to which the humans on board, excluding herself, had no access, all thanks to the parts of alien technology that had been used to build her.

Originally, it had been thought to only be a power source of tremendous measure, but Tabea had found out that there was much more to her. Calliope had a personality and free will. There were limits to what she could willfully do, due to the terrestrial tech used in her build, which gave her constrictions and more power to her crew. Not much was officially known about Calliope's core, but she'd been marketed as a ship with unlimited possibilities. It had been an experiment to begin with, just to see if Humanity had the capabilities of harnessing another race's technology, even though the core's origins were still unknown. Humanity had done plenty of trading with other races, like the Kinjo-unk, who considered themselves Earth's protectors and guardians, and the Crippnerasale, who were closely allied as well, but even they could not identify the original creators.

"Callaghan is going crazy, by the way," Calliope noted. *"He's not picked up on your signal yet and he's been tearing his hair out since you lost contact."*

Fully aware of why Calliope had made the prodding comment, Tabea chose not to react.

"Hammond isn't doing all that much better," the commentary continued. *"But he's focusing on keeping Akari away from Callaghan."*

"You're such a gossip," Tabea chided her, though she was feeling better with every word her friend shared with her.

"You know you love it."

Tabea gave her a mental shrug. She wasn't about to deny it. Otherwise, Calliope might actually stop.

"Nerissa, on the other hand, is loving it."

"Of course she is." Tabea sighed.

"She hopes you don't come back, but she's also annoyed that you'll get a medal for a valiant death. She's also annoyed you dragged Shinay with you. Vince is terribly worried,

though. I think he was planning to ask you out."

Tabea frowned.

"How do you even know this stuff?"

"People talk. And I overhear."

Tabea could practically hear the smug expression Calliope would have been making had she been human. Admittedly, it wasn't their fault. Excepting the senior officers, no one knew that Tabea was a space witch who could communicate with the ship, and as a result, none of the ordinary crew members had any idea that the *Calliope* had a mind to begin with. Why should they expect her to listen to their private conversations?

"You really should respect their privacy, you know," Tabea argued halfheartedly. Calliope could do whatever she wanted. And she couldn't exactly help that she heard everything that happened in her own body.

It made keeping secrets a pain.

"Your head feels a bit muddled." Calliope abruptly changed the subject, sounding genuinely concerned.

Tabea lifted her hand to the wound on her forehead. It still hurt when she touched it.

"It was a little rocky here for a while," she explained.

Shinay was beginning to stir next to her.

"You should really be more careful, you know. There are sentient beings here who worry about you. By the way, you're almost here."

Just as Calliope said those words, she came into Tabea's vision as she glided out from behind a planetoid. Majestically, she was lit up by starlight, her sleek gray and blue coating creating the optical illusion of water rippling all along her surface.

Tabea found herself thinking of a giant, mechanical mermaid and laughed at herself for the thought. The sound woke up Shinay, whose expression turned from surprise to a relieved smile the instant she saw the ship.

Tabea's heart soared.

"Welcome home."

CHAPTER 3

FINALLY, TABEA WAS FEELING BETTER.

Docking had gone smoothly. The team of medics had rushed in right away to get the three travelers to the med bay in order to examine them, and that was where Tabea had spent the last several hours. After tending to the most obvious wounds and injuries, the medics had performed various other tests to ensure there wasn't any other lasting damage.

A lot of rest had been prescribed for Tabea's concussion, and after taking some little white pills and a refreshing shower, she was beginning to feel like a new person. Calliope had left her to her own devices, which she was thankful for. There was a little nagging voice that told her that she should probably rest her abilities a little longer, considering how much she had strained herself.

Shinay had undergone the same procedure as her, while the unconscious survivor had been put in quarantine and intensive care.

For the moment, Tabea and Shinay were also kept in the med bay, for observation, as they had been told. At least there were books for entertainment and comfortable beds. It was just after Tabea had picked up a novel and began flicking through the first few pages that the door flung open and allowed Callaghan to enter.

His hair was unkempt and his uniform not as cleanly pressed as usual. That aside, he exuded the same normal calm energy he did any other day.

Both Tabea and Shinay jumped to their feet and saluted.

"Good day, sir!"

Callaghan grimaced.

"Stop, please, and sit down." He took a seat in one of the visitor chairs while the two women sat back onto their respective beds. "First of all, well done on saving that young man. Second, I'm glad you're both safe. You can write up a written report when you're feeling better, but for now, I'd like you to just tell me everything that happened."

His concerned gaze flicked between them.

Tabea glanced at Shinay, who shrugged and smirked before taking the lead on recounting their recent adventure. Tabea would occasionally jump in with a comment, but as Shinay's tale largely sang her praise, she was mostly kept too busy by blushing and trying to hide her embarrassment to get involved.

Shinay seemed to find pleasure in outlining and dissecting everything Tabea had done over the course of their little trip, pointing out her quick wit under pressure and her ability to make fast and precise decisions. It was wholly and entirely unnecessary and Tabea would have preferred to have been unconscious for all of it so she wouldn't have been forced to listen to it.

"I'm not surprised." Callaghan smiled after Shinay had finished.

Tabea stoically kept her gaze on the ground. There was no way she could survive looking him in the eyes right now. A million responses flooded through her mind, but all of them sounded clichéd and too much resembling false modesty. Instead, she chose to say nothing, lest her voice should tremble or fail.

"Still can't handle praise, huh?"

Tabea could practically hear the smirk on his face.

"I'll accept it when I know I deserve it," she grumbled. "But this is just... It's just too much. Most of it is just down to my powers, anyway."

"Except for your presence of mind after the blast and the commanding of the pod," Shinay reminded her.

Tabea fidgeted a little.

"Fine." She sighed. "I'll admit that was pretty awesome."

Finally, she looked up at the other two, grinning, matching the twinkle in their eyes.

"Where has all that modesty gone?" Callaghan teased.

"Guess it got left behind when we were blasted away by that explosion."

They all laughed. After a moment, Callaghan collected himself and turned more somber.

"I'm glad you're safe, but I'm still concerned about what happened on that ship. We're too far a distance away to contact Earth, or even the last outpost. It would have been the same for them, so I doubt any transmission made it out."

Shinay pursed her lips. "It did look like there was an attack."

Tabea bit the inside of her cheek, remembering the scene on the *Sonata* — all the blood floating through the empty hull — and felt sick to her stomach. "Almost like an invasion. It was like a slaughter... He's got the marks to prove it."

She nodded toward one of the walls, behind which, she knew, lay the young man they had saved.

Shinay breathed in meaningfully, and her brown gaze became steelier.

"It could have been pirates."

"But would they really aim to destroy the ship?" Tabea countered. Admittedly, she didn't have a lot of experience with space piracy — she'd been lucky enough to never have any such encounter in her two years aboard — but slaughtering the entire crew of an extremely large spaceship and then *not* taking it over just didn't seem to make much sense. "What would they have to gain from that? They didn't even scavenge any parts."

Callaghan had crossed his arms, listening to them contemplatively. But now he uncrossed them and planted them on his hips instead.

"It's still too early to tell," he decided. "We'll just have to wait until that young man wakes up and gives us his own account. But until then, we should stay watchful."

They nodded.

"Tabea." Callaghan's gray eyes fixed on her directly, and an apologetic smile played around his lips. "I'm afraid for the next little while you'll have to go back to routine duty."

She nodded. After her little stunt and what Calliope had told her about the reactions of other cadets, it wasn't surprising.

"I don't want anyone feeling like I'm favoring you," he went on.

"It doesn't stop him from doing it, though."

The words had entered Tabea's mind snippily and she had to force herself not to roll her eyes.

"Shush it, you," she chided Calliope.

"What? It's true and you know it."

"Someone might start wondering why and then it won't be long until someone outside of the inner circle figures out that you have…" He glanced behind him as though to check to make sure there was definitely no one else in the room.

Tabea nodded and smirked.

"Got it. Ix-nay on the itch-way."

Callaghan grinned, relieved, and after patting her on the shoulder and nodding to Shinay, he left.

The navigator, on the other hand, fixed her attention on Tabea, and, when the door fell back into place, raised her eyebrow.

"How much did she have to say?"

"Lots," Calliope chimed in.

Tabea sighed and lay back down, closing her eyes. "Too much."

"Anything useful?"

It was no secret amongst those who knew her abilities that Calliope frequently chatted with her, and that it could be quite frustrating from time to time. Apparently, she also had a telltale sign in her face when it happened. Something about her eyes becoming glassy—a lot more awkward when in mid-conversation. The other cadets just put it down to her being a daydreamer, so it was no big deal when she zoned out for a moment during an argument with the ship.

Nerissa had taken to calling her "Space Cadet." A very clever name considering their situation. Very clever indeed. At least, she seemed to think so.

Groaning internally, Tabea remembered what her routine duties entailed: scrubbing the machine rooms and checking all valves on a regular basis, making sure that they stayed at the right pressure. The air vents and other pipes would need to be cleaned also. She'd been enjoying passing those responsibilities to Nerissa while she'd been on duty on the bridge, but there was no helping it.

It was only a pity that she wouldn't get the chance to speak with the young man. It was more than just mere curiosity. It felt important. She didn't know what, but something drew her toward him, and it wasn't just that he'd been her damsel in distress. Finding out what had happened to him seemed... vital.

"Trust your instincts." Calliope turned her inner monologue into a dialogue. *"You, more than anyone else, can feel connections."*

"What does that even mean?"

Of course this was the moment the ship decided to keep things to herself.

"Well?" Shinay asked, raising an eyebrow.

With a start, Tabea realized she had never answered her question, being too preoccupied with Calliope's constant interruptions and her own qualms about the next few days.

She tilted her head. "Can't you guess?"

Shinay grinned and lay back in her bed. "You're going to have to learn how to balance that. Both of you.

Calliope, I know you can hear me." She was now facing the ceiling, speaking louder to the room at large. "You're gonna need to figure out when you need to leave her alone."

"I know perfectly well when to stop, thank you very much."

"She's sulking now," Tabea informed Shinay.

"Am not!"

Shinay shrugged. "Doesn't really work when I can't hear her either way. Though if you two ever figure out a way she can communicate without having to go through you, I'm sure everyone on the bridge would appreciate it."

Tabea nodded. It would make her life easier as well. For one thing, she would no longer need to keep her conversations hidden. And she wouldn't be the only one able to relay some of the information that only the ship could pick up on, but none of the terrestrial radars or scanners.

"We've still got some time till we're cleared," Shinay went on. "Want to do another astro-navigation lesson?"

"Absolutely!" The words had left Tabea's mouth before she'd even fully registered the question.

"That must've been so cool; it's like a movie!"

"It kinda was, but more so in hindsight, you know?"

Vincent, one of Tabea's co-workers in the engineering team, had bugged her for every detail of her adventure as soon as she had shown up for work. He had insisted that he would not budge from her side until he had heard every detail, and he'd kept true to his word. They had worked alongside each other more or less all morning, which was probably for the best, seeing as Tabea hadn't done the routine checks in a while and he was able to remind her of some details that had slipped her mind.

These checks were much less routine to her than they were to him. Though he was in charge of overseeing them and making sure they were done correctly on this mission, he didn't seem to be tired of them at all. Instead, he appeared to take enjoyment from showing her little tricks on how to make it go more smoothly.

In the meantime, he had also had plenty of time to ask a million and one questions about the recent trip. Everyone knew about it, like Calliope had predicted, and everyone was talking about it. As long as Nerissa wasn't around, Tabea was more than happy to share details of the endeavor, at least the ones that didn't involve her technomancy.

"I can imagine. It must have been super scary!" Vincent looked at her with pity.

"There wasn't that much time to be scared, really," Tabea argued. "That is, until we woke up in the middle of nowhere."

She laughed and Vincent joined in.

"Man." He sighed. "You're so lucky."

Tabea looked up from the circuit board with which she had been fiddling. "Come again?"

"I mean it! It's like you're always in the middle of whatever exciting thing is happening. Like before, remember on the Moleus mission?"

A glint of admiration had sneaked into his blue eyes as he wiped a strawberry blond lock of hair out of his face. Tabea turned to face him directly and with a dark expression, beckoned him to lean into her. Looking him straight in the eyes, she spoke quietly, keeping her voice as unemotive as possible. "That's because I have a secret. A deep, dark secret."

She glanced from side to side, as if to check if anyone was listening. Then she leaned in farther, Vincent hanging on every word that dropped from her lips.

"I have had a curse laid upon me," she whispered. "And now, space itself is pulling at me, trying to mold me to fit into the fabric of its very being. It's folding around me, talking to me, trying to make me more than I thought I was. It's making these things happen around me to claim me. I'm not lucky. I'm cursed."

She held his stunned gaze for one more long and heavy moment before she flashed him her brightest smile and straightened up, laughing. After only a moment, he joined in.

"Ever considered a career in acting?" he asked, poking her in the side. "You almost had me going there!"

"Only almost?" She playfully raised an eyebrow.

He grinned and checked his watch. "Lunchtime."

Growling, Tabea's stomach announced loudly that it agreed with this assessment. Determined to finish their task before their break, they went back to work.

A short while later, they walked into the canteen that was already bustling with people and energy. They joined the queue and were immediately drawn into a conversation with two other people working on the ship, Marco and Felicitas. Tabea didn't know them very well, but as far as she remembered, they both worked as Juniors in the medical department, and this was their first mission on the *Calliope*. She'd seen them around on the ship, but she normally didn't have much business in the med bay. It was a miracle she even remembered their names.

"Have you both heard about the handsome stranger Officer Shinay brought back from that crazy rescue mission?" Felicitas asked, her hazel eyes sparkling as she tied her long, brown hair into a ponytail. She wore the same uniform as Tabea, but it definitely suited her bronze skin tone better.

Marco clapped her shoulder playfully. "Oh, come on. Who hasn't?"

He turned to Vincent, the white of his teeth creating a stark contrast to his dark skin as he grinned. "Knowing Vince, he's already on the case to find out more."

Vincent sighed dramatically. "You know me so well. I do in fact already have some more information. But speaking of, are you guys in the med team working with him? Any juicy tidbits you wouldn't mind sharing with an old friend?"

"Afraid we're not able to say much. He doesn't seem to want to talk to anyone." Marco shrugged.

"But he's awake?"

Three pairs of eyes turned to face Tabea. She blushed and bit her lip, chiding herself for her outburst.

Marco frowned. "Yeah, he's awake. But aren't you—"

"Of course she is!" Felicitas chimed in cheerfully. "You're the girl who came in with him and Officer Shinay. The one who was on the mission, right?"

Tabea didn't dare to meet her eye. She would have liked to disappear into the ground, but two hands on her shoulders kept her where she was.

"The one and only," Vincent declared, smiling widely. "Marco and Feli, meet Tabea. She's on my team, though she mostly works on the bridge with Hammond."

"Tabea." Felicitas and Marco shared a meaningful look, one with excitement, the other skeptical.

"Oh, so Her Highness eats with the common folk now, does she?"

Nerissa's voice was unmistakable in her grating frequency. Normally, Tabea would have groaned inwardly, but right now, she was glad for the distraction.

"What's up, Rissa?" Vincent smiled brightly at her and she returned the gesture. Then she turned back to Tabea and her hazel eyes became cold as ice.

"Just wondering what little Miss Favorite Space Cadet is doing, eating with the rest of us." She chuckled, flicking her brown hair over her shoulder. "Oh wait, that's right. She got demoted."

"*So much for not noticing favoritism,*" Tabea thought inwardly.

"*Told ya,*" Calliope was quick to chime in.

"*Really? Now? You've been quiet all day and* now *you want to join in?*"

"*It seemed like fun.*"

"And not only that, but her place was finally given to someone who actually deserves it. How are those simulators coming along?"

Nerissa beamed at her, clearly feeling too much glee to portray anything except Schadenfreude.

"Terrible as always." Tabea beamed back. "Can't deal with those suckers at all!"

Nerissa scoffed.

"Well, don't think we didn't notice that you're having to take remedial lessons with some of the officers. We all know you failed some of the exams."

She was referring to the final examinations at the Academy. Truthfully, Tabea had missed them because, at the time, she'd been on a mission with Callaghan and it had taken longer than originally expected. But she had passed all the exams at a later date with flying colors, with the exception of the simulator tests, which she had only barely scraped a pass on because she had given up on trying to finish it and had ended up using her powers to convince the simulator that she was doing things right. Something about simulators just didn't feel right. Never had, never would.

That being said, her current study sessions had nothing to do with that. She was working on passing the officer's examinations so Callaghan wouldn't need to make exceptions for her anymore.

"*Rissa.*" Vince's warning tone made her stop. With a last hateful glance at Tabea, she shrugged and stalked away to meet her friends at one of the tables.

Felicitas whistled through her teeth. "She, like, really, really hates you, huh?"

"*Hey. Other people notice it too!*" Calliope chirped.

"*She's not exactly trying to hide it anymore.*"

"She's not normally like this." Vincent defended her. "She's actually really nice."

"Sure she is," Marco grumbled darkly. Felicitas elbowed him in the side.

"You're just sour because she turned you down. Shouldn't have asked her out if you couldn't handle the rejection."

"She does take her job very seriously." Vincent continued. "Her mom was one of the top engineers on the *Babylonia* before making captain." He shrugged. "She just wants to live up to that, I think."

"I'd love it if she could do that without trying to drag me down," Tabea muttered. If anyone had heard her, they didn't react.

They had finally reached the food dispensers and all four were busying themselves with ordering their meals.

Tabea was already steering to a table in the back, where she saw her friend Besma, but Vincent hesitated.

"Marco!" he yelled as the other young man turned to join some of the other medical team. "Still down for that game later?"

Marco gave him a thumb up. "You're on."

Tabea shot a questioning glance at Felicitas, but the other girl just shrugged.

"What was that about?" Tabea asked Vincent when he caught up with her.

"Holo-hockey. We're in a league, you know."

"Oh, yeah, I think I knew that. So a league, huh? Like professional?"

He waved her suggestion away. "Nothing like that, but it *is* the highest-ranking amateur league in the Northern Hemisphere. The winners get to play the best of the South and the winners of that get to play the colonies."

Tabea whistled. "That's nothing to sniff at."

His chuffed smirk was enough to prove that he felt the same.

Since global warming had made large stretches of Earth uninhabitable, including the entire equator, over time, governments and countries had dissipated, instead forming two large nations on the planet: the Northern Hemisphere, and the Southern Hemisphere, along with plenty of colonies on the other planets in Earth's solar system and a few outposts in other parts of the Milky Way. Most of the people serving on the *Calliope* had gone to the Academy of the Northern Hemisphere, but there were always exceptions, like Felicitas, based on her accent, and the officer Maya Glaucia.

Chatting easily, they made their way over to Besma and took their seats beside her.

"Slumming it with the rest of us today, huh?" she grinned, her dark almond shaped eyes narrowing in jest, and nudged Tabea with her elbow. As usual, she wore her tight black curls openly, tied only by a pastel-colored headscarf that complemented her dark skin.

Tabea groaned. "Not you too!"

"What? You just haven't been around much lately."

"I guess."

Sullenly, Tabea fished a potato from her stew and let it dissipate in her mouth. For one moment only, she was allowed to enjoy her meal in peace before Besma's curiosity got the better of her.

"So go on, spill! I wanna know the deets!"

Tabea jerked her thumb at Vincent. "Get him to tell you; he's already asked about everything."

"It won't be the same if I don't hear it from you, though."

Vincent chuckled.

"Looks like you're just going to have to deal with it, Tabs."

Tabea sighed deeply, but she relented. As patiently

as she could muster, she answered all of Besma's questions in much the same way as she had done for Vincent. As a result, lunchtime was over before she could finish her meal.

"Take another five," Vincent told her as he got to his feet to carry away his tray. "I can manage that long without you."

He winked and Tabea nodded gratefully.

"And tonight, you can answer the rest of my questions," Besma added cheerfully.

"Don't you have some piloting to do?" Tabea yelled after her as they both left her at the table.

The lack of response left her attention to her meal, which she gulped down quickly. The mess had mostly emptied by the time she was ready to put away her tray. Only a few stragglers were scattered among the tables, most of them wolfing down the remains of their food, but a few seemed to be only starting their break now. On her way out, Tabea passed by a table housing a lone figure: Felicitas. When Tabea passed her, along with a friendly nod, Felicitas' hand shot out and clasped Tabea's arm.

"You need to come with me," she whispered, getting to her feet. Her breathing was fast and her palms sweaty — clearly, she was nervous.

Tabea didn't hesitate.

"Let me just tell Vince. He'll be looking for me otherwise."

The other girl shook her head and glanced around, her brows knitting together.

"There's no time. We've got to use this window. I don't know how long Marco can distract Zhen."

Tabea thought fast.

They were about to do something they could get in trouble for; that much was obvious. But Felicitas and Marco had deemed it important enough that they would trust her, a person they had only just met, to not report them. Chances were high that Vincent had some kind of inkling about what they needed from her also.

Tabea did recall that he had checked his com-watch a lot throughout the morning.

Felicitas was pulling gently on her arm and without resistance, Tabea let herself be led out of the room.

"He's been saying nothing but your name since he woke up, you know."

Calliope's words came sudden and unexpectedly. She didn't need to explain whom she was talking about. There was really only one option.

"Why didn't you tell me?" Tabea chided her and she could almost feel the mental shrug.

"It didn't seem like it would be constructive. Not like you could have gotten to him on your own either way."

"I could have with you."

"And you never would have taken the route; let's be honest here. You have far too much respect for Callaghan to disobey him without reason."

The reminder of Callaghan slowed Tabea down for a moment.

He hadn't given her permission to talk to the survivor. In fact, he had actively put her into a position where she wouldn't have any access whatsoever. Why? Didn't he trust her? What was it he worried about? And how would he react if he found out that she had gone behind his back?

But she also felt like the young man was her responsibility. She was the one who had saved him, after all. When he had woken up in the pod, she had promised him he was safe, and the smile they had shared had sealed that oath. And evidently, he seemed to want some form of contact with her also. Why else would he repeat her name to everyone?

Felicitas and Marco had given her an opening. She needed to use it and pray that Callaghan would forgive her.

Chapter 4

Tabea followed Felicitas all the way to the med bay. There, they tiptoed past a room with its door ajar, from which they could clearly make out Marco's voice and that of Officer Zhen, the head of the medical team.

Felicitas only turned once, briefly, to put her finger on her lips. She didn't need to. Tabea was already moving as quietly as she could.

They turned two more corners before Felicitas entered an access code into the panels of the quarantine area.

Tabea squeezed her arm.

"Is this okay?" she mouthed as she pointed at the warning signs for radiation and infections. Felicitas only smiled and nodded.

Relieved that it seemed to be only a precaution, Tabea swiftly followed her inside and allowed the door to *whoosh* shut behind her.

Ahead, there were three rooms, each of them preluded by a decontamination shower, currently out of use. Upon a sign from Felicitas, Tabea made her way through the second one and into the room behind it. Her new friend remained behind and left through the door, presumably to keep watch, though not before shooting Tabea one more curious look.

The young man was lying in one of the med pods with his eyes closed, and Tabea approached gingerly.

He was looking much better. His torn clothing had been replaced by a medical gown, and all of his wounds had been bandaged properly. He had been cleaned, too—no more soot and grime on his skin like before. Even his hair had been brushed, though it did little to tame his ginger curls.

When Tabea cleared her throat, his ice-blue eyes flashed open and laid on her. They reminded her a little of Callaghan's. He smiled.

"Tabea," he said. His voice was hoarse, as though his vocal cords were still recuperating from screaming for a long time.

She nodded.

"Hello." Awkwardly, she looked around the pod. There wasn't much space to move in here. "I hear you've been asking for me."

He chuckled.

"I wondered how long it would take someone to get you."

Her gaze flicked back to him. According to Calliope and Felicitas, this was the first time he had said anything else than her name since waking.

"*So he does know how to speak.*"

Ignoring Calliope, Tabea stared at him, trying to find answers written in his face.

"Why did you want to talk to me? You could have

spoken to any of the officers on board."

His smile faded and a sense of fear and sadness filled his eyes as he half-blinked, as though to suppress a memory. He shuddered.

"I can't trust them. You're the only one I can trust. You saved me."

"That's a can of worms if ever I heard one," Calliope chimed in helpfully.

"Agreed."

His hands were trembling. Tabea couldn't imagine what horrors he must have endured. Though, considering the scene she'd arrived at... Maybe she had a vague idea. Her stomach was in turmoil as she placed her hands on his, trying to warm his ice-cold digits.

"You're safe here," she promised earnestly. "Everyone here on this ship only wants to help. But you need to let us."

He shook his head, more violently than she'd thought he could.

"That's what we thought on the Sonata. We were a team, a family, but... But..." He choked up. His breathing rate had increased and Tabea wasn't too fond of the loud, more frequent beeping from the screen monitoring his heartrate. He coughed, his eyes squeezed shut, and she was left to awkwardly rub his back.

He reminded her of her younger brother, Dorian, back when he'd still been too young to see her as anything other than his older sister. Years ago, while he'd been sick with the flu, he'd woken up from a nightmare, and she'd tried to comfort him in much the same way she was now trying to do with this young man.

"They came," he whispered, his wide eyes staring directly into Tabea's, one of his hands clutching hers. "There was a traitor, and they..." He faltered.

His grip was tight, squeezing so hard, it hurt. But Tabea didn't withdraw her hand. Instead, she placed her other hand on his and smiled reassuringly, all the while her mind jumped and bounced like crazy, trying to make sense of what he was saying. There had been a traitor on his ship? Her heart pounded at the thought. Who were *they*?

"It's over. You're safe here," she repeated. Right now, she needed to calm him down. He was still healing and clearly not in a state of mind that would allow her to find out much more about what had happened.

He didn't seem convinced, but the beeping gradually slowed again, and he was no longer panting as he lay back in his pod.

"What's your name?" Tabea asked, hoping that a change in subject would help him feel at ease.

"You..." He spoke too quietly for her to hear.

"Yuri?" she guessed, and he nodded.

"Yuri."

"Oh, like Gagarin?"

He granted her an uncertain smile and inclined his head in the affirmative.

"I guess your parents were hoping you'd make it into the space core, huh?" She chuckled and he joined in.

"I guess so."

"Do you have any siblings?" If she could make him feel at ease with mundane conversation that made him think of his family back home, he was more likely to find the strength to speak about what had happened on his ship later. At least that was her plan.

He slowly shook his head. "So far, I'm the only one."

She raised an eyebrow playfully.

"*So far*? You think your parents are going to have more children while you're away?"

He shrugged. "I think it's possible. If I am successful, I am sure they will."

Her heart dropped down into her stomach. His tone of voice was so defeatist, so sad, it made the meaning of his words ring home all the more. She sighed, dropping her own smile.

"Your parents are only interested in accomplishments too, huh?"

She bit her lip to stop herself from sharing her own sob story with him, but she couldn't stop herself from thinking about it. Her parents would never be interested in Tabea's path, not with her sister, Ella, being a prominent political figure and her elder brother, Nick, a renowned epidemiologist who had led the team that had created the vaccine for the worst pandemic the Saturnian colonies had ever seen. And then there was Dorian, of course. The youngest of their group who was competing in intergalactic sports competitions, even though he was only fourteen. A simple member of the Space Core was nothing in comparison to these three.

Yuri nodded and tilted his head to one side as he watched Tabea with warm eyes.

"Do you have siblings?"

The way he said the word sounded foreign, like he was still testing the pronunciation.

"Three of them. But we aren't close."

Tabea laughed, hoping to suppress the unwelcome memories that had forced their way into her consciousness.

"But we're like a family here." She gestured at the ship in general. "So that's all I need."

"You might want to cut the chitchat," Calliope interrupted. *"Zhen is on his way."*

Panic took a hold of Tabea's heart. She couldn't be found in here. Not only would she be in a mountain of trouble, so would Felicitas and Marco, and even Vincent for not reporting her absence.

"I have to go," she told Yuri hurriedly as she rose to her feet.

His grip on her hand remained.

"Will you come back?" he asked, his eyes pleading more than his words. "I need to talk more with you."

Tabea smiled, gently prying her hand from his.

"As soon as I can."

The door to the quarantine area burst open.

"Hurry! We gotta go!" Felicitas whisper shouted.

Tabea flashed Yuri one last smile before running out after Felicitas, following her sprint around various corners until, finally, Felicitas came to a halt, panting, as she stemmed her upper body on her legs.

"Nice getaway. But there's someone about to come around the corner."

Grateful for the warning, Tabea glanced around hurriedly, spotted a supply closet, and pulled Felicitas inside with her. She closed the door just in time as footfalls rounded the corner and briskly moved past them. Once they had left, both girls let out a heavy sigh and left the closet.

"Let's talk about this later," Felicitas said, an

intensity to her gaze unexpected to Tabea. "I'll come by your room around seven."

Tabea didn't even try to get out of it. She owed Felicitas this much, at least, for giving her the opportunity to talk with Yuri.

"Thank you."

The afternoon passed quickly and quietly, and Vincent thankfully didn't ask too many questions about Tabea's prolonged absence after lunch. Even Calliope held back on her commentary.

Besma monopolized Tabea's attention during dinner, asking more questions about her recent adventure.

"So, is he really as good-looking as the rumors say?" she asked, her dark eyes glittering with curiosity. Tabea shrugged, somewhat annoyed at the world in general that this was the main point of interest regarding the new addition to their crew.

"I was too busy dragging him from an exploding ship to notice," she said pointedly, raising her eyebrows a little.

Besma grimaced.

"You've got a point. Do you know where he's from? And what happened there, do you know?"

Tabea shrugged helplessly. "I really don't see how you expect me to know anything about him—he's been unconscious for most of our acquaintance. All I know is that Yu... You're all far more interested in him than what happened on the ship. Don't you think it's really scary?"

"That was close," Calliope trilled.

"I know. Do you think they noticed?"

"Nope. But I do think they noticed that you've zoned out again."

"And whose fault is that?"

While Calliope seemed to have pretended to not have heard her, Tabea focused back on her audible conversation. Both Besma and Vincent were watching her, leaning together.

"You think she's picturing the end of the world?" Besma asked, covering her mouth with a hand.

Vincent nodded, though there was a hint of worry in his lightly furrowed brows.

"It must have been horrible."

"I'm back, guys. You don't have to talk like I'm not here." Tabea sighed. "I just think it's worrisome that something like this could happen without anyone hearing about it, that's all."

The conversation moved on to lighter topics, but Tabea was distracted. She glanced to the other side of the mess, where Felicitas was sitting along with Marco and two other cadet medics. Felicitas wasn't looking her way, but Tabea wondered if she really would come by that evening to speak about Yuri.

Then Nerissa walked through Tabea's field of vision.

"You guys will never believe it," she said loudly, beaming as she took a seat with some other cadets. Her gaze flicked to Tabea for long enough to show her that she wasn't going to like what was going to come next. "I was working on the bridge this afternoon. Hammond called for me personally!"

She was speaking loud enough for all tables in the vicinity to hear her.

"Wow, Rissa, that's awesome!" Loïc, another engineering cadet, said, his brown eyes wide with wonder. "I wish that'd happen to me some time. Congrats!"

Nerissa awarded him a pleased smile and patted his shoulder.

"Don't worry, if you work hard, I'm sure you'll get there soon."

Another girl sighed.

"I'm not sure that's true," she said wistfully, twirling a strand of her straight black hair around her finger. "Between you and Tabea, I don't think anyone else on the engineering team even stands a chance."

"Well, Vince does, doesn't he? He's just as good as those two," a young, tall man named Jonathan chimed in. Tabea recognized him as being a junior cadet in the weapons and defense sector who was often called to take over for Glaucia. With his dark skin and green eyes, he had been the subject of many a cadet's crush Calliope had gossiped about in Tabea's time aboard.

She glanced at Vincent, who was still deep in a conversation with Besma. Apparently, they hadn't noticed the conversation going around the mess.

"*I* think there couldn't be *anyone* more deserving than Vincent," Nerissa agreed, with a hard glance at Tabea. "After all, he's focused *all* of his studies on this, and he's never missed any lectures or failed any exams."

The jab at Tabea couldn't be more obvious. From the moment Tabea had switched from the pilot's course to the engineering course, Nerissa had hated her and tried to show her at every step how little she thought of her.

If it had been up to Tabea, she never would have

made the switch — it had been Callaghan's idea because he'd thought it could help with her powers to understand the mechanics better. And since on her first mission, he'd taken her along as part of the engineering team, even though she'd been in the pilot's track, it had just kind of stuck.

"Listening to this is just going to make you feel bad." Calliope reached out, her voice gentle in Tabea's head, comforting. *"You should stop."*

Tabea nodded mentally. *"I know you're right. And I should be above this. But it just irks me, you know? What did I ever do to her? And it's not like I don't work hard."*

"I know. Your friends know, too. As do the officers. So what does it matter what Nerissa thinks?"

Even though Tabea knew that Calliope was right, she still found it difficult to just accept it. It would never be easy to ignore Nerissa's spiteful comments. Not for as long as Tabea felt like there was even a grain of truth in them.

With a sigh, she finally picked up her tray.

"I better go study," she told Vincent and Besma. "Shinay wants me to memorize the names of all the planetoids and moons in the Caperius System by our next lesson."

A few understanding and sympathetic looks and words from them, and she was off.

She walked briskly to get back to her cabin, relieved that at least for a few minutes, she would have some peace and quiet and time to sort her own thoughts. She did start her alone time by studying a little, but she was also less in need of it than she had claimed. It was more revision than anything else.

After a half hour or so, she put her notes away and

lay down on the bed, staring at the ceiling. Yuri's words replayed in her mind.

They came. There was a traitor.

"*They*" were bound to be an alien race, but as to which one, Tabea could only venture a guess. It was almost definitely not the Moleus. They were newly allied with Humanity and similar in shape and appearance, meaning they didn't have the kind of claws that could leave behind gashing wounds like Yuri had presented. It was unlikely to have been one of Earth's other allies, either, so the Kinjo-unk and the Crippnerasale were out too. Both the Zutani as well as the Penyales were a possibility, but it didn't seem like their styles. For all she knew, it might have been a race Humanity had not yet encountered. Of the sixteen known races in the universe, Humanity had only really interacted with eight. The other half were too far away to reach within a lifetime using human technology.

What bothered her most about his words was that he had spoken about a traitor. Did that mean a human on board his ship had joined enemy forces and aided in the slaughter of their entire crew? But why?

And why go through so much effort? The Penyales and Zutani hated Humanity, sure, but they would have opted for an outright attack like in the past. They certainly wouldn't have wasted time on infiltration. So why?

Her thoughts were disrupted by a knock on her door.

"Come on in," she called, and the door slid into the wall, revealing Felicitas.

She stepped in hurriedly and waited for the door to shut before addressing Tabea.

A wide grin spread across her features.

"He talked to you, didn't he?"

Tabea nodded. "His name is Yuri."

"That's a nice name." Felicitas tilted her head to one side, her hair hanging loose, her lips slightly parted and her hazel eyes directed upward. "Did he... Did you talk about anything else? I mean, did he say what happened?"

His words flashed through Tabea's mind once more.

There was a traitor.

She shook her head.

"Not much, really. We didn't have much time. I was mostly just trying to put him at ease."

Felicitas looked disappointed. "Oh."

"Has he started talking to the doctor yet?"

"No, he won't say a word. Well..." Felicitas shot her a knowing smirk. "At least not anything except your name."

"Still?"

"That's surprising," Calliope chimed in. *"You'd think he'd stop that now."*

Felicitas sat down on the desk chair.

"Officer Shinay even came by in the afternoon and tried. Zhen thought that maybe the problem was that he only wanted to talk to one of the people who saved him. But she couldn't get him to say anything except your name, either."

Frowning, Tabea pursed her lips. It didn't make any sense. Unless... he might not have noticed Shinay in his semi-conscious state in the pod. But still. Why refuse communication?

"Why? Why won't he talk?"

"That's what I'd like to know, too," Calliope said dryly.

"What's so special about you, Tabea?"

Felicitas tilted her head, smiling curiously with slightly narrowed eyes. If Nerissa had said the same words, it would have been just an insult, a slight, but when Felicitas said them, it was clear that she could feel her secret. She sensed there was something Tabea wasn't telling her, and she wanted to know just what it was.

Tabea shrugged.

"Beats me. I assumed the same thing Zhen did, and that Yuri just didn't know Shinay's name."

"Hmm." Felicitas looked pensive. A moment of silence reigned between them.

Tabea thought of the weight of responsibility she was feeling for Yuri. She wanted to make him trust people. She wanted to help him find his way out of the nightmares he was undoubtedly facing every time he closed his eyes.

"Thank you," she said quietly. "Thanks for helping me talk to him. I was worried, but he seems to be doing better than I thought."

Felicitas flashed her a smile.

"It was my pleasure. I think I'd feel the same in your shoes." Then, suddenly, she jumped back to her feet and stretched out her hand to take Tabea's. "So, same time tomorrow?"

"Wait, really?"

"Well, yeah. You're still worried about him, aren't you? You said you had to make him feel at ease, so he clearly doesn't think it's over. He won't talk to anyone but you, which means you're the only person he trusts, for whatever reason that is. And besides, if you can find out just what happened, then we can make sure to report it and prevent it from happening to any other ships. It's a win-win."

Tabea laughed to herself quietly, though she felt relieved that Felicitas seemed to be on her wavelength.

"Let me guess. You just love being part of a secret mission, don't you?"

Felicitas narrowed her eyes and gave an impish grin. "Well, who wouldn't?"

Chapter 5

Routine checks really weren't so bad. At least, that was what Tabea tried to tell herself.

If nothing else, they gave her ample time to sort out her muddled thoughts and finally spend more time talking with friends. After all, that was something that working on the bridge with Callaghan and the senior officers just didn't allow often, especially with so much extra study work he and Calliope had been piling onto her.

It was nice as a break, but if this were to be going on for too long, she would lose her mind with boredom.

She had only just made it to lunchtime when she started wondering how long it would take until Callaghan would call her back to the bridge, or at least get her to resume her lesson plan. At least she had Yuri to think about for the moment, and boy, was there a lot to reflect on.

For once, she escaped Nerissa's snide comments at lunchtime due to the girl's absence and got to enjoy it to the fullest with Besma and Vincent.

"I just want a boyfriend already," Besma mumbled

into her mashed peas. "I mean, it feels like everyone in the pilot's core is dating, so what's wrong with me?"

"Well," Tabea interjected, "I wouldn't say *everyone*. Akari is still single."

Besma rolled her eyes.

"Yeah, but we all know it's only a matter of time for her and Callaghan to get together. I mean, it's so obvious. He's just playing hard to get."

Vincent raised an eyebrow. "Is that right? Tabs?"

Tabea almost choked on her potato with laughter. The coughing and laughing brought tears to her eyes as Vincent slapped her back to clear her throat.

Finally, she could sit up with a sigh, still feeling giddy at the thought of Callaghan doing anything like "playing hard to get." Since his wife had died from an illness a decade earlier, he'd never shown romantic interest in another person, and if he had, Tabea would have been the first to notice. She spent enough time with him, after all.

"If that's what he's doing, he may have put his settings to extreme difficulty."

"Ah, yes, a famous example of a one-sided love, I believe." Vincent nodded sagely.

"Well, whatever," Besma murmured, staring darkly at her cup filled with juice. "It doesn't change the fact that I won't have a date to take to the party."

Tabea and Vincent watched her for a moment before exchanging a glance.

"What about Nick?" Vincent suggested.

Besma only grunted and laid her head on her crossed arms on the table.

Tabea frowned. "Weren't you getting along real well a few weeks ago? Like, flirting and stuff? I was sure he'd be asking you out any day."

"Oh, he did."

"And?"

"And he also asked out Bianca. And did I mention that I found out *afterward* that he also has girlfriends back on Earth in both hemispheres, *and* one on Jupiter, *and* another one on a different ship? For all we know, he's got twenty girlfriends all strewn about the known galaxies!"

Tabea winced as she thought of how that revelation must have gone and felt a weight of guilt settle itself in her chest as she realized that this was the first she'd heard of it, even though it had happened a while ago. She hadn't been there to comfort her friend, not even to hear about the disaster.

"But didn't he also send you those poems and presents? And I'm sure I've heard him say that he broke it off with the other girls for your benefit," Vincent noted.

Both girls stared at him.

"You don't actually think that makes it better, do you?" Tabea asked incredulously. "I mean, that he would even do it in the first place is despicable. It would be one thing if he were upfront about it, but like this...?"

Besma nodded in agreement. "Yeah, how can I possibly ever trust him now? I don't want to date someone like that! Also, think of the other girls, if it's even true that he broke it off, like... Imagine, just outta nowhere, he turns around to his girlfriends and says, 'Hey hon, haven't seen you in months. Gotta break up now. There's a girl on this ship I wanna date right now, but she won't date me because I'm with you.' Well, that's a fun feeling."

Vincent raised his hands in defense. "Okay, okay, I got it. Nick bad. No dating Nick. Is there anyone else you might consider, even just as a date for the one evening?"

Besma looked blank. "I guess I'd say you'd be okay, because you're fun and stuff, but I know you're taking Tabs, so..."

Tabea stood alert, and her eyes darted between the two of them. "Who's taking Tabs to the what now?" she asked.

Vincent blushed. "I was gonna ask tomorrow." He shot Besma an annoyed glance, but she only shrugged. He sheepishly turned back to Tabea. "Will you? Go with me, I mean?"

"*Oooooh,*" Calliope teased. "*Told you he likes you.*"

Tabea grimaced, secretly relieved that she could turn him down easily.

"Can't. I volunteered for the skeleton crew ages ago. Someone's still got to handle the ship and"—she pushed up her sleeve and presented her biceps—"I'm the right girl for the job."

"*No date for you, huh?*" Calliope asked, amused. Tabea had to keep from smirking.

"*You can be my date, Callie.*"

"*It would be my pleasure.*"

"So you two should go together and have lots of fun!"

She gave them both her brightest smile before checking her watch. Time to go. Felicitas was waiting for her.

"I gotta take care of something. I'll just be a few minutes late, kay?"

Vincent jumped up at the same time as her. "Hold up, I'll join you. See you later, Bes-Bes."

Besma only gave them a halfhearted wave as she returned her attention to her food. Vincent followed Tabea to the tray disposal, keeping a half-step behind her, even though she was walking excruciatingly slowly. While trying to spot Felicitas in the hall, she frantically thought up different ways to ward off Vincent. But as it turned out, she didn't need them.

"Don't worry," he said. "Marco told me. I'll help."

Vincent had moved close to whisper the words into her ear and she whirled around to look at him. He returned her gaze earnestly and seriously.

Then a little smile cracked his expression. "You didn't think I wouldn't notice, did you? It was obvious from the way you were talking yesterday that you wanted to see how he's doing. And Marco told me that he actually spoke to you, the guy. So, since you're the only one he'll talk to, we gotta make it happen, right?"

"Right."

Truth be told, Tabea was relieved that she wouldn't need to hide this from her friend. Besides, with more people helping and keeping a lookout, there was a higher chance she wouldn't be caught.

Together, they walked to the meeting point near the med bay Vincent and Marco had agreed on, where they waited for Marco and Felicitas, chatting easily, as though they had just run into one another in the hallway. Almost as soon as the four of them stood together, Marco leaned in, creating a huddle, and wandered from one set of eyes to the next.

"Felicitas is distracting Zhen this time. It'd be too weird if I kept going to him every day."

"So what's the battle-plan?" Vincent asked and the two boys shared a grin.

"You gotta stay around here in case Feli can't keep Zhen busy. Come up with some questions to ask him, like make up some symptoms and stuff."

Vincent saluted playfully, and they split.

Tabea followed Marco through the hallways, all the way to the containment area, where he opened the door for her.

"I'll get you if I hear from the others." He grinned. They were all far too excited about going on a secret mission of sorts, though Tabea had to admit to herself that she was really no different. Her veins were pumping with excitement, with *expectation*. Even though the air was still, she felt as though she could sense the winds of change blowing past her.

Without further ado, she entered the room and headed straight for Yuri's pod.

"I'll keep a look out as well," Calliope promised.

"Thank you."

"Hey, Yuri." Tabea greeted the young man with a smile.

"You came back!"

"I promised, didn't I?"

A smile made the corners of his eyes wrinkle and his nose twitch.

"Anyway, how are you feeling?" She scanned the monitors around the med pod, all of them only spouting gibberish to her. Perhaps she ought to branch out into getting more knowledge in that field also.

"You have more than enough on your plate already." Calliope cut into her thoughts. *"You don't need to be a one-person crew, you know."*

"*I know,*" Tabea said reluctantly. "*But it would be so useful.*"

Yuri stemmed himself up into a seated position, wincing slightly as he tensed his torso.

"Feeling great." He grimaced. "I'm sure I could run all the way from here to the Suprial System."

Tabea tilted her head to one side, trying to remember her astronomy lessons with Shinay.

"Suprial System?"

"*It's a system at the border of your known galaxies,*" Calliope chimed in helpfully. "*It's in free space.*"

What an odd reference to use.

"*And how do you know that?*"

Calliope didn't respond.

Yuri looked embarrassed. "Yeah, um, one of my crewmates told me this story, you see, and it was set in a place with that name, and uh..."

He shrugged helplessly, though his eyes had a nervous quality to them, shifting ever so slightly and not looking directly at her. There was a darkness in his demeanor, something that made the air around him feel heavy.

Tabea reached out for him and placed a hand on his arm.

He flinched.

"It must be hard," she said, searching and finding his gaze. "Finding yourself alone on a different ship, feeling like you need to justify everything that's different."

He dropped his gaze. "I'm not completely alone."

"No, that's right. I'm here with you. And everyone else will also be — once you let them."

He looked back up, smiling gingerly.

"So you know I haven't spoken to anyone else, huh?"

"Why is that?" Tabea asked. "They're all trying to help. But they need to know what happened."

He shook his head violently and a wildness returned to his eyes.

"You don't understand. It's not safe. You must feel it, too. Why else would you need to come here secretly? Your masters, your officers, they don't want you to talk to me. They know that it's all I want, so why wouldn't they try it?

"You could have told them, after last time. You could have told them that we spoke. But I don't think you did. Why not? All I can think is that you believe me, and you realize that there might actually be a traitor on board this ship as well."

His words ebbed away. Then he looked up at her seriously, his eyes filled with sadness, and said quietly, "That there is a chance the same thing might happen here."

Flashbacks of his ship, floating in empty space, dead, flooded Tabea's mind. Images of the inside, the marks of fighting on every wall, and the blood still trapped inside the rooms, just floating in the void, tears from huge, razor-sharp claw cuts in all that remained of the ship.

The thought merged with her imagination, and suddenly, it was Vincent, she saw hanging, trapped like Yuri had been, injuries all over his body while Besma's lifeless body floated nearby, her blood creating one large pool of red in the center of the room.

The image almost brought tears to her eyes, and it instilled fear in her heart. She couldn't let that happen.

"Tell me everything," she said earnestly, blinking away the burning sensation in her eyes. "Let's prevent this from happening ever again."

Yuri nodded and took a deep breath before looking around the room once, nervously checking to make sure they were the only two people inside.

"I was working in the engine room, together with two others," he began. "A woman came in, and she knocked out the other two with one strike of a loose pipe. I tried to stop her, and we wrestled for a moment, but..." He stopped for a moment and stared at his hands, as though he couldn't believe his own weakness. "She got the better of me. When I came to, alarms were ringing, and there was smoke everywhere."

He gulped and Tabea resisted the urge to lean forward and hug him. He closed his eyes, his brows twitching as he recalled the events.

"There were some fires near the engines, and all I could think was that I had to get the others out of there. I couldn't carry them, but I was somehow able to drag them both to the next room. That's when I heard the screaming. I rounded a corner and there she was again, that woman, leading a group of..." He hesitated, and then whispered, "Monsters."

Tabea could see his pupils moving wildly underneath the lids, just as if he were working through a nightmare. Something that wasn't too far off the truth, either. She didn't doubt he was plagued by bad dreams whenever he closed his eyes.

"She was showing them where to go, letting them kill everyone in their path..."

He turned up his face to the ceiling, staring at it as

tears welled up, and he sniffed.

"I ran." His voice broke. "I ran as fast as I could, taking hallways I knew weren't used often, trying to avoid *them*, always moving to where I couldn't hear screaming."

He breathed deeply, and Tabea squeezed his arm, trying to remind him that he was safe now, that the horrors were over.

"Who were they?" she finally asked, but he shook his head.

"I don't know. I really don't. Pirates, maybe? There was a variety of races, and a lot of things I've never seen before. They had space witches too, I'm sure. But that woman, she was with them. I'd seen her before. I'd watched her have meals with us, laugh with my crewmates. She was normal, a member of the crew. But she brought *them* to us."

Tabea couldn't resist her urge any longer and she leaned forward to hug him.

"You're safe," she promised. "We won't let anything like that happen here."

"How can you be so sure?" he whispered and Tabea smiled sadly, sorrow filling her heart at his past, at what she couldn't do for him.

"That's a secret."

"So? What did he say?"

After not having exchanged a single word about their little secret mission all afternoon and dinner, Felicitas, Marco, and Vincent had met up with Tabea in her room in the evening.

Tabea had fought with herself the entire time, wondering if she should talk to Callaghan and tell him what Yuri had shared but simultaneously worried about betraying Yuri's trust and getting in trouble for breaking the rules. Then again, it was important information. She'd begged Yuri to share it with Shinay, but she didn't have much hope that he would actually do it. He seemed to distrust everyone except her and after what he had gone through, she really couldn't blame him.

Her eyes passed slowly over her three co-conspirators. She'd known Vincent for long enough to know he was trustworthy, and she had the same feeling about the other two, especially since Vincent and Marco seemed to have known each other for quite a while as well.

"One of his crewmembers betrayed them and allowed the attackers to infiltrate easily. He doesn't know why, but he got the impression that they were searching for something. They may have been pirates."

She spoke matter of factly, trying to compress his horrendous tale in a few words that carried all the essential meaning.

"A human?" Felicitas covered her mouth with her hand in shock. The two young men just stared at Tabea.

Vincent sighed. "No wonder he doesn't trust anyone aboard," he mumbled. "He can't be sure that there aren't more pirates out there. Especially if they were searching for something."

Tabea nodded somberly.

"What I wanna know," Marco said, crossing his arms, "is what exactly they were looking for."

"And if they found it," Felicitas added.

A pregnant pause followed.

What did it mean if the pirates had found what they'd sought? What did it mean if they hadn't?

"Was the Sonata carrying any special cargo?" Vincent frowned. "They must have had a reason for infiltrating her specifically."

Tabea shook her head.

"There's no way for us to find out. We'd need to connect with the headquarters back on Earth, or even one of the colony outposts, but we're way out of range for that. Plus, Callaghan or Szkarisov would need to be the one asking. They're the only ones with the right access codes."

"Really?" Vincent seemed honestly surprised. "I didn't know it was that classified."

"How do you even know this stuff?" There was something akin to admiration in Marco's gaze.

Tabea shrugged, thinking fast to come up with a plausible explanation.

"Well, Callaghan was my mentor at the Academy. I guess I picked up more from him than I thought."

Vincent turned to the other two. "She was a scholarship student," he explained. "She got the Asimov Grant and Callaghan was the one organizing it at the time."

Marco gave an impressed whistle. "Not bad. No wonder you seem so close."

Tabea couldn't help but perk up at those words.

"So, what do we do now?"

Another pause followed Marco's question. Felicitas shifted her weight uncomfortably, Marco wouldn't look at anyone, and Vincent kept messing with his blond curls every few seconds. None of them seemed to want to make a decision.

"I think it's up to you."

Tabea sighed. "Let's wait until tomorrow evening," she said. "I have a study session with Shinay, so I can kind of test the field. If Yuri doesn't talk to her by then, I'll go to Callaghan directly. He needs to know about this."

"Okay, but why wait?" Marco scowled, his arms still crossed. "Wouldn't it be better to go to him, like, right now?"

Tabea and Felicitas both grimaced.

"I don't want to get in trouble," Tabea said. "And I've asked Yuri to talk to Shinay. If he talks to her directly, we don't have to do anything, and none would be the wiser."

Marco didn't seem appeased by her explanation.

"I think tonight would be better," he mumbled, but he left it at that. Vincent took a step toward him and clapped him consolatory on his shoulder.

With that, their meeting was adjourned, and the guys left. Felicitas hesitated, however. She was about to follow the boys out when she stopped and turned around again, allowing the door to shut. Her brows were furrowed as she looked at Tabea.

"I'm worried," she admitted. "And I think not knowing why the Sonata was attacked is worrying me the most. What if we're next? What if the pirates get to three more ships before we even find out? What if this isn't actually pirates but the first step of an all-out attack against Humanity by one of the other races?"

A knot formed in Tabea's stomach as she listened to Felicitas' concerns. They all felt so familiar to her. The same questions had been swirling around in her head, too, and she couldn't get rid of them, no matter what she did. Still, at the very least, no one could do to the *Calliope* what had been done to the *Sonata*. She would never allow that to happen.

Walking toward Felicitas with a somber expression, she said, "There are many things we don't know about right now, many variables we can't control. But I guarantee you, Callaghan will do everything in his power to put an end to this—whatever it is."

She threw her arms around Felicitas to hug her tightly. Through the embrace, she could feel a small amount of trembling in the other girl and she squeezed tighter.

"It's gonna be okay."

Felicitas nodded and smiled at her when they stepped apart. "Somehow, when you say it, it becomes easy to believe." With another little wave, she opened the door again. "See you tomorrow."

The door slid closed and Tabea was left alone. The silence felt weird, almost stifling, and she felt the need to do something, but she couldn't think of what. She accessed her com pad and checked her messages. Nothing new.

The pit in her stomach still remained, wobbling around just a little, leaving her unsatisfied and anxious about the situation.

"*Callie?*" she asked. "*Can I talk to you?*"

"*Do you even need to ask?*"

She locked her door, lay down on her bed, and closed her eyes, making sure that one hand touched the wall of her room. The physical connection wasn't needed, but it made it easier to merge. She let her mind go, feeling the connections, the currents of energy pulsing through the ship. Entering them with her mind, she was carried along by the never-ending stream.

Calliope was all around her, their energies twirling together, twisting and weaving a bond. They became part of one another. It made communication more wholesome because it was easier to feel the meaning of words. Connecting with Calliope in this way was exhausting, but she could already do it for much longer than she had managed two years ago. It remained Tabea's favorite way to train her powers to this day.

"*Felicitas and Marco are trustworthy, right?*" Tabea asked.

"*You could check their digital communication to find out,*" Calliope replied, both amused and daring.

"*But wouldn't that mean that I don't trust them?*"

"*Do you trust them?*"

Tabea hesitated. She thought of Felicitas' smile, and of their willingness and initiative to help her talk to Yuri, even though it could get them into deep trouble, as well as the vulnerability she had just shown her.

"*Yeah, I think I do.*"

"*Then that's why you haven't felt the need to check.*"

Tabea almost found herself sighing with relief, but the knot in her stomach was not yet gone.

"*What about Yuri?*"

Unease spread around Tabea, a feeling that did not originate within herself. It was a sentiment dripping with suspicion, with caution.

"*You don't trust him,*" Tabea realized, with surprise. Throughout all of this, it had never occurred to her that Calliope might not have considered Yuri genuine.

Calliope hesitated to respond.

"*Did you wonder why Callaghan doesn't want you to*

speak with him? It's clear that he intentionally kept you away from him, why he didn't give into the repeated requests for you."

"You think he doesn't trust him, either," Tabea said. *"But he doesn't know what happened on that ship. He doesn't know that Yuri's innocent!"*

"And you don't, either."

Tabea swallowed her reply. As much as she wanted to believe in Yuri, Calliope had a point. She only knew about what he had told her. How much of that might have been imagined, misremembered, or made up, she had no way of knowing.

Still. The pain in Yuri's eyes, the hurt in his voice and everything about the way he acted, it all sent the same message. And all Tabea wanted to do as a result was to reassure him and make him believe that he really was in a safe haven, that the cause for his nightmares was over.

Either way, tomorrow, Callaghan would hear Yuri's story, and then the decision of what to do with that information would be left up to him.

Chapter 6

THEY DIDN'T SPEAK ABOUT THEIR DECISION ALL throughout the morning. Instead, Vincent and Tabea worked alongside one another, only chatting about mundane things, partially because they were joined by Loïc.

At lunch time, Besma arrived a little later than usual and slammed her tray onto the table before she took her seat with them, a sour expression on her face.

"What's up?" Tabea asked, but Besma only awarded her a glare with flared nostrils.

"Um... Is everything okay?" Vincent ventured as well, but he received much the same treatment as Tabea had.

They exchanged a glance.

Besma started to eat her meal, scratching along the plate and skewering her food a little more forcefully than strictly necessary, pointedly ignoring both of them.

"Bes-Bes, are you okay?" Vincent asked, lowering his head so he could look at Besma properly. She whipped her head away, almost like in a cartoon.

"Yeah. You can talk to us. We're your friends."

Tabea watched her with concern. What could possibly have happened to make her so upset?

Besma dropped her cutlery to glare at Tabea.

"Oh, are you?" Her chin was jutted forward, and small pools appeared in her eyes. "Or have you found someone better?"

A pit opened in Tabea's heart. Had she done something to hurt her friend? She wracked her brain to think of what might have happened to give Besma the impression that she was being replaced, but she couldn't think of anything. Helplessly, she glanced at Vincent, who shrugged, just as clueless as her.

"What are you talking about?" she asked, but that only made Besma's lips quiver.

"Don't pretend like you don't know," she said. "Yesterday was meant to be girls' night."

A dim sense of realization dawned on Tabea. Right. The third of the month. Girls' night. And she hadn't gone to Besma's room to watch a movie with her because she'd been too preoccupied with the Yuri situation. Guilt flushed over her. She should have canceled, at least, or rescheduled, but she'd completely forgotten.

"When you didn't show, I thought that maybe you'd fallen asleep because you were tired, so I came to check on you," Besma continued quietly. "But then I was in front of your room, and I heard all of you. You" — she glanced at both of them — "and your new BFFs from the medical team. So what? Am I not good enough for you anymore? Are you" — her lip quivered, and she took a deep breath — "cutting me out?"

Tabea didn't hold back. She flung her arms around Besma.

"No, no, of course not," she cried. "I'm so sorry. I didn't mean to make you feel left out, I promise. This wasn't... I mean..."

She looked to Vincent for help.

"They asked us to join them for a double-date," he said.

A moment of silence followed his words.

"*A date, huh?*" Calliope asked. "*Oh, that poor, sweet, innocent summer child.*"

Even Tabea had to groan inwardly at his explanation. Sure, it was plausible, but there was no way Besma would believe it. She knew that Tabea had no interest in romance.

"A double date?" Besma repeated, her trembling finally dying down as she processed the information. Apparently satisfied with the explanation, she nodded and turned to Tabea, a sour look still in the lines around her lips.

"Well, you could have told me, at least," she chided her.

Tabea was quick to reply once she got over her surprise. "I know, and I'm really, really sorry. I want to make it up to you. Reschedule for tomorrow night?"

"Why not tonight?"

Besma pouted, though she already looked somewhat appeased.

"I can't, I have class with Shinay and she'll literally come and drag me to hell mid-movie if I skip."

Smiling apologetically, Tabea wrinkled her nose to give her words more punch. Her plan succeeded. Besma giggled.

"Well, no one wants that."

Relieved that the tension was broken and that she

was forgiven, Tabea returned to her meal. She still felt bad about lying to her friend, and for keeping secrets from her, but four people who knew were already more than she was comfortable with, and Besma wasn't exactly known for keeping secrets.

Some girls sat down on the neighboring table.

"And then they took her to see that guy, the one Officer Shinay saved. It's, like, totally proof, right?"

"Oh, for sure. Rissa's gonna be promoted to the core crew for sure. She's the best candidate anyway."

"Yeah, she's worked, like, so hard."

"She really deserves it."

"Totally. And Callaghan's, like, totally showing his trust in her."

"You think they're gonna announce it at the party?"

"Oh, gosh, I didn't even think of that! Yeah, that'd be, like, totally the perfect time!"

"I'm so jealous."

The two girls giggled.

Without meaning to, Tabea had listened to their entire conversation. Her mouth was dry, and her appetite suddenly gone. Her muscles felt heavy, and she couldn't even lift her glass anymore. She tried to bring another forkful of food to her mouth, but somehow, she lost the grip on it, and it clattered on the floor.

The mess was suddenly silent, and Tabea felt their eyes on her as she picked up her fork.

Besma reached over to touch her arm. "Hey, are you okay?" she whispered, and Tabea nodded numbly.

Trying not to look up, she felt the heat rising to her cheeks and ears.

"Sorry, Tabea," one of the girls said. "Better luck

next time?"

"You'll totally get your shot after you finish the exams."

Tabea only nodded. She appreciated that they were trying to make her feel better, but they didn't understand that she wasn't worried about the promotion. It was about Callaghan's trust. She'd already betrayed it by going to see Yuri without permission, and even without knowing that, he'd put his trust in someone else. How much would she lose when she told him the truth? The thought made her feel numb all over. The words of her fellow crewmembers only reached her ears as a low buzz as she tried to calm down.

Breathe.

Inhale, exhale. Focus.

She stood up, the chair scratching noisily along the ground, put her tray away, and left the mess hall.

Why *Nerissa* of all people? Why did it have to be her?

"I'm sure there's a good reason." Calliope tried to soothe her.

"Yeah. I'm sure there is."

Why would Callaghan allow Nerissa to meet with Yuri, but keep her, Tabea, away from him, even though Yuri asked for her and she *wanted* to speak with him? Why was she reduced to going about things secretly, having to break the rules, while Nerissa was allowed to just go ahead? She didn't even have anything to do with the situation! She hadn't seen the ship; she didn't know what state he'd been in. There was no way she could understand what nightmares still plagued him now.

And all this after Tabea had asked Yuri to open up and speak about what had happened.

Nerissa would absolutely take credit for that.

Yes, she was good. She possessed natural talent, the kind Tabea could only dream of. Not only that, but she was also a hard worker. Tabea couldn't deny that, in theory, Nerissa was the perfect candidate for the core crew.

But she was just so mean!

"He wouldn't talk with her."

Tabea stopped her stride.

"What?"

"Yuri. He didn't talk to her."

"He didn't?"

Tabea's chest suddenly started to feel lighter.

"No, he only kept asking for you."

"If you knew all this, why didn't you tell me?"

"I didn't think it would do you any good. And I think I was right," Calliope said dryly. *"Jealousy isn't a good look for you."*

"It's not a good look for anyone, and I'm not jealous."

Calliope only laughed.

The end of her shift came around, and Tabea headed closer toward the bridge, where the ship's library and officer's quarters could be found. She walked the hallways slowly, contemplatively, only occasionally nodding to other juniors or cadets passing her to go to the mess hall.

On days when she had her lessons with Shinay, they usually ate together as well, and whenever Tabea was working on the bridge, she ate with all the officers in their canteen. Callaghan always figured it made more sense, timing wise, since the cadet's mess was located on the other end of the ship.

As she walked through empty hallways, Tabea fretted about the upcoming conversation, phrasing and rephrasing her explanations over and over. What was the best way to bring up Yuri without immediately getting into trouble? And how soon? She could mention it immediately before her lesson even began, or she could wait and have her class, when maybe Shinay would broach the subject, to make it easier.

Long before she felt she was ready, Tabea had arrived at the door to Shinay's quarters and knocked.

"Come in."

The door slid aside and Tabea joined Shinay at a table at the side of her room. Being an officer, Shinay had quarters were much larger than Tabea's, including more furniture. She was still wearing most of her uniform, her long braid hanging over her shoulder, but she had gotten rid of her jacket, making the whole situation feel less formal in her white T-shirt.

Shinay pointed at the two set, covered plates in front of her. "Let's eat first this time. I'm famished."

They unveiled their plates and the rich, sweet scent of a roast with a side of carrots and broccoli seeped up Tabea's nose.

An unwilling sigh escaped her lips. The food in the general mess hall wasn't bad by any standard, but there was always something special about the officer's dishes, something fancy. Perhaps it was only in her own mind, but she nevertheless appreciated them.

"How is it, being back on the floor?" Shinay asked

between bites.

Tabea shrugged. "It's fine. It's nice to spend some more time with my friends."

Shinay chuckled quietly to herself, her fork halfway up to her mouth. "You're bored out of your mind, aren't you?"

Tabea cracked a smile as well, feeling a little guilty about her secret excursions. "I wouldn't exactly say that," she said, "but it is very quiet."

"Then I expect you've had plenty of time to revise your astronomy, right?"

There was a glint of knowledge in Shinay's gaze, something in the quirking of her lips that seemed to say that she knew exactly what Tabea had been up to.

"Um, yeah."

This was followed by series of questions about the Sunflower Galaxy, which Tabea managed to answer at least mostly correctly, followed by some more questions about the Caperius system.

Then Shinay leaned back in her chair, watching Tabea for a minute, her arms crossed and her expression serious.

"We've been here for an hour now, and you haven't yet asked about that young man you saved," Shinay said eventually. "Now, doesn't that strike you as a little strange?"

Tabea wouldn't look her in the eye. She couldn't lie to her. Not if she wanted to tell her and Callaghan what Yuri had told her.

She gulped. "His name is Yuri, and there are some things I need to tell you and Callaghan."

Shinay sighed. "We should have known there was no way to keep you away."

She tapped on her com-watch and selected Callaghan's contact. His face appeared on the small screen only moments later.

"Yes?"

"I have a sneaky mouse here with me, and she needs to talk to you, now."

Callaghan only nodded and ended the call.

"So…" Shinay returned her attention back to Tabea. "He really does talk to you, huh? We were starting to worry that he had brain damage. I'm surprised he recognized you."

Something clicked.

"That's why you brought in Nerissa, isn't it? To see if he would actually recognize if it was me?"

Shinay nodded. It was true that both Nerissa and Tabea had a similar build and general looks — they both had the same chin-length, light brown hair and the same, yellow-based skin tone. The main difference were their eye-colors — Tabea's were plain brown, while Nerissa had hazel eyes.

It made her wonder if Yuri would have mistaken them if Nerissa had met him before Tabea had come to see him. Somehow, she doubted it. He seemed too certain about her, too instantly confident.

The door opened and Callaghan entered, his expression grave. He gave Tabea a stern look but waited until the door had closed to speak.

"Why is it that you must always be at the center of trouble?" he asked darkly. Tabea cringed. Of course he would know immediately why she was here. Guilt once more washed over her, and she wouldn't meet his eyes. She didn't think she could take it if he looked like he was disappointed in her.

"Don't worry so much," Calliope told her. *"He already knows you too well to expect anything else."*

"And how exactly is that meant to be making me feel better?" Tabea shot back. She watched as Shinay and Callaghan shared a long look, both with serious, grave expressions.

"He talked to her," Shinay said after a long moment of silence, raising an eyebrow meaningfully. Callaghan's eyes fell back on Tabea, but he gave no other indication that he had heard Shinay.

"I know I didn't explicitly order you *not* to talk to him, but I expect you *know* you broke some rules. What have you got to say for yourself?"

Tabea took a deep breath. Despite the guilt she was feeling, she knew that she'd had to do what she'd done. And she knew equally well that she would do it all over again, even though she hated going behind Callaghan's back. This was one of those moments where she needed to show strength and summon her stubborn side, use it to its full potential to justify her actions. It was important, after all. Determined not to be dismissed, she met Callaghan's gaze, steady and serious.

"He asked for me."

"I'm aware. Don't you think I would have gotten you if I thought it would do some good?"

"But you didn't. And yet, he spoke to me."

Callaghan didn't respond, but his brooding presence seemed to grow into a cloud that enveloped the whole room. Tabea almost imagined that she could feel the crackling energy around her.

"He's really mad," Calliope said helpfully. *"A lot angrier than I thought he'd be. Good luck!"*

"You know, I really couldn't tell. Thanks for that."

Tabea suppressed an eyeroll and continued. "Yuri told me what happened on his ship, what he experienced."

Callaghan's eyes narrowed slightly, but he still wouldn't say anything. Taking this as a sign to continue, Tabea spoke evenly, without faltering.

"There was a human in his crew who helped a group of other races to infiltrate the ship. He thinks they might have been pirates looking for something. That's the reason why he won't talk. He's afraid the same thing will happen again. He doesn't know who's trustworthy and who's not."

Tabea waited a moment to let the information sink in.

"I tried to get him to talk to you guys" — she turned to Shinay — "but I guess he still wouldn't."

Finally, Callaghan sighed and took a seat in a chair as well. "First of all, you are still in trouble, and we'll deal with your punishment later."

Even though his tone and expression were stern, there was a warmth to his gaze that told Tabea that whatever punishment she may need to endure, he accepted that she might have made the right call. He wasn't disappointed in her. As relief flooded over her, her whole body relaxed, and she felt like a mountain's worth of weight had been lifted off her shoulders.

Tabea found herself surprised. While she'd known that Callaghan's opinion was important to her, she hadn't realized how much the fear for his approval had really affected her.

"It's 'cause you loooove him."

"Shush, you. This is important."

"Second, thank you for sharing this information. Third, I don't want you to speak to him alone anymore, and yes, this time, this is an active order. One of the officers always has to be present."

Tabea's eyes lit up. "You mean I can talk to him officially now?"

He nodded hesitantly. "We've tried all we could, but for some reason, he's fixated on you."

Shinay narrowed her eyes. "I don't like it."

"I don't, either. There's something about this entire situation that sits wrong with me, and until I can figure out why exactly that is, I need you to be careful."

Callaghan didn't need to continue the sentence, Tabea understood. But he needn't have worried. She hadn't even revealed her secrets to her friends; she sure wasn't about to tell a stranger.

"Over the weekend, you'll be on the night shift," Callaghan continued. "But on Monday, I want you to report back to the bridge. In the meantime, no more unsupervised visits, understand?"

Tabea nodded earnestly.

"And keep everything you've heard from him to yourself," Shinay added. She must have noticed Tabea's micro-flinch because she raised an eyebrow. "Who else was involved?"

Hoping that her phrasing would ensure that her friends wouldn't get in trouble, Tabea said slowly, "I told Felicitas and Marco from the medical team, and Vincent from the engineering team."

Shinay sighed.

"I'll talk to them."

Besma was waiting in front of her door when Tabea returned to her room. Grinning, she held up some chocolates and her entertainment pad.

"Up for girls' night?"

Tabea met her smile. "You bet. Five minutes?"

Besma went back to her own room while Tabea got changed into her pajamas before joining her. Girls' night meant being comfortable and talking about nonsense. Sometimes it could go on for so long that Tabea barely managed to get back to her own room. On more than one occasion, she had even fallen asleep in Besma's bed.

It was a tradition that had started in their early years at the Academy, and they'd kept it up whenever possible since then.

Besma had built a "cave corner," as she called it, next to her bed. Really, all it meant was that there was a sort of pillow and blanket fort—another tradition that had lasted. Seeing Tabea come in, Besma grinned and produced a thermos, swiftly pouring the contents into two cups. The sweet scent of chocolate drifted across the room easily and made Tabea's mouth water. Within seconds, she'd taken her place next to her friend on the pillows and took the cup of hot chocolate, smelling it with bliss.

"So..." Besma's eyes sparkled. "Tell me about the double date."

Tabea almost choked on her drink and she coughed, tears coming to her eyes as she tried to free her lungs.

Vincent's excuse for her blunder had completely slipped her mind. But the memory came back with a vengeance, and she struggled to come up with a suitable answer that wasn't an outright lie but would satisfy Besma. Somehow, she didn't want to tell her that she'd been seeing Yuri without telling her. Even though it only meant keeping yet more secrets, divulging that information now, while they finally had the opportunity to just have fun together, felt like the wrong thing to do.

"It hasn't happened yet," she settled eventually.

"Aw, you're blushing!" Besma giggled.

Tabea managed a crooked smile. Blood shot to her face whenever she was nervous; she was only lucky that Besma had misinterpreted the color.

Dropping her gaze, Tabea said quietly, "I'm not sure it's a good idea, though. I don't wanna give Vince any... false hopes, you know?"

She glanced up to find Besma nodding sympathetically with a pitying smile.

"Of course. But you guys are only going because they asked you to, right? So I'm sure he understands. He's known you for long enough, after all."

In theory, Besma was right. In practice, though... Even though the double date was fake and would never take place, Tabea knew that Vincent did have hopes. He was terrible at hiding them. So far, it had been an uphill struggle to find a way to turn him down that didn't hurt him so much that she would lose his friendship.

"Enough about me." Tabea grimaced. "What's new with you? It's been a while, so update me. What's going on in the pilot's core?"

Suddenly, romance was forgotten and Besma's lips trembled as she tried to contain the wide smile that was threatening to break free on her face. The look in her eyes became determined and proud, taking on a piercing quality that Tabea only ever saw when Besma's ambition awoke.

"I got news this afternoon," Besma admitted. "But Akari wants me to take more shifts on the bridge."

Tabea gaped at her. Only a moment later, her own smile matched Tabea's wide, winning grin in size.

"That's amazing!"

She knew more than anyone how much Besma had been wanting to be recognized. Her abilities matched her ambition. With the exception of Tabea, Besma was one of the best pilot cadets in their year, although that didn't mean much on the *Calliope*, where everyone had come from the top of the curve. As Humanity's most prized possession, the *Calliope* was also its most powerful, able to travel faster and farther than other terrestrial ships. Her full potential had yet to be uncovered.

Besma deserved to be on the bridge. Perhaps that even meant that Tabea could finally reveal her powers to her friend. She would have done it long ago, but Callaghan had warned her not to, and, trusting his judgement, Tabea had acquiesced.

"I'm so proud of you," Tabea exclaimed as she threw her arms around Besma. "When do you start?"

"Monday."

Tabea's heart soared. Monday. She'd been told to report back to the bridge then as well. With any luck, they might both be working at the same time.

"So where were you earlier?" Besma peered at her face with unconcealed curiosity. "You took longer than normal. Did Shinay chew you out or something?"

Tabea made a face. She should have known Besma

would notice. After all, getting chewed out had added almost an extra hour to her lesson time.

"I kinda messed something up, but I don't want to get into it right now." Tabea sighed. "Callaghan's putting me on the night shift for the weekend."

Meeting Besma's gaze, she grimaced. Night shifts were her least favorite, especially for routine checks. There was no more boring job on the ship, as least not for her. Though it seemed she wasn't the only one who felt that way because Besma also immediately dropped back into a sympathetic expression.

"Ouch, it must have been something real bad for him to put *you* on the night shift." She leaned back into the pillows and went back to sipping her chocolate.

Tabea pouted at her. "You know, a little more sympathy would have been nice."

Besma smirked at her, an evil glint in her eye. "What? Is little 'Miss Favorite' upset that she can also get punished?"

Tabea threw a pillow at her face, but Besma blocked it easily, countering with a pillow of her own swiftly.

It escalated quickly.

After beating each other into near oblivion with pillows, both girls sank into the blankets, panting with exhaustion.

"That takes me back," Tabea mumbled, staring at the ceiling. She could feel Besma nod beside her.

"You really took me by surprise back then," she said, glancing over. "You were this new, shy, anxious girl and there I was, just being nice."

Tabea smirked at her and raised an eyebrow. "Not *that* nice, either. You had it coming."

They both laughed as they remembered their first

sleepover at the Academy. Tabea hadn't even been there for a week yet, but she'd found it difficult to talk to people. She'd never spoken up because she'd been afraid of being ridiculed, being told she didn't know what she was talking about, and that she should be quiet. After all, her elder siblings were fond of saying things like that.

Besma had been the first person to reach out, inviting her to her room. Tabea couldn't even remember what exactly it was that had set her off, but Besma had said something that had driven her into a frenzy, and before she'd known it, she'd been pillow fencing with Besma, both fighting and beating each other until they'd been out of breath, much like today, except with a lot more anger.

It had been the first time in a long while that Tabea had felt confident coming out of her shell, and it had marked the foundation of their friendship.

"Oh, I just remembered." Besma rolled onto her front to face Tabea, bursting with excitement. "I wanted to tell you. Did you hear what Bianca told Charlotte?"

Rolling onto her front as well, Tabea shook her head.

"She said that she and Loïc went to daycare together."

Nodding, Tabea encouraged Besma to continue. Even though she didn't really have a vested interest in either of these people, she knew that Besma wouldn't be able to rest easy until she got it off her chest.

"*She's a girl after my own heart.*" Calliope spoke up for the first time that evening.

"And guess what—apparently, he made her promise that they'd get married when they're all grown up."

"*I'm sure. You two would have a blast just gossiping at*

each other," Tabea responded dryly.

"And what's wrong with that?"

"And now, the other day, he asked her to the dance, so Bianca thinks that he's actually planning on holding her to that promise from when they were four!"

Besma watched her expectantly, but Tabea really wasn't sure how she was meant to react. Was she meant to be shocked? Happy and excited? Gleeful? Should she just find it funny, or was she meant to be angry at Loïc's audacity? It was a mystery.

"No way," she said, hoping that answer covered most of those options.

"Yes way. Isn't it romantic?" Besma sighed and lay back down with a wistful smile. "I wish I had a childhood sweetheart like that."

Once again, Tabea felt out of her depth. Still, she knew what was expected of her as a best friend.

"Don't worry." She sidled closer and wrapped an arm around Besma, giving her a peck on the dark cheek. "You'll find someone who's going to be perfect for you."

"You know," Besma said, smiling, "when you say it like that, it's suddenly so easy to believe."

She grew silent for a moment, and then squeezed Tabea's arm.

"I'm sorry for always getting overexcited about Vince," she said quietly. "I know it doesn't work like that for you. I just can't help myself."

"That's fine." Tabea cuddled into her shoulder. "I know you understand, and I don't mind that much." She glanced at the dark entertainment pad, already set up for the perfect viewing angle. "Movie?"

CHAPTER 7

AT DINNER—BREAKFAST FOR TABEA ON FRIDAY, Besma suddenly appeared, later than usual, her uniform crisp and her straight, black hair wet.

Tabea raised an eyebrow at her. "Just take a shower?"

"I asked Akari to let me switch to the night shift for the weekend as well," Besma explained with a shrug and a smirk. "It'll be nice to have you to myself for a bit," she added before she laughed embarrassedly. "It seems like you're always surrounded by so many people, and while it's not like I don't like Vince, it's nice that it can be just the two of us for a while, you know?"

The weekend passed quietly—Tabea did her routine checks quickly, with the assistance of her technomancy powers. Unlike during the day shift, the night shift was composed of less than a third of the normal crew, which rotated on a regular basis with others from the day shift.

While it meant that she was able to work more effectively and more peacefully, it also meant that she had more time to be bored, and that, that was the real punishment.

It didn't even really make sense. In space, night and day didn't exist, not as real times anyway. Out here, they could spend weeks in the direct light of a star, or months too far from any star to consider it anything but darkness. But somewhere along the way, the Space Core Initiative had decided that it was better for morale and the mental health of the Space travelers if they could hold on to the same measure of time for the duration of their travels. And so, they had decided that a ship would stick to the same night and day schedule that would have been the case on the space port of their origin.

There were of course captains who disregarded it and had a full crew working around the clock, but Callaghan believed that there was a large social aspect to a crew that trusted each other and therefore worked well together. Even with this mindset, he still ensured that there were more than enough people working to keep the ship running smoothly. His methods also accommodated people who preferred a quieter and less social workspace.

As promised, Tabea also didn't make any more secret visits to speak with Yuri. She did, however, ask Calliope occasionally if there were any changes to his state or situation and let her friends know about the newest development.

At mealtimes, the mess hall felt strangely empty. Not even half the tables had someone sitting at them, and even then, it was usually only one or two people at a time. Tabea was immensely grateful to have Besma to share those times with. If she hadn't, she was sure it would have felt a little lonely, even with Calliope as her constant companion.

It was around two in the morning on Monday when a knock on the wall disturbed Tabea as she went through the final checks with Calliope.

Callaghan stood in the doorway, watching her with a gentle smile, still wearing his uniform despite the late hour.

"Bored yet?" he asked, smirking.

Tabea made a face. "You have no idea."

"Good. Then I expect you've finished up for the night, yeah?"

Seeing one of his eyebrows raised up playfully, Tabea felt her heart warm. Her punishment was over. She nodded and stepped toward him.

"Meet you in the training hall?" she asked, looking up at him, her head tilted to one side.

"See you there in ten."

After only seven minutes, Tabea entered the empty training hall, where Callaghan was waiting for her, his gray and clover-green training gear matching hers. His eyes closed, he was sitting on the ground, cross-legged, and wordlessly, Tabea took a seat beside him, copying his pose and shutting her eyes. She listened to the sound of his slow and steady breathing and focused on her own. Inhale, hold, exhale, hold—and repeat.

She made a note of every part of her body, in particular those responding to her chakras, allowing energy to flow past them, pool in them, before moving on.

When she felt settled and calm, she opened her eyes to find Callaghan watching her.

"It looks like it gets easier every time," he noted. Tabea couldn't disagree. She'd struggled with this part in the beginning, always feeling fidgety, finding it difficult to let her thoughts ebb away, but practicing with him time and time again had made it feel more natural.

They rose to their feet and after going through some of the warm-up movements, they began circling each other with slow, steady steps. Tabea watched his torso to detect any hint of movement before it happened. She felt sure of herself, at ease, and completely ready for anything. Before long, Callaghan launched his attack. Tabea sidestepped his grasp, moved into his arm, one of her hands holding it in place, the other arm reaching across his front, before twisting her body so he was pushed over her outstretched leg behind him. Falling didn't make him lose his momentum, however. He used the fall to roll out of her grasp and back to his feet right away, and this time, it was Tabea who tried to grasp him without losing the flow in her movements. They were precise actions, every one of them accompanied by the energy flowing through her body.

It made her feel like water, swept along with the waves of the ocean, along currents and never stopping for even a moment. The energy continued to pass from one place to the next, never still, never halting, never weakening.

Even though they were both moving quickly, focusing on the power surging through her body, imagined or not, made time go slower. In this state, Tabea's mind was working faster than her body, analyzing openings, projecting the path of her flow before her body had even moved an inch.

Teaching her martial arts had never been one of Callaghan's responsibilities as her mentor, but it was at the core of what had brought them close together. He had hosted a workshop at the Academy once, and Tabea had been brought along by Besma. After the workshop, he had offered a training camp over the holidays at his home to anyone who'd been interested. However, with her as the only exception, everyone had preferred to go home to see their families. So Tabea had ended up staying at Callaghan's house for two weeks on her own, and outside of their training sessions, they'd quickly realized that they got along better than expected. Tabea enjoyed learning about all he could teach her—and Callaghan knew a lot about everything—and he seemed to appreciate her ideas and viewpoints on philosophical and moral debates. Needless to say, they found they shared an interest in entertainment as well. Since then, she'd rarely spent her holidays with her blood relatives.

"You're doing well," he said, watching her form. "I'm starting to think I have nothing more to teach you."

This elicited a bright laugh from Tabea. "You haven't taught me anything new in, like, two years, you know."

"Really? That long?" Frowning, he scratched the back of his head as if he were trying to remember.

Tabea dropped her stance and crossed over to him. They'd been at it for a while now and sweat was making her gray T-shirt cling to her body.

"How about a break?" she suggested.

They sat down at the hall's side, just looking into the empty room, gulping back the waters Callaghan had brought. Then he glanced at her from the side.

"How are you doing, kiddo?"

Tabea only shrugged. "I think I'm fine. I'm training

with Callie again, and I seem to have recovered all of my health." Her hand reached up to the stitches in her forehead. "This is almost as good as new as well."

He nodded, satisfied, and there was a warmth in his gaze that Tabea couldn't help but smile about.

"Any trouble with the exam material?"

Tabea glanced at him. If she said that she was finding any of it difficult, he would be the first to jump in to offer to help her. Yet even if she had problems, she could never put that on him. He was busy enough just being captain.

"None whatsoever."

He smirked. "Good, because I'm planning to have you sit the test when we finish the mission."

Tabea sat up straighter and stared at him. "You mean on the next mission, I could be one of your officers?" she asked, not quite daring to get excited.

He smirked, amused. "That's what I'm counting on."

Tabea jumped to her feet, energy and motivation surging through her body as she bounced on the spot. Even her hair was getting charged enough to start floating up.

"Oh, thank you, thank you, thank you!"

The officer's exams required an officer to recommend a junior cadet to take them. They would only ever arrange for the exam if they truly thought the candidate ready and their personality capable of handling the pressure. Which meant that despite Tabea's rogue actions and her recklessness, Callaghan still thought that she was ready to be an officer.

"Calm down." He laughed. "It wasn't just down to me, you know. Hammond threatened that if I didn't let you sit the exam, he was going to sponsor you instead."

Tabea's hands dropped at her side and she stood still as the realization hit her.

"You're *sponsoring* me?"

None of the Academy's exams were free. As a student, she'd been lucky to be there on her scholarship, but it had reached its end when she'd become an official cadet. She'd assumed she was going to use her savings from her time aboard the *Calliope* to pay for the exam.

"Of course." He reached out a hand and she took it, pulling him to his feet so they both stood, facing each other. Tabea had to tilt her head back to look at his bearded face, always carrying such a gentle expression. "Your family wasn't going to help you out, right?"

He always knew.

"Just, uh…" he added, hurriedly, as if he'd only just realized. "Don't tell anyone about it. This is just between you and me." His eyes looked up and to the right. "And Hammond."

Tabea raised an eyebrow.

"And Shinay?" she asked. "And Szkarisov? And Glaucia? And Akari? And Zhen?"

Callaghan's gaze came back to meet hers for a second before dropping.

"Them too," he grumbled, defeated. "They all offered to chip in."

Knowing that she was so well regarded in the officer's circles made Tabea's heart soar. They all had been present for each and every one of her missions on the *Calliope,* and they all had been around when she'd first tapped into her power. They all knew her secret, and they all respected her ability — whether or not she was a space witch. Some of them, like Akari, had taught her back at the Academy as well. They'd been together for a long time, and Tabea cherished them almost as much as Callaghan. That they all wanted her to join them on the bridge for good meant to world to her.

Callaghan dropped back into a fighting stance.

"All right, break's over. Let's get back to it."

Tabea was delighted to wake up Monday morning after a nap following her training session with Callaghan, knowing that she was back to working on the bridge.

Getting dressed in a hurry and wolfing down her breakfast with her friends, she was ready for work well before she needed to be. Despite the lack of sleep, she felt energized and ready to face the day head on.

Callaghan wasn't there yet. The bridge was manned by the early shift—some senior officers from the core crew like the arms and defense officer, Maya Glaucia, and Andrej Szkarisov at the communications deck. The rest were deputy officers. Besma was already sitting in the pilot's seat, only granting Tabea a brief smile before turning her attention back to the screens and controls in front of her. A glance at the engineering controls destroyed Tabea's good mood, however. Instead of Grant Smith, whom she had been expecting, Nerissa was busy at the controls, moving the power around to where it was needed. It was highly uncommon for a cadet to command the engineering station on their own for a whole shift and it stung to see Nerissa receive the same privilege as Tabea.

Sullenly, she took a seat beside Nerissa, watching her hands move swiftly across the board. Every action exuded certainty, and, to her dismay, Tabea couldn't detect any traces of hesitation. Nerissa was working fast and efficiently — and evidently flawlessly. *Great.*

Nerissa glanced up for a second when she got the chance, but instead of the glowering look accompanied by a snide remark that Tabea had been expecting, Nerissa only returned her attention to her work.

"Grant is sick," she said. "They asked me to fill in for him until he's better."

It didn't sound like bragging. There was a lightness to her tone, a glow in her expression that only spoke of happiness, of joy, perhaps even a touch of relief.

Still, Tabea was irked by her words. *Grant?* She called Smith by his first name? How close were they? Who else on the officer's team was she on a first name basis with?

If the list included Callaghan, Tabea would need to throw up and call in sick for a month, at the very least.

Still, while she didn't like the thought of it, Tabea supposed she could work alongside Nerissa while they were both on the bridge. But it also meant that there was no way she could use her powers openly, not even if Callaghan didn't think it was an issue. She would never, ever, allow Nerissa to find out about her secret. There was no telling what that girl might do with it.

They didn't need to sit silently beside each other for long. Shinay and Callaghan arrived shortly, accompanied by Zhen, and waved Tabea over.

"Our guest is ready to leave quarantine," Callaghan told her.

Zhen was fidgeting with a checkered handkerchief,

twisting it in his hands as he looked from his captain to Tabea.

"He needs to start moving about. The constant lying still is causing his muscles to degrade. Normally, I would suggest physiotherapy, but..."

"But we also need to open up more communication. We need him to trust us, and we need him to give us a more detailed report." Shinay completed his words with a little more certainty, though the lack of force in her tone and frequent glances at Callaghan suggested that she wasn't entirely comfortable with the plan, either.

"How can I help?" Tabea asked, standing ready to attention.

Callaghan hesitated and rubbed his stubble, as though he were fighting with himself. Then he let his hand drop and he sighed.

"We need you to be our liaison. In other words, you're to look after him, make sure he's comfortable with his surroundings and relay any questions and answers between him and us. I'll be having some of the officers accompany you on a rotational basis, and" — he glanced at Shinay, who gave him a meaningful look— "on occasion we'll also be leaving you alone with him. It would seem like we don't trust him if we didn't."

"I'll be keeping a closer eye on you those times."

Tabea nodded. Callaghan was going through a lot of trouble for this. Ordering his officers to come with her meant pulling in some of the juniors for shifts in the bridge, which would be a fantastic opportunity for them, but it left him with crew members he didn't know as well, members whose limitations he didn't know, which made hairy situations all that much more stressful.

"*Thanks, Callie, but I really don't think I'll need that much looking after.*"

"*Well, you say that now, but you know what can happen between a young man and a young woman behind closed doors.*"

Tabea suppressed a laugh, almost choking on the snort she held back. She'd never been the kind to be interested in the opposite sex, or any sex, for that matter, so the notion of suddenly changing her mind because of a stranger, as mysterious and enticing as Yuri might have been, seemed ridiculously funny.

Callaghan frowned. "Are you all right?"

Tabea did her best to wave his concern away and added quietly so only he could hear, "Callie says she'll be making sure nothing indecent happens when you leave us alone."

A small smile cracked on Callaghan's lips as well, though his furrowed brows still spoke of a certain level of concern.

"Well, I'm certainly glad to hear that," he said.

"*Of course he is. No father likes to see his daughter fooling around with a young man whose character they can't judge.*"

"*Oh hush, you! We're not even related. And you know perfectly well it's not like that.*"

"*Do I?*"

"So, when do you want me to start? I guess I should begin by giving him a tour of the ship, yeah?"

"Not too much detail," Shinay warned. "Just the common areas—he doesn't need to know the more specialized districts of the ship."

"That includes the rooms concerning engineers, even if he is one himself," Callaghan added, clearly remembering the story Tabea had shared with him. "And he'll be leaving the med bay later today. I'd like you to go with Zhen when that happens and accompany them to the young man's temporary quarters."

Tabea nodded.

"Hammond will join you for the tour after."

"Hammond?" Tabea glanced to the Engineering station, where Nerissa was still toiling away. "But who…?"

"We have another junior in mind whom Hammond vouched for."

Names and faces flashed through Tabea's mind. "Who?"

She could only think of two people besides herself who might be able to handle it easily.

"It's your friend, actually. Vincent Soucroix."

Warmth flooded through her body and an involuntary smile crept onto her face. He was the first person she'd thought of, and he was more than ready to handle this responsibility. He was diligent and had experience. He'd been promoted to junior on her very first mission, the Harvius VI mission two years ago, and since then, he'd hardly spent any time back on Earth. When he wasn't on the *Calliope*, he was on the *Mercutia*, a smaller ship that dealt with trading between Earth and her colonies.

Thinking of the goofy face he'd make when he found out, she smirked.

"Can I tell him?"

Chapter 8

Walking through the medical bay accompanied by a senior officer made Tabea nervous. It felt weird, not having to sneak into the quarantined area, and she kept obsessing about whether Yuri would talk to her the same way as before if they weren't alone.

Along the way, she saw Felicitas carrying some equipment to another room. She watched as Tabea passed, gaping at them. Tabea gave her a small, almost apologetic, wave, before following Zhen into the restricted area.

Yuri was awake when they entered. He was sitting up in his pod, reading some book that didn't have a title on the auburn spine.

Tabea's breath was going faster, and she kept glancing at Zhen. Would Yuri still acknowledge her? Her mouth felt dry, and she thought her steps, and her heart, and her breathing, and the rustling of her clothes all created an ear-shatteringly loud cacophony of sound.

Then Yuri looked up at her, and he smiled, a warm, friendly smile, one that betrayed excitement in his blue eyes by the way the skin around them wrinkled.

"Tabea," he said.

"Hi, Yuri."

The breath was stuck in her throat. Would he say anything except her name?

"How are you?" she asked.

Yuri raised an eyebrow and only smiled. Tabea's heart sank. She glanced at Zhen again, who was standing nearby, watching silently but with interest.

"I came to show you your new room," she continued, hoping that eventually Yuri would give up his stupid silent charade and just talk, trusting anyone or not.

"Thank you."

The words lifted a weight off Tabea's chest, and she beamed at him, suddenly able to breathe freely again. "My pleasure! Come on."

She took his hand and helped him get up. Meanwhile, Zhen had crossed the room to retrieve a spare uniform from a closet, which he was now holding out for Yuri to take, a small smile playing around his lips as well.

"Later, I'll be showing you around the ship," Tabea said, feeling giddy with relief. She could practically bounce.

"I'd like that a lot. Thank you so much, Tabea."

He was talking. Callaghan's trust in her had not been misplaced. He spoke with her, clearly and audibly, even though Zhen was right there.

"If you have any more problems with your injuries or feel otherwise unwell, please come back any time," Zhen said meaningfully as he stepped forward.

Yuri nodded. "I will, thank you. Officer Zhen, isn't it?"

Not only was he talking with her, but he opened up to other people as well! This was truly the best possible outcome. Though she had to wonder—would he still talk to Zhen if she weren't around? At this point, it would seem silly not to.

They took the quickest path to his new quarters, which were on the other side of the ship to her own. They barely met anyone along the way, since it was mid-shift and they were using the personal corridors rather than the ones people needed for work.

There, Tabea gave him a quick overview of what he had at his disposal: a small bathroom of his own, since he was a guest, a desk and chair, a bed with a small shelf above where he could store his personal belongings—not that he had any right now—a small touch screen integrated into the wall, which included the ship's messaging system and location data, as well as a calendar and some other small features, including light switch and dimmer, thermostat, and entertainment. He was given three sets of uniforms as well as three sets of casual clothes to wear in the evenings or at night. Generally, his room appeared to be something halfway between a normal room like Tabea's and that of an officer. She envied him slightly for the benefit of his own bathroom and shower. She had to share hers with three other girls in her hallway, one of whom was Besma.

While she showed Yuri his room, Hammond and Zhen switched out their babysitting duty.

"You're the infamous Yuri I've heard so much about, then." Hammond was leaning in the doorframe, looking Yuri up and down. "Our Tabea's gonna look after you just fine, so ye made a good choice, trustin' in her."

He wiggled his gray eyebrows meaningfully, and Tabea groaned inwardly.

"Though you might have some competition—she's a popular lass."

This time, she couldn't hold back the eyeroll.

"Please stop, you old coot," she grumbled. "You're gonna give him the wrong idea."

"What?" Hammond grinned. "That there are several young people aboard who wouldn't mind takin' ye out? 'Cause that'd be the right idea."

Tabea settled for a sigh and disregarded his words. She turned to Yuri instead. "Let me show you where the mess hall is. We'll be eating there when you're not with officers."

He nodded and followed her out of the room, only pausing to shake Hammond's hand. "It's a pleasure to meet you, sir."

Hammond's eyebrows rose. "Ah, ye're a polite one, aren't ya? Well, the name's Hammond. Pleasure's all mine."

And on they went.

After the mess hall, Tabea showed Yuri the rec hall and the gym and ended her little tour in the library.

"So…" She turned to him, letting her arms fall at her sides. "Any questions so far?"

"Hmm, let's see." Yuri stroked his chin as he looked around the book-covered hall. Some desks were located in the back to allow people to study there. Admittedly, Tabea didn't spend as much time here as she ought to have.

"I've been wondering," he said. "What's this ship's type? It doesn't look anything like the Sonata."

"Oh, of course, she's a unique model, so you wouldn't have seen it before. It's the Calliope."

Tabea beamed at him with pride, but he didn't seem quite as excited as she had expected. The *Calliope* was a famous prototype. After all, it was the first time that Humanity had managed to incorporate alien technology into terrestrial tech and make it work, even if they didn't know how or why. She was more powerful than any of the purely mechanical starships Earth created, and Tabea knew better than anyone that she had far more dormant potential, tempered by the terrestrial tech that enforced restrictions on her.

"He doesn't know me."

Calliope sounded hesitant, as though she were having thoughts she was keeping to herself. If Tabea were to merge with her, then she'd be able to feel them at least, but as it were, she could only tell that her friend wasn't sharing everything.

"The *Calliope*," Tabea repeated with more emphasis. Maybe he just hadn't heard her properly the first time.

Yuri's look of confusion turned into understanding quickly.

"Oh, of course! Sorry, it took me a moment." He nodded emphatically and smiled, reassured. Still, he didn't seem as impressed as she had anticipated, she noticed sullenly.

While Yuri turned to look at the books covering the walls, Hammond leaned into her, whispering.

"No need to look so disappointed, lass. Not everyone's quite as enticed by ships as you are."

So her feelings had been written on her face as clearly as the words in the books surrounding them.

"But it's the *Calliope*," she said, somehow feeling

slighted and hurt. "And he's an *engineer*. How can he not want to know more about how she works?"

Hammond shrugged. "Maybe he does, but this is all still new to him. I bet he's still processin' everthin' that's happened."

Tabea sighed. He was probably right.

Hammond took over from there and brought them to the bridge, where Callaghan properly welcomed Yuri to the ship, introducing him to all his present officers, and insisted that he dine with him and Hammond tonight.

"Will Tabea join us?" Yuri asked, shooting her a brief smile.

Callaghan didn't hesitate in his reply. "Of course. Unless she has other plans." But even so, the little line that had developed in his forehead didn't escape Tabea's notice. He was concerned, undoubtedly about Yuri.

Calliope's earlier comment about fatherly feelings and protectiveness came to her mind, but she shook it off. No way that was true.

Maya Glaucia ended up present for the dinner as well, and Tabea had the suspicion that she'd been invited so Tabea wouldn't be the only female in attendance, not that it mattered to her.

Callaghan had arranged for the meal to be taken in the officer's meeting room. When Tabea arrived with Hammond and Yuri, the other two were already seated, deep in conversation. Callaghan had been frowning, but his face smoothed over when he saw her, and he smiled at them. They took their seats, exchanging some meaningless small talk.

"What do you think of the ship?" Callaghan asked, and the proud glow in his eyes didn't escape Tabea. He loved the *Calliope* almost as much as she did.

Yuri smiled politely. "It's very impressive. Much bigger than the Sonata." His response was just as disappointing as his previous reaction to finding out what ship he was on.

"I would be very interested in seeing how it was engineered, if I may."

Tabea barely dared to breathe. That, after Callaghan had explicitly asked her to leave those parts of the ship out of her tour. His smile suddenly regained its cautious nature.

"All in due time," he said, reaching across the table to uncover the dishes. "For the moment, you should focus on resting and regaining your strength. Let's start by getting some real food into you, young man."

A smooth coverup. Callaghan gained time and Yuri was in no position to press the point. Tabea almost wanted to sigh in relief. A nudge from her side made her attention switch from those two to Glaucia, who smiled at her, curiously.

"Have you watched *The Soul of Space* yet?"

"Oh! Yes! I watched it just the other night with Besma. Thank you for the recommendation!"

"Didn't you just love the visuals?" Glaucia sighed dreamily. "I know we can see things like that for real, but on the screen it just looks ten times more beautiful, don't you think?"

Tabea thought back on the movie. The plot had been simple, but Glaucia was right; the visuals had been stunning. Real records of space mixed with CGI to enhance the effects, no doubt.

"I guess they have to romanticize it more," she said, shrugging.

Hammond cut in. "It is that kinda film, for sure." Both women turned to him in surprise.

"You've seen it?" Tabea asked incredulously.

Startled, he looked at her, almost seeming a little hurt. "I'm a romantic myself, you know. And I can appreciate aesthetics as much as the next guy. My Holly always says I'm *too much* of a romantic."

Tabea and Glaucia exchanged a glance. One eyebrow raised, Glaucia challenged Hammond. "Is that why you chose to live your life out here in space?"

Hammond shrugged. "What can I say? Space is my mistress. Holly understands that."

They laughed and Tabea suddenly became aware of how much she had missed this — just chatting with the officers over dinner, even though it had been nice to be with her friends for a while.

"I think the same could be said for all of us." Glaucia sighed wistfully and grimaced. "But not all of our partners are so understanding as your wife."

Besma had told Tabea about the rumors going around — that after Glaucia had come home after her last mission, she'd found out that her fiancée had been cheating on her with a lunarian beauty queen. Tabea didn't know how much truth there was to the story, but looking at Maya Glaucia's expression then, she would have bet that there was at least a kernel of truth in there.

"*What about you?*" Calliope asked teasingly. "*Is space your mistress, too?*"

Tabea smirked inwardly. *"According to you, it sure should be."*

"Or is it that you're mistress to space?"

"And now you're getting far too philosophical," Tabea chided her friend. *"Next you're going to ask me what it means to have a bond with space. And what space even is."*

"You know," Calliope said slowly, *"It might not be so bad for you to actually think on that. You might find it more useful than you'd think."*

Tabea didn't know how to respond to that. Instead, she focused back on the conversation around the table, which, she suddenly realized, she had neglected.

"Right?" Yuri was looking at her expectantly, as was Callaghan.

Dang. She'd missed something that had been directed at her. Smiling bewilderingly, she blinked twice. "Sorry, what did you say? I must have zoned out just now."

She laughed, trying to make light of it. Everyone here bar Yuri would know exactly why she hadn't been paying attention anyway. She really ought to practice keeping her attention on her surroundings even while speaking with Calliope.

"No worries." Yuri smiled gently back at her. "I was just telling the captain that you promised to introduce me to your friends to help me settle in."

"Oh, yes, that's right."

She glanced at Callaghan, who gave her the tiniest nod with a microscopic eyebrow twitch. He was asking her to be careful. She narrowed her eyes slightly to show him she'd understood.

"I was wondering…" Yuri turned back to Callaghan, his manner hesitant and yet fearfully determined.

"Where is this ship headed? Have the terrestrial forces been informed yet of what's happened?"

Callaghan took his time in preparing an answer. Everyone was watching him as he chewed his food calmly and deliberately.

"It's just that... I think we have to do everything in our power to make sure it doesn't happen again, you know?" Yuri continued, his hands gripping the cutlery ever tighter, so his knuckles stood out white. His shoulders were tense as well, so tense, in fact, Tabea thought she could see them trembling.

"We've taken all necessary precautions for the moment," Callaghan eventually responded, his direct gaze staring Yuri down, though not angry, not cold, just certain. It was a tone of voice that didn't invite an argument; instead of provocation, it was merely fact. "But while we are on the subject, I want to talk to you about what exactly happened tomorrow in my office so we can take more measures, should they be needed. I have no doubt that with your help, we can figure this out."

Yuri gulped visibly, and Tabea glanced between him and Callaghan. Then Yuri turned his eyes to her, a message written clearly in his expression—panic and fear. Hammond noticed, too. He clapped Yuri on the back.

"I'm sure Tabea here can come along if it makes you feel calmer." Hammond turned to Callaghan, one eyebrow raised. "Isn't that right, Jim?"

Callaghan only inclined his head at the comment. Tabea smiled at Yuri and put a hand on his, though he was still gripping his knife with it.

She leaned forward to catch his gaze. "Don't worry.

You won't be alone."

Before long, the dinner was over, and Yuri retired almost immediately, clearly tired out after his intense exchange with Callaghan.

It was still earlier in the evening than Tabea had expected to be getting back to her room, so she used this opportunity to take a nice, hot shower and then hoped to lounge around on her bed, intent on doing nothing more than playing around a little with her powers and chatting with Calliope. Unfortunately, something else was waiting for her instead.

Felicitas was already lingering in front of her room, practically bouncing on the spot. Resigned to her fate, Tabea let her inside.

Felicitas could barely wait for the door to be shut— she was almost vibrating with urgency.

"So?" she asked as the door locked. Her eyes were fixed on Tabea, her lips slightly parted, and she made a few tiny nodding movements with her head, probably without even realizing.

Tabea raised an eyebrow, amused by her new friend's obvious excitement.

"So?" she echoed.

Felicitas let her hands drop and she gave up on the wordless prompting.

"Well, what happened with Yuri? We saw you, you know, showing him the ship and stuff. Does that mean he talks to everyone now? And what's going to happen? Is he joining the crew?"

Tabea's lips curled into a smile.

"I've no idea. But you certainly sound like you want him to join us."

Felicitas averted her gaze, scrutinizing the air above Tabea's head.

"*Poor Marco.*" Calliope sighed. "*He doesn't stand a chance against the mysterious stranger.*"

"Well, you know, it's just that he's all alone, and after all that effort we put in, I just think it'd be nice to have him with us for a while."

Tabea only snorted.

"Plus, I suppooooose he's pretty good-looking," Felicitas added, grinning at Tabea. "You can't tell me you haven't noticed."

"*She's going to get jealous of you pretty soon.*"

"*Stop your prophesizing,*" Tabea chided Calliope gently.

"*It's pure math. She's got a crush on your survivor, and you spend a lot of time with him. Never mind that you're his savior, and he's clearly singling you out.*"

Tabea hesitated.

"*You're reading too much into it,*" she said, lacking conviction. A pit was forming in her stomach, still subtle and small, but it was there, the size of a pin, perhaps.

"Hello? Earth to Tabea?" Felicitas was waving her hand in front of Tabea's face.

"*You're doing it again,*" Calliope said helpfully.

Tabea wished she could shoot her an annoyed glare. "*Well, you're at least partially to blame.*"

"Sorry, sorry." Tabea smiled apologetically. "I guess I zoned out just now."

Felicitas leaned back, not quite satisfied. A little tick in her brows remained. Then she grinned.

"You were imagining Yuri topless, weren't you?"

Tabea had to let her words run through her mind a second time before she could grasp their meaning. "What? No!"

But Felicitas was continuing, without even listening. "Oh, you just know he's got crazy pecs under there. Makes you just wanna touch them and feel them when he tenses them."

She bit her lip and Tabea had to suppress an eyeroll. She'd never understand the joy people gained from objectifying others.

Meanwhile, Felicitas continued to ramble on about her little fantasy and all Tabea could do was let her talk.

Eventually, the girl stopped herself. "What are you doing tomorrow?" she asked, watching Tabea eagerly.

Tabea shrugged. "Callaghan's probably going to let me know in the morning."

Felicitas crossed the distance between them and clasped her hands around Tabea's. "Oh, please, please, please bring him to lunch so I can sit with you! I sooooo want to talk to him, and, well"—she paused to give a little girly giggle—"I kinda want the other girls to *see* me talking with him."

"*She's blushing,*" Tabea reported, surprised. "*She's actually blushing.*"

Calliope's response was swift and smug.

"*Told ya.*"

Chapter 9

Tabea spent her morning sitting beside Yuri in Callaghan's office while her mentor and Szkarisov asked him question after question. Mostly, they were mundane queries concerning information Callaghan required to make his official report to the Space Core headquarters on Earth. This included the exact code of the ship, a piece of info Yuri had trouble remembering, the name of his captain, which he promptly provided, a full account of the incident, including a detailed description of the woman who had betrayed them, as well as her name and role on the *Sonata*.

No matter what Yuri said, Callaghan didn't show any emotions on his face. He only periodically looked down as he scribbled into his little blue notebook.

Szkarisov acted similarly. He was leaning on the edge of a smaller table behind Callaghan, his arms crossed and his gaze neutral, but fixed on Yuri. Only once did it flick to Tabea, to study her as well.

Meanwhile, Yuri couldn't hide his nervousness. He was fidgeting and kept glancing to her, a helpless cry in his eyes whenever their gazes met. Still, he responded to Callaghan to the best of his ability, promptly answering whatever he could and visibly straining his memory whenever something wasn't as clear in his mind.

Callaghan never seemed satisfied.

Tabea wanted to call him out on it, chiding him for his insensitive behavior toward Yuri, to take Yuri's hand and guide him back to the library, where he had seemed the most at ease since arriving on the ship. But she restrained herself. Callaghan had his reasons for acting the way he did, as did Szkarisov. She respected them both too much to jeopardize whatever they were trying to achieve here. Not once did she interrupt. Instead, she settled for giving Yuri reassuring smiles whenever he glanced at her.

Finally, the interview, or interrogation, as Tabea called it in her head, finished.

"Well then," Callaghan said, a smile finally lifting his features. "Care for some lunch?"

He directed his question to everyone in the room and Tabea breathed out with relief. Simultaneously, her stomach decided to respond in her stead and growled as loudly as it could. Her ears turning hot, Tabea clutched her belly quickly.

"Maybe a little?" she said and was received with laughter. Then she remembered Felicitas' request. "Any chance I could take Yuri to the mess hall? I think it might feel more normal to eat with the other cadets and juniors there."

Callaghan hesitated and exchanged a glance with Szkarisov, who shrugged and tilted his head. Then he returned his gaze to Tabea, intensely locking her down, as if to put unspoken instructions in her head.

"We'll be straight back afterward," she promised,

hoping that was what he wanted to hear.

Eventually, he nodded slowly. "Officer Akari will be waiting to accompany you in the afternoon. Come by the bridge whenever you're done."

Before he could say anything else, Tabea jumped up, taking Yuri by the arm and almost pulling him out of the room.

Yuri walked silently alongside her through the hallways, but eventually, he said, "He doesn't like me, does he? He doesn't trust me."

"*Hypocritical much?*" Calliope chimed in.

Tabea stopped and shook her head with more confidence than she was feeling.

"No, that's not it," she argued. "He's just..." She paused, struggling to find the right words. "Cautious."

Yuri gave her a sad, crooked smile. "It's a good quality to have, but, in this case, it means the same thing."

Tabea's shoulders sagged. What could she possibly say to that?

"And he holds you in high regard," he continued, giving her a strange, pensive look.

Tabea was quick to laugh and wave the suggestion away. "It's just because I'm the only person you'll talk to." She lifted her eyebrows at him to drive the slight reprimand home. He wouldn't even speak to Shinay this morning when she'd picked him up from his room until the moment Tabea had arrived.

Yuri watched her for a moment longer, but then he shrugged, and they headed on their way to the mess hall.

Felicitas was already occupying an otherwise empty table close to the line for the food and frantically waved at them when they entered.

"*She picked the seats that where you can best be seen,*" Calliope noted, full of glee.

"*Yup.*"

Tabea was unimpressed. She'd have preferred to be in a corner somewhere, ideally her usual table, the one that drew the least amount of attention and had the quietest, most relaxing atmosphere because it was far away from the entries and exits, the food, and the bathrooms. It was like an isle of tranquility in a room where silence was unheard of.

Still, she steered toward the table, resigned to her fate. This was a favor to Felicitas, after all.

"*You're too nice.*" Calliope sighed.

"*We're friends. It's what friends do.*"

"*Friends, huh?*"

The unspoken words hung in Tabea's mind, lingering, expanding. *Friends.*

But still, she held firmly to her belief. So what if she'd only really known Felicitas for a week? All friendships had to start somewhere.

"We *were friends after our first conversation,*" Tabea reminded Calliope.

"*That was different.*"

Tabea decided to forgo a response and instead introduce Felicitas and Yuri.

"Yuri, this is my friend Felicitas. She's one of the people who helped me sneak in to talk to you before."

"I suppose I should thank you for your kindness," he said, smiling at Felicitas, who blushed at the gesture.

"Why don't you sit down and talk for a moment?" Tabea said to him, feeling like she needed to get away from the situation while she could, even just for a moment. "I'll get us both some food."

He nodded and took a seat across from Felicitas.

As she joined the line to get food, still short at this point of early lunchtime, Tabea noticed with relief that Yuri and Felicitas were talking. Even though Yuri glanced at Tabea a few times, almost as if to reassure himself that she was still there, he responded to everything Felicitas said, even making her laugh as she twirled a strand of her reddish-brown curls around a finger.

Just then, Marco entered the room with a friend, but he stopped dead in the entrance when he saw Felicitas. Tabea watched the blood vanish from his face as he stood there, wide-eyed and still. Then, he gulped and headed for Tabea, joining her in the line.

"So he's free to walk around now?" he asked, and Tabea nodded.

"Sort of. With the exception of right now, an officer has to accompany him at all times, but yeah, he's no longer stuck in a pod."

He nodded, his gaze still fixed on Felicitas.

Tabea sighed. Romance made everything so complicated. Why did people even bother with it?

It was her turn to order. She collected their food and waited for Marco to finish up as well.

"Join us," she said simply. A little buffer would be nice anyway.

He hesitated.

"Come on. Sit with us," Tabea urged, before adding, much quieter, "and ask her to the dance."

He turned his look toward her, undoubtedly surprised, but she ignored it and walked back to their table, taking a seat between Felicitas and Yuri, sliding

Yuri's food in front of him. From there, she gave Marco one more meaningful look, as he remained transfixed in the same spot. A moment later, he was sitting down with them.

"Marco." Tabea introduced him to Yuri. "He also helped me to see you."

They greeted one another and Tabea noted happily that Yuri seemed to feel more and more at ease. Perhaps it really had just been Callaghan's intimidation that had left him so odd before. Perhaps interacting with juniors and cadets was all Yuri needed. After all, from what she understood, these were the kind of people he had mixed with on the *Sonata* as well.

While Marco and Yuri exchanged a few words, Besma arrived in the hall, and, after giving them a surprised look, she collected her food and joined them as well.

"This looks like a party," she said upon sitting down. Then she looked at Yuri, tilting her head to one side as she inspected him, her gaze lingering for a moment on the muscular biceps showing through his shirt. A charming smile flashed across her face and she stretched her hand out to him. "I don't believe we've met before. I'm Besma. Pleased to make your acquaintance."

Tabea felt like banging her head against the table repeatedly. It seemed like every girl on the ship was instantly attracted to Yuri. Well, besides her. She'd seen some of the guys and enbies give him admiring look as well.

"I'm Yuri." He took her hand and shook it. "The pleasure is all mine." He turned to Tabea and smiled. "Let me guess, she also helped?"

Tabea cringed as she shook her head. "She wasn't involved. But she is my best friend."

Besma raised an eyebrow. "Wasn't involved in what?"

Tabea groaned inwardly. Now she'd be mad, and Tabea couldn't blame her. She leaned over to Besma and whispered in her most apologetic tone, "I'll fill you in later, I promise!"

She looked at her pleadingly, and, after a moment, Besma nodded, probably already connecting the dots.

"But you owe me."

Kyoko Akari was much less hands on about her babysitting duty than the other two officers had been, and, upon Yuri's request, they spent the afternoon in the library where he studied several large volumes. After giving him a brief initiation to the ship's library, Tabea left him to it and inspected the shelves herself while Akari sat in an armchair in a far corner, spending her time flicking through who-knew-what on her holopad.

Tabea strolled through the rows of books, her gaze idly passing over the titles, and finally stopped in the fiction section. At random, she selected a book and pulled it out. Jules Verne's *From the Earth to the Moon*. The cover was a beautiful line drawing of Earth with a simple rocket that flew up to a childlike imagined version of the moon, a pristine moon, long before the first colony had been built there.

She opened up the book and read a random sentence, something she couldn't remember having done in a very long time.

Hence shall our projectile take its flight into the regions of the Solar World.

Feeling nostalgic about past times, simpler times before humans had met other life in the universe or even taken to the stars, Tabea took the book to a corner and started to read.

A while later, after she'd returned from the journey of her mind the book had taken her on, she lifted her gaze to see Yuri looking at her. Akari hadn't moved from her spot, though now she had closed her eyes and wore headphones.

"Is it interesting?" Smiling, Yuri pointed at the book in Tabea's hands.

She lifted it up so he could read the title. It didn't seem to have any effect on him. He only tilted his head to the side and continued smiling.

"It's Jules Verne," Tabea explained. "He was a writer, I don't know, maybe like a thousand years ago or so?"

She tried to remember the date. She'd read something else of his, back in school. A lot of his works were considered classics, and even prophetic because he had dreamed things about the future that in his time, had been considered impossible and utter nonsense, but in the end, a lot of his ideas had proven right, or at least close enough to count.

But how long ago? Was it a number with a one or a two in front? Tabea honestly couldn't remember. It had certainly been before so much of Earth had become uninhabitable by warming and been split into the Federal States of the Northern and Southern Hemisphere. Long before Humanity had taken to colonize the rest of their solar system.

Yuri nodded and looked down at his own books.

"I'm afraid I'm not a strong reader," he confessed, and Tabea noticed that he appeared to be mostly looking at sketches, graphs, and blueprints, which were now strewn across the tables in front of him. "It takes me a long time to grasp the meaning behind letters."

"Need any help?"

He shook his head. "I should be fine. But I do have a question."

He glanced at Akari, and, assured that she wasn't paying any attention, he leaned forward. Tabea did the same, meeting him halfway across the table.

"Can I trust you?" he asked quietly, barely above a murmur. He looked directly into Tabea's eyes, determined, and yet still worried. But Tabea nodded seriously. The hairs on her arms stood up from the tension in the air, and she almost felt electricity crackle.

"I need your help. To protect them. But we can't trust anyone else."

He chewed on his lip, seemingly unsure of whether he should continue. Tabea remained silent, hoping that his words would make sense in a moment.

"I heard them, on the Sonata, when I was running through the halls."

He paused, and her breath caught in her throat. This was it. This was the truth he had been keeping back, the reason why Calliope and Callaghan didn't fully trust him. The secret he'd been keeping all this time. She put the book down, intent on granting him her undivided attention.

"I know what they were looking for."

He flinched, his eyes going wide, when Akari sighed

and shifted in her seat.

Tabea reached out to him, placing her hand on his. "It's all right," she promised quietly. "She can't hear us. What is it they were looking for?"

She angled her head to get a better view of Yuri's face. His nostrils were flaring, the white of his eyes showing, and he was breathing heavily. Clearly, even just thinking about it filled him with fear. What could the pirates have expected to find on the *Sonata*? Had they followed a rumor, or did they know of some valuable cargo currently transported on a human vessel?

"Did they find it?" Tabea pressed. She clasped his hand tightly to show him her support, to reassure him as much as she could.

His downcast gaze found his way back up to meet hers as he shook his head.

"Not on the Sonata." He shrugged helplessly, a tremble sneaking into his voice. "I've never even heard of it before. I don't know if it might be real."

"What is it?" she prodded. His evasions induced fear in her, first with a trickle, but the uneasiness grew the longer he waited to tell her. This mysterious item... It was beginning to feel dangerous, like a threat to all of them.

Yuri gulped and took a deep breath. "They're looking for a space witch. A human space witch."

A second ago, Tabea's mind had been filled with millions of ideas, thoughts, fantasies of what he might say, but all of them were washed away within a second, like a tidal wave took away entire cities.

Only emptiness remained behind as she stared at him, struggling to form a single coherent thought. She blinked, thirteen times, her mouth slightly agape.

"What?" she eventually managed.

"I know it sounds crazy—humans can't be space witches, but I guess they think that we have some." He shrugged helplessly, his hand trembling in Tabea's grasp. "And they're looking for them. And they won't stop until they have them all."

Tabea swallowed, hard, trying to make sense of his words in her mind. How could anyone in the universe possibly have found out about her? It was impossible. Unless... Unless Humanity had other space witches besides her. It was possible. If her, why not others as well?

"Whatever you do, DO NOT TELL HIM."

The words were a scream in Tabea's head and without realizing, she'd covered her ears, instinctively trying to keep Calliope's voice out.

"First of all — OW. Secondly, I'm not stupid."

She'd kept her secret so far. None of her friends knew of her abilities. And neither did he.

"Tabea, are you okay?" His head was tilted to the side with concern.

She answered hurriedly. "Yeah, I'm fine. Sorry, I just got this splitting headache all of a sudden."

"Look I know this..." He took a deep breath, biting his lip. "It's a lot, but I'm telling the truth. You believe me, don't you?"

He looked at her pleadingly, and Tabea felt compelled to squeeze his hand, smiling reassuringly.

"Of course I do. But what now?"

"We need to find them," he said simply, full of determination. "We need to check if there's anyone on this ship who might be one. Someone who stands out, who's particularly good at technological stuff, almost like they can talk to it or something."

A shiver ran down her spine when she heard him so aptly describe her ability. It wasn't uncommon—everyone had heard of space witches, technomancers, who could bend technology to their will. There were enough of them in the known universe, after all. Still, it was unnerving.

"And then?" she asked, hoping her voice wasn't shaking.

"Then we need to protect them, keep them safe. Bring them far away from here before the pirates catch up."

Tabea opened her mouth to respond, but she was interrupted by Akari walking over to them.

"All right kiddos. Back to the bridge," she said, waving her holopad. "Callaghan wants to see you."

Yuri gave her one last long look and squeezed her hand, mouthing the word "secret" before getting up and putting his books away.

Tabea was left sitting, waiting, while she held on to her Jules Verne book, her mind racing. She could tell that Calliope was trying to talk to her, but her own mind was in such uproar, the ship couldn't get through. A million voices argued in her mind, and a thousand scenarios from the last two years played in her head as she tried to figure out which one could have given her secret away to the world at large.

And then—were there others like her? Other *humans*?

And if there were, wouldn't Calliope know and have told her?

She followed Yuri and Akari out of the room, unable

to look at or speak with either of them. Akari didn't seem to notice, and Yuri only shot her a few concerned glances.

Tabea barely knew how to move forward. Placing one foot in front of the other had never seemed so difficult. She wasn't sure she'd find her way if she hadn't been following Akari.

Finally, they reached the bridge, where Callaghan waited for them.

"There you are," he said, turning to them. "I've got some..."

He stopped, looking at Tabea, and his brows furrowed in concern. He took a few steps toward her.

"Tabea?" he asked, placing his cold hand on her forehead. Her eyes flickered up to him, but she was barely able to stand up straight, never mind speak. Her body was on fire, and yet freezing cold at the same time. Which way was up? She wasn't sure anymore.

He took his hand away and nodded to Shinay, who was hovering nearby, concern spread across her features also. "Take her to the medical bay."

Shinay didn't waste any time. She placed her arm around Tabea, steadying her with her own body, and guided her out of the room.

All Tabea heard as she left was Yuri quietly saying her name.

CHAPTER 10

TABEA WOKE UP IN THE MEDICAL BAY, STILL feeling tired and groggy. There was a new scrape on her cheek, and her head was thumping in time with her heartbeat. The Jules Verne book was sitting on a small table beside the pod, right next to an untouched glass of water and a box of tissues.

No one was around.

"*What happened?*" she asked.

Calliope's response was prompt and drenched in relief.

"*You worked yourself into a system overload and you overheated.*"

Tabea translated it into human terms. "*So, you're saying that I was getting overly worked up and stressed, so I got a sudden fever?*"

"*That's what I said!*"

Tabea was saved from having to think up a witty retort by the doors opening. Felicitas and Besma were peeking inside. Upon seeing that Tabea was awake, they both entered fully, crossing quickly to her side.

"Hey, Tabs," Besma said meekly. "How are you feeling?"

Tabea slowly propped herself up. "I'm fine, I think. Whoo." She touched her head when the world started spinning. "Sat up too fast."

"You should have said something if you weren't feeling well," Felicitas chided her gently. "To keep quiet until your fever is so high, you're basically falling over... That's not going to be any good to anyone."

Tabea shrugged. "I was fine until the afternoon. I didn't even notice it happening."

"Seriously? That's scary." Besma watched her face in concern. "Are you sure you're fine now?"

"Yes, I'm telling you; I'm totally okay. I'd be ready to go back to work right this second if they'd let me."

"Well, no chance of that happening, missy." Felicitas laughed. "You know, Yuri was asking about you. He's pretty worried."

"Vince is, too," Besma added quickly and forcefully.

"And Marco asked about you, as well." Felicitas shrugged. "Oh, by the way, I gotta tell you. He asked me to go to the dance with him!"

"He did?" Besma asked, her eyes wide and full of excitement. "What did you say?"

Besma could smell gossip a mile away, Tabea was sure. She was glad that those two seemed to have a naturally good rapport with one another. It meant that her new friendships were less likely to put a strain on the old one.

Felicitas shrugged, pursing her lips in semblance of nonchalance. "I said I'd have to think about it. Honestly, I'd like to ask Yuri to go, but I don't know if that's possible, so going with Marco might be nice. But I want to wait a little before I give up on Yuri."

She shot Tabea a mournful glance, as though the

reason Yuri wouldn't join the dance was her fault somehow.

Tabea raised her hands in defense. "Hey. Don't look at me. I'm not even going!"

"Exactly. That's the problem." Felicitas growled. "You're not going, and so Yuri isn't going, either. And if you *were* going, he'd definitely be going with you."

Tabea sighed. There was no way she could win this argument.

"Look, ask Callaghan if he's okay with Yuri going. *Then* ask Yuri. I don't see what I've got to do with it. But if you ask me, I think you'd be better off going with Marco. You guys are so close; you'd be sure to have a good time together."

Felicitas bit her lip as she considered her options, but then she shrugged. "I guess I'll think about it. By the way, he started talking without you around."

Tabea perked up. "He has?"

Besma nodded and sat down on the pod next to her. "Apparently, after you got sick, he asked if he could eat dinner with us, so Callaghan asked Vince to accompany him for the evening."

Warmth filled Tabea's chest when she thought about Yuri finally opening up to more people. But then the feeling was chased away as dread took its place, a strong pull in her chest, trying to tear it open. Her arms felt restless and yet incredibly weak.

He knew about a human space witch.

There might be others, maybe even on this ship.

Tabea had expected Calliope to chime in with something at those thoughts, but the comment didn't come. For some reason, she was holding back again.

"He did act a little weird, though, don't you think?"

Besma directed her question to Felicitas, who was also taking a seat on the side of the pod.

She furrowed her brows and made a pouty face. "I guess so, but like, only a tiny bit. We probably just don't really know him yet. Don't totally *get* him, y'know?"

Tabea chewed on the insides of her cheeks and rubbed her thumbs over one another, trying to keep a calm and composed exterior while adrenaline rushed through her body setting off all sorts of alarms.

"Weird how?" she asked.

"Well," said Besma, "he wanted to know if we knew of anyone who had a habit of talking to computers."

"Yeah, and I was like—only all of us! I yell at my holopad anytime it doesn't load a site properly, or when it's just slow." Felicitas laughed.

"I know, right?" Besma joined in, giggling. "Yesterday I apologized to a chair after I knocked into it! And Tabs, I totally saw you last week when you zoned out, walked into that wall and said, 'Excuse me'!"

"Zoned out, huh?" Felicitas grinned, suddenly peering closer into Tabea's face with unexpected intensity. "That seems to happen a lot to you."

Besma rolled her eyes. "Like you wouldn't believe."

"Hmm," Felicitas said, her eyes narrowing slightly. Tabea's breath was once more stuck in her throat. There was no way Felicitas could know, was there? "You should really get that checked out. That could be an indication of a serious issue, like a brain tumor or something."

Besma's quiet laughter faded instantly. "That's not funny."

"Good, because I'm not joking."

The atmosphere had completely changed. Where previously there had been jovial chatter and laughter, there were now serious looks and held breath.

"Promise me?" Felicitas asked, cocking her head to one side and putting a hand on Tabea's. "I'd hate to think that something happens to my friend because I wasn't paying enough attention."

Tabea nodded and smiled. "I'll ask Zhen to take a look. Promise."

Besma breathed a sigh of relief. "Anyway," she said. "Back to Yuri. You know what he wanted to know? He was asking who the best person on board with machines is. So, I said, it's got to be Hammond, right?"

Felicitas nodded vehemently and added, "And he said, no, not Hammond, I met him and that's not right. Someone newer. And then we were saying, well you've only got three options then—Smith, Nerissa, or Vince."

"And then he got super pensive and barely said another word."

Somehow Tabea felt both glad and hurt that she hadn't appeared in the list. Hurt because her friends didn't think she was one of the best with machines, but glad because it meant there was less suspicion on her.

Unless...

The thought appeared in her mind before she knew it.

Unless one of them is a space witch, too.

The thought of Nerissa being the same as her, as being able to create the same bond with Calliope as she did, made her feel sick to her core. But no, there was no way. There was no other space witch on board this ship. That was something she felt certain Calliope would have known and mentioned. In fact, Tabea would have probably encountered them in her training sessions within the ship's systems at some point over the last two years.

"Hey. Are you okay?" Felicitas was suddenly very close to her face, her brows firmly knit together. "You're super pale again."

Tabea was quick to nod.

"I'm fine. Just getting a little tired again."

The two other girls got to their feet.

"We'll leave you to it then. Make sure to get well soon, 'kay?" Besma waved as they walked to the door. "And I'll come by later with Vince."

And gone they were.

Tabea leaned back, suddenly feeling exhausted, and closed her eyes.

"*Callie?*" she called. "*I don't know what to do.*"

"*Well, you're making a good start, with closing your eyes. Now just lie down and from my understanding, the sleep just happens at some point. It's kind of like a standby mode, right?*"

Tabea had to smile. "*Not that,*" she said. "*I mean about Yuri.*"

Calliope remained silent, but Tabea could feel her hesitation, her troubled haggling with herself.

"*Callie?*" she asked after a moment.

"*I'm here. I just… Can I be honest?*"

"*Always.*"

"*He's not trustworthy.*" Calliope paused, as though she were considering her next words carefully. "*There's something fundamentally wrong about him.*"

Tabea frowned. "*What do you mean?*"

She searched her own memories, but aside from a

few odd behaviors, she could think of nothing. And as far as that went, everyone had little quirks; they were hardly cause for mistrust.

"It's like there are pieces of a hard drive, but the pieces don't slot together properly."

The analogy certainly wasn't helping Tabea understand her friend's issues.

"When they started the first med checks, the scanner malfunctioned," Calliope admitted. *"It shouldn't have; there was nothing wrong with it."*

"A malfunction isn't that weird, though, and it couldn't be his fault. It could have been a fluke."

"Maybe. But he also doesn't seem to know anything about Earth."

"What are you talking about?" This was a point she could argue. *"Of course he knows — it's just that he's from one of the colonies! He knows his captain's name, and his own role on the ship. He knows about his family and about Gagarin. He was even studying about mechanics in the library the other day. He's part of the Space Core."*

A pregnant pause followed her words. Then Calliope sent back a single thought before cutting herself off.

"Are you sure about all that?"

Calliope seemed to have decided to sulk for a while, because she made no attempt to reconnect with Tabea at all while the latter was still kept on bedrest. Tabea didn't want to force it, so she didn't, settling instead for taking apart, reshaping, and rebuilding the appliances around her when no one was around. That and reading

Jules Verne were the only distractions available to alleviate her boredom until Callaghan came by.

He strode in, all confidence and seriousness, and took a seat on the chair beside her bed. They looked at each other for a moment, then he asked, "So?"

Tabea gave him a thumbs-up, and he finally cracked a smile.

"Glad to hear it. You've been overdoing it again, haven't you?"

Tabea shook her head in protest. How could he think that?

"No, I..." She stopped herself. She had gotten a fever. And she'd collapsed. And apparently had been knocked out for quite a while. And there was a damn good reason for it, too.

"You know, you need to look after yourself better. We have no idea how much of an impact your powers have on your body long term, the kind of strain it might be putting you under. You've got to be more careful."

The concern in his voice was heavy.

Tabea averted her gaze and looked at her hands, folded over the bedsheet. Like always, he was only looking out for her.

She considered telling him about what Yuri had shared with her, but her promise to Yuri made her hold back. Before she could fully make up her mind on the matter, Callaghan changed the subject.

"Jules Verne, huh?"

She looked up again to see him pick up the book on her table, a reminiscent smile playing around his lips.

"I loved his books when I was in school. The other kids never really understood why. It was a completely different world back then, wasn't it?"

Tabea nodded. She felt similarly. Even stories like *Around the World in Eighty Days* felt fantastical, not merely fiction, purely because the world, the time they were set in had been so vastly different to human's lives today. For one thing, the countries and nationalities from back then no longer existed and most of the places mentioned had long become part of the ocean floor.

"Have you ever read *Twenty Thousand Leagues Under the Sea*?" Callaghan asked.

"I haven't. What's it about?"

He smiled and got to his feet. "I'll bring it by. By the way," he added, "one of your friends asked if Yuri could join the dance."

He watched her for a moment, as if to gauge her reaction, which, incidentally, was the same thing she was doing watching him.

"I allowed it," he finally said when she gave no answer. "He's been through a lot, and this might help."

He shook his head at the thought and Tabea found herself smiling at the thought that Callaghan appeared to ease up on his distrust, unlike some people she knew.

"Does this change your mind about wanting to go?" he added after a moment, almost shuffling his feet.

Tabea's grin grew broader.

"Oh, stop smirking like that, you brat," he said, narrowing his eyes at her, but he was still smiling.

"It doesn't." She decided to relieve him of his awkward situation. "I wanna be on the bridge, helping out as much as I can with Callie." She rubbed the wall affectionately, hoping that Calliope was paying attention. "I'd rather be with her and you than at any party."

"Well, Hammond shall miss you dearly." Callaghan grinned. "He was hoping to ask you for a dance."

"All the more reason not to go." That was certainly one bullet she had dodged. "I can't dance to save my life."

"Then let's hope you'll never have to."

The next day, Tabea was free to go about her usual business again, so she began by reporting to Callaghan on the bridge.

"It's good to see you up," he said, smiling when she entered. "You're looking much better."

"I feel much better."

She looked around the room. All officers were busy at their controls, including Hammond at the engineering station. He looked up and winked at her when he noticed her, and Shinay gave her a little friendly wave.

"What do you want me to do with Yuri today?" Tabea asked. "Have you planned anything?"

Callaghan shook his head. "Not anymore."

Was that her imagination or did he almost sound apologetic?

"Since he's going to be on board with us from now on, we decided to have him become part of the crew for this trip. Nerissa is showing him the ropes."

Nerissa?

Discontentment once again took hold of Tabea. So Nerissa was the leading engineering junior beside

Vincent, but why did it have to be *her*? Couldn't Vincent have done it?

"He actually requested to spend some time with her. I asked Vincent to look in on them occasionally, just in case."

"I see." She did see. Yuri wanted to check if Nerissa was a space witch. If she was the one who needed to be protected. The thought almost made her laugh, but it didn't make her feel any better. And what did that mean for her? "So…" She trailed off.

Callaghan gestured at the room at large.

"So I figured we could use you here again. It's only officers today, so as long as you feel up for it, you could take over for Hammond. Smith is still sick, after all."

Hammond leaned back in his seat to look at them and sighed. "Aye, I could use a break. Mind cuttin' in for me, lass?"

A chuckle forced itself up Tabea's throat. "Gladly."

Still, a kernel of unease remained. Calliope hadn't spoken to her since their argument in the med bay, and Tabea was dreading the confrontation. Especially since she wasn't even sure at which point it had turned into an argument, and why Calliope had felt so strongly that she had cut the connection.

She took the seat Hammond offered her and placed her hands on the controls. The first few issues she solved manually, waiting for a lull in work before she attempted to reconcile with Calliope.

She worked mechanically, and every movement was made without hesitation or too much thought. She knew her way around these controls—her practice had made it possible.

One by one, the night and early morning shifts

switched out with the day shift. Callaghan hadn't lied—they were all officers. Then, finally, there was a period of quiet for her. As long as she kept an eye on the energy levels, they'd be fine.

She placed a hand on the console and closed her eyes for a moment, feeling the electricity flowing through the ship, the pulsating energy that felt like Calliope's heartbeat. She listened to it, let it resonate through her own body, and then let go of herself, attuning her own energy to match Calliope's before slipping through her hand into the ship herself. She traveled along the wires, the nodes, and connections farther and farther, past the motors Nerissa and Yuri were working on, past Vincent tinkering with a connection, and on farther. Always farther, all the way to the ship's core, the part that had nothing to do with human engineering, the part that was truly all Calliope.

There, she waited.

"*Hey,*" Calliope said eventually.

"*Hey,*" Tabea responded. "*How are you doing?*"

"*I should be asking you.*"

Now that Tabea was no more than energy within Calliope's being, physical actions no longer held any meaning. Still, Tabea shaped some electric impulses to simulate a hug to Calliope, or at least something that held the same feeling, the same meaning as a hug. "*I missed you.*"

"*You're sure you weren't glad to not have me nagging you all the time?*"

"*Well, I mean when you put it like that…*"

"*Hey!*"

"*I was kidding!*" Tabea laughed and Calliope joined in.

There was a pause. Then Calliope said, sullenly, "*I still don't trust him.*"

"*That's okay. You don't have to.*"

"*And there are no other human space witches. It's impossible. There's only you.*"

Tabea sighed. "*That's what I was afraid of. But then how did they find out? Whoever they are?*"

Calliope gave the equivalent impulse to a shrug. "*I don't know. But other space witches could have sensed you, if they were nearby. And if they found something you impacted, they might also have realized.*"

Tabea wanted to shake her head. "*All I ever work with is on board you, or back on Earth. So it's only possible if they were close at some point. But wouldn't they have recognized you then? Or tried to take control?*"

"*Normally, I think so.*" Calliope hesitated. "*I'm worried about you.*"

Tabea thought of everything that was at stake here, all because she was on board this ship, along with these people. If they were attacked, she was relatively certain she could divert some of the danger, but it would still be a hairy situation. And once her secret was out, there was no going back. Ever. Her own race would either cage her to study her and her abilities or use her as a tool.

Certainly, these pirates were out to kill her, to eliminate the threat a human technomancer represented. It was a sign that Humanity was finally able to join in on the larger playing field of intergalactic politics, not just under the protection of other alien races. Even though right now, there was only her.

But the real issue was that if they came to kill her, they would also kill everyone else aboard and destroy the *Calliope*, thereby killing her as well. It was something Tabea didn't want to think about, but her thoughts trailed off that way anyway.

"I'm worried, too," she admitted. *"It's scary."*

"Tabea, more power to the shields!" Callaghan's voice reached her body's ears, and the information reached her mind with minimal delay.

"I've got to go."

"I'll be with you."

In an instant, Tabea was back in her body, but along the way, she already redirected energy to where it needed to be, using her abilities. No need to waste time.

When she returned to her senses, she could feel Calliope's familiar presence in the back of her mind, and she saw small debris hitting the shields ahead of them. They were circling a small planet, turning more swiftly by using its gravitational pull.

Tabea turned one look back to Callaghan and raised one questioning eyebrow. He crossed over to her quickly without ever taking his eyes off the screen ahead of them.

"We've made contact with a ship heading back to the Milky Way. We've passed the information on to them, so we're going back to our own mission."

"Are you sure that's wise?" Tabea asked, keeping her voice low. Callaghan peeled his eyes from the screen and gave her a long, hard look.

"Whether it's wise or not has nothing to do with it. We have a mission, and we need to complete it. If we, on the Calliope, aren't equipped to deal with a group of pirates, then none of Earth's ships are. Especially since we have a secret weapon."

He winked at her and Tabea gulped.

"*Not so secret,*" Calliope said. "*You need to tell him.*"

Tabea opened her mouth to speak, but just then, the door opened, and Nerissa strode in, followed quickly by Yuri. Nerissa was looking mightily pleased, and her grin widened when she saw Tabea looking. Then she dramatically looked away and turned to Callaghan, who came to talk to her.

Tabea reverted her attention to her controls, biting her tongue and trying hard not to overhear their conversation. It would undoubtedly only make her angry.

CHAPTER 11

TABEA MADE SURE TO HAVE BREAKFAST WITH her friends the next morning.

All four of them were talking about the dance scheduled for the next day. The time had passed so much quicker than Tabea had realized. It was hard to believe two weeks had already passed since she'd saved Yuri from the *Sonata*.

"It'll be so much fun!" Besma said, her eyes sparkling.

Felicitas nodded in agreement and stemmed her chin on her hand. "I still remember the last one." She sighed in bliss and closed her eyes. "It was amazing. I just danced all night."

Marco chuckled and threw a meaningful glance at Vincent. "Girls, am-I-right?"

Vincent shrugged. "I don't know. I always have fun." He turned to Tabea. "What about you, Tabs? Like dancing all night till your head's spinning?"

Tabea waved the suggestion away quickly. "Not me, no, sir." She grinned at the boys, remembering the one and only time she'd joined one of the dances. She'd been wearing a dress that had felt weird on her skin, heels that had been hard to walk in and made her feet hurt, and all in all, she'd spent most of the night hovering near the buffet, more interested in the delicacies than any dance. The few times she had been asked to dance hadn't exactly gone well, and she grimaced at the memory. "I've got two left feet. And I prefer to have my peace and quiet."

Besma nudged her in the side. "That's why you volunteered to man the bridge, didn't you?"

"What? You're really not coming?" Felicitas seemed equally surprised and disappointed. "I was hoping you'd changed your mind and go with Yuri."

"I thought you were going to ask him," Tabea said, with a quick glance at Marco to gauge his reaction, but he didn't seem perturbed.

Felicitas listlessly pushed her spoon around the bowl. "I was, but someone else asked him first. I thought it was you being sneaky."

"Tabs wouldn't do something so underhanded!"

Tabea shot Vincent a grateful glance. It was nice to have friends who came to her rescue like that.

Felicitas laughed. "Calm down. It's not like I was mad at her or anything. Anything is fair in love and war."

"Love?" Vincent seemed honestly taken aback and Tabea sighed.

"Not Tabs, you idiot," Besma cut in, calming him down. "She doesn't do love." She shot Tabea a meaningful glance. "Right?"

Tabea was quick to nod her agreement. "Right. No interest here."

"No?" Felicitas watched her for a moment, looking disappointed about the lack of a rival in love, or, at the very least, gossip.

"Then," Marco leaned forward, whispering conspiratorially, "who did ask him?"

Silence washed over them like a gentle wave, as all of them thought about what could have happened.

Then Tabea snorted, before laughing out loud, gaining her a few confused glances from people at other tables. "You guys all love drama far too much."

She grinned into the round of them, and, one by one, they all joined her in laughter. Vincent even had to wipe away a tear from the corner of his eye.

"You're not wrong!" He gasped between bursts of laughter. "But it makes life on board so interesting."

The others nodded their agreement enthusiastically, while Tabea got to her feet and picked up her tray.

"Whatever you say. I'm gonna go now. I've got a lesson with Szkarisov."

"Wait!" Besma shouted. "Are you free tonight?"

Tabea looked back over her shoulder. "I think so?"

A wide grin spread over both Felicitas' and Besma's faces.

"Then make sure you have a pillow fort ready. We've got a new girls' night initiate!"

Humming to herself, Tabea sauntered through the halls. She was in no hurry to get to Szkarisov's office, knowing that she was early.

"You're not curious about who asked him?" Calliope asked.

"I don't have to be." Tabea walked on as if there were no change. *"I already know."*

"Oh?"

"I guarantee you it's Nerissa."

It would be just like her to scoop up the new guy everyone was curious about, thereby putting herself into the spotlight beside him.

Just then, Tabea passed by the open library doors and a single glance inside allowed her to spot Yuri sitting at the same table he had previously occupied when they'd been there together. Aside from him and his pile of reference books, the room appeared to be empty. Even when Tabea glanced up and down the hallway, she could find no trace of Nerissa.

Making up her mind, Tabea stepped inside, crossing the room to Yuri's side. This was probably the best chance she'd get to talk to him without Nerissa overhearing. If he hadn't confided in her already, Tabea preferred to keep the space witch thing a secret.

"Hey, Yuri," she said quietly. He looked up, blinking at her as if his mind were just returning from far away. A cursory glance at the opened books spread before him showed her once more sketches and blueprints — some of Earth and the human colonies, some of terrestrial ships and technology. Rarely had Tabea met someone as dedicated to their job as him.

She smiled at him, amused. "You know, you can take it easy for a while, right? Callaghan may have given you some responsibilities, but no one is expecting more of you than what you would have done before."

"I know." He averted his gaze, his lips pressed together. It was a more abrupt response than Tabea had come to expect from him and, bemused, she took a seat. He seemed frustrated somehow, and something about the disarray on the table told her that it hadn't just become that way when she'd come in. Some books had been swept to the floor, and they were still lying opened, spine up on the floor.

Tabea picked up one of them and carefully smoothed the crumpled pages before closing it.

"What's going on?" she asked, placing the book on the table while peering at Yuri. "Is Nerissa being hard on you?"

He looked up at her, his eyes widened in surprise.

"Nerissa? No, she's wonderful!" Rubbing his temple, he sighed. "It's just... I can't afford to disappoint them." A haunted look snuck into his eyes, but he collected himself quickly. "Anyone, I mean," he added. "Not after what happened before."

Tabea nodded sympathetically. "I get it. But don't overdo it. You saw what happens when people do too much." Pointing at herself, she grimaced.

Now it was him, peering into her face, inspecting every part of her expression.

"How are you doing, by the way? I was worried about you, but the captain didn't want to let me see you."

She gave him a thumbs-up, mimicking a happier expression than she was feeling.

"I'm all good now. I was just doing too much, you know?"

She dropped her smile and got serious again, meeting his gaze evenly.

"But I wanted to talk to you about what you said." She glanced over her shoulder, just to make sure no one had entered the library while they'd been talking. They still retained their privacy. Best get to the point quickly. "Are you sure the pirates were looking for a *human* space witch?"

He only nodded.

"It's just... you know how it sounds, right? Can you remember the exact words they used? Maybe that'll help us figure something out."

"I know it's crazy. There's never been a human space witch before. But..." He took a deep breath and closed his eyes, his brows furrowed as he tried to recall the attack. "They said that there'd been traces of power, a kind of energy signature that couldn't be matched with any other race, so it had to be a human space witch."

He opened his eyes, his gaze dark and sad. While Tabea felt guilty for making him remember, his answer did help her. It was another lead to figuring out why the *Sonata* had been targeted.

His eyes locked onto her intensely. "You'll keep a look out, won't you?"

Tabea nodded, but she gave him an uncertain smile. "I will, but the chances that they were right *and* that there's a technomancer on our ship specifically are pretty low, you know."

"*Low or not doesn't change the fact that he's right,*" Calliope said pensively. "*I still don't like it.*"

Yuri sighed and stretched. "I know. But this ship is all I have right now."

Even though his words seemed to indicate loneliness and desolation, his demeanor only presented determination.

Tabea's reply froze on her tongue when she heard hurried steps approach.

"Yuri!"

Nerissa ran into the room, a broader, truer smile than Tabea had ever seen on her face before as she called. It cooled significantly when she saw Tabea sit beside him.

"Oh," she said, her gaze shifting between her and Yuri. "It's you."

She didn't look any happier to see her than Tabea was feeling, but the quip she expected never came. Instead, Nerissa forced a smile; though far from a real one, it was convincing enough.

"Thanks for keeping him company while I was on the bridge," she chirped. "But don't let us keep you. I'm sure you're busy, too."

Tabea didn't need to be a mind reader to know that Nerissa was trying to get rid of her quickly. Still, it was surprising that she refused to let Yuri see the nastier side of her. She didn't try to hide her disdain for Tabea in front of any of the other cadets, after all.

Still, Nerissa was providing her with an opening. It wasn't like she'd continue the conversation with *her* here. She rose to her feet, smiling at Yuri.

"You're right. I have an appointment with one of the officers. Don't overdo it, Yuri, okay?"

She took her leave.

Even though she picked up her pace and went straight there, she arrived at Szkarisov's office later than anticipated.

He only gave her a stern glance as she entered. "For someone who is good with machines, you really need to improve your watch-reading ability."

Tabea gave him a weak smile. "I'm sorry, something came up and I... lost track of time."

He sighed and took a seat at his desk. Tabea quickly joined him.

"Let's get right back to it, then. Where did we leave

off?"

"You asked me to memorize the short codes used for unusual occurrences," Tabea replied quickly.

"Well then," Szkarisov said, a small smile creeping on his thin lips as he leaned back. "Why don't you give me the codes for a stowaway then?"

Dutifully, Tabea had built the pillow and blanket fort in her room well ahead of the time Besma and Felicitas showed up. She didn't prepare a movie—who knew if all of them liked the same things, after all, and besides, she had the feeling that tonight was going to be more about talking than anything else.

Besma brought hot chocolate in a thermos, while Felicitas brought chips and salted crackers, both girls ready in pajamas. Felicitas' eyes sparkled when she saw the fort, and the first thing she did after pushing her savory treats into Tabea's arms was to throw herself into it.

"Do you know how long it's been since I've been invited to a girls' night?" she asked, sighing contentedly. Tabea and Besma shared a glance.

"Three years?" Besma guessed haphazardly.

"At least." Felicitas groaned. "There are so few girls in the med team, and those who are around don't have time for anything, and definitely not for anything that's fun." She sat up, looking at them expectantly. "So, how does this go?"

Tabea shrugged. "However you want it to go."

"*I* want us to start by having some of this deliciousness," Besma chimed in, holding up her thermos. "I've been dying to have some since I made it and you have no idea what kind of torture it is to smell it and not drink it!"

She planted herself next to Felicitas and began pouring into the cups that Tabea had prepared.

"Wait, we have to cheer to something!" Felicitas interjected when Besma lifted the cup to her mouth.

Tabea pondered for a moment. What was something neutral that everyone liked?

"Mystery and adventure," she said, raising her cup. The other two stared at her for a moment, but then also lifted their own, repeating, "Mystery and adventure!"

They all took a big gulp of the hot chocolate, letting the sweet taste wash over them.

Besma sighed. "So good!"

Felicitas nodded in agreement. "It really is. Nicely done, Bes-Bes."

"Looks like you needn't have worried," Calliope said. *"They're already friends."*

"This is what happens when I spend a day sick in bed, apparently." Tabea thought back to how Vincent and Besma had met and become friends. Incidentally, that had also happened when she'd been sick. *"This is becoming a pattern."*

"So, I gotta ask." Felicitas leaned forward conspiratorially, and Besma and Tabea leaned in as well. "Why did you guys join the space core?"

"Originally, I was meant to go into space law." Tabea pulled a face. "My parents wanted me to support my sister — she's a politician. But I liked flying better." She tried to laugh it off, though the memory of her family created a knot in her stomach. It had been about two years since she'd last spoken to any of them. She'd sent them a message that she'd been accepted into Callaghan's crew, but she'd never even received a response.

A feeling of warmth encroached on her, and she knew it was Calliope trying to comfort her.

"It's okay, Callie."

"I just want you to know I'm here for you. And they are, too."

"I've just always wanted to fly spaceships, since I was a little kid," Besma said cheerfully. "I would have been happy to fly the cruise liners or something, but the Space Core pays better." She shrugged, grinning.

"What about you, Feli?" Tabea turned the question around. "Any particular reason?"

Felicitas groaned. "This is going to sound really stupid," she warned. "So try not to judge me, okay?"

Besma and Tabea exchanged a glance, both of them barely able to anticipate what Felicitas would share.

"So, when I was little, I had this crush on a girl, okay? She was a few years older—I think I was ten when she was admitted to the Academy. She kept writing me letters while she was there, and I just wanted to be with her and share her future and all that, so I applied as well." She shrugged. "Unfortunately, she got pregnant by some doofus just after I joined, and they both dropped out. By then, I already realized I quite liked what I was doing, so I stayed anyway."

"Wow," said Tabea.

"That's... quite something," Besma agreed. "Where is she now?"

Felicitas shrugged again. "I think they moved to Jupiter, but honestly, she could also be dead, for all I know. We didn't really keep in touch after she left."

Suddenly, there was a knock on the door.

"Are we expecting anyone else?" Besma asked, frowning.

As clueless as the other two, Tabea crossed over to the door and peeked out. Or tried to, at least, because the door was pushed open as the new visitors intruded.

"We wanna join!" Marco called out jovially. "We brought offerings!"

He waved chocolates through the air and Besma jumped up, snatching them away from him. Vincent obediently handed over the jellies he had brought as well as Tabea closed the door.

Felicitas frowned at them, her arms crossed.

"My first girls' night and you guys have to crash it? Really?"

"The more the merrier?" Vincent ventured.

"If it makes it any better," Marco said as he strolled over to the fort, "it's our first girls' night as well." He grinned winningly, and the corners of Felicitas' mouth began twitching.

"A warning would have been nice," Tabea chided Vincent gently, though she didn't try to hide the fact that she was enjoying the extra company.

He winked at her. "But then you might have said *no*."

"*He has you there.*"

Tabea sighed dramatically. "Weeeell, I guess since you brought offerings, you can be forgiven just this once."

They joined the others in the fort.

"So," Marco said, poking at the blanket, "what do we do on a girls' night? Do we paint our toes and talk about love, or...?"

Besma and Tabea exchanged a glance before bursting into laughter.

"Did I say something funny?" Marco looked at Vincent, seeking help, but he only shrugged, just as clueless.

"How about ghost stories?" Felicitas suggested, grinning impishly. "Everyone loves a good scare."

Tabea shot finger guns at her. "Now we're talking!"

By the time breakfast came around, the five of them were still laughing and joking around, repeating anecdotes from the previous night. No one had slept over in Tabea's room, but even so, the night had gotten late enough, especially considering that tonight was the dance, meaning another late night was ahead of them.

"But next time, I want a girls' night without you guys crashing," Felicitas declared, growling, though the uplifted corners of her mouth belied her true feelings.

Marco raised his hands up in defense. "Okay, okay, no guys allowed, got it. But you have to admit that it was fun."

He beamed at her and reluctantly, she relented.

"It was. But it just became a party, not a girls' night."

Before he could argue his point further, Felicitas grabbed an apple slice and shoved it into his mouth.

"Handfeeding each other now, are we?" Besma trilled mischievously. Tabea couldn't hide her grin, either.

"No way. Shut up." Felicitas laughed, her tone joking, though Tabea noticed her squeezing Marco's hand under the table. "You know Yuri is the only one for me."

"The only one for what?"

Out of nowhere, Yuri had appeared behind Felicitas, tray in hand. He looked at them curiously, his gaze lingering on Vincent for just a moment too long for Tabea's comfort.

Meanwhile, Felicitas had turned crimson, though Marco wasn't in a much better position.

"Um," she said.

"The only one she would love to tell the mysteries of the ship to," Vincent jumped in helpfully. "Because you're the only one who doesn't know them yet."

All attention dropped from Felicitas and Yuri's eyes were glued to Vincent, who ruffled his blond hair, glancing at Felicitas and Marco. They both watched him with immense relief.

"What mysteries?" Yuri asked, his tone indicating a hunger for knowledge.

Vincent outlined the seven mysteries of the ship, fairy tales made up by crewmembers to scare each other like children. They'd come up in several of the spooky tales they'd shared last night. Everyone on board knew them — the wails of a dead engineer who screamed for help (in reality just the whistling of some rusty tubes that should have been replaced), the stories of a poltergeist who made everything turn on and off at random in a specific room (which had been Tabea and Calliope's fault — the closest they'd ever come to being discovered), and the hallway where you could meet with the personification of death, which would be a sign that you would die before ever meeting your one true love. How that one had come into being, Tabea had no idea. There were others, but she stopped listening, instead focusing more on Yuri's face.

Even though he'd seemed eager to hear about them at first, the longer Vincent talked, the more disappointed he looked.

Finally, Vincent finished, and Tabea looked from one of them to the other, then sighed.

"You wanna sit, Yuri?" she asked, nodding toward his tray of untouched breakfast.

Smiling gratefully, he pulled up a chair and sat between Vincent and Besma.

"So, where did you leave Nerissa?" Tabea asked, trying to sound casual.

Yuri smirked. "You two don't get along very well, do you?"

Several chuckles could be heard from the other people around the table.

"Not any more than fire and water," Besma said, her grin threatening to split her face in half.

"Or cats and dogs," Vincent agreed.

Tabea grimaced. "She told you, huh?"

"No. But she changes around you. As do you."

Tabea didn't know what to respond to that.

"He's right, you know," Vincent said, glancing at her from the side. "Both of you are so nice when apart, but when you come together you both get prickly."

Tabea only grunted discontentedly.

"Why is that?" Yuri's gaze bore into Tabea, trying to see underneath the surface. Tabea shrugged.

"She's never liked me," she said. "But I guess it got worse after I changed tracks." She glanced at her watch and got up with a sigh. "I've gotta go. Callaghan wants to talk to me."

She picked up her tray, leaving Yuri with her

friends.

"I'll see you later," Yuri called after her, but she only waved in response.

Chapter 12

Upon entering the bridge, Tabea playfully saluted to Callaghan.

"Sir, ready for duty, sir!"

He rolled his eyes. "Again?"

She broke into a grin and leaned on his workstation. "What have you got lined up for me today?"

He checked his notes briefly and then nodded toward Hammond at the engineering dock. "Help him out in the morning so he can take a rest. Then you're to take the afternoon off. Relax a little, maybe have a nap." He looked up at her, smiling. "I want you in best shape for tonight. So no playing around with the Calliope, either, you hear?"

"Got it."

She sauntered over to Hammond and looked over his shoulder.

"Make sure you dance a round for me tonight, 'kay?" she asked him.

He made space for her to sit down and grimaced. "Yeah, well, don't expect too much of these old bones."

She looked up at him, smiling. "I won't forgive you if you don't."

He grinned back and ruffled her hair before taking his leave.

Andrej Szkarisov in the seat next to her leaned over. "I'll be working tonight as well," he said. "Swapping out with Callaghan so he can take a break for a while. I'm looking forward to seeing your work up close."

He winked, and Tabea nodded. Outside of her lessons, she didn't know Szkarisov very well, but she knew he was a capable man, again, one of Callaghan's most trusted people. Like all of the senior officers, he'd been part of the crew on her first trip, the Harvius VI mission where her powers had been revealed. Despite his whole work life circling around communication and information exchange, he'd been extremely adept at keeping her secret. They all had. But somehow, it had leaked anyway. Though, apparently, not to Earth.

Briefly, Tabea wondered if he *had* made a transmission about her after all, a piece of information weaving its way thought space, picked up by enemy scanners, revealing her. She dismissed the idea almost as soon as it had appeared in her mind. If that were the case, it would have happened a long time ago.

She spent the morning working normally, trying to avoid using her powers any more than to have conversations with Calliope. By lunchtime, she swapped out with Vincent, while Besma took over for Akari.

Time for Tabea to go. After a quick late lunch, she retreated to her room. Unsure as to how to pass the time, she settled for reading the book Callaghan had lent her. *Twenty Thousand Leagues Under the Sea.*

Deeply engrossed in the story, she barely noticed the time passing. Traveling on the *Nautilus* didn't sound all that dissimilar to travelling on the *Calliope*. Enclosed spaces in hostile territory that, without the right equipment, could quickly kill a person. Vast empty spaces and unknown geography. Submarines were like spaceships of old.

"It's time to go." Calliope finally pulled her from the fictional tale.

Tabea put on the jacket from her uniform again, pushing the tags that had come over her T-shirt back under, and headed for the bridge, with a minor detour to pass by the mess hall where the festivities were to be held. Peppy music was already blaring from speakers distributed around the room. Colored lights had been set up, along with banners and sparkly decorations. All in all, it reminded Tabea a lot of the dances she'd experienced back in school and at the Academy.

She didn't regret missing it one bit.

Delighted about her excuse, she hurried to the bridge to relieve Vincent so he could get ready for the party.

When she got there, only Vincent, Akari, Callaghan, and Szkarisov were left. She tapped Vincent on the shoulder, and he looked up, relieved to see her.

"I'll bring you a snack from the party," he promised before he left. Absentmindedly, Tabea remembered the delicious chocolate puddings that had been served at her last dance. She quickly licked her lips and took her seat. A moment later, Akari, who'd been talking to Callaghan, left, leaving behind only the other three. For the moment, they were only floating in space, the shields up and camouflage turned on—standard protocol.

"Andrej," Callaghan suddenly said. "Go on and

have a bite to eat. If you come back in three to four hours, we'll be golden."

Szkarisov nodded and left as well. Callaghan followed him to the door, locking it after him.

"We don't want any surprises," he explained, indicating the center of the room.

Tabea followed his instruction and sat cross-legged in front of his normal vantage point on the floor, leaning against his station, both hands touching the floor next to her, allowing her to feel the energy, to direct it at will.

Connecting with Calliope was as easy as it had always been, and without lifting a single finger, Tabea accessed the piloting controls and put the ship back in motion slowly but keeping most of the power in the defense systems. She checked the course Shinay had plotted and programmed into her part of the ship's memory and corrected their course according to it. She checked the scanners and radar — nothing to be concerned about. Then she opened her eyes. Callaghan was crouching next to her, observing her closely.

"This never gets old," he said, smiling. "How does it feel?"

Tabea thought about it for a moment.

"It feels right," she said. "Callie and I moving and working as a unit — there's no better feeling."

She smiled at him, her chest light with joy. It had been too long since she'd been allowed to pilot Calliope fully on her own for longer than a few moments. This was a gift, better than any party could ever be.

"It's like we were meant to be one," she continued. "Like she's an extension of myself, two souls, one body." She shrugged. "It probably doesn't make much sense, does it?"

Callaghan fully sat down with a grunt, his arms lazily hanging off his knees.

"Not really," he admitted. "But it does sound nice. I'm glad you have that. I never want you to feel like what you have is a burden."

Tabea shook her head forcefully. "It could never be a burden! Callie is my best friend! More than that, even. She's like..."

The words failed her.

"*Like a sister.*" Calliope came to her aid and Tabea smiled.

"Yes," she agreed. "Like a sister."

And so much more like it than her real siblings had ever been. From them, she'd never experienced the kind of love she shared with Calliope. They'd never been able to think the same way, to meet each other on a plain of mutual understanding and acceptance. At best, Tabea had been met with disinterest.

Again, Callaghan watched her for a moment, nothing indicative of his thoughts, except for a gentle smile.

Meanwhile, Tabea double-checked their course, power levels, and scanners. All clear.

"*Let me know if anything changes,*" she instructed Calliope.

Tabea stood up and held out a hand to help Callaghan up.

"Food?" she asked.

"I'll ask Hammond to bring us some."

A few minutes later, Hammond had come and left again, leaving behind two plates filled to the brim with delicious dishes. Callaghan and Tabea sat on the floor facing each other, eating while chatting about how much Tabea had come along since he'd mentored her at the Academy, and about how long it had been since he'd gotten a good old-fashioned fast-food burger on Earth.

"I think... about two years," he admitted. "My last was just before the Harvius VI mission, when we had the Academy's Christmas party."

"I remember that!" Tabea pointed. "You got really drunk! And danced the bubbletops!"

Callaghan rubbed the bridge of his nose and closed his eyes.

"Please don't remind me. On my way home, I got a craving for oily things and" — he shrugged — "I couldn't stop myself."

Tabea giggled. "You make that sound like that's a bad thing. It's normal, really."

Callaghan threw her a sharp look and raised an eyebrow. "Oh yeah? And how exactly would you know, Miss I'm-Not-of-Drinking-Age-Yet?"

"*Busted,*" Calliope trilled.

"According to movies and TV shows anyway," Tabea added, trying to pretend as though that was what she'd been going to say all along.

Callaghan chuckled but left it at that.

"*Good save.*"

"Speaking of," he continued, "I was wondering if you'd like to come visit my lake house for your birthday. With your friends, of course."

Warmth filled her heart and she nodded.

"I'd love that."

Of course he knew how disappointing a birthday with her family would be, when her sister was about to have a baby, and her elder brother was always busy with work, and her younger brother was being fussed over by their parents while he was taking his final examinations before choosing his future path. She'd be in the way, and a celebration would have been out of the question. Not that she'd ever planned on going back for it.

"*Such a loving and caring father,*" Calliope teased, but this time, Tabea couldn't think of a way to argue. Maybe she didn't want to.

Callaghan checked his watch and picked up the empty plates. "I'll bring these back and ask Szkarisov to come by. Can you manage on your own for fifteen minutes?"

Tabea smirked. "Can the FS-729 fly to the moon and back?"

Callaghan chuckled and left. Tabea returned to her prior position to reconnect with Calliope and checked on the systems. Still, everything was clear.

"*Someone's coming!*"

Calliope's warning didn't come a second too soon. Tabea barely had time to stop the ship and stand up before the door opened.

Yuri peeked in gingerly, but when he saw her, his eyes lit up.

"I'm glad I found you," he said. "I missed you at the party."

"I volunteered to keep an eye on everything," Tabea explained, her heart racing when she thought about how close she had been to maybe being discovered, and by him, of all people!

"On your own?" His eyebrows spoke chronicles of doubt.

"No, Callaghan was here, too. He's just gone to take care of something. I'll be here all night, though. You should go back, enjoy the party."

Yuri shook his head and entered fully, letting the door close behind him. "It wasn't all that much fun without you," he said. "And..." He hesitated.

A thought struck Tabea. "Where's Nerissa?" she asked, observing his reaction closely. "Won't she be looking for you?"

He only shrugged and shuffled his feet. "She's not who I thought she was."

Tabea waited for him to elaborate, a terrible feeling creeping up on her, clawing its way up from the depths in her stomach.

Yuri's eyes lifted to meet hers, steady and strong. Determined. "She's not the space witch."

The world seemed to stand still for a moment. Tabea's heart pounded, like nails being hammered into her coffin.

He took a step toward her. "You are."

Tabea walked backward, her mind racing, her breath barely reaching her lungs.

She chuckled. "That's ridiculous. Me? A space witch? That's a good joke."

She stumbled to the scanner, her eyes falling on what it showed, and her heart seemed to stop.

Nothing was important anymore.

"Callie, why didn't you tell me?"

Calliope didn't respond.

Little red dots moved across the screen, encroaching on their location, coming closer and closer with every passing second.

She whirled around to Yuri. "You have to go get

Callaghan—now! Someone's coming and I don't think they're friendly!"

He didn't move.

"Yuri!"

"Did you know," he said, slowly walking toward her, "that you're the only human space witch to ever have existed? The only being of your race who's ever had the abilities of a technomancer? I'm actually relieved that it's you. That it's not her."

He sighed, looking as though a terrible weight had been lifted from his shoulders.

"That's why you changed tracks, didn't you? Why you became an engineer instead of a pilot. Because you discovered your powers."

"Yuri, I'm serious!"

Her mind was whirling. Calliope still wasn't answering.

Fear washed over her. If he didn't leave right now, she'd have to act and admit that he was right, that she really was what he thought she was.

"*Callie!*" she called again, but she received no answer. She couldn't even feel her presence anymore. Meanwhile, the strange ships approached closer, but one look at the coms' station told her that they hadn't tried to make any contact.

This wasn't a fluke. Despite camouflage mode, the other ships knew exactly where they were. There were three ships, and they were spreading out to surround them.

"Did you also know," Yuri said, "that space witches can feel the power of other space witches? They're drawn to it."

There was no time to lose. Tabea could feel it, like

Yuri said. There were space witches on those ships, one on each. Their power was reaching out to her, trying to subdue her, trying to take control of Calliope, to order her to submit to them. It was like they were spinning a web of silk to lay over her, to dull her senses and overpower her. She could feel it in the air around her — a heaviness, laden with forced tranquility.

But there was no way Tabea would just give in to them, no way she would give up so easily. She thrust her arms to the ground, the force of impact vibrating painfully within her bones. She connected with the ship, a ship that didn't seem to hold Calliope's soul anymore, just a hull.

Fighting off the impulses sent by the other space witches, Tabea merged with it, disregarding that she was outing herself to Yuri. There were more important things to consider right now. She made a note of the location of each of the other ships, then, instead of speeding forward, she made the *Calliope* drop. Ignoring all safety protocols, she prepared for hyper speed.

Callaghan could yell at her later, but she knew they needed to get out of there right this instant, out of the grasp of the other space witches.

She reached out tendrils of her power to the other ships, infiltrating them from the parts farthest away from their own space witches' powers, and took over from the inside, just enough to plant the order to resist in them, to resist the technomancers, to resist following Calliope.

She could feel the anger of the other space witches when she retreated; she felt it like they burnt her arms and legs, but Tabea pressed on, teeth and fists clenched.

She needed to get everyone out of there.

She initiated the jump and opened her eyes, feeling sick to her stomach, dizzy, disoriented. And there Yuri stood, watching her, a satisfied, gleeful grin on his face.

He crossed over to her side as she lost her balance, just in time to catch her.

"That was magnificent," he whispered. "Utterly sublime."

Tabea's lips were moving, but she knew that no sound came from them.

"Callie. Callaghan. Please..."

Her vision had given way to millions of colored dots, blinking happily. After a moment, they faded to black and white. All sounds were suddenly harsher and louder, and quieter all at the same time.

Tabea's entire body was screaming in pain at every breath.

"But you know," Yuri said, "that was only just the beginning."

And then, there was only darkness.

PART 2

Two Years Earlier

LED LIGHTS WERE BLINKING FRANTICALLY IN yellow, red, and blue, accompanied by a shrill alarm that seemed intent on shattering Tabea's eardrums. She hammered on the controls, hectically trying everything she could think of to stop the systems from going out. A fading green light to her left told her that the shields were failing, while a bright orange glow on her right informed her of the overheating engine. Her mind raced through all the books and lessons she had worked through about these kinds of situations, but none of them helped. In fact, they only added more confusion. The screen in front of her showed how she was plunging through space, right through an asteroid field. Tremors went through the entire ship any time some of the small debris hit the shields. By some miracle, the larger rocks had missed her. So far.

She closed her eyes and held her breath, praying that she would come out the other side unscathed. She knew she should be doing something, acting to direct the ship, but she couldn't move. Her hands trembled, weak and disobedient. She cursed herself for her nervousness, her fear, her inability to work around it, but it was in vain. She was stuck praying that some otherworldly force named Luck would save her.

A moment later, the vibrations and shaking stopped, and Tabea dared to open her eyes again.

Vast, empty space lay in front of her, calm and undisturbed. She sagged in relief, a sigh escaping her lips. Somehow, miraculously, she had made it through the asteroid field.

She almost felt like laughing.

But the sound caught in her throat when a small movement on the side of the screen caught her eye. It took her a moment to recognize the danger—a large asteroid, probably about half the size of the ship, was hurtling directly toward her.

She should have done something—anything—but she froze, staring at the large space rock. It connected with the ship, a loud, screeching, scraping sound mixed with millions of alarm sirens going off at the same time ringing in Tabea's ears. As she was violently thrown around in her seat, all the screens and lights died.

She didn't move for a long time, even after the tremors had stopped. She sat in her chair, hands clasped around the armrests, knuckles white. She focused on her breathing but found it difficult to avoid crying from shock.

The airlock opened, letting in the gleam of bright halogen lights. Callaghan peeked in, a frown on his face. He reached inside, and Tabea took his hand gratefully, letting him help her out. Even though it had only been a simulation exercise, she was still unsteady.

The simulators were designed to look and feel as real as possible, to prepare the cadets for missions and actual space travel. Sure, most of the youngsters had traveled with large commercial liners like the FS72 at some point in the past, but the Space Core's ships were a different story.

"That was less than ideal," Callaghan informed her, skimming the charts the simulator was coughing up.

"I know," Tabea replied, hardening her jaw and looking down at her shoes. Even after three years at the Academy, she just couldn't pass the simulator tests. She crashed every time. Every. Single. Time.

Something about it made her nervous, and she blanked, forgetting everything she had learned.

"I'm sorry," she added for good measure. She felt guilty for having let him down. He was always the first to believe in her, and the first to help if she needed it.

Callaghan looked up at her and sighed.

"Don't apologize. And stand up straight," he ordered. Tabea straightened her shoulders and put her feet together. "Maybe we just need to work on your confidence," he mused, eyeing her up.

"Yessir!"

"Take five and then go on to the hangars. I'll be there in half an hour. Get yourself a HN64 ready."

Tabea saluted and fled the room. With every step she moved toward the hangars at the other edge of the campus, she felt better. While she was terrible at spacecraft simulators, when it came to actually flying a machine, she was unbeatable. The aircrafts were a different model, designed for terrestrial flight, not space, but the concepts were the same. She nodded to people here and there on her way over but didn't stop to speak with anyone. This day was too important. Callaghan would be deciding whether she would be allowed to join him on his next space mission. She had aced the written exam and spectacularly failed the simulator, but after the flying test, perhaps he would consider it worth a shot. As he had said himself, maybe she just needed more confidence. The simulators flustered her. They didn't feel right.

Just before she reached the hangars, a wall of rain caught up with her, soaking her before she ever made it inside the hall. It was a good thing she was changing into her flight suit now anyway. She took a few minutes to dry off her cropped, brown hair, but she was ready beside her HN64 when Callaghan arrived under a large umbrella.

His expression was grim.

"We're going to have to reschedule, I'm afraid," he said.

Tabea's expression fell. *No, he couldn't!*

"But why?"

He jerked back with his thumb. "Weather. Have you seen the storm? The winds are blowing like crazy, and visibility is next to zero. There's no way you can handle it. We're going to have to take a rain check."

He chuckled at the pun, but Tabea didn't have a mind for laughing. She had to do her tests today. If she didn't, they wouldn't have the opportunity until Callaghan returned from his mission, and that would obviously be too late. Besides... Maybe she could make up for her earlier blunder.

"Sir!" She saluted. "Requesting permission to continue with the test!"

Callaghan raised an eyebrow. "Didn't you hear me?"

Tabea lowered her hand. "I did," she said, meeting his gaze earnestly. "But I know I can do it. Please let me prove it."

Callaghan crossed his arms, regarding her critically. "You know what you're asking is completely irresponsible, right?"

"In space, we don't always have the choice to do the responsible thing, sir," she fired back.

A smile cracked on his lips. "Throwing my own words back in my face, are you?"

Tabea nodded, mirroring his smile, and he sighed.

"A little theory test, then," he said.

Tabea cocked her head, uncertain about what he was going to ask. She'd already completed the written examination. What did he want from her now?

"I want to see how much study you've been doing outside of your normal classes."

She gulped. He could ask about absolutely anything. This was about stuff that wasn't on the curriculum. For all she knew, he could ask her about alien abductions from centuries ago.

He watched her, an impish glint in his eye. "Tell me about five other races in the known universe. And what you know about them."

Tabea didn't have to think. The answers shot to her mind and out of her mouth before she realized.

"The Penyales, the Crippnerasale, the Zutani, the Kinjo-unk, and the Moleus. The Crippnerasale and the Kinjo-unk are allies to Humanity, the Moleus are neutral, but the Zutani and Penyales are hostile toward Humanity. We first encountered the Crippnerasale when they were crossing our galaxy on their way to an intergalactic marriage, though it came to some confusion because they have a strong resemblance to cows, so some people thoughts they were genetically engineered bovines that came from a secret lab in a country that was called Russia. The Kinjo-unk—"

"All right, I think that's enough!" Callaghan interrupted her, laughing. "You've proven yourself. But if you damage the ship, you're staying grounded for at least a year, you hear me?"

Tabea smirked confidently.

"Yessir!"

Driving out to the launchpad, Tabea was aware of a queasy feeling growing in her stomach. The rain battered against the window, and she could even see lightning, followed by rolling thunder. Even just driving, she felt the wind pressing against her aircraft, steering her off course.

Still.

She was confident she could do it. She had never claimed it would be easy.

Callaghan was standing on the launchpad, holding a tablet with which he could track her flight. He had given up on his umbrella after it had been blown inside out the instant he had stepped outside. Their eyes met, and Tabea nodded.

She would prove to him what she could do, what he had taught her. He knew her potential.

He gave her the signal, and Tabea powered up the plane. Within seconds, she was in the air. Up here, the wind's strength was even worse, and as Callaghan had predicted, the rain made it impossible to see anything. She was left trusting her instincts and the system indicators. The comms in her ear crackled, and she heard Callaghan's voice.

"Clean start," he said. "Not bad. Now I want you to do a sharp turn to fly back across the hangars."

Tabea flipped a few switches and leaned into the curve. A second later, she shot overhead Callaghan.

"Now, a loop."

She did as she was told, moving at speeds that made it impossible to even feel the momentary change in gravity.

"Now go high in a spiral. Fifteen thousand feet should do it."

She circled as tightly as she could, constantly aiming up, corkscrewing her way into the sky, directly toward a dark cloud. The winds were trying to push her out of her spiral, make her fly toward the mountains inland, but she held her course steady. She was still spiraling when she noticed that her hair was standing up on end, electrified. Callaghan's voice rang through the comms, but only in broken words and crackling.

This was bad. Something wasn't right here. An ordinary storm shouldn't have had this kind of impact.

Tabea reacted fast, flicking switches, turning off the engines to drop, but she wasn't fast enough.

A web, a net of electricity, covered the cloud in front of her, sparking, connecting, illuminating everything as though it were the brightest day, and then racing toward her at the speed of light. The lightning impacted with the HN64 as Tabea shielded her eyes, blinded. Impossibly, the currents ran through the plane and seared into her; she saw the sparking net of electricity run across the instruments and even her own hands, although she felt it before she saw the periwinkle light.

She squealed in pain and pressed her eyes shut. A

moment later, she felt the shift in gravity, as the seatbelt pulled her down with the ship. She tore her eyes open, panicked. The lightning had disappeared alongside the pain, and she was falling away from the clouds — and falling fast.

Her hands moved faster than her mind, turning all engines back on, straightening the aircraft, activating the shields — but the plane wasn't reacting.

"No, no, no, no!" Tabea muttered angrily under her breath. "Work, dammit! Don't you dare crash!" Her fingers tingled, and her mind was spinning, but the plane obeyed. The engines flared to life, and the aircraft lifted up its nuzzle just in time, traveling parallel to the ground with barely twenty meters to spare before she made it gain some height again.

Letting out a sigh of relief as she tested the controls to make sure they were all still functioning, Tabea set course to land. She reached safe ground without any further incidents. Callaghan ran toward her as she debarked the HN64, his face a mask of panic.

"Tabea, are you all right? Are you hurt?"

He grasped her shoulders, holding her at arm's length to look her up and down, searching for any injury.

Tabea smiled at him crookedly. "I'm fine," she said, though her shaking legs betrayed her. "And so is the plane, I think! The only casualties are the comms."

Relief visibly flooded over him and his shoulders relaxed. "I'll have the mechanics take a look at it, though." He frowned at the aircraft. "That shouldn't have happened. But those were some good reactions." He beamed at her. "Now onto your last test."

Another test?

Well, at least she hadn't completely failed yet.

"Fix the comms by tomorrow. Here's the other half." He handed his own earpiece to her. "Well done," he added. "Now you should get some rest. Get yourself checked out by the nurse, and we'll talk more tomorrow at fourteen hundred."

Tabea nodded and walked alongside him to the main complex. Suddenly, she realized how exhausted she was. This flight had taken a lot out of her, and she was only beginning to process what had happened in the first place.

It should have been impossible for the HN64 to be struck by lightning, and much less to conduct it all the way to her. That web... She had never seen anything like it. She half-considered asking Callaghan, mentioning it to him, but he would surely have her hospitalized, denying her the chance to join the expedition altogether. Even now, as they were walking, he was shooting her several worried glances.

It wasn't something she could take a chance on. Not now.

The nurse sent her straight to bed. He didn't find anything explicitly wrong with Tabea, except for unusually high blood pressure, but he prescribed plenty of rest and fluids.

Now, Tabea sat at her desk in her quarters, staring at the comms, her heart still beating at racing speed and her mouth dry. How could her plane get hit and permeated by lightning? They were designed for all types of weather, with clear precautions regarding conducting materials. Even so, she should have been more careful. She really should have had the shields up, flying straight into a lightning storm. At least her save had proven to Callaghan that she was definitely able to function under pressure. Now he wanted to put her engineering abilities to the test. It wasn't something she had a particular talent for, but one of Callaghan's mechanics, Hammond, had shown her a few of his tricks over the years.

She sighed and decided it was about time to get a start on fixing the little earpieces. She grabbed her tools from a drawer, starting with the scanner to check for the finer damage that she wouldn't be able to see with her bare eyes. While the scan ran its course, she went to take a shower.

The hot water pouring down over her shoulders felt nice, as though it were washing away the day's events and the stress that had come with it. Soon, she felt her muscles relax and her pulse slow down. Her breathing slowing to a normal rate, she let her thoughts take their own course until they had all passed and what was left was only the noise of the shower. The sound infiltrated her mind, taking over until it was the only thing she could perceive. The drops hitting the floor brought back the memory of the rain pelting against the cockpit. The bright flashing light blinding her, too fast to react. The searing pain surging throughout her entire body as the current ran through her.

She opened her eyes, her breathing as fast as her pulse. She forced herself to calm down again and began inspecting her body. She didn't have any marks as people hit by lightning usually did, possibly because she'd been in the aircraft at the time. When she was satisfied with the lack of signs of the incident, she turned the water off but remained standing there for a moment, dripping, eyes closed, waiting for herself to calm down fully. But the calm didn't come. After a few minutes, she sighed and gave up, dried off hurriedly, threw on a comfortable, loose tracksuit, and dropped onto her desk chair again. A green message across the device announced that the scan had finished.

Zero errors detected.

Tabea frowned and opened the file for a manual check. That was impossible. If there was nothing wrong with them, they would have been working. But she couldn't find any more than the scan had shown.

Testing them to see if she had missed something earlier on, she confirmed what she already knew: They were broken, but somehow, the scans didn't show anything. Furious and frustrated about her inability to find the problem, she launched into a three-hour frenzy, trying anything she could think of to fix the earpieces

Finally, she leaned back in her chair, defeated, twirled the comms around her fingers, and mumbled, "Why aren't you working?"

As she said the words, her fingers began to prickle, similar to the way they had done just before the electric current had run through them. Still staring at the comms, she then saw tiny sparks of lightning pass between herself and the objects.

Suddenly, she understood. She knew it. She felt it.

She couldn't put it into words, couldn't explain it, but an inherent knowledge had taken up residence in her mind, knowledge about why the comms weren't working and what she could do to change that.

"Work," she commanded. Another spark passed from her fingers to the comms and somehow, she knew that they were fixed. Not quite trusting this sudden instinct, she tested them once again.

It worked.

Adrenaline rushed through her body, a mixture of curiosity and disbelief taking a hold of her.

What was going on?

And more importantly, what else could she do?

The alarm clock next to her bed caught her eye. She furrowed her brows in concentration, stretched out her hand toward it without touching it, and said, "Set the alarm for thirty seconds from now."

Electricity played around her fingertips for a moment, creating a visible web of yellow, blue, and purple before uniting and reaching in one white bolt toward the clock, engulfing it for a split second in another web of light, then dissipating. Tabea held her breath, waiting to see what would happen, counting down in her head.

Right on time, the alarm rang out.

"Stop," she demanded, and a lightning bolt shot out from her hand, silencing the clock.

Tabea sank to the floor, staring at her hand in disbelief.

No. Way.

She was one of them.

She had read about them and their abilities.

Humans had encountered extraterrestrials with this ability some years ago, the ability to fully comprehend and command electronics at will. The ability was extremely rare in aliens, but in humans, it was unheard of. The name for beings with this power inspired fear and awe in equal terms.

Other races in the universe called them space witches. But Humanity had a different name for them.

"Technomancer," Tabea whispered. She stared at her hands, clenching and unclenching them as she tested the word in her head. She had to say it out loud to believe it. "I'm a... technomancer?"

Fear washed over her in rippling tidal waves that swept away the strength from her bones.

What did this mean?

Was she even still human?

Could this strange power kill her or change her life forever?

But along with the fear came excitement.

What were the limits of her power?

What would Callaghan think?

Didn't this make her some kind of superhero?

She forced herself to stay calm and think about it logically. Despite not being the weakest of the space traveling races, among humans, technomancers were met with fear. Even half a dozen of them could easily destroy all of human civilization. So how would the people react to a technomancer of their own kind?

The military would undoubtedly try to use it to their advantage, though in what way, Tabea wasn't sure. They might try to figure out how she'd gotten her ability and how to replicate it. Or they might force her into constant labor at the frontier, whether she wanted to go or not. Either way, she was sure she would lose her autonomy.

It was best to keep it a secret. But perhaps she could tell at least Callaghan...?

By the time she had finished that thought, she was

toppling over, her eyes closing. She was asleep before she could even feel the impact of the floor.

Morning sun tickled Tabea's nose, and she blinked, waking up slowly. Her back ached, as did her head, and her limbs felt like they weighed several tons. She sat up carefully, looking around, still half asleep.

Why was she lying on the floor?

Then the previous day's excitement flooded back all at once. The test, the lightning, the technomancy.

It had to have been a dream. It was impossible.

Right?

Hesitantly, and scared of even the memory, Tabea got to her feet and peeked at the comms sitting innocently on her desk. Gingerly, she picked them up and tested.

They worked. And if they worked, then...

Her eyes fell on her clock and reality caught up with her. Cursing, she threw on her uniform and grabbed the comms before racing to Callaghan's office as fast as a cockroach. She was late — again.

She barged into the room, panting and sweating. Callaghan was sitting at his desk, reading some report. He casually glanced up at her.

"Some people might knock," he noted, smiling. "Go on. Close the door."

Tabea nodded, still out of breath, gasping for air, and shut it behind her before taking a seat across from her mentor.

He eyed her up with a concerned look. "The nurse said you didn't have any injuries. How are you feeling?" he asked.

Tabea gave him a smile. "Perfectly fine," she lied. "A-okay. The same as always."

Callaghan laughed. "Glad to hear it! Did you get a chance to look at the comms?"

Tabea nodded and produced them. She hesitated for a moment, but then laid them on the table, praying that there wouldn't be another random spark between them and her hands.

Callaghan took one of the pieces and placed it into his ear. Tabea took the other.

"Can you hear me?" she asked gingerly.

"Loud and clear." She heard Callaghan in her ear and in front of her. "Good job!"

The praise formed a knot in her stomach that reached all the way to her throat, making her feel lightheaded.

"Thank you," she said quietly, guiltily.

"So, in light of everything, including the three years we've been working together," Callaghan continued, "you'll be allowed to join the Harvius VI mission, if that's what you want."

Tabea's head shot up and she stared at him. He was really going to take her. She nodded violently. "Yes, absolutely, please, thank you!" she stammered.

"Since you haven't passed the simulator test yet, you'll be coming as a cadet engineer instead of pilot but doubling as a general assistant. Are you all right with that?"

"Yessir! I am very grateful for this opportunity!"

The twenty-four hours until launch were busy with preparation. Tabea had to pack, read up on her duties, report for a meeting with the head engineer, Hammond, and help load the spacecraft. It was the *K.L.I.O.P.*, otherwise known as the *Calliope*, the most impressive starship ever built on Earth. Alien technology had been used to enhance her abilities beyond what human technology alone could do. Some of it had come from treaties with friendly galaxies, such as the Kinjo-unk, and others had been taken from fallen enemies.

Tabea didn't even get a moment to breathe all day until just before she went to bed that evening. But despite her exhaustion, her mind refused to take a break from fretting about her newfound ability. She needed to train it secretly. Since she didn't know whether this was something that might suddenly surge out of her, or how it might affect her in the long run, she needed to take every precaution she could. It was vital that she knew what exactly she could do, and at what range. And if she could do it without sparking lightnings that everyone could see.

The reports she had read on technomancy in the past had been vague, to say the least. Perhaps she might gain something from doing a little research. Sadly, she knew that she wouldn't have a chance to visit the library before they were going to leave for their mission; heck, she had barely found the time to send a message to her parents to inform them of the huge honor and opportunity she'd been given. She'd just about managed to tell Besma in passing that Callaghan was taking her, and even though her friend couldn't hide her envy, it was clear that she was also happy for

Tabea. Going on this trip was already an incredible milestone, but this, this power, that was something else entirely. She needed to keep it a secret, no matter what. There was no way to tell how others might react to it, no way to tell what would happen to her if she were found out.

Determined, Tabea looked around her room, jutting forward her lower lip.

Bring it on.

There was something she was itching to find out about her ability. She'd been thinking about it all day. After a moment, she found the perfect test subject.

She grabbed an old-fashioned radio and a hammer from her drawer and brought the tool down on the device with force, destroying it completely. Once it was all scattered on her desk in the tiniest pieces, she held out her hand over it.

Closing her eyes, she imagined the radio, and what it was meant to do. Then she ordered the pieces to reassemble. When she felt the now-familiar prickle on her fingertips, she opened her eyes again. Lightning was pulling the pieces together as if by magnetism, sealing cracks that she had caused until the radio sat in front of her again, looking as though she had never smashed it in the first place, perhaps even a little newer than before.

She turned the knob and peppy music blared out of the speakers.

Fatigue washed over her, but she forced herself to stay upright. One more thing.

She destroyed the radio again, and, this time, told the bits what she wanted them to be—she wanted them to assemble an alarm clock. This time, however, she instinctively knew that to fulfill her order, she needed another piece. A piece that could be found in her flashlight.

She took the lamp off the shelf and ordered it to disassemble. When she opened her eyes, the individual components lay in a heap on the table. Then she requested an alarm clock again, holding her hands over both piles. This time, it worked, though she didn't even have the energy to be happy about it anymore.

By now she was dangerously swaying back and forth, barely able to keep her eyes open, never mind keep her balance. She dropped onto the bed and fell asleep instantly.

Tabea reported for duty first thing in the morning. Her supervisor, Hammond, was an older man close to retirement who had already seen far too much in his lifetime. Crow's feet crowded the corners of his eyes and his forehead was lined with age. Yet his blue eyes still kept their youthful sparkle. She'd known Hammond for a while as one of Callaghan's most trusted crew members, and she'd always liked the man, so getting to work under his supervision was a pleasure to her.

He was in the progress of giving her a tour of the *Calliope*'s interior when the ship took off. The motors began humming in the engine room, and the circuits came to life while the floor rumbled uncomfortably.

"Already?" Hammond glanced at his watch. "Ah yes. That's right. Glad I got Smith to take on the starting shift, or we'd be having a problem now." He winked at Tabea.

"Is it always like this?" Tabea asked, gesturing toward the ground. An unsettling, queasy feeling had placed itself in her ribcage at the thought. Commercial liners rumbled often—she'd experienced that before—but they were only meant to travel for short spans of time, while this mission through the vast infinity of space would take a minimum of two weeks. Luckily, Hammond shook his head.

"Not at all. We're still in the atmosphere is all." He tapped lovingly against a wall. "She's not built for the resistance, see. There're too many planetary forces here."

"You mean gravity, the air, the atmosphere, and such?"

"Someone paid attention in class! Yep, that's exactly right."

He beckoned her and walked briskly onward. "Come on. There's something you've gotta see."

Tabea followed him closely until they had reached the bridge. Callaghan was there, sitting at the helm, concentrating on watching several screens. He glanced up when Hammond and Tabea entered and gave her a quick smile before turning his attention back to the screens and yelling out orders at the half dozen other people sitting at screens around him.

Tabea's eyes were fixed on a screen ahead of her that played the live recording of the backward-facing cameras.

Earth was rapidly shrinking until the fields and towns, oceans and continents were no more distinguishable, and it became a blue pearl floating in nothingness with a backdrop of millions of glimmering stars.

Along the horizon, the Aurora Borealis floated gently over the world, an ethereal silk curtain of rainbow light caressing the Earth ever-so-softly. There were also clusters of thick clouds, black and charged, even from above, lightning sparking throughout them.

Tabea had barely had a chance to take it all in when they shot past the moon, an even smaller, white pearl, where a commercial liner seemed to just land in the colony's port.

The smaller Earth became, the more it looked like a drop of water hanging in space. Other planets came into view as well—red, orange, blue, green... A whole string of colorful pearls creating a celestial bond, the sparkle of the billions of suns in the background only adding to the magic of the view.

It wasn't the first time Tabea had seen this view, but she found it just as breathtaking as before.

Only now, as they shot past Pluto, did she notice that the ship's rumble had dissipated. The *Calliope* was calm, as though she weren't moving at all.

Callaghan turned the back screen off and allowed an uninhibited view of space ahead of them.

Tabea had seen the view on photos and videos, even holograms, but seeing it for real was something else— the view only visible from the edge of the galaxy and beyond. It felt fake somehow, as though her brain was only partially able to comprehend it. Galaxies, millions of them, clustered together in the distance, some of them colored in reds or greens, others just bright. It looked as though someone had stolen the irises of thousands of eyes and expanded them, letting them create their own worlds out here, in the vast infinity of space.

Callaghan stepped up next to her.

"Beautiful, isn't it?" he asked proudly, his gaze directed forward, looking ahead with equal measures of confidence and awe.

Tabea could only nod. She didn't trust herself to still have command of her own voice. Happiness washed over her, and she forced herself to avert her eyes from the view, lest she should shed tears of joy. She'd made it. She was finally out here, at what people used to call the final frontier. All that hard work at the Academy… it had paid off. She was on board one of the proudest ships of Humanity's construction, on her first mission outside of the solar system. Heck, outside of the Milky Way!

Innumerable possibilities pushed their way into her consciousness, making promises of what the future might hold, whispering about things she'd only ever read about. It was starting to become difficult to not start giddily bouncing around.

It was only then that she noticed that Hammond had left her side and had taken one of the seats, studying a small screen.

"The next engineering shift should be an easy one, so I'd like you to take it, just so you can get a feel for the controls. Hammond will walk you through it. Have you seen your quarters yet?" Callaghan nudged his head toward the door.

"Yeah, I'm all settled in."

It was a small room, basically only a closet-sized bed with a low ceiling. But she wouldn't be spending a lot of time there anyway. At least if she had anything to say about it.

"In that case, you should take a few hours to have some food and get better acquainted with the ship."

"I will, sir, thank you."

She turned to leave the bridge, but Callaghan called her back.

"Oh, Tabea? One more thing."

She glanced back at him with a questioning glance. He was smiling.

"Drop the 'sir.' You're a part of my crew now."

Her heartbeat rising proudly, she nodded and left, compelling herself not to turn back around to look at the incredible view again. She'd get to see it plenty.

Wandering down the halls toward her room, she let her fingers trail along the ship's wall. If she didn't reassure herself that she was really here, on this amazing ship in outer space, she feared she might just wake up from her dream. The hallways were a pleasant gray tone, not too bright to appear white or glaring, but not too dark to seem gloomy either. She spotted a group of young cadets, barely two years older than her, and a blond one caught her eye. He smiled brightly, a gesture that made his blue eyes sparkle, and beckoned her over.

Hesitantly, she stepped closer.

"You're Tabea, right?" he asked, a small lilt ringing in his voice.

She felt just as much surprise as his two friends, it seemed.

"Tabea?" one of them asked, staring at the blond guy. "*The* Tabea?" He turned to her, as if he expected a response.

Uncomfortably, Tabea shifted her weight. "Um... Maybe?"

Her mind raced through thousands of possibilities why these guys might know her name and whether it was a good thing.

The blond guy laughed. "You're kind of famous, you know?"

Oh, no. Her secret was out. Someone had seen her do her experiments last night. How long would it take for the rumors to spread to Callaghan? What would happen then?

Tabea gulped, blood draining from her face as she scanned her surroundings to look for a way out.

"No kidding," the third guy said. "You're like the best pilot the Academy's seen in ten years or something. It's no wonder Callaghan became your mentor."

Tabea's shoulder had never relaxed so fast. She practically sank into herself, fatigue mixed with relief washing over her in tidal waves.

"Oh." She sighed and managed a smile. "I just got lucky."

The blond guy laughed. "You win the Solar Race and you just call yourself lucky? You must truly be something else!"

Ah yes, the race that had won her the scholarship to the Academy. Without it, she never could have trained to become a Space Core pilot, even though working aboard as an engineer cadet looked like a step away from that.

Flying had always come naturally to her, so winning the race against the other human colonies just hadn't seemed like a big deal to her. Her family certainly hadn't considered it one.

"I'm Vincent Soucroix." He stuck his hand out to her

with a big smirk and she shook it.

"You already know my name." She grinned, cocking her head to one side. "But it's nice to meet you."

One of the guys tapped Vincent on the shoulder and he nodded.

"Well, we've got to go, but I look forward to getting to know you better."

He winked, and then the group left.

Tabea went on her own way, her chest feeling lighter. She'd just made a new friend, right? Her first friend in a real crew. While she loved talking to Callaghan and Hammond, it was nice to have the option of hanging out with someone closer to her own age.

Still, the encounter had left her yearning for a little bit of privacy and alone time before she could venture to the noisy canteen, so she veered off to head back to her room.

After shutting the hatch, she lay down on the bed for a few moments, trying to catch up with herself. She was here, on a spaceship, and outside the galaxy! She'd been on a cruise liner before, but only as a child and never outside of the Milky Way, or even the solar system. Really, she had only ever visited the colony on Mars where her aunt lived, and once she'd been to Saturn for a class field trip.

The *Calliope*... Like everyone on Earth, she'd known about her, had followed her first launch on the live screenings. She was a strong ship, intricate, and complex. Even the people who had built her weren't fully aware of what she was capable of because of the alien tech embedded inside her. They were open about it; in fact, she had been advertised with that in mind.

Unlimited potential, they had said. Infinite possibilities.

Tabea wondered if that was true. She turned on her side and placed her hand on the smooth, cool wall.

What if… she could find out?

She closed her eyes and waited for the familiar energy at her fingertips. She wanted to know the *Calliope*, understand her.

No information reached her. The spaceship was a larger object than the small items she had experimented with before. Maybe it just took more effort, more power, so she pressed more. A part of her self slipped through her hand into the ship, whizzing around with the electrical currents. She traveled through every part of the ship, through the engines, through the bridge with all its screens, through every notch. She traveled through terrestrial technology — familiar, and simple — and then she reached the parts made with alien tech.

It was fundamentally different.

The currents there were pulsating with a regularity that reminded Tabea of a heartbeat. They didn't follow logical paths anymore but seemed to decide randomly which way to flow. Only the human tech around it kept it somewhat in check. It was unstructured at first glance, yet Tabea suddenly understood.

"Hello there."

When Tabea came to her senses, waking up from a deep sleep, her hair was standing in all directions, charged with static. The hours she had been given had also passed. Without time to think about what she had seen and felt, she hurried back to the bridge. On the way, she forced her hair down and tied it into a bun.

The ship was alive.

The thought forced itself to the front of her mind, despite her efforts not to think about it.

The ship had a mind, and she could communicate with it.

However, she now saw a pattern in her sudden sleeping spells. The more she used her technomancy, the more she exhausted herself. Every time, she seemed to pass out from the stress it put on her mind and body. Perhaps she would get better at it with some proper training.

"You look like you've got a bad case of space sickness," Callaghan noted, frowning, when she entered the bridge. Tabea shook her head, gently slapping some red back into her cheeks.

"I'm fine. Just a little tired. I'm sorry I'm late."

Hammond got up from his seat in front of several screens and consoles. "No worries, lass. You're here now, so let's get crackin'!"

She took the offered seat and Hammond talked her through the controls. The moment she touched them, she already knew their purpose, but she let him continue to explain without interruptions. She didn't want to have to justify knowing too much about the ship already. Besides, Callaghan was watching, and she wanted to show him her best behavior, so he didn't regret taking her along.

"All right, so if you pull this lever..." Hammond's voice sank into the background as Tabea's fingers began to prickle. Except that this time, it didn't come from her, which only left one possibility: The *Calliope* was reaching out to her, trying to speak with her. Tabea ignored it, hiding her hands, lest a spark should give her away. She couldn't chance it. Not now.

The prickling faded, and before long, Hammond allowed her to take the controls and translate everything Callaghan called out into actions. Instinctively, she followed his orders flawlessly.

Hammond whistled through his teeth. "You're a natural!" he said. "Took me ages to get used to the system!"

"You explained it really well," Tabea muttered, not meeting his eye.

"We're entering Moleus' territory now," Callaghan announced.

Tabea tensed up, remembering what she had read on them.

The Moleus were a neutral race of humanoid aliens with antennas where a human would have ears. They had seven digits at every extremity, and their skin was smoother, with a strong, green tint. What worried Tabea was that their territory was adjacent to that of the Zutani, a race that hated humans and had been at war with them since their first encounter. They were vicious and not generally well-liked around the known galaxies.

They were already about a quarter of the way to Harvius VI's galaxy, and Tabea felt a mixture of excitement and nervousness pass through her.

"*Tabea.*"

"Hmm?" Tabea shot up, trying to see who had called her.

"Did you say something?" Hammond asked.

"Uh, no, sorry."

Tabea looked back at her screens. Her fingertips

were tingling but thankfully not yet throwing sparks. She curled them over the controls to hide anything that might pass from her to the ship.

"*Tabea*," the voice said again, urgency permeating through it.

The ship. *Calliope*. Tabea was tingling all over now. And the feeling on her scalp told her that her hair was beginning to rise up.

"*What?*" she asked, annoyed, glancing at Hammond to see if he was noticing anything while forcing her breathing to stay calm.

"*Your enemies are near.*"

"What?" she shrieked. Several heads turned toward her. Callaghan strode to her side with two lunges.

"What's wrong? Are the engines all right?"

She blinked up at him with wide eyes, panic slowing down her thinking. Her lips trembled as she fumbled to find the right words.

"Uh, yes. Yes. But, uh, enemies."

"What are you talking about?" Callaghan frowned, though his demeanor was alert.

"*What enemies? The Zutani?*" she asked Calliope.

"*No, not them. They call themselves the mancrushers.*"

"The Penyales?" Tabea's eyes widened, and a cold shiver went down her spine. Both Hammond and Callaghan sharply took in a breath. The bridge was suddenly dead silent.

"*Yes.*"

"Where?"

"*They are in camouflage mode, waiting just outside the reach of your terrestrial radars.*"

Panting, Tabea turned to Callaghan, chilled to her bone.

"Some Penyali ships are waiting for us in camouflage mode. We're headed right for them."

"The scans aren't showing anything," an officer yelled from across the bridge.

Callaghan looked at Tabea contemplatively. "Why would you think that?" he asked sternly.

She didn't have to respond. The ship shook as the base shields were hit by enemy fire. Callaghan reacted quickly, as did Tabea.

"Shields up!" they both ordered simultaneously.

"They... They're already up," the arms and defense officer, Glaucia, said, bewildered.

"*Avoid enemy fire at all costs,*" Tabea asked Calliope.

"The ship is moving on her own!" the pilot, Kyoko Akari, screamed.

Callaghan grinded his teeth, his eyes narrowing.

"They have a space witch," he growled. Tabea flinched but stayed quiet.

"No..." Akari stammered. "We seem to be avoiding their hits..."

"*Talk to them.*"

Tabea stared at the console in front of her.

"*Talk to who? I don't speak any Penyali languages!*"

"*Not the Penyales. Their ships. If you demand, they must obey.*"

Hammond pushed her out of the seat. "This is a job for someone with a little more experience. Sorry, lass."

Forlorn, she stood behind him for a moment.

What should she do?

"*I can't evade them all; there are too many.*" Calliope told her. "*You have to do something.*"

Tabea clenched her fists. How? Why now? Her first mission, too. She didn't even know if she could do anything, and if she did and it worked, her secret would be out.

But she didn't have a choice.

The ship trembled, and the lights flickered for an instant as they were hit by another salvo.

"Shields at fifty percent," Glaucia yelled, her voice shaking.

Tabea relocated to the center of the room so she would have the best view of all the screens and the front window.

"Tabea, get to the emergency capsules—now!" Callaghan shouted, but she ignored him. She knelt to the floor, stretched out her hands, and concentrated. It was easier this time than it had been before. Before she knew it, a part of her had already merged with Calliope again. She connected with the weapons system and used it and the radar to pinpoint the locations of the enemy ships, enhancing the range with some of Calliope's untapped potential.

Then she let go of the crackling energy that had been building up inside her. She thrust both hands onto the ground, letting all energy flow through it and toward the weapons. Lightning was sparking and cracking in the air around her. She lost her own vision, but she saw what Calliope saw. All her lightning energy was directed toward the four enemy ships. The bolts shot out of Calliope's weapon's dock, brightening up the vacuum between them and the other ships before connecting with them.

Tabea could feel them, the way she felt Calliope.

"*Leave,*" she ordered. "*Cease fire and leave. Go to your home planets and stay there. Never attack this ship again.*"

She enforced the command with as much power as

she could, although she didn't know for how long it would keep its effect.

The ships obeyed. Their attack stopped as they veered off.

Tabea severed her connection with Calliope and the other ships as they warped away, and her senses returned. Everyone was staring at her. Before she could say anything, she toppled over, caught by Callaghan just before she hit the ground.

"Tabea."

Callaghan's voice was gentle, caring. Something cool was placed on her forehead. Her eyes flickered open.

"Hi," she croaked. Her voice felt raw and her mouth dry and fuzzy.

"They ran off," he told her, almost casually. "Just like that."

"Just like that," Tabea repeated. He threw a sharp gaze at her.

"Something tells me you had something to do with it."

"I..." Tabea began, hoping to find an excuse quickly, but she faltered. No excuse in the world was going to get her out of this one.

"You're a technomancer," Callaghan concluded.

"The lightning..." she said, looking at her hands. Her throat was closing up, and her hearing and vision became dulled.

"I figured as much." Callaghan sighed. "And I understand why you didn't say anything. But don't you worry." He smiled at her. "I only ever hire people I trust completely, all my officers included. They won't say a word to anyone."

Tabea nodded, tears welling up in her eyes.

"Including me," he continued. "I'll guard your secret with everything I have. You saved our lives today. Thank you."

"I… is it okay?" Tabea asked, finally looking at him, though he was only a colored blob through her tears.

"More than that," he said, smiling. "It's absolutely incredible! If you wouldn't mind, I'd like to talk to you about it some more. A lot more, actually." He paused for a moment before continuing. "And I would like to invite you to be a full member of the crew, if you're keen."

He waited again, searching her face for an answer.

"*Say yes,*" Calliope chimed in. "*It's your destiny.*"

"*My destiny?*" Tabea asked.

"*Yes, to be the Spark in the Universe. You need to be in space to be a space witch.*"

Reassured by the feeling of Calliope's words, Tabea dried her tears and looked Callaghan straight in the eyes.

"Count me in."

PART 3

Chapter 13

Blazing fires danced in the darkness, twisting and bulging, like a red and white mass of magma expanding outward, the stone cracking with red and yellow flames. Stars were extinguished, hidden in the scorching light that blackened the vast void.

Everything was nothing, yet the emptiness began to disappear from spaces in the inferno, as though it were pulled from existence one electron at a time.

Tabea floated alone, watching this terrifying spectacle with horror. Screams filled her ears, cries for help, voices calling out her name, begging her to help them, to save them. Calliope screeched in pain, Callaghan begged, whimpering, Besma sobbed wordlessly—there was no end to them. Each sound chipped another piece of Tabea's heart away until all she was left with were shattered pieces, a broken mirror.

Then the shards, floating in the emptiness in front of her, where the fiery spectacle had taken place only moment before, reflected light and darkness as they turned and twirled—a dance to an unheard, disharmonious melody, written from the fear and pain in Tabea's soul.

One by one, each of the pieces reflected a face back to her, a face of a person she loved and cared for. There were Callaghan, Hammond and Shinay, Besma, Vincent and Yuri, Felicitas and Marco, her parents and her siblings, and, finally, Calliope, not as a clear image, but as a feeling. As the face that existed in Tabea's mind, but not in reality.

The shards disintegrated, slowly at first, then rapidly, until nothing but stardust was left. Tabea tried to reach out for it, capture it, keep it, to save whatever was left of her friends, but she couldn't reach. She was left alone, floating in eternal space, lonely and full of guilt and pain.

Her head pounded.

Bang. Bang. Bang.

Her ankles and wrists throbbed, and burned, and then a shock flitted through her entire body, forcing a scream from her lungs.

Bang. Bang. Bang.

She was alone again, and there was nothing more she could do.

When she opened her eyes, all she could focus on was her pounding headache.

Bang. Bang. Bang.

Her eyes stared blankly at the blue ceiling above her, barely even registering the color. Her mouth was parched, but the thought of drinking brought only queasiness.

She closed her eyes, wishing for the sweet release of death. Her entire body was aching, muscles and joints screaming at her, even though she wasn't using them. Her bones felt cold while her skin felt hot, so very hot.

And all the time, the pain in her head persisted, threatening to stay forever.

Bang. Bang. Bang.

The blue became everything, swallowed up her entire world and her along with it. It was like a black hole, pulling her into its orbit, grabbing her, sucking her in with incessant force, until there was nothing left of her.

Bang. Bang. Bang.

Even her own body no longer seemed real to her. Did she even have one? Did this pain truly belong to her, or was she projecting, experiencing someone else's agony?

Bang. Bang. Bang.

She was hardly sure if she even was Tabea. This didn't seem like something that would happen to her. Tabea lived safely on a starship with her mentor and friends; she wasn't the kind of person who found herself in sudden, unexpected agony that barely left her room to breathe, never mind hold a clear thought.

Bang. Bang. Bang.

Darkness came once more, engulfing her in a terrible embrace.

When she came to again, there was no more pain, but she barely noticed. Even though she'd just woken up, she was exhausted, and her hair was sticking to her face with sweat. The blue ceiling greeted her like an old enemy. Familiar and comforting in its presence, but no less hateful.

Her thoughts were scrambled, and her mouth was

parched. Water. Water would help. She was sure of it. She always kept a glass on her bedside table. She only needed to reach out her hand to —

Her muscles refused to move. No matter how hard she willed herself to budge, she accomplished nothing. She continued to lie motionless, just like a porcelain doll. Had she not finished with the nightmares? Was she experiencing sleep paralysis? Now that she thought about it, her ceiling wasn't blue. It had never been blue. It was meant to be a sleek silvery gray, like the rest of the *Calliope*, meaning that this wasn't her room. Where was she?

Expending an extreme amount of effort that left her breathless and had sweat running down her temples, she finally managed to turn her head after several minutes. She closed her eyes for a few moments to rest and to allow herself to catch her breath. Opening them again, she found herself in an unfamiliar environment; a room in all blue and purple, filled with unfamiliar equipment.

Even though she didn't recognize anything, and it all felt alien to her in its shapes and placement, the room reminded her of a medical bay. It looked too clinical to be anything but science related. Too pristine.

She was lying on something resembling a bed — it was soft, warm, and wrapped around her, like leaves around a flower bud. *Cocoon* was probably a more apt description. The smell in the air resembled ethanol or some other form of antiseptic.

Large containers holding a gel-like substance leaned against the wall, and a flowery scythe pattern made up what she assumed was a doorway with throngs extending inward that all overlapped at the tips. The other wall had several apparatuses mounted on it, decorated with strange symbols etched into them all over.

"*Callie?*" she asked gingerly.

A searing shot of pain exploded in her head, making her lose all her senses for a moment. Instinctively, she squeezed her eyes shut and bit her tongue, so she tasted the warm, iron taste of her blood. The pain subsided quickly, leaving behind only relief.

Okay, what was that? She had to assume the pain was connected to trying to build a mental connection with Calliope, so she wouldn't be trying that again anytime soon. Her heart was racing as she tried to figure out what was going on, her gut twisting and turning as she considered the possibilities.

Something weird was happening here, that much a toddler could tell.

She closed her eyes, recalling her latest memories to piece together what was going on.

The dance had been happening, and she'd volunteered to man the bridge. Callaghan had joined her, and they'd had a nice dinner and conversation, just the two of them. Well, three of them if she counted Calliope.

Then he'd had to leave and... And Yuri had shown up. And there'd been an attack, but she'd gotten them all out of danger. Because of that, he'd figured out that she was a space witch. He knew. And then... Then what?

She drew a blank.

As much as she wracked her brain, she couldn't remember what had happened then. But whatever it was, it had brought her here, wherever "here" was. She wondered how much time had passed. It couldn't have been more than a few days. Probably less, although she was feeling nauseous at the thought of food, which could mean that she was either sick or she hadn't eaten in quite a while and was left overly hungry.

Swallowing made her throat hurt. It was too dry. She still needed water. Surely, she could find some around here somewhere? But before she could go on a scavenger hunt to find anything, she needed to regain control over her limbs.

Priorities set, Tabea got to work and concentrated on first small body parts, like making her finger twitch, before moving onto tensing other muscles gently, without demanding too much of them.

All of them were tense, and they screamed at her with painful neurological messages when she ordered them to move. Still, she persisted. She didn't have a choice.

By the time she managed to lift up one arm below the elbow, she was exhausted. Sweat drenched the plain robe she wore—soft, light material she didn't recognize, and a design that seemed unusual as well, though she couldn't inspect it properly in her current state.

Exhaustion had made her eyelids heavy, and she relented to let them shut for a quick nap. Perhaps a little rest would return the energy she so sorely lacked.

She was awoken by the feeling of a pinprick in her temple. Opening her eyes and seeing the creature holding her up, she couldn't even hold back a scream.

It was a being without nose or ears, and it was all eyes — four of them, yellow in color, and a large, sharp-toothed mouth that almost seemed to split the periwinkle, fine-scaled face in half. The head ended in several jags, almost like a dragon's spines.

Apparently almost as shocked as she was, it dropped her back onto her bedstead and took a few paces back, all four diagonally slit eyes wide open.

Its claws, three digits, one of which had a large, sharp talon extending from it, were clasped in front of its chest with spindly arms that were jointed and seemingly muscled like those of a human. It was standing upright, standing on two jerboa-like legs, with three-pronged clawed feet that were individually wrapped in cloth. At first glance, they looked remarkably like the feet of large, ground-dwelling terrestrial birds. A scaled and spiny tail extended from its behind to the ground for balance, its tip flicking from side to side nervously, like a cat.

It wore a robe, seemingly from a similar material as her own gown but fashioned in a more practical manner. The wrapping reminded Tabea of something between a toga and a mummy's bandages.

As she stared at the creature, the extra-terrestrial, slowly realizing that it must have been a sentient person, she tried to figure out which species they belonged to, mentally running through the different descriptions she had learned.

"It's okay. Everything is fine. Don't be scared. Please don't hurt me." The words, although clearly using the sounds of a strange, foreign language, made perfect sense in Tabea's mind.

But no matter who they were, they clearly didn't

intend to harm her. Instead, they were almost huddled near the wall, watching her every movement with eagle's eyes, giving Tabea the distinct impression that they feared her, for whatever reason.

Tabea tried to smile, but moving her mouth was hard. Only after a moment did it occur to her that this species might not recognize the meaning behind a smile, since their own anatomy was so clearly different to hers. She settled for closing her eyes slowly. Surely obviously lowering her defenses for a moment should be a sign of peace?

Not that she was in any condition to be a threat to anyone. Besides, she thought giddily, it was insane to think that anyone with claws like that would consider her a threat at any time, never mind in her current state.

Her act apparently calmed the extra-terrestrial down because they stepped closer again.

"I'm Sh't'ani," they said. "And please don't tell anyone about this. I was just meant to put the transmittal unit in you while you were asleep. I'm not meant to even be talking to you."

They paused and watched Tabea for a moment, their head tilted to one side, eyes open and wakeful with curiosity. "I've never met a human before. You don't really eat our eggs after throwing them in hot water, do you?"

There was a hesitant note to their voice, just enough to suggest that while they didn't actually think it was true, there was the tiniest fear that it might be after all.

Tabea didn't have the strength to respond, but she was able to manage the tiniest shake of her head. She hoped that Sh't'ani would keep talking. At this point, anything might help her to remember what had happened and where she was now, never mind her friends and Calliope.

But Sh't'ani didn't do her that favor. Instead, their shoulders released some tension, and two flaps between their eyes and mouth Tabea hadn't noticed before flared. Then the door opened as the prongs making up the floral pattern retracted outward into the walls, ceiling, and ground.

Sh't'ani gave one quick glance at the two newcomers before lowering their head and rushing out past them.

They were members of the same species, one dressed in navy cloth, fashioned to sit tightly on the body, likely to allow for better movement, perhaps a combatant or engineer, while the other wore a long, bright yellow robe with a hood that covered almost their entire body.

The one dressed in navy walked with their claws behind their back, the rest of their body tensed. They had watchful eyes that narrowed when fixing their diagonally slit pupils on Tabea. The other one in the bright robe seemed a lot more relaxed, though their gaze was no less piercing.

Neither of them appeared as friendly or chatty as Sh't'ani had been.

Tabea gulped and tried to sit up. It was hard, and she was afraid her elbows would buckle, but she managed, just about. Still, she felt as weak and vulnerable as a newborn kitten.

Despite the preparations at the Academy, Tabea had only encountered an extra-terrestrial once before, a special guest of Callaghan's from the Moleus. She had no idea what customs to employ for these new acquaintances, however.

They watched her in silence for a few moments, and Tabea felt as though she were a piece in a gallery, inspected and observed, but not interacted with.

She cleared her throat.

"Um... Hi." Her voice came out a lot weaker and scratchier than she would have liked, but there was nothing she could do about that. Her body wasn't in good condition, and she was already expending far more energy than she had reserves for. It was only the need to find out what had happened and where she was that kept her going right now and pulling on the last bits of energy she could muster.

"I believe that was a human greeting," the gold-robed alien said.

The one clad in navy nodded.

"I'm aware."

Another silence ensued, during which Tabea knew even less what to do with herself. Her head was starting to spin again, and she wished they would leave. All she wanted was to sleep some more and then try talking to Sh't'ani again. They seemed a lot more willing to have a conversation than these two. Nevertheless, she still needed to try.

"Who are you?" she asked. It wasn't the politest of questions, but it was direct and uncomplicated, and about all she could manage right about now.

After what seemed like an eternity, the one in navy finally spoke, but Tabea's eyes kept returning to the one in gold. There was something about them, something familiar that drew her toward them.

"I'm General P'cha'me. This," — they referred to the one dressed in the fancy golden robe — "is High Priest C'ru. We are part of the Penyali star force, and we've been looking for you."

CHAPTER 14

"DOES YOUR RACE HAVE NAMES FOR THE INDI-vidual, or should we refer to you as 'human?'"

Tabea's mind was whirring with confusion and fear rushed over her.

The Penyales. She was on board of a Penyali ship, facing two of the infamous mancrushers. She didn't know of a single story where a human had survived a face-to-face encounter with a Penyali and live to talk about it. Until now, she hadn't even known what they looked like.

And they'd been looking for her.

Even though her body was sluggish and weak, her mind operated at lightning speed, connecting the dots that had led to her presence in this room.

It must have been the Harvius VI mission. The one and only time she'd encountered Penyali ships. And she'd ordered them to turn away and never bother them again, overpowering the strength and will of the technomancers on board their ships.

Heat and cold rushed through her body at the same time. She was going to die.

They'd tracked her down to end her.

Then the High Priest spoke with a gentle voice. "It is tired and afraid. We must let it rest a while and allow it to calm down." They said it to the general, but their meaning was clear in Tabea's mind as well. It was a higher voice than that of the general, and she instinctively wanted to attribute femininity to it, but she didn't know if that was true for the Penyales.

The general nodded, and they both retreated, leaving Tabea behind alone with a quickly beating heart and several more budding questions.

Exhausted, she dropped back down on her bed and closed her eyes. Pearls of sweat had formed on her forehead and shivers were running up and down her entire body.

It was clear to her now that the Penyales didn't want to cause her immediate harm. For the moment, she seemed to be in a sort of safe position, but why that was, she couldn't tell. The only thing she could think of would be that her abilities as a space witch made her seem more valuable than a mere human, whom they despised as a rule, at least as far as she'd been told. Now, a tiny voice in the back of her mind questioned even that. Sh't'ani didn't seem to hate her. At most, they'd seemed to be wary, maybe even scared. The High priest, C'ru, had also shown a significant lack of ill will toward her. So, if not the entire race, perhaps at least this ship, didn't want all of Humanity to perish.

Having expended more energy than she had saved up, that was the last thought she could form before drifting into unconsciousness once more.

Something Tabea presumed to be food had been placed on a small stand next to her bed while she'd been asleep. It looked terrible — a green-brown mass of lumpy liquid — but it smelled delicious. Having a much easier time using her muscles now, Tabea sat up slowly and, allowing a moment for the dizziness to pass, picked up the bowl with the straw and tentatively sucked on it. Savory, thick liquid, akin to a stew or soup, flowed into Tabea's mouth. It was spicier than she'd expected, and richer. Some lumps came up in the straw and burst in her mouth, releasing some floury substance.

Tabea found herself briefly concerned, thinking that she might have just allowed herself to be drugged, poisoned, or inserted with nanobots, but her stomach was protesting too loudly for her to stop herself or to make herself throw up what she'd already ingested.

She was in their power. They could make her take whatever they wanted, especially right now when her strength was at its lowest. Besides, if she didn't eat, she would only get weaker and she didn't exactly have a lot of options left.

Thusly reasoning with herself, she finished the entire bowl. Only then did she notice the closed hourglass-shaped cup with a straw beside it on the stand. Based on the positioning, it was probably a drink.

The first sip confirmed it — plain water. Just what she needed.

Refreshed and re-energized, Tabea decided it was finally time for action. She'd been lying about immobile for long enough.

Determined, she swung her legs over the side of her sleeping pod just as the door opened. Tabea recognized

Sh't'ani instantly. The slight shading of their scales and the gentle curves in their face made them unmistakable, never mind the humble manner in which they held themself.

Their eyes became round with surprise.

"Oh, you're awake!"

Tabea curled her lips up in a smile and closed her eyes for a moment but made sure not to show teeth until she knew more about how Penyali body language differed from humans.

Then she cleared her throat. "Hello, Sh't'ani."

Sh't'ani's eyes widened and glittered as their tail began to swish from side to side slowly. "You remember my name! I didn't think you would."

Tabea chuckled. It was nice talking to someone who seemed to be so genuine. With the other two, it was obvious that they had motives they hadn't disclosed to her, plans beyond just keeping her here.

"My name is Tabea. Did you make this?"

She gestured toward the tray with her breakfast, and Sh't'ani nodded and cast their eyes down, though their tail continued swaying.

"I hope you liked it."

"It was delicious."

The tail flicked faster now.

A moment of silence followed where they both seemed to want to speak, but neither knew what to say. Tabea decided that frankness was the best way to move forward, and she had accumulated a lot of questions that needed answering.

"Sh't'ani." She looked the Penyali directly in the eyes, well, the bottom left one, anyway. "Why am I here? And where are my friends?"

The tail froze.

"Um." Their voice was shaking. "I don't... I can't..."

Sh't'ani took several tiny steps backward but made no real attempt to leave. Tabea decided she could stand to prod a little more. She gestured around the room helplessly.

"I just don't understand how I got here. The last thing I remember is warping my ship away from an attack, and then I woke up here. *On a Penyali ship.* I thought your species was supposed to hate mine, but here we are, you feeding me delicious food. I was told that if I ever met people from your galaxy, I wouldn't live long enough to even see your faces. And if I'm here, then my crew has to be as well, right?"

Sh't'ani still shuffled around for a moment, but they didn't seem to see a way out of the situation. "I don't know much. I'm just a guard-nurse, so I don't get included in the plans and bigger decisions. But I know that General P'cha'me has been trying to find you for a long time."

She'd known it.

"She's had a suspicion that the first human space witch had been chosen by the universe for a while now, and then we found you."

Sh't'ani briefly fell into silence and an ice-cold shiver ran down Tabea's spine.

"And your friends... I truly don't know. I haven't been told anything else." After hesitating for a moment, Sh't'ani's eyes widened again, and their tail perked up. "But please don't think that we attacked you! This ship has not been in any battle recently. We found you in an escape pod!"

Tabea flopped in her seat. She understood no more

226

than she had before. She'd been in an escape pod? Why?

She couldn't remember entering one. It made no sense that she would have been alone, either. If the *Calliope* had been in trouble serious enough for Tabea to leave her friends behind, then others would have shared the pod with her.

And if Sh't'ani was to be believed that they hadn't attacked the *Calliope*... then that meant someone else had been after them. Images of the *Sonata* as Tabea had found her flashed through her mind. Could it have been the pirates? She gulped, trying to calm her rapidly increasing breathing and heartbeat.

Right now, she couldn't do anything.

She also still didn't know what General P'cha'me's plans were for her going forward. Time to consider her options.

"Are you allowed to take me outside of this room?" she asked.

"I wasn't explicitly forbidden from it, but I'm certain you are not permitted to roam around alone. And"— Sh't'ani looked her up and down, a critical look in their eyes, a long, vertical furrow down the center of their face—"I don't know if you're really in the right shape yet. From my understanding of human physique, limited as it may be, you haven't yet fully rested up."

Tabea smiled and jumped down from her bedstead. Her knees wobbled on impact, but she was standing and determined to remain on her feet. She couldn't just sit by and do nothing. She needed to collect as much information as she possibly could, as quickly as she was able.

For all she knew, her friends' lives might be in

danger. The Penyales apparently had a reason to keep her alive, but the same might not be true for the rest of her crew, or for Calliope, if Sh't'ani was wrong, and they were in fact on this ship somewhere.

The thought of her best friend sent a jab through her chest. She hadn't been able to connect with her earlier, but maybe now…?

Acting on impulse, Tabea sent her essence out with the mission to sense and follow traces of Calliope's energy. She didn't get very far.

Shock ran through her body, rendering her limbs limp and weak, setting explosive fires in her brain, and making her feel sick to her stomach.

It was only a few moments later when Tabea realized she was leaning over a bowl Sh't'ani was holding while keeping her hair out of her face, that she noticed she was emptying the slim contents her stomach had been holding. Weakly, she leaned back, wiped her mouth with her sleeve, and closed her eyes.

Still. She still couldn't use her abilities. They were there, she could feel them, but for some reason, she was unable to use them without essentially destroying her body.

"You won't be able to use technomancy here, human."

High Priest C'ru's voice came from the entry way, where they stood, looking down on Tabea, but not unkindly. Their lilac eyes portrayed something Tabea was beginning to recognize as good humor. Their tail was swaying slightly, similar to the way Sh't'ani's had done earlier.

"Why not?" Tabea croaked wearily. Her vision was beginning to blur again. She didn't know how long she'd be able to stay conscious.

"You're a space witch," C'ru said simply. "You didn't think we'd let you come on our ship without taking some precautions, did you? We can't have you just take control of our ship."

Their eyes narrowed as they watched Tabea.

Tabea nodded. "If I promise not to do that, can you take whatever this is away?"

C'ru scoffed. "We know your kind can and will lie. We cannot believe that you would keep your word."

Tabea hadn't forgotten. One thing that was universally known about the Penyali was that they, unlike most other species, were factually incapable of telling untruths. It was only to be expected that this knowledge would have installed a natural distrust toward others in them.

It's like the boy who cried wolf.

The thought popped into Tabea's mind before she knew where it had even come from. It was no less true. She wanted to rise up, to retort, to insist on her trustworthiness, but the earlier shock was taking its toll, and once more, she faded into darkness, sinking against Sh't'ani in the process. The last thing she noticed was the guard-nurse's gentle touch and smell — earthy and foresty.

Waking up in the now familiar room, Tabea was alone again.

There was no confusion in her mind as to where she was and what she needed to do. No matter how well-meaning the Penyales on this ship might have been, she had no guarantee they would remain that way. They were the mancrushers, after all. And she needed to find her friends. Sh't'ani might not know where they were, but that wasn't to say that someone else might not, and since she couldn't use her powers to either ask the ship or at least check the systems, she would need to do this the old-fashioned way.

Determined, she swung her legs out of bed and crossed the room toward the entry way. There had to be a simple mechanism here somewhere. It was too bad she had yet to see someone open the door from the inside. She touched and tested the door itself and the wall around it, concentrating on finding something that would activate the mechanism to open the door.

There was a small hole in the wall, and Tabea wondered if it was designed for one of the Penyali talons. If that was the only way to open the door, she'd be in trouble. Frowning, she looked around the room. If she could find something long, thin, and slightly bent, she might be able to test her theory and perhaps even open the door. But the closest thing she could find to what she needed was the straw from the water cup Sh't'ani had left for her.

It'll have to do.

She jerked it into the hole and started wiggling it around. The straw bent and squished too much to do anything useful, and Tabea only hoped this didn't work like an old-fashioned lock. Additionally, if it was based on biometric recognition, she didn't stand a chance, either.

Just as she gave up with the straw for the moment, the door opened and Sh't'ani came in, holding a tray with another bowl. Startled, they stumbled a step back when Tabea stood right in their way.

"Hey, Sh't'ani," Tabea said. "Any chance you could let me out of this room today?"

She glanced at the remarkably unremarkable hallway behind the Penyali nurse.

Sh't'ani nodded, and their tail flicked happily.

"Yes! I received permission from my superiors to take you on a tour of the ship. You will even get your own quarters."

While Tabea was happy to hear the news, she couldn't silence a little voice that told her that this was far too familiar, yet twisted in a way. For the moment, she couldn't quite pinpoint why that was the case.

Sh't'ani waited for Tabea to have her meal and then offered her a set of fresh clothing. "I will take you to the sanitary stalls, first. Then you shall see your new quarters."

Eagerly, Tabea grabbed the pile they were holding out to her and followed Sh't'ani outside. Incidentally, the lock for the door was activated the way she had expected, by inserting a talon into the hole and flicking the wrist thirty degrees.

Tabea watched the swift, elegant movement, and a thought occurred to her.

"Sh't'ani, your race has genders, right?"

Sh't'ani glanced over their shoulder. "We do. Five of them. How many do humans have?"

There was a curious glint in their eye as they watched Tabea.

They continued their conversation in the hallway — a gray corridor that could have belonged to any spaceship Tabea had ever seen, including the *Calliope*.

"It's a little complicated. Historically, only two were

accepted by a lot of cultures, but we now know that there are many more, though almost none of them are named. Honestly, I really couldn't put a number on it."

"I see. In that case, which are those two historical genders?"

Even though Sh't'ani was leading the way, they kept looking back at Tabea, speaking with enthusiasm and genuine curiosity.

"Male and female, I guess." Thinking of her own difficulty to attribute genders to the Penyales, Tabea added, "I'm female."

"How interesting! Our general is also female! High Priest C'ru is what you would call male. I am qurusanne. You know, there is a race that has no genders at all — they don't believe in the concept."

"Oh, yeah, the Crippnerasale. I've heard of that before, too."

They fell into silence and Tabea used the opportunity to really look around. While the hallways were bland and common, she noticed that all doorways had same petal-blade pattern. They were certainly prettier than the doors back on the *Calliope*, or on Earth, but Tabea was itching to find out how exactly the mechanism worked. If she couldn't use her powers, at least she'd like to take one of them apart, or see a blueprint.

"In here are the sanitary stalls. I'll be right outside, so if you need anything, please shout."

Sh't'ani opened the door for her, and Tabea entered, curious as to what she would find.

She hadn't really expected genuine stalls — cabins made from some material resembling plastic, about the size of a very small bathroom back on Earth. Ten of them were lined up in a row, each with swinging doors with a primitive triple-thronged sliding lock. Currently, none of them were in use, so Tabea had free choice. She peeked into two or three, but they were identical to one another—a sort of stool that she assumed to be the lavatory, separated from the shower by two plastic-like dividers, and a small bench between the two. The setup reminded her strangely of camping sites back on Earth, the kind she'd visited with Callaghan in preparation for her survival training. However, unlike those, there was a small bowl with what could only be soap in the shower here. Also, judging by the orifices around the walls of the shower cabin, the water was sprayed from the sides here.

Suddenly realizing that she really needed to use the bathroom, Tabea decided to stop sightseeing and get to business. After figuring out how to flush with some difficulty, she discarded the robe she had been wearing since she'd awoken on this ship. Smelling herself for the first time in a while, she made a face. She was *ripe*. Grateful that Sh't'ani had brought up the subject of showering without an awkward conversation, Tabea made use of the opportunity she'd been given and enjoyed the shower to its full potential once she'd figured out the pulls and levers that made it work, without scorching herself.

Feeling refreshed, she put on the golden-threaded garment Sh't'ani had provided for her—the same look as High Priest C'ru. She wondered if it was a space witch thing. Donning the robe, she realized she may need to request needle and thread, as the tail flap at the back of the robe didn't quite fulfill its intended purpose in her case, and the robe was a little too long for her.

Now, being out of isolation and having regained her strength, feeling refreshed, old thoughts popped back into Tabea's mind and took their seat in the forefront of her consciousness.

She knew the Penyales wanted her, had *sought* her. But she also knew that, as a race, they despised humans and thought them the scum of the universe, wanting to eradicate their existence, if at all possible. Additionally, there might have been pirates, potentially also looking for her. Keeping those things in mind, she needed to find out what had happened to her friends and find them — fast. A tiny voice in the back of her mind added the clause *if they're even still alive*, but she silenced that thought quickly. There was no way she would allow herself to believe anything other than her friends being alive unless proven otherwise. She couldn't.

But finding them was her top priority nonetheless because something *could* still happen to them.

First things first. Sh't'ani was definitely Tabea's best bet for information, innocent as they appeared, and they seemed to be willing to show her around and help her. The first step would therefore be to find out what had happened after she had lost consciousness, how she had ended up in an escape pod and then on the Penyali ship. During that process, she should also find out what had happened to Calliope and her crew, which would then give her a decent starting point for her search.

The vague plan in mind, Tabea left the sanitary stalls and rejoined Sh't'ani in the hallway. They were fumbling with a small device, a ring around one of their talons that seemed to have two buttons on it and could project a small holographic screen to about hand's width over the claw.

"What's that?" Tabea ogled it curiously, but to her disappointment, Sh't'ani wiped the holoscreen away and hid their claw behind their back.

"It's just my ring."

"Your ring?" Tabea stared at them, confused and intrigued.

"Yeah, my cellular molecular ring. Do humans not have that?"

The claw came back forward, and Sh't'ani fumbled with it, twisting it around their claw in thought.

Tabea only shook her head, eyeing the ring intensely and wishing she were allowed to take it apart to figure out what exactly it did and how it worked.

"It's a communication device firstly." Sh't'ani stretched out their talon and pressed a button so the holoscreen returned. It showed what Tabea presumed to be the home screen. There were several icons and text symbols spread across it, though they didn't make a lot of sense to her. "But these days it can really be used for anything. It's a light source, and it has entertainment options as well."

Tabea nodded vigorously. It was a phone. An alien version of a phone that might even use similar technology to Earth's communication devices, such as the holopads. Fascinating.

Sh't'ani's eyes fell on one of the symbols on the screen, and their nostrils flared. Then they grabbed Tabea by the wrist and pulled her behind them before she could react.

"We have to hurry," they huffed. "General P'cha'me wants to talk to you in your quarters. I need to get you there before she arrives."

Rushing through hallways and taking turn after turn, Tabea noticed how exhausted she was. Walking around for long stretches of time didn't seem to be in her cards just yet. How long had she been unconscious that her muscles and stamina had deteriorated so much?

Finally, Sh't'ani opened a door and led Tabea inside. It was a small sky-blue room, with a flower-shaped bedstead similar to the one she had been using thus far, equipped with many pillows and some blankets. Other than that, a chest, inset into the wall, and a small bedside table, the room was empty.

Sh't'ani crossed the room to open the chest. Several garments like the one Tabea was wearing had been stuffed inside.

"Here's fresh clothing whenever you need it, and here" — they strode over to a button near the door, with speakers next to it — "is how you can call me if you need anything." Their eyes flicked to their ring. "I've got to go now, but just wait here. General P'cha'me will be by at any moment."

Tabea only had the time to nod before they were gone. The door closed behind them, and she was left behind, uncertain as to how long she'd have to wait, or how to pass the time. With nothing else to do but contemplate her own exhaustion, she lay down on the bed and closed her eyes. Entering a sort of trance-like state where she wasn't quite asleep, but still resting, she started to feel the energy surrounding her.

Little sparks of electricity all around, bumping into each other, constantly in motion. Her own body, a pool of them. As she watched, no, *felt*, their dance, a though entered her mind.

Does energy have memory?

But before she could continue with that train of thought, she was disrupted by the door opening.

General P'cha'me strode in, the same poise as always, and looked around the room critically. Finally, her lilac gaze fell on Tabea.

"Come with me."

CHAPTER 15

GENERAL P'CHA'ME STRODE OUT OF THE ROOM, not even bothering to so much as look around to see if Tabea had followed. They walked through several more blue hallways without encountering anyone else and finished in a tiny, empty room with a light reddish glow that only had the one door.

"Top floor," General P'cha'me ordered, and Tabea could feel the slightest hint of movement in the ground, though it was so faint, she wasn't entirely sure if she had imagined it. When the door opened again, Tabea was greeted with the sight of another hallway, though this one was distinctly prettier.

Someone had taken the trouble to line the walls with all sorts of small plants, none of which were types Tabea recognized. Lichen grew across the walls in different colors, almost creating the illusion of paintings. All of this was topped off by the soft light beaming from the ceiling, accentuating the luscious green of the plants.

Only when Tabea stumbled forward in awe did she notice that the ground was soft, and a glance confirmed that it was overgrown with moss and short grass. The general glanced at her as she gaped at her surroundings but didn't say a word. Tabea made a mental note to ask Sh't'ani about this floor later when she had a chance. Something about her aura made Tabea think General P'cha'me was the kind of person who wouldn't take kindly to too many questions.

She followed her down the wondrous hallway and into a room resembling an office. There was a table, several seats clearly designed for Penyali physique—with a groove for their tail—some shelves holding items whose origin and purpose didn't immediately reveal themselves to Tabea, and High Priest C'ru.

He stood up when they entered and gave the tiniest bow of his head to the general before his piercing amber gaze fell on Tabea.

"The robe's color suits you," he said lightly. "But the shape does not."

Tabea grimaced. "I know," she said. "Am I allowed to make alterations?"

The question was directed at both of them. The general only shrugged, clearly not intending to bother with petty business of this sort, and C'ru only barely stifled his tail from swinging wildly as he replied.

"You may."

The door shut behind her, and P'cha'me gestured to one of the seats. It wasn't the most comfortable place for her to sit, seeing as it wasn't shaped for her body, but P'cha'me's harsh gaze on her made her comply without showing any sign of discomfort.

For a few moments, Tabea watched the general pace back and forth, all the while the tip of her tail was flicking in irritation. Then she gave a sigh and turned to Tabea briskly, pinning her down with a glare. Tabea's mouth went dry as she steeled herself for whatever was to come.

"We need your help as a space witch."

"Huh?" Tabea was taken aback. She didn't know what she had expected, but a plea for help certainly hadn't been among the possibilities. An order or demand, maybe, even threats. But never a request.

"In the past, our race was led by fools. As a result, our planet of origin was turned into uninhabitable land. It used to be known as 'the Viridian planet'. Now we call it 'the brown planet' because nothing can live there anymore."

That glare bore into Tabea's soul, and even though P'cha'me wasn't the most expressive of the Penyali she'd met, there were traces of emotion dancing in the depths of her eyes. Anger, mostly. Perhaps some sadness and regret.

"We want to return the planet to its former state so that our people may return to their origins, but our space witches do not have enough power to make that happen on their own." She glanced to C'ru who only lowered his head. "That's why we need your help."

Memories of Earth's development came flashing into Tabea's mind. The destruction of the atmosphere, the ever-increasing warming, first so fast, now artificially slowed. The large stretches of the planet that had become deadly purely because of heat, and other stretches that had become charged with nuclear radiation during World Wars Three and Four.

The Viridian planet sounded a lot like where Earth was heading. Of course, Humanity had been lucky to slow the murderous warming and destruction of the planet, but only thanks to the Kinjo-Unks' help.

Apparently, the Penyales hadn't been so lucky to receive help. Even the thought of losing Earth, her home planet, her species' planet of origin, to those forces that had been induced by Humanity itself made her chest ache. She could only imagine how the Penyales might have been feeling. And her throat choked up.

"My help," Tabea repeated, trying to wrap her head around the request. "To basically turn back time on a planet?"

P'cha'me looked to C'ru, who cut in.

"Not quite. You know we space witches control energy, correct? It's where technomancy comes in. Technology works with electricity, energy. This, however, is a much purer form of what it means to be a space witch. This is taking out the electricity and the metal and focusing on the pure energy. The idea is to draw out the nuclear energy residue in the soil and at the planet's core and creating a shield around its atmosphere so the planet can recover and return to its former glory, given the time."

Now things were starting to make a little more sense.

"But why do you need my help for that? You have plenty of space witches, don't you? And I'm just human."

C'ru gave her a strange look—his eyes narrowed slightly, and his head tilted to one side.

"It's *because* you're human we need your help."

Tabea frowned at them, her eyes flicking between them.

"I don't get it."

"You have more power than we've ever seen in a

space witch," C'ru admitted after a moment's hesitation. "We've seen you overpower several experienced space witches with ease, without formal training, even though you're the only human space witch to have ever come into existence."

Tabea thought back to the few times she had exerted her will over other space witches over the past two years. C'ru was right. It *had* been easy. She'd always assumed that it was her tactical approach, finding back entrances and such, that had allowed her to exert her own will over theirs. But apparently, she'd been wrong. No wonder they had made such a big deal of keeping her power subdued while aboard this ship.

She tried to consider her options. The fact that she'd been asked for help, rather than forced, seemed like a good sign. Perhaps the animosity between humans and Penyales might have been partially caused by a misunderstanding, or perhaps the work of a politician who'd broken a promise early on in the intergalactic relationship, thereby unwittingly condemning the rest of their people for eternity in the eyes of the creatures who could never lie.

And perhaps her helping them might mend those burnt bridges.

She stopped herself at that thought. While she sympathized with their desire to regain their original planet, this was no time for developing a hero complex. Only because they *thought* she had the ability to do something great, didn't mean that she actually *did*. And one little action by her, put in a corner as she was, would be unlikely to solve a blood feud that had raged for generations.

Besides, the real question was what would happen if

she refused. For all she knew, they might kill her, having outlasted her usefulness. They'd searched for her to get a hold of her powers. If she didn't use them for their sake, what good was she to them? She might just as well be another random human, liable to lie and deceive at any given moment.

She decided to take a leap.

"If I try to help you," — she kept her eyes locked on those of General P'cha'me — "will you help me? I need to find my crew and ship."

P'cha'me held her gaze steadily. "We have already sent out vessels to search for your ship."

Surprised at how forthcoming the general was, Tabea nodded gratefully before turning to C'ru, realizing now just why he had felt familiar when they'd first met. It was his energy signature. He, like her, was a space witch.

"While you say that I have a lot of power, I know very little about being a space witch. I hope you or one of the other space witches will be able to teach me so I can better help your planet."

C'ru nodded, his eyes narrowed and tail swaying happily from side to side. "I will give you all the guidance you need personally."

All Tabea could think about was that Calliope would be so pleased to hear that. It looked like she would finally make some real progress in learning about her powers.

Back in her room, Tabea looked at the scriptures C'ru had left with her. They were on a little disk with a button in the center that would show the information on a holoscreen. Admittedly, Tabea had always preferred the old-fashioned method of printed paper, but this was a much more efficient method of storing and sharing information. And it gave her something to do.

C'ru hadn't wasted time before giving her learning materials. Of course, for the moment, all of it was purely theoretical, but the chance to learn more about what it meant to be a space witch was already more than enough for the moment while the Penyales looked for her friends. Still, thinking of the Penyales of all races to be helping her felt odd to her. With everything she knew about the interactions their races had had in the past, she knew something was wrong about this situation. She was likely only in this privileged position thanks to her being a space witch.

P'cha'me had informed her that they were to arrive and stop on Cerulean, one of the planets in Penyali territory, in a few days' time. Viridian was the next planet over, so Cerulean was the ideal place to lodge and train for the real attempt to revivify the planet and to wait to hear about the *Calliope* and her crew. Since she was in Penyali hands, there was no other way out either way.

Tabea clicked one of the buttons and the holoscreen appeared. Once again, she was grateful for the translator Sh't'ani had inserted in her temple that instantly translated everything in her mind. It meant that even though she could tell that the shapes and direction of the writing didn't seem familiar, she could still understand the meaning without problems.

Apparently, this was a text on space witch lore.

Some of it sounded oddly familiar and Tabea was hit with a spell of homesickness as she remembered Calliope teaching her on the same subject.

Lying on her bed, Tabea finally gave in to Calliope's nagging and started their training session.

She allowed herself to merge with Calliope whole, so their thoughts and bodies were shared. She loved the feeling of being one with Callie – the sparks that flew around them at impossible speeds, the way she stopped seeing the world, but felt it instead. Feeling so close to Callie, she knew nothing could ever come between them. It was a state of lightness and heaviness at the same time and if it didn't exhaust her so much, she'd be doing it every day.

"Took you long enough," Calliope teased, and Tabea giggled.

"I'm here now, aren't I?"

Calliope didn't respond, but instead manifested as a shape in Tabea's mind, electric blue with never-ending bright yellow lights flashing throughout her body.

"Now let's see. What do you want to practice today?"

Tabea hesitated to ask the question that had been bugging her since she first tapped into her powers last month. It had been such a sudden change and she still couldn't fully believe that Callaghan had accepted her so readily, as had the other officers, Hammond especially. She'd been so lucky to have such an incredible mentor and work with wonderful people like these, and she wanted to make sure she could be the best asset they ever had.

But to be that, she needed to get proper control and understanding of her abilities.

"I want to know what it means to be a space witch," *she said.* "I mean, what does it mean to be a technomancer? Is there something I have to keep in mind? Rules of some sort?"

Calliope watched her carefully for a moment, or at least, her essence did. Observing, was probably a more accurate term. "How about we start by discussing what it means?"

Tabea edged closer to Calliope's essence. Vivid images began flashing in her consciousness, matching what Calliope told her about.

"Long ago, the universe was only chaos. Then conscious beings began carving out places for themselves, inflicting order on their homes and everything that was within their reach. Over time, more and more of them appeared until Space found that she could no longer contain herself and introduced new harbingers of chaos into the world.

"She chose certain individuals over time and granted them power, abilities that matched her own, in the hopes that they use these gifts to create balance."

Tabea found herself taken aback by that thought.

"Balance?" *she asked.* "That doesn't make any sense. Why would Space want balance if she wants chaos?"

Even without a face, Tabea could feel Calliope's smirk.

"It's so human of you to think that way."

"And what's wrong with that?"

Calliope laughed softly before continuing. "Chaos has its own order, real balance, whereas forcibly created order by conscious thought complicated things and actually creates real chaos, thereby offsetting the balance."

Tabea sighed, feeling her head spinning, even in her current state of being. "Now you really don't make any sense anymore. Plus, I don't see what that has to do with me."

"It'll make sense in time, I promise. But for now, the important thing for you to realize is that Space chose you. It wasn't by accident that you received these abilities, and technomancy is only one of the many things you're capable of."

Tabea read the same story Calliope had told her about in their early days together in this scripture. It used different words and a lot more detail with an actual legend and love story woven around it, but the essence of the tale remained the same.

Space herself chose her heralds, granting them power beyond the capabilities of any race, when she found individuals she considered worthy. This particular scripture even mentioned a specific amount of all the space witches that could exist at any given time. Only one hundred and twelve. One hundred and twelve individuals across all the different species in the universe. The tale continued to mention that these one hundred and twelve individuals needed to come together every one hundred and twelve millennia to restore balance. Outside of those times, the space witches were free to follow their own agendas completely and wholly.

Tabea set the scripture aside to stare at the ceiling.

While it was a nice story, it was less than helpful. So she'd been chosen by Space. Great. But why? And why were her powers apparently stronger than those of other races? Why was she the first and only human space witch? And most of all, how was this story going to help her become stronger? Besides, it still didn't explain any of the juxtapositions of balance and chaos and order. It was all a bit nonsensical as far as she was concerned.

She also sincerely doubted that there were in fact only one hundred and twelve space witches around. There had to be more for sure.

She sighed. Her stomach announced itself with a ferocity she hadn't expected, and she glanced hopefully at the door. Now... Trying to read another scripture, or maybe check if Sh't'ani could get some food for her? She was still more or less confined to her quarters. At least, she hadn't been shown how to open the door herself and she hadn't been able to make it happen, either.

Her complaining stomach convinced her to check in with Sh't'ani, and she crossed the room quickly to press the button meant to summon the Penyali nurse. P'cha'me had informed her that Sh't'ani was to be her keeper—her line of contact and guardian, available to bring her whatever she needed. In other words, they were meant to be what Tabea had been for Yuri back on the *Calliope* the first few days after he'd left the med bay.

She sighed and pressed the button that would alert Sh't'ani, though she felt awkward doing it. But she had to. She didn't know how frequently the Penyales needed nourishment, and how long it might take to prepare something for her. For all she knew, they only ate once a month.

Her stomach growled once again, so loudly, it almost covered up Sh't'ani's voice from behind the door.

"I am here!"

The door whooshed open, and they entered, looking concerned and a little frazzled. Tabea felt a smidge of guilt at having called them, but she knew it had to be done.

"Hey, could I have something to eat?" she asked, tilting her head ever-so-slightly. She chuckled with embarrassment. "I'm kinda hungry."

Sh't'ani's eyes widened, and their nostrils flared before they started to knock their head with their fists.

"Stupid, stupid! I knew I forgot something!" They rushed off, without another word, leaving Tabea behind with the door open.

Tabea, startled, hesitated for only a moment. She went through the door and looked around the blue hallway. Which way should she go?

Following instinct, she went left—the opposite way Sh't'ani had taken.

The hallway was winding upward ever so slightly, an incline and curve small enough to be barely noticeable.

Not for the first time, Tabea wondered how big this ship actually was. It had become clear to her early on that this ship was several times larger than the *Calliope* was. In fact, she wouldn't be surprised if the *Calliope* could fit into the landing bay.

She was reminded of old movies from Earth, movies of alien invasions, long before anyone had made contact with the other races in the universe. This ship could easily be the size of one of the motherships that had been depicted in those films. It was laughable, really. By now Tabea knew more than anyone that the term "mothership" made no sense. No race lived purely nomadically, and most fleets consisted of multiple even-sized ships, especially when it came to long-distance space travel.

Suddenly, she heard voices. She pressed herself into a niche in the wall, beside what appeared to be some sort of drinking fountain.

The two Penyales, deep in conversation, passed her quickly.

As they walked by, Tabea watched them closely and tried to catch snippets from their dialogue.

She thought they looked young, younger than C'ru and P'cha'me, at least. It was like their scales were smoother, less coarse, and they moved more like cadets sauntering through the halls, lacking the gravitas and authority officers possessed.

"…it's just so dull, y'know? Same thing every day."

"I hear you. Mentor K'lani recommended this mission to me because it was supposed to be different. She said it would be good experience—but look at this!"

"I know! It's the same as always. I could've gone on the Mercut'cha mission, y'know."

"Whoa, really? Sorry to hear you had to miss out."

"Me too. And I haven't even gotten to see the Gemini."

"Me, neither. And hey, did you know…"

Their voices became too faint to make out much more.

Tabea remained in her hiding spot just a moment longer to make sure they were really gone and listened out for more footsteps. When she didn't hear anything, she continued her journey to explore the ship. The farther she went, the more elaborate the blue hallways became. It was subtle at first. The lighting became more refracted, creating patterns on the walls and floor that reminded her a lot of those seen on an ocean floor when the sunlight was refracted by the waves. Once she had made the connection with the lighting, she also noticed the scent. Unmistakably salty with a slight hint of algae.

So far, she had only passed corridors and closed doors, which she had no way to open. Occasionally, Penyales passed her, and she tried to hide behind corners and between some of the items spread along the sides of the hallway.

After she'd walked for what felt like an eternity, still no step closer to having found anything useful, she considered going back but found the thought of it dreadful and regressive. Besides, she wasn't even sure if she'd find the right door again. Unfortunately, she hadn't thought of making a note of what the hallway looked like right outside her room, not that she'd be able to open the door to get inside.

The only option left was to continue and hope that she either found something interesting or that she ran into Sh't'ani, rather than someone else who might still be feeling resentful toward humans.

Determined to make the most of her temporary freedom aboard the ship, Tabea pressed on, keeping a lookout for whatever may be of use at some point while trying to create a mental map of the place.

Eventually, she came by a frequently used door. She lingered nearby in hiding for a while, watching the comings and goings of the Penyali cadets. As she waited, her heart was pounding in her throat and thoughts of what might happen to her if one of them should find her raced through her mind. After all, she didn't know if the cadets had been briefed that there was a human aboard. None of the ones she had spied on along her way to this point had spoken about her, unlike with Yuri's arrival on the *Calliope*, which led her to believe that she might be a well-kept secret at the current time. Nervous about her situation, Tabea pulled up her hood, hoping the shadow would obscure her face enough to not immediately stand out as a different species. She could only hope that her comparatively small stature and lack of tail wouldn't be enough to give her away.

Thus preparing herself, Tabea took a deep breath and stepped out of her hiding place. She forced herself to stay at a relaxed stance and then strode toward the permanently open doorway, keeping her head low.

Even so, she could hear snippets of confused conversation around her.

"Hey. What's a kid doing here?"

"A space witch? And such a young one!"

"Wow, they really start recruiting right after they leave the crib these days, huh?

"Don't you think there's something weird about that one?"

She didn't react to any of it, even when some of them tried to speak to her directly. She just kept walking, pushing past the string of Penyali crew members and into the hall they were leaving. It was vast, with a large circular podium in the center, which, upon closer inspection, seemed to be the setup for a holographic projection. Otherwise, there was no furniture in the room. An assembly hall, perhaps? There was a walkway with railings on a second level to allow for a better view of the currently inactive hologram, and on both levels, many doors led away from the hall. Four of them were open, including the one through which Tabea had just entered. Only one of them was on the upper level.

There were still a decent number of Penyales in the hall, but it was nevertheless emptying rapidly. After taking a quick overview of her situation, Tabea hurried to get up one of the three sets of stairs around the circular outline to get onto the balcony level and headed straight for the only door open on the upper level.

At this point, she wasn't even sure anymore what she was hoping to accomplish. But anything seemed better than to just be cooped up inside a tiny room without a way to find out anything about her own situation.

As she passed through the throng of Penyales heading out into a somewhat familiar green hallway, Tabea spared a brief thought for Sh't'ani. Hopefully, they wouldn't get in trouble for this. Also, how long would it take for them to raise an alarm because Tabea had gone missing? And what would happen then?

The realization that she had acted willfully and irrationally hit Tabea to the core of her stomach, and she felt sick. Why had she rushed out without thinking? She imagined Calliope's amused voice answering her.

"It's what you always do."

A heavy sigh escaped her lips before she could help herself. What she wouldn't give to truly hear Calliope's voice, to have her fill the emptiness in Tabea's mind, return her internal monologue to dialogue.

She'd gotten so used to it over the past two years, thinking just by herself was feeling... lonely.

Out in the green passageway, she headed the direction fewer of the Penyales were taking. She felt safer walking on her own. Soon enough, she had managed to shake off even the last of the other race.

She left the hood of her robe up, just to be safe. It had disguised her surprisingly well, even if it did make her appear like a child. It was one risk less to worry about.

She looked at her current surroundings; vines and lichen covered the walls so that almost none of the green paint was even visible. The scent of forest and earth seeped into her nose when she breathed in deeply, but it was eerily quiet.

Then her stomach growled, and a wave of weakness rushed over her. She'd forgotten over the adrenaline rushing through her body. She still needed food, and she supposed she also didn't have a lot of energy left right now.

While she was wrapped up in thoughts about her condition, she bumped into someone. Two claws clasped around her shoulders immediately and ice-cold shivers ran through her entire body. She'd been caught!

"So, humans are rebellious—that's interesting."

Tabea looked up at the familiar voice. C'ru was looking down at her curiously, observantly.

"Um," Tabea began, but she could think of no way to justify herself. "I had to go to the bathroom?"

"And that," C'ru countered, "would be a classic example of your human lies, yes?"

A hardness had entered his eyes and voice and Tabea bit the inside of her lip.

"I'm sorry," she said, not knowing where to go from

there. Undoubtedly, C'ru had found her by using his own abilities as a space witch after Sh't'ani had reported her missing.

A moment of silence ensued, and then C'ru sighed.

"Let's bring you back."

CHAPTER 16

SH'T'ANI WAS ALREADY THERE WHEN TABEA awoke again. Since the Penyali didn't have the same measurement of time, Tabea wasn't sure how long she'd been asleep, or if it was even a new day. Either way, Sh't'ani looked as though they hadn't slept a wink in two days. Their eyes were bloodshot and droopy, and their tail hung down listlessly.

Tabea felt instant guilt shoot through her body.

"Good morning, T'bea," Sh't'ani said, setting down a tray with what must have been breakfast.

Tabea thought for a moment to correct their pronunciation of her name but decided against it. It was probably easier for them this way and it wasn't too different from the norm. Besides, she still felt bad for having gotten them in trouble.

"Good morning," she said instead. "How are you feeling?"

Sh't'ani looked at her, their eyes widened in surprise at the question.

"What an odd question! I suppose I feel guilty for having let down my superiors—and wary. I don't understand you, so I can't predict how you will act.

Physically, however, I am well."

"I'm sorry for having gotten you in trouble. That wasn't my intention."

Sh't'ani's eyes narrowed warily. "High Priest C'ru warned me that humans are well versed in the art of deception. Is this one such tactic?"

Involuntarily, a smile appeared on Tabea's lips, and she chuckled. "No, I'm serious, I promise. I feel bad."

Sh't'ani watched her with contemplation. Then they tilted their head to one side. "Does your kind show their teeth when they lie? Or when they are upset?"

This caused Tabea to almost choke on laughter and she bent over, clutching her stomach, unable to stop herself. Sh't'ani fussed around her immediately.

"Are you all right? Are you hurt?"

"Yeah, I'm good." Tabea forced herself to stop, even though the laughter had brought a tear to her eye. She didn't know why it had affected her so much — it hadn't even been that funny. "The teeth thing is our way of showing we're happy. We call it a 'smile.' I think it's comparable to your tail swinging."

Sh't'ani stepped back, clearly relieved their charge wasn't going to be sick. Then they opened their mouth and showed rows upon rows of sharp, pointed teeth. "Like this?"

"Almost." Tabea grinned. Sh't'ani's tail was swinging from side to side again. Apparently, they were enjoying themself. Tabea was glad for it. Maybe this wasn't so bad, and they would both be able to learn from each other's cultures.

She pointed at the tray Sh't'ani had set down.

"Would you care to join me for breakfast?"

"I..." Sh't'ani hesitated, their claws fidgeting around

for a moment before they seemed to come to a conclusion. They nodded and took a seat, determined. "I suppose I could."

Tabea smiled again, glad she no longer needed to suppress the action for their benefit. Just being able to smile made her feel better about her situation.

As they shared the food, Tabea decided it was a good opportunity to ask Sh't'ani for some information.

"Are there any plans for me today?"

"Yes, you are to start your training with High Priest C'ru. I don't know the details, but apparently, it's going to be something big and important."

Tabea allowed herself to contemplate that for a moment. What had General P'cha'me told her? They needed her help to bring back a planet from nuclear and climate destruction. How exactly one could train for that, she still wasn't entirely sure. Well, she would find out soon enough.

"I see. And do you know where that training will take place?" she asked, hoping to perhaps learn a little more about the geography of the ship.

"I'll be bringing you to the Carnelian level. That's where the training room has been set up."

"The Carnelian level?" Sudden acknowledgement flooded through Tabea's mind. Hallways that were full of plants and almost resembled a jungle, hallways in blue with the smell of the ocean and lights that gave the same impression. "Ah, I get it. The different levels on this ship are all mimicking different planetary biomes, right?"

"Yes—they are meant to represent some of the planets in our territory. Right now we're on the Azure level, named after the water planet Azure. It's a wonderful place, with magnificent cities that thrive on the ocean floor. Most people from there develop webs between their fingers, like this."

As their tail swished happily from side to side, they held up their hand, the talons spread out, so Tabea could see the translucent webbing that stretched between them. She wondered if they could also breathe underwater. She knew that the Penyales were one of the few races that didn't need spacesuits—their scales kept them safe from pressure imbalances and the cold, and they could hold their breath for a long time. Perhaps Viridian, too, had originally been a water planet. She wondered if it would be rude to ask.

"So, is Azure where you're from then?" she asked instead.

Suddenly, Sh't'ani seemed embarrassed. They cast down their eyes and covered their hand quickly, shoving it into their lap.

"No, I have never been there. I'm from Vermillion, actually. But my paternal unit was from Azure. I've always wanted to visit."

Why was Sh't'ani acting so weirdly about not being from Azure? Was there something shameful about it that only someone knowing the culture would understand?

"Well, then, why don't you?" Tabea asked, tilting her head slightly in what she hoped was an encouraging fashion.

Sh't'ani pressed their eyes shut. "No, I couldn't! It wouldn't be right—I don't deserve to live, or even *visit* such beauty. I am already honored enough to visit Cerulean!"

"But why not? If it's something you want...?"

Something about the way Sh't'ani looked at her then made her falter. As a complete outsider, someone who had no idea about what the Penyales valued, she had no right to push them. But she couldn't help still feeling like they were being too hard on themself, like they considered themself below others, and it made her sad. Especially since Sh't'ani seemed like a nice person.

She stopped pressing the point. They finished their meal in silence and then got ready. Before long, Tabea was following Sh't'ani down several pathways and down into a red corridor. The walls were less defined and reminded her more of tunnels carved into a mountain. It was hotter here, and like on the Azure level, the lighting created patterns. Although here it reminded her of the fiery depths of a volcano.

What kind of planet is Vermillion?

They passed a few Penyales along the way, but Tabea had made sure to put up her hood, so they received no more than a few curious glances.

Soon they had reached their destination.

The room they entered was large—perhaps almost as big as the hall Tabea had stumbled into before. About a dozen Penyales in short, green garments were milling about, busy working at the many technological stations spread around the room. Tabea briefly wondered if those loose wires with a headset but no screen were their version of a computer.

Then her eyes fell on a large, spherical contraption in the center of the room. The outside walls were completely transparent, with a gap just large enough for one adult Penyali to enter. However, there was a ring, seemingly made from metal, stretching from the ground on the left to the top right of the sphere. Above a chair inside, Tabea saw hundreds of wires with connectors hanging, connected to the bubble all around.

At the back of the room, three Penyales in golden robes were speaking privately, but when they noticed Sh't'ani and Tabea, they turned and came their way.

"Tabea, I hope you slept well," C'ru said, watching her. "May I introduce to you two other space witches of the Penyali empire? This is O'kirat'li and this is To'a. They will be assisting with today's experiment."

"Experiment?" Tabea took a step back. All her instincts riled up at the word and screamed at her to run out right this instant.

C'ru tilted his head to one side. "Why, yes. We need to measure how much power you truly hold so we can construct a container in which to store it. This is all in preparation for returning Viridian to us, and it is just as vital as actual training."

Something in his words clicked with her.

"I'll need to use my powers," she said, a little ray of hope rising in her chest.

"Naturally, we will be removing the limiters as soon as the exercise begins to use your abilities to the fullest of your potential."

While Tabea still wasn't thrilled about being part of this experiment, she was starting to see the need for it — and not only for them.

Even if it was only for a moment, she would regain control of her powers. She could send parts of herself out and maybe find traces of Calliope. If she was anywhere near in space, she would sense her, and that would give her a lead. Perhaps she would even be able to direct General P'cha'me toward her.

New determination filled her.

"Let's do it."

C'ru inclined his head and gestured toward the orb with the chair. They walked over together.

"And this thing will measure the amount of energy I can hold, or something?" Tabea eyed the connectors critically as C'ru strapped her into the chair and attached all the little suckers to her temples and other body parts. Soon her entire body was covered in wires.

"More or less, yes. It will gauge how much energy you can control and absorb at any given time."

Her stomach was feeling a little unsettled. This seemed like a bad idea and she wondered if she could still jump ship. But based on her precarious situation on board, she probably didn't have the luxury of choice, at least not if she wanted General P'cha'me to keep her promise and continue to search for Calliope.

"Okay."

Tabea didn't resist when C'ru strapped her arms and legs to the chair. Nor did she react when he placed a talon on her forehead.

The spot he touched began to prickle, and very soon, energy, sent by him, flowed through her body, numbing her, though not in a painful way. When he retracted his claw, he put the last connector in the same spot and left the sphere. He nodded to some of the Penyales in green—scientists or engineers, Tabea guessed.

Then lights flashed in Tabea's vision as the ring started to move. First, it was sluggish, like watching a coin in slow motion at the end of its spin, but it gradually got faster and faster. Eventually, Tabea couldn't even see the ring anymore. All she could see was flashing and blurry motion.

Then excruciating pain exploded into her body. She felt like she were being simultaneously being supercharged and drained of all energy in the universe. It didn't feel like burning or freezing, but instead she felt like her whole body was being torn apart, cut, and shredded into tiny pieces that could float away in the wind.

Her body was being pulverized, taken apart, atom by atom, only to be reassembled under high tension.

She couldn't breathe, she couldn't make a sound. All her senses had left her, except for the sensation of unimaginable pain. Her eyes were wide open, but she could see nothing. Sounds held no more meaning than taste or smell. They were gone, irrelevant to her existence, if it even was existence at all. Perhaps this was the truth of what came after death: never-ceasing, inexplicable agony.

Tabea felt the connection to the universe, but the universe was screaming at her, beating her and shooting her — destroying every part of her that was Tabea, to leave behind only energy.

If she were the sun, this would be the supernova.

"Calliope!"

It was a plea for help, as well as a desperate attempt at establishing a connection, sourced from a desire deep within her, lacking any real thought or conscious effort.

Rage surged up inside of her body as instinct took over. This pain — the universe didn't inflict this on her. The machine did. And *machines* she could control.

She focused on her breathing first. Where before she had been hyperventilating, now she forced herself to slowly suck in air, hold it for a moment, and then let it out, taking her time. She concentrated on pushing the energy out of her body, to block the entry points so the pain would stop. Then, when the pain had been minimized, she let go of her body and entered the machine—became one with its currents and simple mind.

Except she could feel a pull that was trying to drag her back into her own body. Surprised at the sensation—a first for her—she allowed it to happen.

The moment she was one with her body again, C'ru was in front of her, a claw to her face. Almost instantly, her connections with the machine and the universe were completely severed. Left behind was only a feeling of emptiness, utter exhaustion, and a mind-numbing migraine.

C'ru took off the suckers, but when Tabea tried to get to her feet, her body refused to obey. All she succeeded in was falling forward, passing out before she hit the floor.

It was a deep sleep. There were no dreams, not really.

But there were voices.

Her own, calling for Calliope, and then a million others with whom she had to compete to be heard. She tried shouting louder, but she never managed to shout over them.

Then she saw the constellation of Gemini, as seen from Earth. Both twins looked at her, and then turned to sneer at her, but for what reason, she didn't know.

Finally, Calliope appeared, but she was swallowed

by the celestial twins before Tabea could even call out her name another time.

Then, a memory.

As they entered the atmosphere, Tabea stood beside Callaghan, nervously trying to ignore the ship's sudden rumbling. But she failed.

"Is this okay?" *she asked Calliope.* "You're not falling apart or anything, are you?"

Calliope only chuckled in response. "You'll get used to it."

How she was ever supposed to treat this like it was normal, Tabea didn't know. She watched as the Earth rapidly grew ahead of them, how more and more details became visible.

"You should get your things ready," *Callaghan said.* "And I'd like you to come by my office in the morning, okay? Rest up well tonight."

A little disappointed that she wasn't going to be watching the landing from the bridge, Tabea nodded and retreated, but not without one last glance at the screens Callaghan was observing.

So much had happened over this comparatively short Harvius VI mission. She'd only been gone two weeks, but it felt like she belonged on the Calliope, *ever traveling through space. It was profoundly saddening to know that the mission was over, and that she would have to leave the ship, returning to her studies at the Academy. As she mulled this over, she got completely lost in thought packing, and before she knew it, the rumbling had stopped.*

A knock on her door pulled her from her own head.

"Yeah?" *she called, pushing her bag closed.*

The door opened to let Vincent peek inside. He was a proper cadet on this mission, having just finished his final examinations at the Academy top of his class. Being a member of Hammond's team, he'd helped Tabea whenever she'd struggled with anything and made her feel right at home. Unlike the officers, he didn't know her secret, but his open and uncomplicated nature had immediately earned him her high regard.

"Ready?" he asked, smiling. "We're good to go."

Tabea grabbed her bag and flashed him a smile of her own. "Yup. All good."

But before she followed him out of the room, she hesitated.

"Are you going to be okay?"

"Of course I will. Don't worry." Calliope's assured response did little to ease Tabea's heart. Why was it that she felt like she was abandoning a friend? She may have talked a lot with the Calliope over the past weeks, but at the end of the day, she was only a ship. An inanimate object controlled by people. And yet, thinking about her that way felt wrong.

Still, she couldn't very well live on the Calliope while she was on Earth. Besides, she had duties and responsibilities. So, she nodded and followed Vincent out.

"I'll come visit soon," she promised as she left.

"I know you will."

Besma waited anxiously by the hangars as Tabea and Vincent came out.

She leapt at Tabea, throwing her arms around her neck.

"Oh my gosh, how was it? Tell me everything!"

Tabea laughed. "Can you let me arrive first? How about we talk about it over girls's night?"

Besma nodded vigorously. "It's set up and ready." Her

gaze flicked to Vincent. "And who is this?"

Quickly, Tabea made to introduce them, but he held Besma's interest for no longer than that one moment before she turned back to Tabea.

"Oh, guess what! Lou and Marianne – they got into serious trouble for you wouldn't believe what!"

Tabea gave Vincent a quick, apologetic smile before following Besma toward the Academy buildings. He only grinned and nodded in response before heading the other direction, toward the temporary accommodations granted to officers, juniors, and cadets just before, after, and between missions.

The entire way back to their dorms, Tabea barely even got a word in, and Besma was too busy rattling off various rumors and everything that had happened in the few days Tabea had been gone to notice her friend was barely listening. Tabea's thoughts were mostly with the Calliope, *wondering how she felt being left alone in the hangars. Could the other ships talk? Could they communicate with each other the same way Tabea communicated with Calliope? She hadn't really thought to ask before.*

Lost in thought, Tabea ran into someone, and, stumbling back, she recognized Nerissa, the girl at the top of their year in everything except piloting, which was Tabea's field of expertise. Her eyes narrowed when she saw Tabea.

"Oh," she said. "It's you."

Her voice was cold, as per usual. They hadn't exactly met many times, but there'd been an instant dislike between the two girls, which Tabea put down to the fact that she was the reason Nerissa couldn't get the perfect academic record of being top of the class at everything. Luckily, that didn't matter since they weren't following the same track. So even though they didn't like each other, they still remained civil and polite but distant with each other.

"How was the mission?" she asked, watching Tabea closely, a slight frown on her face. "I sincerely hope you didn't cause Captain Callaghan and Officer Hammond any trouble."

From what Tabea knew, Nerissa was also aiming to become part of Callaghan's crew one day, working under Hammond. Then again, who wasn't? Working on the Calliope was one of the biggest honors any cadet and junior in the Space Core could have.

Tabea briefly thought back over her adventure – aside from briefly taking control of the Calliope to ward off the Penyali attack, she'd been a picture-perfect cadet.

"It was good," Tabea said, careful about what she said. "I learned a lot."

Nerissa's eyes narrowed further as she contemplated Tabea. "Good for you," she said, though it sounded like she'd meant the opposite.

Tabea watched after her as she walked away, a little stunned. "Is it just me, or was she even colder than usual?"

Besma shrugged. "I think she's just bummed that she wasn't the first from our year who got to go on a mission. She does have the highest grades, after all. Can't really blame her, either. All of us are a little jealous, you know." She gave her a sidelong glance. "And you better believe you're going to tell me everything in excruciating detail."

Tabea knocked on Callaghan's door, feeling guilty. In the end, she'd made the snap decision not to tell Besma about her new abilities. She hadn't gotten the chance before the Harvius VI mission, and now, after everything that had happened, somehow she wanted to clear it with Callaghan and the Calliope first, as though it were their secret just as *much as it was hers.*

"Come in," he said, and Tabea slowly pushed the door open, peeking her head through the crack.

"Is now a good time?"

He only gave her a large, beaming smile, and waved her in. "There are a few things I need to discuss with you," he said. "But first things first. Would you like to join us on the Calliope on our mission next month?"

Tabea's breath caught in her throat. He'd asked her before if she wanted to stay on and become a full member of the crew, but she hadn't expected to join another mission until she'd graduated as a cadet, at minimum.

"It would be another short mission — this one is meant to last three weeks, though. And you would need to continue your lessons with officers on board so you don't fall behind."

He raised his eyebrow questioningly, but she only stared at him.

"Tabea?"

"Oh." She caught herself and stood to attention, saluting. "Yes, sir! I would be honored to be a part of your crew again, sir!"

She broke into a grin as he made a face.

"Please stop that. You know I hate it when you talk to me like that."

Tabea only chuckled.

"There's another thing," he continued. "I'm sure it goes without saying, but you can't tell anyone about your... situation. It doesn't matter how trustworthy they are, the more people know, the higher the chance of the wrong people finding out. Because of that" — he took a deep breath — "I would like you to switch from the piloting track to the engineering track."

Tabea's good mood froze. She loved flying. She loved the freedom that came with it. As a pilot, she'd be able to fly in space, in the atmosphere, and on any of the other colonies. As an engineer... she wouldn't.

"Why?" She couldn't bring out more than that one word. It didn't make any sense. People didn't just switch tracks. Not when they were as good at something as she was. She was the Academy's star pilot pupil! Why would she ever want to give that up?

Callaghan sighed, watching her apologetically. "I've talked about this with Hammond and Akari, and they both agree. It would be safer for you. If someone saw you do something strange with technology, being an engineer could cover it up, but as a pilot... There would be questions."

He paused to give her a moment to take it in.

"I don't expect you to give it up altogether. There are sidetracks you can do once you have your cadetship. The only difference would be that for the rest of your studies at the Academy, the focus would shift. You'd be spending more time learning about technology and less time flying, but according to Akari, you don't need any more flying lessons to ace your exams."

Tabea's heart was breaking. She understood the need for safety, but at the same time, she couldn't help feeling like a part of her was being stolen away. She'd always found solace in flying. In fact, right now, all she wanted to do was take one of the planes and soar over the mountains, ignore the world for a little while and just focus on the air.

Flying was what had gotten her here.

In more ways than one.

"What about my scholarship?" Her voice almost cracked. She'd been accepted as a pilot, not an engineer. Her family would never pay for the rest of her tuition; they'd made that clear with their silence. She'd sent off a message to them about the Harvius VI mission before she'd left and another one the moment she'd come back, but she still hadn't received *any response. Nothing.*

"Don't worry about that," he said earnestly. "If it should be taken away, then I will pay for you instead. Even without these powers, you're far too valuable to lose."

He smiled gently, and it warmed Tabea to know that he thought of her so highly.

She didn't have much of a choice, though, did she? He was right. It was safer. And it would allow her to train this new ability better, to get a better grasp of it, understand how it worked and how much she could do.

She nodded. "Okay."

CHAPTER 17

BANG. BANG. BANG.

A familiar blue room awaited Tabea along with a pounding drum in her head when she awoke. Sh't'ani was also there, seemingly asleep in a chair in a corner of the room. Their eyes were closed, and their head slanted. For the first time, Tabea saw them in a slouch, their body completely relaxed. It created a stark contrast to their normal, rigid posture.

Bang. Bang. Bang.

Tabea's head was tilted to the side, but she couldn't move it of her own accord, no matter how hard she tried. The same was true for the rest of her limbs. Like the first time she had awoken in this room, she had no control over her muscles, but they all ached like she had run fifteen marathons in a row without prior training.

Bang. Bang. Bang.

At least this time, she knew why. The electrical currents she'd been subjected to had gone through her muscles first, spasming them so they'd been in constant action. She had no idea how long she'd been in the activated sphere, so maybe the marathon comparison wasn't all that far off.

But that left her to wonder—had they put her into that device before, without her knowledge or consent?

Bang. Bang. Bang.

She'd barely formed that thought when drowsiness and darkness claimed her again.

Regaining motion in her limbs was easier and faster this time—almost as if her body remembered how to heal better than it had before. The next time Tabea awoke, she could already move her head and her limbs again, though she was still too weak and in too much pain to sit or even prop herself up. At least the throbbing headache had faded.

Sh't'ani was still beside her, awake this time, and ready to jump into action with a drink, gently lifting the cup's straw to Tabea's lips. "Drink. It will give you strength."

Tabea didn't need to be asked twice. She yearned for that sustenance and refreshment. Like before, her mouth was as parched as Earth's equator.

The liquid had a fruiter taste to it than before—perhaps a vitamin supplement, or an alien fruit juice, Tabea wasn't sure. Either way, it was delicious, even though every gulp she took hurt deep in her throat.

"Thank you."

Sh't'ani smiled—the human way—and Tabea snorted.

"You don't have to force yourself to mimic me," she said.

"I want to," Sh't'ani asserted. "You don't have a tail,

so you can't do what we do, but I think it will help us understand each other better if we try to be the same."

Tabea shook her head, trying to think of a way to make Sh't'ani understand.

"Look, it's not that we need to be the same. We're so different. Why change that? We can have understanding without being the same. Don't you think it would be more enriching if we celebrate and acknowledge our differences instead of erasing them?"

Sh't'ani only tilted their head to one side.

"Like, I know that you're showing that you're happy when you swing your tail and you know that I'm happy when I smile. As long as we both know that, what's wrong with both of us just continuing to emote the way that feels natural to us?"

Sh't'ani contemplated this for a moment. "I suppose you might be right," they relented.

"Good," Tabea said, and she smiled, noticing Sh't'ani's swinging tail.

A cough forced its way up her throat, spluttering, her throat burning like glowing embers.

"How are you feeling?" they asked, their eyes full of concern for her.

Tabea made a face. "Terrible."

"Wait, take this. It should ease the pain and let you sleep."

Sh't'ani held up a little white pill in their claw, and Tabea allowed them to place it on her tongue before they helped her wash it down with the juice, though swallowing remained painful.

It took effect quickly.

Her eyes grew heavy and her mind sluggish. Before long, she was gone once more.

A spark floating in emptiness was all that Tabea could make out. The void was limitless, and time and space held no meaning. She'd been there forever, just waiting, watching, expecting. There'd been no light. No darkness, either. Nothing.

But then, this spark appeared. It didn't grow, it didn't arrive, it just... began to exist. Though small and lacking a distinct shape, it radiated warmth. Not physically, but one that reached into Tabea's innermost being.

The feeling it emanated was as familiar to Tabea as if it were her own body.

"*Calliope*," she whispered into the void, reaching out to grasp the spark.

"*I'm here*," Calliope responded, and hearing her familiar voice almost broke Tabea. Even though she had no body, she choked up, and her shoulders began to tremble. Any vision she'd had was blurred by tears rushing to her eyes. "*I'm so glad you're alive*," Calliope continued. "*Callaghan is —*"

Whatever connection they'd had was suddenly cut off as Tabea was yanked from her sleep.

No. No!

What was going on with Callaghan? What had happened?

She needed to speak with Calliope, to find out!

Unwittingly, she started to reach out, trying to connect with her friend, no matter how far away she might be, but her attempt was cut short immediately by another blast of pain that almost knocked her out again.

"T'bea!" Sh't'ani shrieked upon seeing Tabea's eyes roll back in her head. "What's wrong?"

The pain subsided quickly, just like before, and Tabea took a few deep breaths to ease the process.

"I'm okay," she said. "I promise. What did you need?"

"I'm sorry to wake you." Sh't'ani winced. "But High Priest C'ru wanted to know how you are. He wants to know if you're ready for some training."

Still recovering from the shock to her system, Tabea first thought of of the sphere, and fear washed over her. There was no way she would enter that torture device voluntarily another time. Absolutely not.

Then again, it would mean taking off the limiter to her powers, which would allow her to try reaching out again, just to see if maybe she could connect with Calliope and find out what had happened to her captain.

"What kind of training?" she asked, covering up her emotions to the best of her abilities.

"I don't know. He said he wants to come talk to you in a little while to see for himself if you're ready to continue yet. I figured you should probably eat something first."

They shoved a tray with some form of stew toward her. Tabea propped herself up and managed to sit. Her muscles were still aching, but she was clearly regaining her strength faster this time.

As much as she didn't like the idea of having to return to whatever C'ru apparently considered "training," she was glad that he planned on coming to see her first. At least she'd have a chance to prepare herself and find out what exactly he was planning for her. In the worst-case scenario, she could always play up the pain and exhaustion she was feeling. There was enough of it, after all.

She cocked her head to one side and smiled at Sh't'ani. "Eat with me?"

This time, they obliged quickly. Tabea was glad that one by one, they were demolishing the barrier between them set up by their difference in race. She found herself genuinely liking her minder. Sh't'ani had a good heart. They reminded her a little of Calliope, when they had first met.

The thought of her friend brought a pang to Tabea's chest, and she remembered her dream. It had just been a dream, after all. She couldn't connect with Calliope, so it couldn't possibly have been real. More than likely, it had only been her subconscious giving a voice to her fears and desires. Yearning grew, and Tabea was quick to swallow the tears that were starting to force their way up. How long until she would be united with her friend again? Until she was truly allowed to search for her and feel her presence? She'd tried, in the sphere, but had been cut off before accomplishing anything. And now, who could say if C'ru would really give her another chance?

She guiltily reminded herself that she *had* tried to disassemble the machine that was so important to the Penyales, but, she justified herself, that was only because it had been causing her agony.

It all boiled down to her situation being frustrating.

She listlessly chewed on a crust of what appeared to be bread, or something like it, anyway. The flavor was barely even making it into her consciousness.

She set it down, even the last remnant of appetite

gone.

Sh't'ani met her gaze instantly.

"Let's go." She sighed.

This time, Sh't'ani led her back up to the green level, and Tabea could barely contain a breath of relief when she glimpsed the emerald hallway. She followed them obediently to what she assumed to be C'ru's quarters. Sh't'ani opened the door, gave a bow, and left, but not before giving Tabea a shark-toothed smile.

Tabea entered the room, where C'ru sat on a stool, watching a holo-screen intently. One of the other space witches was also present, though Tabea had no recollection of their name. They closed the door after she came in and gestured to a stool opposite from C'ru.

After a split second of hesitation, during which she wondered if there was more torture in store for her today, she jutted her chin forward and strode decisively to take the seat.

C'ru took several more moments of swiping things across his screen — graphs and images that made no real sense to Tabea — before he glanced up at her.

"I trust you've been indulging in the reading material I provided for you?"

Tabea grimaced. "I haven't exactly been in a suitable state for reading," she said, glaring at him accusingly. "But I did read one of them."

C'ru sighed, deeply, as though he were disappointed in her abilities. "I suppose I should have seen that coming. I thought you would be able to withstand the energy better, but I suppose I overestimated your potential."

His degrading tone infuriated her, giving birth to a red-hot ball of fire and spikes that rose from her stomach, but she wouldn't let herself show it. Only her fists clenched, so much that her fingernails dug painfully into her skin. She needed the sensation to keep her wits about her.

"Which scroll did you study?"

She forced herself to keep her tone and gaze cool and calm. "It was about how space witches came into being."

"Ah, yes, that is a good one to teach you about what we stand for."

"Yeah, about that. It didn't exactly make a lot of sense. And, only one hundred and twelve of us in the universe? That doesn't seem right."

C'ru shut off his holoscreen and set it aside to lean across the table, closer to Tabea. "It's not," he admitted. "There are many more. But the number is only symbolic. It will all make sense in time."

He paused, as though he expected Tabea to reply, except that she couldn't think of anything to say. Instead, they only stared at one another until the other space witch in the room knocked on the wall with their tail. Finally, C'ru broke eye contact.

"So," Tabea said, "what are we doing today?"

"Today, we are going to train."

Tabea gulped. She was moments away from asking if that meant returning to the machine before she caught herself. She'd be damned if she was going to show weakness in front of C'ru, especially after the way he'd behaved toward her.

She pushed her shoulders back, bracing herself for whatever was to come. "Let's begin, then."

C'ru watched her pensively for a moment before bringing up his holoscreen again, tapping and swiping faster than Tabea could follow. "You're in no shape to move about very much. We'll stay here for this exercise," he eventually said, blinking at the other space witch with all four eyes.

They sat down, cross-legged, and brought their fists together before closing their eyes. Tabea was still frowning and wondering what they were doing when C'ru placed one talon on her forehead, like before.

The connections she had with the world around her returned to her senses, the ones made from energy, except not all of them. She could only sense the contents of the room and a fraction of the ship. When she inspected the barrier with her mind, she discovered that it emanated from the space witch on the floor. She could feel their energy as clearly as if it were painted in the air. There were insets in the walls, floor, and ceiling of the room that amplified the bubble they had created. But even still, it seemed weak to Tabea, almost flimsy. Perhaps like a durable silk—strong enough to withstand a lot of pressure and tension, but not nearly robust enough to withstand her if she chose to tear through it with everything she had.

It was a satisfactory piece of knowledge.

But she needed to play nice. Besides, she got the impression that perhaps it might be wiser not to let on that this was no prison for her. For all she knew, she might need them to underestimate her in the future.

She felt a foreign energy approach her, first testing the currents that ran along the outside of her body, gingerly, as though it expected her to lash out. Then, it merged some of its tendrils with hers, and flowed into her. She allowed it to happen.

"Can you hear me?"

Even though there was no physical voice, Tabea recognized it with ease.

"*I didn't know space witches could communicate with each other this way,*" she said, tilting her head slightly.

C'ru was watching her closely. "*There is much you don't know. But I am pleased that you possess this ability. It will make my tasks easier.*"

He placed an item on the table. It looked foreign to Tabea, and looking at it from the outside, she couldn't even fathom what it was meant to be or do, but she could feel energy radiating from it.

"*What is it?*" she asked, and C'ru's tail flicked with amusement.

"*That is what I want you to tell me.*"

Her eyes flicked up at him, warily.

"*It is of Penyali origin,*" he said. "*We use it on our planets. I want you to use your* sight *to inspect it and figure out what it does, without taking it apart.*"

Tabea frowned at him and reflected on how she had been training her powers so far. Calliope had made her create things mostly. Work on her stamina. Create and repurpose. But she'd never needed to figure out what something did before. Then again, there weren't that many alien technologies aboard, with the exception of Calliope herself.

She let her gaze fall onto the object in front of her. The shape reminded her of what people used to believe alien spaceships had looked like — like a flying saucer — except that the bottom and top were flat, not rounded. She couldn't make out any buttons on the device, and she didn't detect any sensors, either. Its coating was of a dark gray color, with a metallic sheen. Platinum or steel, perhaps?

He'd said to use her sight. What an interesting term to use.

She closed her eyes and concentrated on the object in front of her, reaching out for it with her energy, gently engulfing it, and finding the right frequency of resonance. It was easy to merge with it, even though it didn't have a consciousness like Calliope.

It only took her an instant to find out everything there was to know about the small device, and exactly how it was powered.

She opened her eyes and a smirk had stolen its way onto her face as she triumphantly looked back at C'ru. He was still watching her closely.

"That was fast," he said. *"Are you sure you comprehend it fully?"*

"I'm sure."

He leaned back, his condescending eyes never leaving Tabea's. *"Then tell me."*

Tabea decided that since they were already using such a convenient method of communication, she might as well take full advantage of it, especially since she would find it troublesome to find the right terms for some of the components and interactions of the energy.

Instead of replying with words, she gave C'ru images and abstract concepts, explaining that way how the device could absorb memories from a person and replay them whenever they wished. There was a special function to allow it to record dreams, which could be replayed as a hologram. But both memories and dreams could also be redirected to a person's mind while they were sleeping, which would then turn them into another dream. It tapped into the electricity that powered a person's body, intercepting and recording impulses before sending them on.

"*With slight adjustments, it could even put new memories and ideas into a person's mind,*" she added verbally, not wanting to explain how exactly those adjustments could be made if C'ru didn't already know.

She was impressed with the device — Earth certainly had nothing like it. Then again, that may have also been for the best. Humans would definitely find a way to abuse it, much in the same way Tabea had discovered it could be altered.

C'ru blinked twice, surprised.

"*What is it called?*" Tabea asked.

"*It's a Gram. It's how the youth record their lives when they still believe they are important, before they find the universe.*"

Tabea had to suppress a chuckle that was pressing against the back of her throat. It was a diary. An alien diary. But it had the potential to be so much more...! She thought of people who had lost a loved one — how much joy it would give them to be able to relive a treasured memory, awake or asleep. She thought of criminal cases that could be resolved so much easier. Of course, memory was always subjective, even a device like this couldn't change that, but it would weed out the lies at least, no matter how convincing they were.

But no. Instead, it was used to record teenage angst and fantasies.

No matter how different some races appeared, in the end, teenagers were all the same.

She sighed, exhaustion catching up with her. Not being fully healed yet, she had less energy and stamina than she usually did. Even though the exercise had been a simple one, it had drained her quickly. Her eyes were burning, and she could tell that her body was beginning to sway back and forth.

C'ru was still watching her carefully.

"Let's stop there for today. Rest, and we will continue tomorrow," he said out loud.

Sh't'ani, who had been waiting in front of the room, brought Tabea back to her own quarters. Tabea wasn't able to even stay awake long enough to notice them leave again.

Listlessly, Tabea pushed around the food on her plate as she haphazardly listened to her family's conversation around her.

"Daryl said that, really?" Her mother gave a high-pitched laugh.

"Yes, isn't it droll?" Ella giggled.

Tabea didn't think it was all that funny. Daryl, Ella's husband, had suggested that with Tabea getting a scholarship to attend the Academy, she might be acting in diplomatic functions someday. And, if she became a captain, or even an officer, that might very well happen. It was one of the things they studied for at the Academy as well, not that her family would know that.

"I couldn't imagine our Bea having any interest in dealing with intergalactic issues, isn't that right?" Even though Ella's question was directed at Tabea, she didn't wait for a reply. Turning to Dorian, she said, "By the way, Dory, have you been practicing your languages?"

Dorian, the youngest of the siblings nodded, grinning proudly. "You bet. I'm gonna make tons of connections at the

Intergals."

He was referring to the intergalactic sports championships. An event he hadn't even qualified for yet.

Meanwhile, Tabea took actual lessons on alien languages and cultures at the Academy and was almost certain to encounter other races in the future. Not that it mattered.

"There's a good boy." Their mother sighed, smiling. "Helping each other out so well…"

Her eyes fell on Tabea and hardened a little. "You could take a page from his book," she said pointedly, nodding toward Dorian.

That was enough.

"Hey, Dorian," Tabea said, snapping her head to her brother. "Don'kal bet'chuna te hem?"

She'd asked if she could borrow his book in the common dialect of the Kinjo-Unk, but he only stared at her blankly. After a moment, a cocky grin formed on his face.

"Gesundheit."

Tabea didn't even bother to check if Ella had understood. She'd never bothered to learn any other languages herself, after all. She had interpreters for that.

"Does anyone want to know how my first term at the Academy was?" she asked instead, already knowing what the answer would be.

Her mother gave her a strained smile. "Sure, honey. But can you clear the table first?"

Before Tabea even had a chance to move, her father came in the door.

"Quick, he's coming!"

Everyone stormed out, leaving Tabea behind on her own. While she guessed that "he" was her brother Nick, she didn't know why it was such a big deal. He lived only two streets over, after all. She followed her family, finding them surrounding her elder brother, as he beamed back at them.

"I got it," he said. "I've signed the lease."

He looked so proud, as did everyone else. It was good for him, but it wasn't that big a deal. He'd gotten a license to open up his own lab — that had been the hard part. But that was already last year's news. This was just him signing the lease of a space. It was nice, certainly, but it wasn't nice enough to warrant this parade.

"When do you get the new equipment?" their mother asked, hanging on his every word.

"Monday. And Wednesday I can give you all a tour. Well..." His eyes fell on Tabea. "Except Bea. I didn't know you were going to be here this week, so I don't have clearance for you."

Of course he hadn't known. It wasn't like she'd sent them all messages telling them weeks ago. Oh, wait.

She should have realized coming back was a bad idea. What had she hoped for? That people would listen to her for once? That anyone was interested in what she wanted and thought? What a joke.

She left her family to celebrate her brother's "achievement" and went back to clearing the table in the dining room.

Two weeks later, she was back, standing in front of the Academy's doors. Throughout the holiday, not once had any member of her family asked any questions about her time at the Academy or made any comment about her scholarship. Really, conversations had been minimal either way.

She'd almost forgotten what it was like. Almost.

"Morning, trooper," Callaghan suddenly said from behind her. She turned her head to face him, surprised he'd been able to sneak up on her.

"Morning," she said.

They began walking toward the building together.

"How was your break?" he asked. "Did you have a nice time? You went to visit your family, right?"

Tabea nodded, surprised that he remembered what she had done during her time away. After all, he'd been on a space traveling mission — her life was hardly a comparison for that.

"It was fine," she said quietly, not looking at him. Silence followed her words for a few moments.

Then he said, "Do you have a little time now? Why don't we go to the hangars and take a quick flight? I bet you've missed being in the air."

She looked up at him, surprised, and he winked at her.

Only a few minutes later, they were getting a plane ready, her as the pilot, he as her co-pilot, there for safety.

Without prompting, Tabea started up the plane and rolled across the runway. First slowly, then faster and faster, before she could pull up the nuzzle. She lost her anger and her sadness as she left the ground, and around her, there was only air. Soaring above the clouds, she began to feel free again, her worries dropping away as if nothing that happened mattered.

"All right," Callaghan's voice reached her ears through the comms. "Let's make this a little more exciting. You know the drill."

And she did.

Beginning with a barrel roll toward the sea, she swerved into a swooping dive above the water but pulled up again just before touching the waves. Then she corkscrewed her way back up into the clouds in tight spirals all the way until they broke out into the endless blue.

"Now that's more like it."

Sensing that he wasn't talking about her flying, Tabea glanced at him, puzzled. He was smiling at her.

"That confident smirk of yours suits you much better," he said, and only now did Tabea realize that she was indeed smiling, grinning with joy at what she could do, knowing she was good at it. Really good. "It's more like you."

He gestured toward the sky ahead of them with a flick of his index finger.

"And at this rate, you'll be an officer of the Space Core in no time. If you keep this up, I might have to fight with some of the other captains to get you on my crew."

Even though she knew he was joking, the praise filled her with warmth. Before she brought the plane back down to the ground, any trace of discontent and unhappiness her visit at her family's had created had been whisked away by the wind and Callaghan's words.

Chapter 18

"*I HAVE ANOTHER TASK FOR YOU*," C'RU SAID when Tabea was back in his office for another training session during what she assumed to be the next day. "*I want you to leave your body.*"

A simple task—something Tabea had done millions of times with Calliope. Now that she was feeling more rested, the pain more subdued every time she awoke from her memory-plagued slumbers, it should be a breeze.

She reached out to the fraction of the ship available to her and—

"*Stop!*" C'ru got in her way. "*Not like this. I want you to leave your body without going somewhere else. Watch.*"

Tabea made sure to keep her senses fully trained on C'ru, reaching out with tendrils of her power to merge with his energy just enough to detect his every movement.

Her skin heated up as she sensed the shift in his energy. His essence left his body, heading toward the ship, but, at the last instant, it veered away and moved to the center of the room to remain there, though not quite motionless. He fizzled, spinning and twisting in ways that kept the energy going. Her eyes still closed, Tabea reached out for him with her hand, but she stopped just short of him. The air was charged and the hairs all along her body were standing upright, sending shivers down her spine. Suddenly, the air was difficult to breathe. She flinched back, and the sensation disappeared.

She'd done something like this before when she'd reached out her tendrils into outer space, approaching Yuri's ship, for example, but back then, a part of her had always been connected to her body still. And it had been outer space, not a pressurized, controlled environment. How much would that impact?

She had to try. If C'ru could do it, she could too. They were both space witches, after all.

She concentrated as much as she could, visualizing herself, her essence, as a ball of orange energy in her core. When she felt that she had accumulated all of herself, she soared up, through the top of her head, instead of her feet or hands like she would have normally done.

At first, it didn't work. She reached her head but could get no farther. It was like there was nowhere to go. But there had to be a way.

Tabea reminded herself of what she'd felt C'ru do. All she had to do was mimic his actions. A different approach was needed.

Instead of trying to force herself into the air, she directed her attention and will *past* the empty space, toward the ceiling. Gathering herself, she launched the second attempt. This time, she was more successful. She headed straight for the ceiling, veering away in the last moment just as she had felt C'ru do, and then...

Forces kept pulling her back.

It was more difficult to push through air than space. She felt like she was an insect, trying to burrow its way through jelly, pushing, only to be pushed back. Tendrils escaped, reached up, trying to pull the rest of her back into her body or into the ship, but it wasn't like she could hold on to something—it wasn't a physical thing. She tried, and fought, and forced herself to keep going, but even though she managed to inch forward a little, she never made it fully out of her body. The connection was too strong, and this environment too unwelcoming. Why that was the case, she had no idea.

"Enough."

C'ru's voice finally made it through to her, and she stopped pushing, allowing herself to be gently nudged back into her normal state. She regained full feeling of her body, her limbs trembling and weak, her hair wet from sweat. Her eyes were burning, and she could barely keep them open.

His tail twitched and he seemed oddly satisfied. "It seems we have found something you need to work on."

"What is your world like?" Sh't'ani asked as they sat down for another meal together. It seemed to have become a tradition to share dinner together, and Tabea was quite pleased about it. She preferred the company of the Penyali nurse to being on her own, enduring her thoughts alone without Calliope's comments.

"I heard it is a water planet, like Cerulean, is that true?" Their eyes sparkled as they watched Tabea.

"Well, I haven't seen Cerulean yet, so I wouldn't really know…" Tabea scratched her nose, thinking about how to respond to Sh't'ani's question. She reflected on the blue pearl she called home. "I guess it is mostly water. More so now than it was a thousand years ago, anyway. And life on our planet all came from the ocean, so…" She trailed off, hoping to have answered Sh't'ani's question because thinking of Earth, she suddenly felt awkward and somewhat homesick. The question of whether she'd ever get to see her home again became a prevalent ache in the forefront of her mind.

Sh't'ani's gaze dropped to Tabea's hand and a crease in the shape of a cross appeared between their four eyes. Tabea suspected it was their version of a frown.

"But you don't have webs between your digits."

Feeling embarrassed, Tabea laughed and rubbed her hands together, almost as if trying to hide their weblessness.

"Well, we left the water a long time ago. We're not able to live underwater anymore, you know?"

"I see." They looked disappointed — their tail drooped to the floor and curled around their chair, as the crease in their face disappeared. But just as quickly, the tail jumped up again, the tip swaying back and forth. "But you have underwater cities, don't you?"

Tabea grimaced as she thought about the ruins of the lost cities and the few coastal cities that had been partially inserted into the water.

"We do now," she said. "But we didn't use to. Relatively recently, our planet changed, which meant that there was a sudden increase of water and it took some of the cities by the seaside and swallowed them up. After that, we built a few buildings that could be sustained underwater. But it's uncommon still."

She thought of the lost cities—names that carried a strangely hollow nostalgia; names that sounded great in history but meant nothing to her. New York, Tokyo, Brussels, Rio de Janeiro. They all had ceased to exist long ago, swallowed up by the ocean that was taking back the planet from Humanity.

"Would you tell me about your planet some more?" Sh't'ani asked, their head slightly tilted as they pleaded.

Tabea began by describing the fields and forests around where she'd grown up—their luscious green and beautiful mix of colors every year—and went on to talk about the mountains, and then to the oceans, and finally, she spoke about the cities and the colonies.

Here, Sh't'ani cut in for the first time, having quietly and happily listened up to that point.

"How are your people segregated?" they asked. "Which kind is better?"

"Better?" Tabea looked up at them, shocked. "What are you talking about?"

"Well, which kind of your people have more worth?" Sh't'ani pressed.

"More worth?" Tabea echoed, incredulous. Then, she said firmly, "No one. No one has more or less worth. Inequality exists, but not because anyone is 'better.' Whenever there is inequality, it's because someone is selfish."

Anger rose in her stomach, not directed at Sh't'ani, but at the system that had clearly made them think that there was such a thing as a difference in the worth of a life. As far as the Penyales went, Sh't'ani clearly thought of themself as worth less than someone who had been born to a water planet. Their own webbing probably made them almost royalty on their home planet, though. Tabea's insides broiled around, with magma and cacti, burning her veins and pricking every part of her.

This was not okay.

Sh't'ani watched her for a moment, only to sigh wistfully.

"Your home sounds so nice," they said quietly. "So different."

Tabea was left alone for the better part of what she suspected to be several days. Sh't'ani couldn't spend much time with her, aside from bringing her food, due to having other, undefined "responsibilities."

Tabea used that time to read through more of the holoscrolls. Only once she was called back to C'ru's quarters to practice the out-of-body exercise. After she had rested and the pain had almost completely gone, she managed, though it didn't come as easily to her as most other space witch things.

She missed spending time with Sh't'ani, if only to learn more about the Penyales. But, as that was not possible, Tabea, left to her own devices, was only able to spend her time with study.

It wasn't that the scrolls weren't interesting—full of history, legends and theoretical principles, as well as teachings for the space witch talents—but Tabea could only take in so much information in one go. Besides, it wasn't like she could try out the techniques described in the scrolls with her powers being blocked. Incidentally, that was one skill she was particularly interested in learning about. If only to find out how to unblock herself.

There were plenty of other abilities that seemed impossible—like moving whole planets from their gravitational pull or sensing the electrical impulses of every being in the universe, manipulating water by using electrons. There were also certain things that she had before considered amongst the undoable that had been proven to be possible, such as telepathic communication by reading and interpreting the electric impulses of another being's nervous system.

She also learned more about the legend she'd read before, in particular about the notion of one hundred and twelve space witches overall. One scroll suggested that, while there were thousands, perhaps even millions, of space witches in the universe, there were only one hundred and twelve who were truly beloved and chosen by Space itself, and henceforth much more powerful than the rest and the only *true* space witches.

Another scroll taught her that different species had different affinities for these powers, and that purely by species, one could be more powerful than another, and that some species, such as Humanity, simply didn't have any affinity for it and could therefore never produce a space witch in their current stage of evolution. Well, she sure had proven that one wrong.

But enough was enough. Tabea paced up and down in her room, contemplating her situation and what she could do with it. There wasn't much. She didn't have access to her powers, Sh't'ani was busy, and the door was shut.

Finally, she sighed and flopped back onto her bed. If she couldn't use her powers, or even tinker with anything, she might try to do something that approximated the feeling.

She slid onto the floor and crossed her legs, keeping her back straight and regulating her breathing. As her lungs expanded and contracted slowly, Tabea imagined energy flowing through her and directed it to accumulate in her chakras, though she was careful not to use her powers to make that happen for real. Even without it, she felt the spots on her body pulsating, her skin prickling.

Then, out of nowhere, images flashed into her mind.

Yuri, standing with her on Calliope's bridge.

That was only just the beginning.

The glint in his eye—admiration mixed with something else—relief, perhaps? Greed? She couldn't tell.

The image gave way to the faces of Callaghan, Shinay, Felicitas, Vincent, Besma, Marco, Hammond, and, finally, Nerissa.

They're all here.

Calliope.

More faces of the crew flashed through Tabea's mind.

Everyone is here.

Calliope's familiar energy was just out of reach, so comforting and yet almost torturous.

We're not giving up on you.

A jolt of agony was sent through her whole body, centering on her head. Like a migraine, it immobilized her, and before she even realized what was happening, she was curled up on the floor, clutching her head with her hands, while tears flowed incessantly across her face, and she gasped for air.

Her imagination had always been too vivid for her own good.

She missed her friends so much, Calliope in particular, that she'd imagined talking to her while she'd been meditating, and as a result, she'd tried to reach out subconsciously. Her previous experience should have taught her not to try that again.

Eventually, the pain subsided, leaving her cradling herself and panting. Sweat beads of exhaustion formed on her temple and forehead and her eyes burned when she opened them. Powerless to resist, Tabea let them remain shut to allow herself even the smallest of relief. Perhaps a nap might help her recover.

Using the last of her remaining strength, she climbed into bed and snuggled into the soft cushioning.

The ship rumbled.

Sh't'ani rushed in, their tail swinging happily.

"We have arrived," they chirped, helping Tabea up while she rubbed the sleep out of her eyes.

"Arrived?" she asked.

"Yes, to Cerulean, the nearest planet to Viridian—this ship's home base. It's General P'cha'me's home planet."

Based on the Penyali naming system...

"It's a water planet?" Tabea asked, her head tilted to one side slightly.

"It is. With the most magnificent cities you can imagine."

Her mood significantly improved instantly. She'd get off this ship and get to finally see a little more of Penyali culture and customs! Not only that, but being stationary on a planet would mean that if her friends were found, she'd get the message sooner than if she were constantly moving around.

Tabea was ready to go, but Sh't'ani beckoned her to stay.

"We need to wait until the majority of the crew has left, to avoid the chaos," they explained.

Even though Tabea couldn't wait to leave this room and ship behind to see the blue waters of Cerulean and ask about her friends again, she didn't have a choice but to comply and wait.

She decided to pass the time by asking Sh't'ani about Penyali customs, culture, and communities.

"What do you guys do for fun?" she asked.

"Exercise," Sh't'ani responded without hesitation. "We love to swim and climb. They're our most highly regarded sports. Some prefer to tend to gardens, however."

"Gardening? Really?"

"Oh, yes. General P'cha'me, for example, is said to have a magnificent garden."

Somehow Tabea found it difficult to imagine the general, as cool and distant as she was, in a bountiful garden, raking weeds and carefully tending to flowers.

"What about you? What do you like to do, Sh't'ani?"

This caused the Penyali nurse to pause and reflect. "I'd like to be good at gardening," they admitted. "But I'm afraid I'm very bad at it. Everything I touch seems to die."

They looked at their talons and seemed utterly

helpless, in the most endearing manner.

"But I do have something else I like," Sh't'ani said, looking up gingerly. They leaned in to Tabea. "But it's a secret, so you cannot tell anyone. I like to read."

Tabea blinked a few times, trying to understand if she'd heard correctly.

"You like to read," she repeated dumbly. "But why is that a secret? Doesn't everyone here read? I like it, too."

Sh't'ani stood back up to their full height, their tail swinging cheerfully.

"Everyone reads for work or to study, but I read for pleasure." They sighed, gazing upward. "I enjoy tales of romance and adventure. And of battles and death. I love letting my mind disappear for a while, to allow it to travel into another world where I can be anything I want."

They closed their eyes in blissful reminiscence before sighing again. Then they shook their head. "But it is not considered proper."

Their tail drooped to the floor. Tabea could barely suppress a smile.

"On my ship we have a library," she said. "One that's filled with all sorts of books, including some tales that I think you might enjoy."

Somehow, she really wanted to give Sh't'ani a book. A good one, with a magnificent, long story that they could lose themself in for a while. Reading was clearly a source of solace for them, a way to escape a society where they were not among the higher classes.

She had gathered by now that Sh't'ani didn't come from a wealthy planet, and they didn't hold a high status in the Penyali star fleet, either, or even on this ship, for that matter.

"I would love to see it." Sh't'ani sighed.

"Maybe you can, if General P'cha'me finds the Calliope."

"Yes, maybe." Sh't'ani didn't seem convinced. There was something nervous about their manner, some shiftiness in their eyes, perhaps. They weren't looking at Tabea head on, but instead, the slit pupils kept diverging to just beyond her.

"I enjoy preparing meals as well," they then said a little too fast, as if to change the subject. "I tried to learn about human dishes to make your food, but I don't think I know enough yet. Can you tell me more about your 'Earth' dishes?"

Tabea obliged gladly, and they spent a long while talking about food.

The time passed quickly and before long, it was their turn to leave the ship. Only then, a worrying thought occurred to Tabea.

"Will I be able to breathe in your atmosphere?"

Whenever she'd alighted a starship in the past, she'd known from Calliope's systems that it was either safe or to bring a space suit. Here, she couldn't even tap into the ship to find out what it gauged.

But Sh't'ani only waved their tail. "General P'cha'me said that it should not be a problem."

Tabea was somewhat reassured, though she wondered how the general could be so certain.

She followed Sh't'ani through the halls of the ship, down pathways she hadn't yet discovered, and into the airlock. It was a small, circular room, clear crystals of some sort inset into the walls all around them, jagged and barely polished. The violet ceiling was a convex shape with thousands of tiny holes. Despite its alien appearance, the function was still clear to Tabea at the first glance, though she couldn't put a finger on how she could tell. It would have been a different matter if she'd had full access to her powers, but even so, it was a feeling more than anything else.

The doors opened slowly, almost hesitantly, yet without a sound. They glided smoothly and Tabea was at first blinded by the bright light streaming through the crack along with a gust of heat. She put up her hand to shield her eyes, squinting to escape the burning pain the light brought with it.

As she followed Sh't'ani forward, she blinked rapidly, trying to get used to the brightness. Then, when her eyes had finally grown accustomed to it, she tried to take it all in with wonder.

They were standing on a rocky shore, lifeless and still, except for the cooling engines and the chattering of some delayed crew members. Most had already vacated the vicinity. A few of them were unloading the ship's cargo, but Tabea didn't get the chance to take a closer look.

Sh't'ani took her hand and pulled her along, excitement betrayed by both their step and by their flicking tail.

"Look," they said, "Look! There is Cerulean's capital: Catha'ris. Isn't it magnificent?"

Tabea couldn't think of the words to form a reply. Her eyes were fixed on the ivory towers reaching into the sky after breaking the water's surface. They looked like curled horns woven together, though Tabea was also reminded of a Narwhal's tusk, an item she had only ever seen in museums, since the animal had long gone extinct.

There were hundreds of towers of different sizes, a little way away from the small island where their ship had landed, which, as Tabea could see now, must be their version of a hangar because she could make out two other ships of similar sizes farther inland near some large sheds or halls and some smaller aircrafts close to the coastal lines. They were shaped like boomerangs, with a slight thickening in the center for the cockpit. One glance at the strange aircrafts made her fingers itch briefly with a flash of desire to pilot one of them for a test flight.

Sh't'ani brought her to the water's edge, where a white bridge stretched between the island and the city of Catha'ris. The bridge looked smooth, but it wasn't slippery. It seemed to have many pores, and the consistency reminded her of a pumice stone, or perhaps corals. Looking at it for too long hurt her eyes because the planet's sun was burning down hard, and the reflection burned. It was hot, too. Tabea was glad she was wearing the Penyali garments because her overalls would have been far too warm for this weather, even if she'd shed some layers. Though more acutely than ever, she was missing the cool feeling of her tags on her chest. If nothing else, at least it would have served as a reminder that she belonged to Humanity's Space Core, even though she was as far away from it and one of its ships as she could be, alone on an alien planet. Although really, she was the alien here.

Sweat was already forming on her upper lip and streaming down her temples. She even had to wipe her forehead with her arm to prevent it from dripping into her eyes.

She peered at the water underneath the bridge. It was crystal clear, and she could easily make out the ground and see the corals, along with creatures that she assumed were the local equivalent of fish. A lot of them had three tentacles, that trailed behind their bodies when they swam, only used when they grabbed something, but they used two flippers on the upper half of their bodies to propel themselves forward. They each had four large eyes, making up about half of their faces, and one large mouth with what Tabea could only assume was a beak like that of an octopus.

There were other creatures as well, but Tabea couldn't get a good look at them. They flitted through the water too quickly and always just at the edge of what she could see.

When they got closer to Catha'ris, she could see more of the city as well. Some boomerang hovercrafts were flitting around in the air above them, but the real city was underneath the waves. The water was deep here — so deep that Tabea wasn't even certain if what she could see was the ocean floor. Among the many towers, she saw transparent tubes that acted as walkways. They were busy, filled with Penyales trying to get from one place to another. But they didn't restrict themselves to the walkways. There were also plenty of submarines — some of the hovercrafts even moving around underwater — and Tabea even saw many Penyales just swimming in the water, using their tails and arms to propel themselves forward.

Calling it magnificent did not do it justice.

Tabea stared at everything, her mouth agape. She'd read about places like this in science fiction and fantasy novels and comics, and she'd read and seen pictures of incredible structures made by other alien species, but nothing had ever come close to give her the impression of something as grand and intricate as this.

Sh't'ani led her across the bridge past the first few buildings, straight toward a thicker, flatter tower, the top of which was level, as if to create a helicopter pad. They entered and immediately, the heat subsided. Instead, there was a cool breeze that even Sh't'ani seemed to enjoy because they blissfully closed their eyes for a moment and stuck up their nose flaps.

C'ru was waiting for them in the large, circular empty room.

His eyes narrowed as his tail flicked when he observed Tabea's awe. He looked pleased, she thought.

"I welcome you to Catha'ris of Cerulean, human. You are the first human space witch to ever set foot on any of our planets."

Tabea noticed that he seemed to feel the need to qualify the fact that she was also a space witch, which meant that she was probably not the first human. Her eyes narrowed slightly. Who had been here before her? And more importantly — why?

She hadn't forgotten about the Penyales' hatred toward humans, and the fact that they were known as "man crushers," even though talking to them in person made that seem almost ridiculous. They had shown her much more hospitality than she ever would have expected — in fact, they hadn't treated her that differently from the way Callaghan had dealt with Yuri, even though he was from the same species and there was no inherent dislike accompanying the acquaintance.

"Thank you. It's a beautiful place and I truly feel

blessed to get to see it." Not a word of that was a lie. "Now that we're here," she continued, "I was wondering if you'd heard anything from your fleets — have you found any trace of my friends?"

C'ru took his claws behind his back and paced slowly toward one of the large, floor-to-ceiling windows to gaze across the city.

"I have received a notification that one of our ships was chasing a band of pirates that we believe may have attacked your ship."

Her heart jumped. It wasn't quite the same as having found her friends, but finding the pirates was already a big step forward!

But it was still a far cry from good news. She remembered the *Sonata* too well to believe that the pirates might not have tried to do the same thing to the *Calliope*. Especially as she was well aware that they had space witches. She could only hope that her connection with Calliope in the past had made the ship strong enough to resist.

She sighed. There was still nothing she could do. "Thank you."

He made a non-committal noise.

"Guardian," he called to Sh't'ani, though he barely even spared them a glance. "Show our guest where she shall be staying for the time being." Then he turned back to Tabea. "I will call on you later today — there are some commitments I need to keep first."

Tabea followed Sh't'ani to a platform, which, when they both stood atop, slowly lowered itself into the floor — an elevator.

Before long, the elevator moved into a see-through tube as well, continuously going down.

Tabea's attention was captured by the view around her, and she couldn't look away. There were signs made from fabric stretching between buildings with messages, akin to billboards, and the whole city seemed to be moving and interacting according to rules that Tabea couldn't make out. Even though it looked chaotic, none of the fish-like submarines or swimming Penyales seemed to be in any danger of crashing into one another. Some sea creatures were making their way between the buildings as well, but there were fewer here than outside of the city limits. Occasionally, she noticed some tufts of what appeared to be some form of seaweed or anemone swaying in the water, often near round windows.

"Say," Sh't'ani said, interrupting her observations, "I know your kind lives out of the water now, but how do you fare underwater?"

Tabea looked up. "Not very well. We can't breathe there, and we can only hold out without air for a few minutes at most."

Sh't'ani turned their head to look at her with all their eyes, wide open. "So fragile! Don't you have problems with heat and cold as well?"

"We do, but we always find ways around that."

Sh't'ani's tail drooped to the floor. "Amazing."

The words were uttered so quietly, that Tabea barely heard them. But as she was about to respond, something caught her eye. Her gaze was drawn to one of the glass tubes where Penyales were crossing from one tower to another, and her breath caught in her throat as her heart sped up. A tuft of ginger hair was peeking out between the scaly heads of the Penyales, and if Tabea wasn't completely mistaken, she recognized it.

Yuri!

She resisted the urge to call out to him—he wouldn't have heard her anyway.

Suddenly, the bright waters around her felt colder, shadier. Perhaps it was because they were reaching new depths, but Tabea felt chills run down her spine as she reflected on what Yuri's presence meant. Could she have been mistaken? She stared at the back of his head, willing him to turn around so she could see his face. He was wearing Penyali robes, just like her, though his were gray. Then, as her elevator passed his height and sank underneath, he finally turned his head to the side, and she could see his profile. Undeniable—it was him. He was conversing with one of the two Penyales flanking him, and there was no way he could see her, even if she signaled.

Then he disappeared from view, but his image remained clearly in her mind.

She wasn't alone.

Yuri was here.

And C'ru, somehow, had lied.

CHAPTER 19

SHE WAS KEPT ON THE OCEAN FLOOR.

Tabea's room was not much larger than her cabin on the spaceship had been, though now it had its own bathroom attached and some form of mechanism in a corner that delivered food at the push of a button without Sh't'ani having to bring it in to her. Learning material had already been prepared and left for her, as had more garments in her size.

But like before, Tabea didn't have free rein. Like before, she wasn't allowed to leave her room, and, like before, when she tried to use her powers, she still only received blinding pain in return.

Even though they had landed on a planet, a place where she couldn't control everything and act akin to a god, she wasn't trusted. Nothing had changed. Nothing except that now, even Sh't'ani wasn't there to keep her company much anymore because they didn't need to bring her food or accompany her to the sanitary stalls.

For four scheduled meals and two long sleeps, Tabea remained locked alone in her room. Not even Sh't'ani came to see her.

There weren't even any windows because her room

was in the center of a large compound building, rising from the ocean floor. A dome that held breathable air covered most of what Sh't'ani called the "inner city," where the main entrances to most important buildings were as well. Apparently, everything that was above the inner city was made up of apartments and smaller shops, only the cheapest above water.

Tabea had given up on pacing. It was too frustrating.

She'd given up on reading, too. Instead, she was staring angrily at the ceiling, as white and pumice stone-like as the bridge. She soon found she was too angry and restless to remain that way and entered her full exercise training routine from back when she'd been training to be a pilot at the Academy, starting with push-ups.

With her body busy with exercise, her mind ran free. Instead of taking advantage of that freedom, it homed in and intensified around the thoughts that kept her so restless.

Yuri was here.

Yuri was here, and it had been kept from her — *continued* to be kept from her.

She didn't believe for a second that C'ru might still not know about Yuri at this point — humans couldn't be visitors so common that the news wouldn't reach him, so why had she not been told about her friend?

She could believe that at the time of their arrival, C'ru may not have heard yet, but by this time, he had to know.

The thought left her with only one possible conclusion. The high priest was purposefully keeping Yuri's presence from her. She'd been making excuses for their distrust of her, for their safety precautions and the isolation they had made her suffer, but she couldn't do that anymore. This was too clear-cut.

She moved on to sit-ups, flexing her abdominal muscles with all the frustration she felt.

Yuri was probably in a similar room as her—a holding cell, she now had to admit to herself with grinding teeth. But why? She understood why she was held here—they needed her. But Yuri wasn't a space witch. What could he possibly have to offer that the Penyales might value? Unless...

A shiver ran down her spine as she spelled out the horrible thought in her mind.

Unless he was insurance.

If she, for any reason, were to refuse to give her help to restore Viridian to its former glory, would they threaten him? Endanger him? Use him to force her?

She'd made it very clear that she would do anything to save her friends, after all.

She moved on to practice her punches and kicks in the air, thrusting her fists forward with all her might, fighting an invisible enemy—perhaps C'ru or P'cha'me.

Perhaps she'd been deceived. She had started to feel comfortable around them, feeling like she might become friends with some of them, Sh't'ani in particular. But in the end, she was a tool for them. And the lives of all her friends weren't worth any more than insects.

Had P'cha'me even sent out a ship to look for them? She had said that she had.

Penyales weren't meant to have the capacity to lie.

Could they have learned?

Or perhaps Yuri had been found the same way she had—in an escape pod floating through space. After all, he had been on the bridge with her. If something had happened there that had made her lose consciousness, it wasn't outside the realm of possibility that he might have tried to get them both to safety.

Whenever she reached the end of her routine, she began anew, continuing this way until she couldn't lift a finger anymore. Drenched with sweat, she pulled open her robe to let air soothe the heat of her body and lay sprawled on her back across the floor.

Her head was beginning to hurt from her frantic, jumping thoughts, her arms heavy from exercise along with labored breathing and her burning eyes. Closing her eyes, she placed her fingers on top of the lids to feel the soothing coolness.

These contemplations were getting her nowhere.

Sh't'ani's face popped into her mind, the genuine curiosity with which they asked questions about Humanity expressed clearly in their earnest eyes.

Sh't'ani, at least, had not deceived her. Of that much Tabea felt certain. Besides, they held too low a rank to have been entrusted with any information about a larger plan, that much had been proven several times. Perhaps she could consider them something akin to a friend at least. The closest thing she could find here, in any case. But where their loyalties would lie in case of a conflict, Tabea didn't dare to think about.

She sat up briskly. These thoughts were only making her more miserable.

She focused on trying to regulate her breathing, on slowing and deepening it. It had been Callaghan who had taught her certain breathing techniques back at the Academy. He was a master in tai chi, and he'd always said that breathing was the essence of everything. It was the essence of life. Any living thing needed to breathe, no matter if it was an animal, a plant, or an extraterrestrial. There was power in one's breathing—a way to increase one's own might and strengthen it, if done correctly.

When she felt that her breathing and heartbeat had slowed to their normal pace, she noted with satisfaction that the cloud in her head had cleared up. She felt more in control of her thoughts and emotions—less desperate and hopeless. Less frustrated.

Now, she had two choices.

She could wait to see whatever the Penyales had in store for her next, or she could work on a way out.

She smirked to herself. As if there were ever any real question in the matter. She'd been a passive player for long enough. But no more.

She almost thought she could feel Calliope cheering her on, sending her positive vibes.

So, what to start with?

Still lying on the floor, she looked around the room.

There wasn't much to go on. There weren't any indentations in the walls that showed panels, or sockets of any sort, but there were the edges to the food mechanism and the corners of the door. The bathroom had the water lines. If she had any tools, that might be something she could work with. Besides, there had to be air vents somewhere. She'd felt the drafts. And seeing as the Penyales were quite significantly larger than her, she dared to wager that it would be easy enough for her to squeeze through. As long as they didn't use any technology unknown to her, that was. If the room was a closed circuit, that was a different matter also.

First and foremost, she needed tools—a commodity the Penyales unsurprisingly hadn't been kind enough to supply her with. She wondered if Sh't'ani would bring her some, if she asked. But then, there was no guarantee that Sh't'ani was still in charge of looking after her. It didn't seem to be needed in this place after all. And even then, she would be asking them to unknowingly betray their superiors, something she couldn't do with a clear conscience. She didn't want to get the one person who'd shown genuine concern for her to get into trouble. Again.

Her head was pounding, and her mouth was dry. She really ought to rehydrate. She pushed herself to a seated position and her eyes fell on the food dispenser.

She stared at it for a moment, allowing the thought to take shape on its own.

Yes. It just might work.

She sprang to her feet and crossed the room. First, she got some water and gulped it down greedily. And then a second cup. Then she pressed the button that ordered food for her. If she only waited a few moments, makeshift tools would be supplied to her in no time.

The cutlery the Penyales supplied her with seemed more akin to chopsticks than the cutlery used on the *Calliope*, but one of them generally also had a small blade at the tip, almost like a scalpel, except blunt. If she could sharpen it on the walls... it might just make the perfect tool for her endeavor.

As expected, she didn't have to wait for long. The food arrived with the same chopstick scalpels they always did. Unfortunately, so did C'ru.

The door opened to let him enter barely thirty seconds after the food arrived. Panicked, Tabea whipped around to him, but she tried to appear composed and aloof. He couldn't know what she was planning, right? Was that a secret space witch power she hadn't read about yet? Mind reading without the two-way telepathy?

"Apologies for the delay. I hope you have not found your accommodations lacking."

He inclined his head, as if to symbolize a tiny bow.

"They're fine," Tabea responded, trying to remember if she'd been told what was next on their list of tests and experiments.

"I am glad to hear it. Please follow me."

He turned and left the room. The door remained open. Hurriedly, Tabea followed. Anything to get out of the room for a little while! And if he wasn't suspecting anything, all the better.

"Where are we going?" she asked as they rounded a few undecorated white hallways.

He didn't even glance at her when he spoke.

"To the training hall. There is one more vital skill you must be taught before we can even fathom the resurrection of our planet."

Tabea jogged beside him in silence for a little while. His stride was long and quick; he must have been in a hurry. Or perhaps he didn't want to give her a chance to look around too much?

If that was his plan, it wasn't working. She was memorizing every turn they took, creating a mental map of the layout in her mind. Before long, they were leaving the building into the underwater dome. Thanks to the clarity of the water, the sun was able to reach even to these depths, but there were extra lights by way of luminescent green plants growing along the dome to enhance the brightness. The color gave the ocean floor an eerie, ethereal quality. Markings from the sun hitting the waves above were drawing an ever-changing mosaic on the ground while white towers reached for the sky all around. There weren't many Penyales around this part of the city, but Tabea had seen before that other parts were bustling with life. She had to admit to herself that she'd like to see those and understand what life in Penyali culture was truly like. Her limited interactions had told her very little.

C'ru led her past various towers until they reached a wide, but flat structure that reminded Tabea of a clam. A giant clam.

C'ru opened a door at its side, and she followed him in without hesitation. He brought her into a large, closed hall, illuminated by some of that green-glowing seaweed. Three other Penyales in priest robes were already waiting there at three corners of the room. Assuming they wanted to keep her power contained to the hall like they had done on the ship before, she suppressed a confident smirk. This might be her chance for escape. If she could break their barrier after her block had been lifted, she could probably command some of the submarines that could help her get to Yuri and then grab one of the shuttles she'd seen on the island to —

She stopped herself from thinking further. She was jumping too far ahead. She didn't even know where Yuri was kept, or if there were any other more of her friends on the planet she needed to save. Perhaps some of them were on different planets altogether but still in Penyali talons.

She needed more information. And a better plan

than to bust out and go gung-ho.

She turned to C'ru, who picked up a metal cylinder from one of the other space witches.

"What you will learn today," he said as he turned back to her, placing his talon on her forehead to release her power, "is how to fill up a container to store your power."

Tabea had powered electronic objects before, but she had never made something to store her power—a battery of cosmic energy. Intrigued by the notion and indulging in her thirst for knowledge, she set aside all thoughts of an escape for the moment and just tried to soak up everything C'ru was about teach her.

"Think of it as a part of your own body, in which you create a bubble of energy. Once it's at the brink of bursting, you sever your connection, stopping the flow, and trap the energy inside. Of course, this wouldn't work without these stones." He pointed at several inlaid plates that at first glance looked purely decorative. Tabea nodded to show she understood.

"What are they?"

"It's a very rare space rock named Plorinium. It can only form the moment when a supernova turns to a black hole. There are several grains set into the walls of this hall. Of course, these plates aren't pure, either. They're normal metal, infused with grains of Plorinium. It's powerful enough that no more is needed."

She thought of their training session in his quarters on the ship. She would have bet her right hand that he personally owned some items with the same properties.

"And they trap our powers, is that right?"

His tail flicked once, something that Tabea

interpreted as a hint of a smile.

"That is correct." He was pleased with the speed with which she picked up his lessons, that much was obvious. "If you remember the first test you performed when joining us, the machine you entered tried to do what you will be doing now: Draw out your power and store it. But because of your inexperience, you almost destroyed it and doomed us all."

The accusation was as clear as day and irked Tabea immensely. Her eyebrows twitched and she clenched her fists, biting her tongue lest she should burst out with something unwise. She took a few breaths until she trusted herself to speak once more.

"Show me."

And he did. It didn't look all that impressive. In fact, not much was visible at all. But Tabea could feel the change. She sensed the power leaving C'ru's body with the hairs all across her body and by the metallic taste in her mouth, and she detected it vanishing into the container, though as soon as it was inside, it stopped existing to her. Then the last tendril of power was severed by the Penyali priest, and it was her turn. He handed her another battery without a word.

She felt a split second of hesitation, thinking about whether she should go ahead with the lesson. After all, what could they do with her power once they had stored it? She would be giving it out of her hands, practically gifting it to them, and while she itched to try it, to learn how to do it, she didn't want to give them something they could use as a weapon, potentially against her own people.

That thought hadn't really occurred to her since her first days on their ship, but now that she knew they'd kept Yuri's presence a secret from her, the distrust rushed back with a vengeance.

She was certain they wouldn't harm her. Oh no, she was far too useful. They'd made it clear that they thought she had a lot more power than their own space witches did—C'ru included—so they couldn't afford hurting her and losing her cooperation. But similarly, they couldn't risk losing her by giving her what she wanted. Meaning, she would likely never see her friends again if she complied.

But it was going to be the same if she refused her help. They would probably switch to threats, then, dangling Yuri and Callaghan and Calliope in front of her, promising terrible, awful things if she wouldn't comply.

She moved the battery from one hand to the other to get a better feeling for it. It didn't have any markings; it was a simple, chrome-colored cylinder, the edges so fine, Tabea thought she might get a cut from them if she didn't handle it carefully.

Determined to make it work, she started the exercise, copying everything she'd seen C'ru do and filling in the gaps with guesswork. Focusing her power first on her hands, she clasped them both around the cylinder and waited until they were almost vibrating with energy. Then she slowly let the energy seep into the container.

Visualizing a growing bubble, she was thrown back to her childhood, long ago, when she'd made soap bubbles with her siblings in the family garden back on Earth. To a time when it hadn't become so painfully obvious that she was the odd one out. Before expectations had been thrust upon her that she always failed to meet and before her siblings had risen to become the self-centered, shade-throwing people they now were. Before she'd joined the piloting races that would earn her the scholarship for the Academy. Before she'd begun to be riddled with self-doubt and inferiority complexes. Before she'd met Besma, and Callaghan, and Calliope.

"Watch, you guys. I'm gonna make the biggest bubble yet!" Nick announced, grinning cockily.

Tabea and Ella put their own bubble-implements down. When Nick showed something, it was worth watching. He always figured out the best ways to do things.

Dramatically, he put his bubble ring up to his mouth and blew gently. The iridescent surface rippled for a moment, threatening to burst, and Tabea found herself enchanted, gripped by the action. Teeth gnawing on her lower lip, she was captivated by her brother and her heart beat as fast as if she were the one doing the blowing.

Would it burst?

Dorian squeaked happily in ignorance in his crib behind them, as babies were wont to do, but Nick wasn't disturbed by it. He shaped a small bubble, and it grew steadily as he increased the airflow. It grew and grew, and Tabea's eyes grew alongside the bubble. This was so big!

It had already lost most of its greens and purples, and it was not much more than a clear, fragile crystal ball in the making now. It had to burst any second now. She held her breath, hoping fervently that Nick would stop in time.

He now blew gentler again, and then he let his breath fade out slowly while moving the ring away from the bubble.

As the soap separated, the bubble shivered and trembled, and for just a moment, it looked like the sudden movement would destroy it. But then the trembling ceased, and the bubble floated away phlegmatically.

Tabea slowly let out her held breath and beamed at her

older brother. "That was amazing, Nick!"

Ella jumped forward as well, her eyes sparkling as she bounced on the spot.

"Show me again! I want to make an even bigger bubble!"

As Nick explained his technique to Ella, Tabea focused on making her own bubbles. Small ones, that still retained all their shiny, shimmering gloriousness. Ones that seemed so full of life as they danced in the light breeze, reflecting the world around them in myriads of colors. Nick's bubble had been impressive, but she preferred these small ones. They were so much prettier.

Occasionally, she would catch one again with her bubble ring and just hold it there in front of her before using that bubble's soap to make dozens more small ones.

Dorian giggled as they danced around him, and he tried to reach for them, only to find that they burst the moment he touched them, which made him gurgle with laughter.

Happy to see her baby brother enjoy them so much, Tabea made sure to make many more tiny bubbles, blowing them his way.

Meanwhile, Ella managed a large bubble of her own, though it still wasn't quite as big as Nick's. Dorian's eyes were caught by the sight and he stared in wonder, ignoring the many small bubbles around.

Tabea took only a moment to imagine how big his smile would be if he found one of those big bubbles close to him, so she decided to make one for him.

She tried, time and time again, but all her big bubbles burst before they ever left the ring. She didn't even manage to make them large enough to compete with Ella's. Frustrated and determined, Tabea kept trying, yet time and time again, they burst, splashing droplets of soapy water to rain down on the grass.

Almost as if the memory triggered something in her

powers, her bubble burst.

With soap bubbles, the worst thing that could happen was getting her hands wet and soapy. But this was not the case here.

The bursting of the bubble severed the used power from her, and it took on a life of its own. She could feel it, still, but she had no control over it anymore. And it went crazy. The bubble hadn't just burst, it had exploded, making the energy shoot out in all directions, striking blindly, zigzagging at random, bouncing off from the walls of the hall, returning back to the center...

The other space witches ran for cover or created flimsy shields with their abilities the moment they realized what was happening. C'ru released the power from his own battery and shaped it as a cloak around himself as protection.

For a moment, Tabea could do no more than watch as her power went wild. She watched the reactions of everyone else there, C'ru in particular, and then caught herself in her bewilderment. She had to act.

Sending out more tendrils of her power, like a hundred-armed octopus, she reached out to catch all the kinetic projectiles, absorbing them back into her own pool instantly. That alone wasn't quite enough to absorb all of the impact, so instead of taking it back inside of her, she reminded herself of Callaghan's tai chi lessons, and let the energy flow around her, guiding it around herself while controlling her breathing. Round and around again until the force behind it lessened. Only then did she fully internalize her power once more.

She looked up.

The room had been devastated. The lesser space witches had huddled together, joining forces to create a protective dome around them. C'ru was the only one who hadn't joined them, instead using his own power as his only protective measure.

The hall had been torn to shreds.

Any item that had been there before, like the tables and benches at the sides, had been thrown around and bashed against the walls, shattered into pieces.

The doors had been torn from their hinges and lay scattered across the room. Though they had held up, even the walls had taken considerable damage, seen not only in the scratches and dents created by the furniture blasting through the room, but also huge gashes, as though a beast had tried to claw its way out.

Taking in the devastation she had caused, Tabea gulped. This was not what she had intended. She hadn't even known that she could cause something like this with her abilities in the first place, and this had only been a fraction of her full potential, she was well aware. What if she ever lost control—truly lost control? She didn't dare to think about it.

She started to feel faint and dizzy, but she could still hold up. Spots appeared at the edges of her vision, but she wasn't going to faint. Not this time. She looked to C'ru, her expression undoubtedly fearful and worried. Neither his own expression, nor his tail betrayed anything of his thoughts on the situation.

Wordlessly, he crossed over to her, placed a talon on her forehead, and sealed her power away once more.

Chapter 20

"*I CAN FEEL YOU.*"

Only those words reached Tabea. But those words alone were a comfort to her nonetheless. They were in her mind when she woke up, remaining as a memory. But more important than the words themselves was the feeling attached to them.

Calliope.

Calliope had sent them, and they had reached her, of that much Tabea was certain. It wasn't just a dream; the sensation was too strong, too real, almost as if the molecules of her innermost being were still charged with Calliope's energy.

She wondered if, perhaps, C'ru in his rush, hadn't fully sealed away her powers. Or if, by separating and unleashing parts of said power, she had been able to create and establish a momentary connection.

Whichever it was, it gave her hope.

Yesterday, after the incident in the training hall, C'ru had marched her straight back to her room, without so much as saying a word. She'd been too exhausted to resist or attempt an escape, never mind that she wouldn't have been able to save Yuri.

"I can feel you."

Knowing that she might have lost her chance would have been a blow to her, if it hadn't been for those words.

Tabea was still lying in bed, staring at the ceiling, when the door opened, and Sh't'ani entered, their tail swinging hesitantly.

An involuntary smile came to Tabea's face. "Sh't'ani, I was wondering when I'd get to see you again!"

It wasn't a lie.

Their tail now swung more forcefully, and their eyes sparkled. "Me too," they admitted. "I wanted to talk more with you, but I couldn't come sooner. I..." A troubled look crossed their face for only a moment. "Wasn't permitted."

"Well," Tabea said, looking around the room for a moment, and then patting the bed beside her, "take a seat and we'll do just that."

The door shut and Sh't'ani took the offered place. "C'ru ordered me to check in on you and monitor your condition." They gazed critically at Tabea's face but then gave a huff as their shoulders sagged. "But I can't gauge the way humans look when they're healthy to when they're unwell."

They diverted their eyes, kicking one clawed foot forward dejectedly. Their tail drooped down, but the tip of it seemed to be under tension still. Tabea thought they looked angry, or annoyed, possibly with themself.

"I'm doing great," she promised. "I'm just a little concerned, you know?"

"Concerned?" Sh't'ani looked up at her, with evident surprise. "Does the food not contain enough nourishment?"

"That's not it. Just... You know that C'ru promised to look for my friends, right?"

Sh't'ani nodded hesitantly, the troubled look returning to their eyes along with the frowny cross between them.

Suddenly, Tabea had doubts about whether she should proceed. Was it really wise to share this piece of information with them? They might seem friendly, but at the end of the day, they were on opposite sides, weren't they?

No matter how friendly and nice Sh't'ani was, Tabea could never know for certain if she could trust them. She'd put her trust in C'ru, and he had clearly betrayed it, in a way that she hadn't considered possible.

"There is something I need to tell you," Sh't'ani blurted out.

Tabea looked up, surprised.

"I know I shouldn't," Sh't'ani continued, "and I've been ordered not to, but it feels wrong to keep it from you."

Tabea remained silent, allowing for Sh't'ani's outburst to continue untethered.

"I thought it odd for High Priest C'ru to tell me to stop looking after you, and I was unhappy about not being able to continue our conversations, or at least say goodbye, so I went for a dive. Then I saw some activity by the underwater halls near the hangars, and they should have been abandoned. Normally, I wouldn't have thought anything by it, but... When I first brought you here..." Their voice failed. Their talons trembled, as did their tail, and their eyes flicked from side to side, as if desperately searching for anything to hang on to in the room. Something akin to fear had crossed into their expression, visible to Tabea in their mouth pressed into a thin line and flaring nostrils, and something about their demeanor spoke of broken trust and shattered truths.

The pieces snapped together for Tabea.

"You saw him too, didn't you?"

Sh't'ani nodded.

"I saw a human, walking with my comrades. And I saw your face, too. I wasn't sure if it was distress at the time, but I guessed."

Their voice was quiet now, as though it could somehow make it less true.

Tabea no longer felt like she had to steer clear of Sh't'ani. After all, they had just proven to be a much-welcomed ally in a time of uncertainty. They had willfully broken a command from a superior officer because they felt it was *right*. They didn't want to keep secrets from her. In essence, Sh't'ani had just betrayed their race for *her* sake.

Warmth filled Tabea's chest, but there was an uneasiness there, too, one she chose to ignore for the moment. She couldn't think about what this betrayal might mean to Sh't'ani right now. Not when she was dependent on it.

"His name is Yuri," she said. "He's one of my friends."

Sh't'ani's nose flaps flared. "I thought so."

Tabea locked her eyes on to those of her ally, her friend. A plan was forming in her head, and she had just figured out the first step.

"Can you bring me to him?"

After Sh't'ani left to investigate Yuri's whereabouts, Tabea was left alone for what felt like the rest of the day, and the day after. She used that time to work on her previous plan of escape, just in case. Getting the tools had proven easier than expected, but the work she was doing on the food dispenser wasn't quite as simple, especially without taking it out of commission entirely.

Finally, she managed to take it off, only to discover that only two small tubes led through the walls, much too small to be of any use to her, so she remounted the dispenser to the best of her abilities, thankful for the engineering lessons in which Hammond had forced her not to use her powers. Mildly discouraged, she found herself with nothing left to do except another training and then breathing session.

It was during her breathing exercises that she heard it: a scratching in the walls. It was quiet, almost unnoticeable, and if she hadn't been hyper aware of the sounds of her surroundings while trying to meditate, she wouldn't even have noticed it.

She placed her ear against the wall in several places, trying to pin down the exact location where the sound originated. Eventually, she figured out where it was loudest, high up on the wall between her bedstead and the food dispenser. She had to stand on a chair to reach it. Determined, she used the scalpel side of her tools and worked away on the wall. Surprisingly, she cut through it easily here, though in other places where she had tried, including near the food dispenser, it had been almost impossible, as the wall there had been made of stone. Even so, one of her tools broke.

It was different material than the stone, designed to look and feel the same but significantly more fragile and easier to cut. It wasn't long until she had uncovered what she'd been looking for before: an air vent. And as expected, it was large enough to hold someone like her, though there was still a grid before it. The scratching sounds had vanished and reappeared several times, and now Tabea was certain. Someone or something was traveling through the vents, and she was going to find out who or what.

She worked away at loosening the sides, but all she succeeded in was her other tool breaking. She cursed herself under her breath, for not having prepared a third in advance. Using the food dispenser now to get one would take too long and be too loud.

The sounds were still approaching. It wasn't long before she could make out whispering.

"Can't you go a bit faster?"

"Don't *rush* me! I'm *trying* to be *quiet* here!"

Tabea frowned. Something about them seemed familiar.

She peered into what she could make out of the shaft. It was lined by metal, or so it seemed, and what she could tell by the reflections of it in the meager light shining in via her room told her that there was a tunnel connected to her vent, which, really, was only logical.

The sounds were still approaching.

"Seriously, give me some *space* here. *Some* of us are trying to *save* our asses here!"

"Sorry, it's just... I'm getting nervous. I feel like something's following us."

"There's nothing following us."

Tabea could practically *hear* the eyeroll, and it

reminded her of a person she had never expected to be missing. But it couldn't be, could it?

The sounds were ever approaching and then, suddenly, they stopped. Tabea was staring at the face at the back of the tunnel, the familiar face staring right back at her. She wasn't sure who was more surprised.

"Hey. What's going on? Why did you stop?"

Tabea gulped, but she couldn't tear her eyes away. "Nerissa?"

Her old rival regained her composure quickly and scoffed. "Should have known we'd find you here, alive and kicking."

She changed direction to head toward Tabea. And following her was another familiar face.

"*Besma*?" Tabea's surprise only grew with every moment. Her heart was undecided when it came to what to feel and remained numb in shock.

"Tabea!" Besma almost yelled, her entire face brightening up. Then, pushing past Nerissa and directly to the vent's grid, she peered into Tabea's face, before bursting into tears. "I didn't think I'd ever get to see you again!"

Tabea, moved by her friend's emotions, felt her tears welling up as well. "Me too," she mumbled. "They said..." Her voice faltered.

Nerissa pushed Besma aside to get to the vent, and with a few practiced movements, she removed the grid and lowered herself into the room. She glanced around unemotively and then shrugged, only granting Tabea a half-glance, though Tabea felt as though she wasn't quite as indifferent as she pretended.

"Everyone thinks you're dead," she said, matter-of-fact.

Tabea nodded. That wasn't entirely surprising. "Is…Is everyone okay?"

Nerissa shrugged. "Everyone is alive, if that's what you mean. Though none of us really know why. They've been keeping us prisoner, just about fed, and telling us that we'll serve a greater purpose."

Nerissa's entire body trembled with undisguised anger.

"Most of the officers have been hurt—badly," Besma added. "Vince and Callaghan, too."

Tabea's hands clenched to fists. How could she ever have been so foolish as to trust the Penyales for even a moment? "What happened?"

"Because you were the only one on the bridge during the party," — Nerissa flashed her an icy glare — "no one entirely knows. But there was a sudden, unscheduled hyperjump. The officers brought the ship back under control, but then we were ambushed by pirates."

She paused, looking around the room again, almost as if to find her next words.

"We all fought them as much as we could, but they took us prisoner. We assumed they'd killed you during the attack. Apparently, they were looking for a space witch." She gave a dry, humorless laugh. "It's such a joke. A human space witch? Yeah right, as if."

Tabea didn't laugh. Nothing about this was funny.

"It wasn't long before *their* ship was attacked by the Penyales, and they pulled us to this planet and told us we were going to make a difference in the world, that we just needed to help them."

"To be fair, they weren't hostile," Besma said quietly. Her demeanor was dejected and Tabea missed her usual happy self that only worried about dances and being the best pilot she could be. There were lines on her face that hadn't been there before, and a haunted look in her eyes.

This was her fault.

"Maybe not, but they're not much better, either, keeping us here against our will." Nerissa hissed. "And they're keeping us like animals, you realize that, don't you?"

Tabea braced her heart against the pain she was sure would come if she dwelt on the new information. Guilt washed over her, threatening to drown her in a sea of sorrow. Everything about this was her fault.

"I think it's Yuri," Besma said quietly.

"Huh?"

"The space witch. I think they were looking for him, like before. And that's why the Penyales took him away."

Nerissa didn't answer, but a slight inclination in her head made it seem as though she were agreeing.

Her eyes turned on Tabea and she stemmed her hands on her hips. "So how did *you* end up here?"

"I..." Tabea stopped herself. She was the space witch who had put everyone in danger. If she disclosed that information now, there was no telling what would happen. And yet, without it, how could she explain why she was here?

She decided to stick to as much of the truth as she could.

"I'm not sure. The last thing I remember is Yuri and I being on the bridge and trying to escape from an attack by doing a hyper jump. I blacked out almost right after and then woke up on a Penyali ship."

She left out the fact that she'd been found in an escape pod. It would just make them think that she'd intentionally escaped on her own when the pirates attacked again, and she would never do that. Then she thought about Yuri, and about his being here and having been with her then.

"I bet Yuri knows what happened," she said. "And I have a friend who's going to find out where he is."

"A friend?" Nerissa's eyes narrowed as she frowned. "What kind of 'friend'?"

Instead of explaining the details, Tabea reinforced her words with a determined gaze toward Nerissa's and Besma's eyes. "Someone I trust."

Nerissa didn't seem convinced, but Besma let out a little giggle.

"Leave it to Tabs to make friends wherever."

Tabea forced a smile. Then she looked at the vent. "I'm guessing you two decided to go on a reconnaissance mission to plan an escape?"

Nerissa jutted her chin forward and glared at Tabea defiantly. "Someone had to do it. I'm the best cadet engineer on the ship, and Besma could pilot if we found a ship or some other vehicle."

Tabea's heart almost stopped. "Calliope's not with you?" Her voice was shaking.

"Of course not. You don't think they'd let us keep our ship, do you? Besides, it was totally wrecked during the battles; it's basically scrap now. Our only chance is to steal one of their ships and figure out how they work."

Tabea felt faint. Calliope—scrap. Her knees were growing weak, and tears were pushing their way into her eyes. Suddenly, the air was so much heavier, it became difficult to breathe. It couldn't be true. Hadn't she only heard her friend's voice the other night? No, Calliope was still alive. She was still functioning and just waiting for her to get to her. She had to be.

"We should go."

Nerissa turned back to the vent and was halfway through climbing in when Besma asked, "Tabs, aren't you coming?"

Tabea, still rooted to the spot, shook her head. This was her fault. She had to fix it. But she had to save everyone. Somehow.

"I've got to find Yuri first. My friend promised to help me. It'll be easier and faster than going blind. But..." She paused. "If you can find any trace of the Calliope, please let me know. I need to know."

If even just her core were still whole, Tabea could fix this. As long as Calliope's center hadn't been hurt, she could use her powers and make everything right again.

Nerissa scowled. "I doubt it, but okay." She hesitated, and then stepped back into the room. "Just tell me one thing. Why are they keeping your separate? What makes you so special? Why did you disappear but Yuri didn't?" She gestured at the room and Tabea's robe. "Why are they treating you differently to the rest of us?"

This was it. Tabea didn't know how to explain it without either feigning complete ignorance or by telling the truth. Besma was watching her with confused curiosity as well. Heat and cold chased one another in her body like a red fox and an arctic fox.

Besma would know she was lying. Besma, who had suffered because of her. Who trusted her. Who was her friend.

Tabea closed her eyes in defeat and took a deep breath.

"They want my help," she said, quietly. "We had a deal—I help them, and they find you for me so we can go home. They never told me that they already had you."

"And why," Nerissa said as she paced slowly into the room, approaching Tabea, "would they need *your* help?"

Despite the turmoil in her gut, Tabea forced herself to meet Nerissa's gaze. "I think you already know."

"Spell it out, then."

Tabea's fingers trembled, as did her legs. She felt so weak. *So guilty.* "They need my power. Because I'm a space witch."

Chapter 21

Silence followed her confession.

It was Besma who finally broke it.

"Tabs." She shook her head and squeezed her eyes shut. "That doesn't make any sense. Humans *can't* be space witches. It's impossible."

Tabea granted her a small, mirthless smirk. "I thought so too. Until my accident."

Besma looked puzzled for a moment until her hands flew to her mouth as her eyes widened in shocked realization. "When the lightning hit you…?"

"Back at the Academy?" Nerissa whirled around, her eyes aflame with fury and disbelief. "*That's* when you became a space witch?"

"Yeah. It was just before the Harvius VI mission, and there was an incident then."

"Callaghan knew, then." Nerissa's voice was dry, unemotive.

Tabea looked to the ground, grimacing. "All the officers know."

"And that's why you changed from the pilot's track to the engineering path!" Besma pieced the past together.

335

Tabea nodded, feeling a mixture of relief and shame at finally telling someone else the truth. "It was easier to cover up that way."

Nerissa began to giggle, but it quickly gave way to open laughter. Besma and Tabea shared a confused glance and watched her doubling over, clutching her stomach. She was laughing so hard that she even shed some tears. After a few minutes, she finally let up and sat down, wiping her eyes, grinning.

"What's so funny?" Tabea asked gingerly.

"I'm still the best," Nerissa said simply.

"What?"

"I don't have to hate you anymore. But I still don't like you, okay? I've always resented you for being a prissy pilot girl who decided to change her path on a whim, even though she was the ace in her original field. And now she was there, trying to show everyone up in a new field as well. It just bugged me so much because it didn't make any sense. Why, just why? And how? I work harder than anyone—I know I'm the best—but you always trumped me. So I hated you. But now that I know why you were better with machines, I just can't be angry. You're a freaking technomancer. That's basically cheating."

"You were *jealous*?"

Tabea thought back to all the times Nerissa had made her life hell. All that for petty jealousy? She'd guessed as much before, but she hadn't really believed that she'd been right. That it was all there was to it. Then again, what if their roles had been reversed? If Nerissa had suddenly taken Tabea's spot as the Academy's ace pilot without warning, she was sure that her reaction would have been similar resentment.

Nerissa shrugged.

"Even without it, I don't like you," she reminded her, but her grin remained.

Tabea chuckled and offered her rival a hand up. "That's okay. I don't really like you either," she said cheerfully.

They grinned at each other for a moment, united in shared dislike and respect for one another.

"Um, sorry, but can this wait?" Besma interrupted, waving her hand around. "Trying to escape an alien planet here? Saving everyone?"

Her frown brought the other two back into the moment.

Nerissa glanced at Tabea. "Can you do some space witchery to get us a ship and out?"

"No, their space witches blocked my power, so I can't use it. But if you can find Calliope, I'm sure she can help us."

"You talk like it's a person," Nerissa noted, frowning.

"She is. She's like my second half."

Nerissa sighed. "I don't get it, but—fine. You find Yuri, we'll try to find the ship, and you try to get your powers back or whatever. I don't know how they work, but I'm guessing they'll be coming in handy to escape from here."

She turned back to the vent and climbed in. Glowering, Besma turned to Tabea one last time before following Nerissa.

"There's a lot going on right now, and now isn't the time, but when all this is over, you and I are going to have words because I'm really, seriously mad at you. Don't you dare get yourself killed before we have our argument, you hear me?"

Tabea nodded, feeling relieved somehow. "You stay safe, too."

It couldn't have been another day before Sh't'ani returned to Tabea's room.

"I think I have found your friend," they said hesitantly. Their tail was hanging low, but it twitched at the tip, as if they weren't quite content with what they had found.

Tabea crossed over to them quickly, frowning. "What's wrong?"

Sh't'ani fumbled with their words for a moment, trying to find the right thing to say.

"Something about it doesn't feel right." They paused, nostrils flaring. "He is not kept like you are, and he regularly gets visits from P'cha'me and some scientists. It doesn't make sense."

While even Tabea would admit that it did seem odd, if Sh't'ani couldn't put a claw on it, she definitely wouldn't be able to. Instead, she decided to focus on the important matter at hand.

"Do you think you'll be able to get me to him?"

Sh't'ani hesitated, but then they relented. "If we time it right, yes."

"Okay. Could you also get me my old clothes back? The ones I wore when I first arrived on your ship?"

Their tail perked up. "I can," Sh't'ani assured instantly. "I kept your robes in case you ever got sad."

The notion gave Tabea pause, and she felt her heart melt a little.

"You're such a sweetheart!" She flung her arms around Sh't'ani in an embrace, though the Penyali was clearly startled by the action and tensed up. After a moment, their limbs relaxed a little, and they tried to mimic the gesture.

"I like this," they said. "But what is it for?"

Tabea laughed and let go, putting a step of distance between them. "It's a sign of affection. And you're my friend, aren't you?"

"Your friend?"

The words had a clear reaction on Sh't'ani. At first, their tail was completely still, but then it perked up and began waving around frantically, swishing from side to side so much, Tabea thought it could have tripped up an oncoming army.

"We're friends!"

Sh't'ani repeated those words to themself multiple times, and Tabea could only watch and marvel with a smile. Although seeing it also made her a little sad. There was too much happiness there for something that should have been as simple as friendship, and her earlier impression of Sh't'ani not being valued a lot, especially on this planet where they were apparently considered lower class due to their origin, increased with every moment.

When Sh't'ani had calmed down, they turned to Tabea once more before leaving. "I will get everything ready, and I will come for you later today so we can go to your friend."

Tabea nodded, delighted.

Not long now until she would find Yuri once more and find out why he was kept separately.

Deciding that she should be at the top of her strength

when that was going to come to pass, she lay down for a nap.

She dreamed of the night of the ball—her sudden inability to communicate with Calliope, from the moment Yuri had appeared, and his demeanor once he had discovered her secret.

"Don't trust him."

Calliope's voice rang out clearly in Tabea's mind.

She woke up, Callie's voice still lingering in her frontal lobe.

She remembered fully now. She remembered exactly what had happened on the ship, and she no longer doubted that her waking up in Penyali custody hadn't been an accident. Yuri had had something to do with it. And when she saw him later, she would find out just what that was.

For the first time, she began to wonder if she'd been lured into a trap when she'd jumped away from the attacking ships with the *Calliope*.

Remembering it felt strange. It seemed like eons had passed since that day, like an entirely different lifetime. And yet the ripples it had caused still traveled, still affected everything around her, changing her viewpoint with every passing moment.

It was a relief to know that her friends were on the same planet as she was. At least she could be certain that they were alive and nearby. This way, she could work to get away together with them, instead of alone. While it did seem like it would make things more complicated, it was reassuring to know she wasn't alone here.

Sh't'ani arrived eventually. They looked nervous, the tip of their tail twitching, their eyes flicking around constantly. They handed Tabea her old clothes, and without ceremony, Tabea put them on, the familiar, stiff, green uniform just as unflattering as ever, and yet so welcome to her. Sh't'ani had even kept her tags, and Tabea gratefully put them around her neck again, letting them rest against her bare skin. Once she had changed clothes, she pulled the robe over her head and pulled up the hood. Being able to change her outfit quickly in a pinch might come in handy. Plus, even just knowing that she was wearing her uniform again was a comfort to her. Somehow it made her feel more in control and filled her with confidence.

She followed Sh't'ani out quietly and they rushed through empty hallways. They didn't pass a single soul, and the only other Penyales Tabea saw in the building had their backs to them and were far ahead.

They went out into the dome, which was similarly quiet, and into another tower, where they entered some form of elevator and rose several levels.

The entire time, Sh't'ani continued to seem nervous, constantly looking around, checking their surroundings, evidently expecting to be caught. While it didn't help to reassure Tabea, she still thought it was good to see that her new friend wasn't overly comfortable with sneaking around and doing things they shouldn't have been. It made them more trustworthy.

Before long, they were making their way through the glass tunnels and had to pass the first other Penyales. Tabea kept her head low, to cast her face in shadows underneath the hood, and stepped in behind Sh't'ani.

Even though her heart pounded so loud, she thought it must have rumbled like an earthquake, they passed one another without incident.

The next encounter soon followed, however, and that time Tabea received an odd look. She held her breath, expecting to have been exposed. Luckily, they lost interest quickly, probably not noticing much aside from her small stature as they passed them by.

Sh't'ani and Tabea entered another building. At first glance, the interior appeared similar to the one where Tabea had been kept—built from the same type of material, and the same kind of design—but there were significantly more Penyales afoot here.

Tabea stuck close to Sh't'ani and they somehow managed to avoid most closer encounters, slipping past people, taking corners, and waiting for others to pass, until they reached a darker hallway. It was narrow, and Tabea would likely have walked past it, barely even noticing it was there, if Sh't'ani hadn't stopped in front of it and then, after conspicuously looking around, ushered Tabea inside.

"I'll wait here," they whispered. "It's the door on the right—it should open with this."

They handed her a hollow, ornamental talon, possibly some form of jewelry for Penyales to wear over their own claws like humans wore rings. Tabea accepted it and hurried down the hallway quickly, getting more nervous with every step.

She'd been so looking forward to seeing Yuri again, and to ensure herself that he was doing all right, that he hadn't been mistreated and that he was unharmed. But now, after her dream, her memory of that night returning, there was a part of her that wasn't sure if she ought to be happy to see him.

What if he had truly betrayed her and all those she held dear? What if he wasn't whom she had thought he was? Callaghan and Calliope had been wary of him—had they reason to be? Now that all those questions had formed in her mind, it was difficult to push them back and when she stood in front of his door, seconds away from opening it, she hesitated.

There was no guarantee as to what she would find behind that door. But she still had to check. Because Yuri was her friend, too, and she still couldn't shake the feeling of being responsible for him.

Determined and bracing for the worst, she opened the door, slipped in, and closed it behind her before she really took a look around.

The room she discovered was much like her own—though filled with more things. There were books—human books, actual paper and ink writings—and various pieces of technology strewn across the desk. Yuri sat at it, his back to her to begin with, but he turned around when the door closed and now stared at her openly, slightly shocked.

"Tabea." He gasped. "What are you doing here?"

She smiled at him—an involuntary reaction. With two steps, she was beside him and hugged him, unable to restrain herself.

"I'm so happy to see you!"

He barely reacted—evidently still in shock. But when Tabea pulled back to look at his face, she noticed that his expression had darkened.

"Is this another test?" he asked. "There's no need. I haven't gone human."

Confused, Tabea took a step back. "What are you talking about?" she asked carefully. The terrible feeling was once more rising in her stomach. She wasn't going to like this. Not one bit. "Yuri, it really is me."

His face was still, as if it were made from stone.

"You shouldn't be here," he said eventually. His voice was even; it no longer portrayed any emotion. "You need to go back. The Penyales need your help, after all. They won't be able to do it without you."

Her voice got caught in her throat. "How do you know that?"

He didn't reply.

Tabea stood firm and glared at him. "Who are you? Who are you, really?"

He met her stare for a moment, but then he dropped his eyes. "There is no point in telling you. It wouldn't do you any good. And as soon as they find out you were here, your life among the Penyales will change from what it was before. You won't even have a single thought to spare for something like me."

"Is that a threat?" She narrowed her eyes, watching him carefully.

"No. It's a prediction. I know how they work. If you want my advice, take one of the ships and blow yourself up. It's a kinder fate than what they have in store for you."

Even though his words were spoken evenly, Tabea detected truth in them. There was pain in his eyes—a glimmer of something else. Fear, perhaps?

"Who are you?" she asked again, but he shook his head.

"I told you—forget about it. Forget you ever met me. All you need to know is that I'm the reason you're here.

I brought them to you. And I doomed you and all your friends."

Bitterness seeped through his words, and he turned his back on her.

He was right. He was the reason she was here; he was the reason why her crew was imprisoned. Logically, Tabea knew that she had no reason to care about what happened to him. But she couldn't stop herself from still caring about him, against all odds. She wasn't about to go anywhere. At least not without finding out the whole truth.

"Tell me. Tell me why, at least."

Tiredly, he looked up at her. "They wanted you. So they came for you."

Tabea watched him silently for a moment, trying to piece together the puzzle. Things Calliope had told her before, things she hadn't listened to. Things that were now becoming apparent.

"You're not from Earth," she eventually said quietly. "You're not human."

He looked up at her, his pained expression making her heart stop for a moment. There was infinite sadness in his eyes, so much that she almost forgot why she was here and wanted to throw her arms around him once more to comfort him.

"No," he agreed. "I'm not. I'm not anything." He sighed, a sound that could have made ghosts cry, and gestured to the room at large. "I was created here, on this planet, designed to lie and betray." His gaze returned to her, and a bitter smile developed on his lips. "And I fulfilled my mission."

Tabea remembered the *Sonata*, and the claw marks that had been scattered across the walls. Her throat seemed to close up as she realized the implications.

"There never were any pirates, were there? You were the one who infiltrated the Sonata and it was the Penyales who came, wasn't it?"

He gave her a long, hard look. "What good will it do you to find out all the details of what did and didn't happen? You're here—stuck just as much as the rest of us. There's nothing you can do anymore. You're in their power. All you can do is give up and just do what they ask." He stood up. "You need to go. P'cha'me's probably on her way here again to ask me about Humanity. Don't let her catch you."

He crossed the room to the door, tapping it meaningfully, and, for a lack of knowing what to do, Tabea left. But before the door closed again, separating them, she turned to him once more, filled with determination.

"We're getting out of here," she promised, glaring and pushing her shoulders back. "With everyone. You better start deciding whose side you want to be on."

Then, the door was closed, and Tabea turned to Sh't'ani who was still waiting for her.

"Let's go back."

Trying to make up her mind, Tabea paced in her room. Sh't'ani had left her for the moment, which suited her just fine. She needed to get her thoughts in order. Yuri was a genetically engineered life form, designed specifically to get her trust so he could bring her here. The infiltration had worked almost too well. And she'd fallen for it, completely and utterly, despite

Calliope's repeated warnings. Even Callaghan, despite his initial distrust, had fallen under Yuri's spell.

And yet, Tabea couldn't bring herself to hate him. *They*, he'd said. Never *we*. He was just as much a prisoner of the Penyales as she was.

She fully intended to go back and talk to him again, but that would be the last chance for him to explain to her exactly what had happened. While it wasn't relevant for their escape, she *needed* to know. The gaps in her memory were too confusing, too scary. And she *deserved* the truth after everything he'd done.

Despite everything, she wanted to trust him. But she knew she couldn't. It created a whirlwind of emotion inside of her and she threw herself at the questions of when he'd been genuine, and when all he'd done was an act.

The door opened and Sh't'ani entered, twiddling their talons uncomfortably, interrupting her frantic thoughts.

"Your Yuri..." they said. "He asked me to give this to you."

They held out a letter, but before Tabea could take it from their claws, the door opened once more, letting C'ru inside. He barely glanced at Sh't'ani, but when he did, a crease appeared between his eyes, and they narrowed. Then he turned to Tabea.

"Let us commence another training session," he said, his tail swinging amiably. "We have much work to do before you can help us."

Tabea nodded, faking enthusiasm. Sh't'ani had somehow made the letter disappear in their robes instantly, and Tabea hoped that there would be an opportunity to read it later on, but the sooner she could get C'ru away from it, the better. Luckily, he gave Sh't'ani such little attention that the detail of the letter seemed to have wholly escaped him.

"Before we go," she asked innocently, "have you heard anything of my crew and our ship?"

He looked at her for a moment, and Tabea was sure that he was assessing his words carefully, trying to determine what he could say to make her believe what he wanted her to think.

"Our ships have caught up with the pirates," he said. "But it seems your friends are not in their custody at this time."

Remarkable, Tabea thought. *He's genuinely not lying.*

But he was nevertheless trying to deceive her. She nodded, casting her gaze down in a show of dejectedness, before looking back up at him. Softly, she said, "Thank you for all that you're doing, C'ru. I so appreciate it."

She tried to sound genuine, not quite knowing how much of a grasp their species had on sarcasm. From what she had learned, it appeared to be more of a human thing.

She followed him out, ready to be trained once more in abilities she hoped to be using to get away from them.

However, he didn't unlock her powers. Not this time. He led her through the halls into an almost empty room within the same building. There, they both took a seat, and C'ru turned on a projection of a three-dimensional hologram that filled the entire room.

"We are here." He pointed at one of the blue planets orbiting slowly around their star. Then his talon wandered to a planet that was slightly farther away from it. "This is Viridian."

He enhanced the image, increasing the size of the planet so Tabea could see it better.

They hadn't been kidding — it really was brown now, the color of clay.

With one movement of his claw, C'ru created an intersection of the planet, showing Tabea the different layers. Inner core, outer core, mantle, and so on. Then, with another movement, he made energy appear. It visualized as golden glittering, and it moved about the projection. The planet's surface was covered, but it had seeped deep into the ground and reached all the way to the core. Without being told, Tabea understood that she would need to draw that energy out somehow. But how exactly she could do that, she didn't know.

"I'm sure you've realized by now that our power is more than to generate and use energy," said C'ru. "More than manipulating energy and bending it to our will. We affect the essence of things."

Tabea nodded, and C'ru continued.

"For this endeavor to work, you will need to create an energy pulse of tremendous force at Viridian's core, to push back the nuclear energy with a sort of forcefield. Then as that energy gets ejected, we need to collect it before it can do harm elsewhere. Our own space witches will assist you with this part, of course."

And that was why he wanted her to learn how to encapsulate energy. In fact, if she encapsulated enough energy, another space witch could use it to create the energy pulse as well, without needing to carry the same power themselves.

"How much power will I need to use?" she asked, inspecting the hologram critically.

C'ru launched into a detailed explanation concerning numbers and techniques, but all that Tabea understood from his lecture was that he vastly underestimated her potential. She could already do far more than he needed.

Chapter 22

Tabea.
I had no choice.
But I do now. If you let me, I will explain everything.
Yuri.

It was only a short note, hardly anything to help Tabea make up her mind, but reading it, she knew she had to speak with Yuri. Even if it was always for her own satisfaction, she needed to know the truth.

She had trudged back after C'ru to her room across the dark ocean floor, only illuminated by the eerie, pale green bioluminescence of seaweed and algae stretching across the dome. Sh't'ani had been waiting for her still, along with Yuri's note.

"Well?" they asked, watching Tabea concerned. "What does he say?"

Tabea only held the note under their nose.

"I'm sorry. I can't read your language," they said apologetically. Suddenly, Tabea was reminded of Yuri in the library, looking only at blueprints and maps. Yes, it made perfect sense now. He'd had rudimentary reading skills, but he'd found it difficult. Nerissa must have helped him get better at it. They'd spent plenty of time in the library together as well, after all.

"He wants to talk to me again," she said. "To explain."

Sh't'ani watched her face carefully. "And do you want that as well?"

Tabea hesitated, even though she'd already made up her mind. With Nerissa and Besma doing all they could, she had to try as well. She cocked her head to the side, looking up at her friend.

"Yes. Will you... help me again?"

Sh't'ani's tail began to swing happily. "I will always help if you ask."

No point in wasting time. Tabea was exhausted, her senses dulled and movements sluggish, but she couldn't afford not to take the chance when the opportunity presented itself. And so, they only waited a short while before heading out.

Sh't'ani led her through the glow back to Yuri's building and straight toward his room. They passed no one.

"I will wait and keep watch," Sh't'ani promised. "Be careful."

Tabea nodded and, once more, entered Yuri's room. He'd been lying on his bed, apparently sleeping, but his eyes snapped open when she entered.

"So," she said, one eyebrow raised. "I guess you've got some explaining to do."

He nodded; his smile pained.

"Starting with the Sonata," she added, locking him into place with her fiercest, iron gaze.

When he began to speak with downcast eyes, she had to step closer and lean in to even hear him.

"It's... complicated. But it boils down to General P'cha'me using the pirates to find you, staying near them with her ship at all times, so C'ru could sense you if you were close. She told them there was a human space witch, and that they were more powerful than any others. After they attacked the Sonata, C'ru sensed your power, and they put me in place to infiltrate your ship."

"But your wounds," Tabea said, frowning. She'd dressed them herself. And he'd been in a critical state—none of that had been fake. "And what if I hadn't been there fast enough? The ship would have blown up no matter what!"

Yuri shrugged. "They had to make it believable. And what is the loss of one pawn, really, in the face of potential success?"

He spoke matter-of-fact, dryly, without emotion. His face didn't give away any part of what he might have been feeling. Unknowingly, Tabea's fists clenched, and her pulse sped up. Despite everything he had done, warmth for Yuri grew in her chest once again, and she choked up on his behalf. To be valued so little and feel the effects... She could relate.

Of course, her own experiences were nothing like his—she knew her family cared about her, in their own way, and they certainly would never leave her to die—but she at least had an inkling of how he must have been feeling. Tears gathered in her eyes as she contemplated his fate.

"But you know," he continued, his gaze taking on a faraway expression, "I really enjoyed my time on your ship. It was nice to feel... like an equal. Appreciated."

She took his hand and squeezed it. She was about to

speak, but the door opened, cutting her off.

"We have to go," Sh't'ani whisper-shouted. "A human has been caught spying in the general's study!"

Their words spurred Yuri into action. Fear entered his eyes, and he leapt to his feet, pushing Tabea out the door. "Go! It'll be even worse for you if they find you here now. Real bad. For all of you."

He gave Sh't'ani the briefest of nods before the door closed between them, shutting him back inside.

Confused, distraught, and worried, they rushed back to Tabea's room, where Sh't'ani left her alone to avoid any risk of suspicion.

Her mind was in turmoil, not only because of the information Yuri had just shared with her.

A human had been caught—was it Besma or Nerissa? Did one of her other crew members go on a reconnaissance mission? What was going to happen to them now?

Her thoughts only revolved around the captured human. What did it mean for them? Would they be killed? Or, as Yuri seemed to have suggested, would something worse happen to them?

Tabea wasn't left alone for long.

Soon the door was opened once more, and C'ru strode in, accompanied by General P'cha'me.

The sight of both of them, their eyes quickly scanning her room, seemed to only prove everything Tabea had learned so far. They'd expected her to be gone, or someone to be here with her. The best she could do was act natural.

"Are we having another lesson?" she asked, feigning ignorance. She forced a yawn.

C'ru narrowed his eyes. "No, not now. Excuse us."

They left once more, but Tabea couldn't get their piercing stares out of her mind for the rest of the night.

Despite her exhaustion, she paced up and down in her room for hours—one eye on the door, and one eye on the ventilation vent. She would have gone through the vents to look for the girls, but she didn't know where they had gone, and Yuri in his vagueness had made it abundantly clear what the Penyales might do if they found her room empty. So she could only hope that whoever was left would come to consult with her. But if they were going to take too long, she was going after them, to hell with Penyali threats.

"Psst, Space Cadet!"

Nerissa was peering through the grid, her usual haughty manner replaced by unease and guilt.

"Don't come into the room," Tabea hissed, trying to keep her mouth as still as possible. She stopped pacing and sat on the bed, picking up a scroll to stare at. "They might have installed some form of surveillance."

In the brief visit the previous night, P'cha'me had touched many items, talons lingering. It would have been easy to plant a bug of some sort.

A brief silence followed her words.

"But won't they be able to hear us then, too, smartass?"

"Maybe," Tabea admitted. "But at least they won't know how I can hear you. And I don't think they understand our language. With any luck, they'll think I'm talking to myself."

Nerissa gave a short, mirthless chuckle but

suppressed it quickly.

"They have Besma."

Even though Tabea had suspected that, hearing the words still caused a piercing pain in her chest. Sweet, always supportive Besma, who loved hot chocolate and bad movies. She bit her lip to stop a wail from getting out.

"How?" she eventually managed to grunt after taking a deep breath.

"We found something that looked like an office, and we tried to do a little snooping to see if we could find a blueprint, or weapons, or anything that could be useful, but then I heard steps approaching. I dived back into the vent, but Besma was still on the other side of the room, and she didn't make it before the door opened."

Tabea remained silent.

"There was a Penyali, scales purple, and it looked at her like… like she was a bug that needed squashing…" Nerissa was getting choked up. "I didn't know what to do—I didn't have any weapons, and the Penyales are strong, and they have talons, and… And Besma glanced at me and gave me a sign to stay put. Tabea, I'm so, so sorry."

There was true emotion in her words. Never had Tabea heard her nemesis speak like that.

"It wasn't your fault," she said. "And we'll get her back. I have… a feeling I may know what they'll try to do to her. So maybe I can stop it."

"How?"

"Yuri… insinuated some things."

"You found him?"

The excitement in Nerissa's voice was unconcealed.

She really likes him, huh?

"I did, but he's—"

She stopped herself. He was what? A traitor? A spy for the Penyales?

But that look on his face when she'd visited. The sadness, the bitterness. And the fact that he was locked in a room just like she was. Whether he was human or not, he was still a prisoner here. Despite everything that had happened, there was still a part of her that wanted to trust him, believe in him, naïve though it was.

"He's in one of the other buildings nearby," she settled on saying. She didn't want to call him a traitor. Not after everything he'd told her.

"But he's all right?"

"Yeah. They're treating him well. He's not hurt, and he's got everything he needs for the moment."

A relieved sigh escaped from the vents.

"Oh, I almost forgot!"

Tabea's ears perked up.

"We found where they brought the ship, but... there may not be much left of it."

"Where?"

"There's a miniature dome where all of us are kept, and there's a building there reaching up from the ocean bed until it's level with the island. The Calliope is there, in a large shed on the island near that tower, but they've pretty much completely dismantled her. Your friends from the med division were the ones who found it, Marco and his girlfriend. They said that the only thing more or less still intact was the energy source."

Relief flooded through Tabea's body. Calliope's core was still whole. Another thought followed quickly. That meant that the terrestrial limiters were gone, and her full potential could be unleashed. If only Tabea could get to her and have complete use of her powers once more, she could create a new ship around her core and help them all flee together.

A plan was slowly beginning to take shape in her mind. It would need to be exacted precisely, and she'd need a lot of luck on her side, but... it could work.

Footfalls interrupted Tabea's thoughts.

"Hide!" she hissed, and the door opened.

A space witch was waiting for her, but it wasn't C'ru. Their scales were a light orange, similar to the color of a flame's sparks.

"High Priest C'ru is requesting your presence," they announced. Tabea got to her feet and followed the space witch out, without even a single glance to the vent where Nerissa was still holding out.

She felt certain that she knew what C'ru wanted to talk about. Aside from getting her to restore Viridian, there was only one other thing they could want from her right now. If she was right, he was going to ask her about how her powers had manifested and then try to artificially recreate the same conditions for Besma. After all, they needed a backup in case something were to go wrong with Tabea. It was comic book logic 101.

Alternatively, he might put her into that machine again and try to siphon off her power to restore their planet himself before she could try to escape. Undoubtedly, they assumed that she'd made contact with the rogue humans traveling through Catha'ris.

The space witch marched quickly, and Tabea had to jog to keep up with their long strides. Once again, she added the new route to her mental map of the city.

As soon as they reached C'ru's office, the space

witch left the two of them alone.

C'ru was deep in meditation when she entered, a sight that made her stomach boil. How could he sit here so peacefully when he'd arranged for a whole ship to be slaughtered and kept all those dear to her prisoner? Still, for want of anything better to do, and to keep up the appearance of ignorance, Tabea sat down on the floor facing him and tried to meditate as well.

Flames and flickers of energy licked at the edges of her consciousness, wanting her to grab them, to hold on to them. Teasing her and taunting her, while begging for her to get a hold of them once more. That she could feel them as clearly as this was already more than she'd experienced in a while, and endorphins rushed through her. She now felt certain that her powers reached her in her sleep and had connected her with Calliope. How else could she have warned her about Yuri?

Though it seemed like C'ru's hold over her was weakening, Tabea made no active attempt at breaking through her barrier. Now was not the right time. Not yet.

She opened her eyes again to find C'ru observing her with open curiosity.

"What do you see when you meditate?" he asked.

"Well, mostly flashes of disconnected images, I guess. Colors, impressions, sometimes memories."

Tabea shrugged. There was no way she'd tell him what she'd discovered.

"Interesting. Then your kind must possess a natural connectedness with the stars."

Tabea frowned and tilted her head. "What do you mean?"

"Our kind does not benefit from meditation unless they are of the chosen ones. Yet humans do. I watched how your body started to relax the longer you were in that trance. The same is not true for us."

Tabea wasn't sure what to make of that information but hadn't Callaghan once mentioned something similar when teaching her about tai chi?

Let the universe's energy flow through your body. It's its natural state – don't fight it.

C'ru shifted his body, as if to go from a relaxed position to talking about business. Tabea followed suit, changing to kneeling so she could sit up straight more easily.

"Since we're on the topic," he said, "I would like to ask you a few questions. Did you always possess your abilities as a space witch?"

Tabea laughed inwardly.

I knew it!

"No, I was born an ordinary human. My abilities didn't manifest for a long time."

"I see, how strange. Was there an event that triggered it?"

Tabea reflected for a moment. How could she best go about this?

"I remember the day, actually," she said slowly. "I had just done an exam, and I'd done really well, and my mentor promised that I would be allowed to go on the next mission with him. I'd just taken a nice, warm shower and had a good meal, and I felt really good, at peace with everything, like everything was right with the universe, and then – bam! There they were."

"I see."

Even though C'ru still appeared curious, he also

seemed ever so slightly disappointed. He'd probably much rather had heard the true story about how she'd gotten zapped by lightning. Definitely an event that was easier to recreate, and so much more painful and dangerous to Besma.

"That suggests a latent possibility for all humans to manifest the powers of a space witch," C'ru noted. "Do you know of any others on your planet?"

Tabea shook her head. It was better not to lie on this point. She didn't want to know what the Penyales might do if they thought there were more of her. And she definitely didn't want to know what they might do to her and her friends if they no longer thought her vital.

"As far as I know, I'm the only one."

"I see."

C'ru got to his feet and moved to his desk, where he jotted something down. Tabea watched him, trying to calculate what his next move would be.

"High Priest C'ru," she said, after a moment. "Do you have any news of my friends?"

His head flicked up, his eyes piercing her. "Most of our ships have returned without finding them," he said, his gaze lingering on her for a moment.

His tone invited no further questions on the matter. Tabea was starting to see a pattern in the way he answered her questions about her friends. It was never a straight *yes* or *no*. Being from a race that couldn't tell untruths, he had become remarkably adept at omitting just the right pieces of information to make her believe what he wanted her to. Knowing that she could gain nothing from continuing in this vein, Tabea opted for a change in subject.

"What did you want to see me for today? Are we having another training session?"

C'ru nodded and crossed the room over to her to help her up. "We're going back to the hall. I want you to master the power storage."

Tabea cheered inwardly, but on the outside, she only followed C'ru obediently, though this time, he led her to a different, shell-shaped hall. The path there was much longer, leading through plenty of tubes, and brought them significantly closer to the hangar island. Large parts of the tunnels were underground on the way there, which led Tabea to believe that they might even be entering a different bubble, possibly the same her friends were being kept in.

The other space witches were already waiting in the hall along the walls. There were twice as many as before, and Tabea could tell which ones had been there last time by the nervous twitching of their tails.

C'ru lifted her power block, and she paid close attention to how the energy around and inside her felt as he did it. Every time he locked or unlocked her powers, it felt like she'd figured out another piece of the puzzle. At this point, she was very close to the full image. Perhaps she could even recreate the effect herself.

Then he showed her once again how to store her power in an object. While he did that, Tabea busied herself with creating a concealed bubble of energy, making sure that there was no way for C'ru or any of the other space witches to detect it, and then trapped it in the tags around her neck, hidden by her space witch's robe. Even though it had no traces of the metal C'ru considered necessary for the trapping of space witch energy, Tabea's bubble stayed put. Clearly, he knew a lot less about how his power worked than he let on.

When he was done with his demonstration, she followed his example openly but made sure to only trap a sliver of her power in the battery, enough to prove to him that she could do it, but not enough to be useful—or dangerous. She faked an exasperated, concentrated expression, even though, after last time's mistakes, she knew exactly what to do, how to do it, and was able to fly through it with ease.

"Done." She sighed, dramatically swaying back and forth and letting her eyes droop.

"I..." She broke off, pretending to almost collapse.

C'ru caught her, his eyes gazing down at her with clear satisfaction. He waved one of the space witches over and locked her powers away again. This time, too, Tabea paid close attention to how he was using his energy.

"Bring her back to her room."

Tabea didn't resist when the space witch picked her up. Her eyes were still trained on C'ru, who regarded the battery she had charged.

As she was carried out, she closed her eyes and went limp, pretending to lose consciousness.

She didn't open them again until she was alone in her room on the bed. Nerissa jumped out of the vent the moment the door closed.

"Tabea, what's wrong? What did they do to you?"

Tabea's eyes flicked open, and she smirked up at Nerissa. "Aw, you care about me! You were meant to stay in the vent, remember?"

"Yeah, well, you don't get to give me orders."

Nerissa glared at her for a moment, but it didn't last long. "What did they want?"

"They want to use Besma as a guinea-pig to see if they can artificially create space witches."

Nerissa's eyes widened. "What are they going to do to her?"

Tabea smirked again, relieved she had bought her friend some time. "Probably treat her really, really well. For a while, at least." She pulled out her tags. "Could you step back for a moment? I need to try something."

Nerissa looked like she wanted to argue, but something in Tabea's expression must have convinced her not to because she stepped back without another word, watching her closely.

The tags felt warm, and not just because they'd been sitting on her skin. They were hotter than that. She looked at them closely. Nothing seemed out of the ordinary otherwise, and she could sense no power from them. This was the moment of truth.

She bent them. Then she bent them back the other way, and she continued to bend them back and forth until, eventually, they broke in two. Only an instant later, power suddenly flowed out of the broken pieces. It was strong, at the edge of visible. Even Nerissa could sense it, judging by the hissing gasp she produced.

Tabea gently grasped at it with her mind and weaved it into her consciousness. She found the lock C'ru had been tending to and instead of picking it, she disintegrated it. No one was ever going to lock her powers away ever again.

She was back. The connections she had washed over her like before—like floodgates that were opened suddenly to connect what never should have been severed.

It was… almost too much.

Tabea dropped to her knees, gasping, yet delighting in the sensation of her powers having returned.

Immediately, she could sense Calliope. Weak but nevertheless there, exactly where Nerissa had told her she would be.

She could also feel the other space witches and knew that she didn't have a lot of time before they would feel her, too. Maybe they already had. Quickly, she concealed her presence as well as she could. It wasn't a guarantee, but it should buy her some time.

She looked up at Nerissa.

"Let's go."

CHAPTER 23

SHE DIDN'T HAVE A PLAN PAST THIS POINT.
Not really, anyway.

It was more of a vague idea of what needed to happen, and Tabea figured that opening that door was a good start. She was reaching out, her palm facing the door, when Nerissa placed a hand on her shoulder to stop her. With a smirk, she passed her, and approached the door herself. She pulled a pin from her hair and inserted it into the hole meant for the Penyali talons. After wriggling it around a little, the door slid open quietly. Tabea silently applauded, and Nerissa mouthed the word, "Engineer," with a little smirk.

Tabea wasn't able to send her power outside for reconnaissance very far—the planet's atmosphere prevented easy travel, and the building was made from some organic material that didn't conduct her energy.

It was almost definitely by design—in a nation with a large number of capable space witches, you didn't want them to seize ultimate power, after all.

She followed Nerissa out into the hall, looking from side to side. No one was around—yet.

Tabea took the path to the left, out of the building

into the dome. Meanwhile, she was repeating her makeshift plan in her mind. Step one: Rescue Besma. Step two: Get to her friends and help them escape. Step Three: Get to the *Calliope* and reassemble her.

After contemplating for a moment, she decided to put Calliope as the first step. If she was ready, an escape would be faster and easier, and Tabea reckoned that it would be simpler to conceal the ship having returned to a functioning state than to move all of the crew from a guarded location. She may not have a lot of time later on, and Calliope would likely require the most of her energy.

Keeping that in mind, she looked for one of the small transporter submarines at the edge of the dome, studiously avoiding the dome's center, where she knew many Penyales to go about their business. They managed to avoid a direct encounter on their way to the dome's edge, though only narrowly, by jumping behind statues depicting epic battles.

She finally found a whole lot of submarines in a small pool that evidently had an opening to the ocean underwater. Unfortunately, this area was busier than the rest of Catha'ris they had traversed. There was a steady coming and going of the transporters, with a stream of Penyales either getting out or getting in.

"Create a diversion," Nerissa whispered. "I have an idea."

Tabea didn't question it. After all, Nerissa wasn't her rival for nothing.

She directed her power at one of the empty pods and commanded it to jump out of the water and into the crowd of waiting Penyales, ideally without hurting anyone. She also requested for another one to force the incoming pods to veer away by getting into their way.

The diversion worked. The pod out of water created chaos as the Penyales stared in disbelief and evaded the thrashing submarine. It almost looked like a fish.

Nerissa was already slipping into a pod on the side of the small pool. Tabea followed quickly, jumping over the bannister, and slid into place next to her.

Staring at the text-based controls in Penyali, Nerissa cursed. "I can't tell how to fly this thing. I'd need more time to figure it out."

Tabea grinned. "Allow me."

She inserted the Penyali talon cover Sh't'ani had given her into the slot that was engineered for it and twisted it forty-five degrees before taking it out. Figuring out the remaining controls came naturally to her—she'd flown many planes before, and any part of the ship she didn't understand, she used her powers to quickly change that fact. Steering it was easy. Like a marlin, they slipped out of the parking lot, into the ocean, and within less than two minutes, they had reached the island.

She shot past it, surfacing on the far side after she had verified that no one was around. They alighted in a small, rocky bay, hidden from direct view.

"What are we doing *here*?" Nerissa asked, her face scrunched up in a frown so familiar to Tabea.

"Getting our ship ready," Tabea merely replied as she left the pod.

Without even sending out her own energy, Tabea could *feel* Calliope. Her essence radiated so much stronger than it had been before—probably because it was no longer blocked by terrestrial technology.

Tabea walked toward her friend with certainty,

Nerissa falling in beside her. A short while later, they had reached a hall by the shore, a hill blocking the view to the rest of the island, and, much to Tabea's surprise and amusement, she saw some small figures scurrying around the outside, peeking into windows. They froze when they noticed them, but Tabea kept going, unbothered.

Soon, they stood face to face.

"Hey, guys." Tabea smirked.

Felicitas and Marco stared at her with wide eyes, flicking to Nerissa for a moment, who shrugged and then stared at Tabea again.

Tears welled up in Felicitas' eyes and she threw her arms around Tabea.

"We thought you were dead!" she cried quietly. Tabea returned the hug and stroked her friend's back reassuringly.

"I'm here," she cooed. "And I'm gonna get all of us out of here."

Nerissa cleared her throat meaningfully.

"I mean *we* are gonna get all of us out of here," Tabea corrected herself, but she couldn't suppress an eyeroll.

"But how are you *here*?" Marco asked, frowning.

"It's a… long story."

"Is there a short version?"

Tabea glanced at Nerissa, who shrugged again. Well, the cat was out of the bag anyway. No point in trying to hide the truth from her friends anymore.

"The short version is that I'm a space witch and they're trying to use my power."

"Wait, really?" Marco gaped at her with equal measures of disbelief and understanding.

"*I knew it!*" Felicitas whispered into Tabea's shoulder. She freed herself and looked up at Tabea. "I knew it!" she repeated.

Marco sighed, shaking his head.

"I guess you called it. I still don't get how that's even possible, though."

Tabea exchanged another glance with Nerissa.

"How could you have possibly guessed that?" Nerissa asked, incredulous.

Felicitas grinned. "When she came back with Yuri and Shinay, she was in the med bay, and Marco and I were in charge of doing radiation tests when they were asleep. All of her test results were weird, and then later, there was—"

Marco interrupted her. "Don't we have something more urgent to deal with than talking about the past?" It earned him a sour glance, but Felicitas relented.

Tabea stepped past them both to peek inside through the window. She saw her immediately—her friend's core, blue light pulsing like a heartbeat, suspended in the air, seemingly held up by nothing other than her own power.

Her heart both leapt and sank seeing Calliope like that. She was incredibly happy to see for herself that her core truly was undamaged, but at the same time, Calliope had been stripped of everything. She was reduced to the innermost part of her being, basically like a ghost without true corporeal form. But Tabea could change that.

All around the hall were parts that had once belonged to Calliope, but far from everything there should have been. Too many components were missing. Tabea gnawed on her lower lip. She would have to cannibalize one of the Penyali ships for parts.

Other than what remained of Calliope, the hall was empty. There weren't even any Penyales around.

She turned to Felicitas and Marco. "How do we get in?"

They shared a look.

"There's a gate around the corner," Felicitas said.

Marco finished her sentence. "But we can't open it—only the Penyales are able to."

Nerissa flexed her fingers with a cocky grin. "Leave it to me!"

She delivered what she'd promised—within seconds of arriving at the gate, it was open, and the four of them could enter.

Tabea looked around the floor, where parts were strewn about carelessly. After a moment, she found what she was looking for. She reached out with her energy and commanded the parts of two connecting communication devices to assemble and come to her. Small parts from all over the hall were lifted off the ground as if by ghost hands and came together in a flash of light. When the light faded, Tabea held two coms in her hands. She handed one to Nerissa, and the other to Marco, turning to him and Felicitas.

"I need you two to look over the hill and tell us if any of the Penyali ships are unguarded. It needs to be one of the larger ones, though. It can't just be a small transporter."

They didn't react. Instead, both of them still stared at her, eyes wide and mouths gaping open.

"That. Was. Awesome." Felicitas breathed eventually. Nerissa rolled her eyes.

"Go already. You can fawn over the little witch

later," she said, ushering the two of them outside.

Once they left, Tabea concentrated and reached out to Calliope, but her friend seemed to have set up some form of barrier that prevented her from merging like they had done in the past.

"*Callie*," Tabea called out softly. "*It's me. I'm here to get you.*"

She reached out gently, instead of trying to force her way in, enveloping Calliope into a sort of hug of energy, taking care to make it feel warm and comforting, instead of like an attempt at merger.

"*I'm sorry it took so long.*"

It took only a moment.

Calliope opened up her barriers, like a flower bud blooming in the light, and returned Tabea's embrace.

"*It was about time,*" she said grumpily, though her bliss was barely disguised. Joyful energy spun around Tabea, weaving in and out with her own, dancing like flower petals carried by the wind.

"*Thank you for helping me before,*" Tabea said, hugging her tighter, a lump growing in her throat.

"*Someone had to do it. There's no way you could've made it on your own.*"

Tabea giggled, and Calliope fell in with her.

Then they became serious again.

With Calliope's aid, Tabea took an account of all the present parts and made an assessment as to what was still missing. She tried to only take into account the necessities to transport all of the crew and the power needed to transport them back into Earth's vicinity.

"*We have to be able to outrun them. We can't just rely on your power,*" Calliope pointed out, so Tabea made a note on creating boosters and hyperdrives with a longer capacity and reach.

"Tabea." Nerissa's voice reached her, muffled, as if she were pressing several pillows around her head or speaking underwater. "They said that there's a ship to the farthest left of here that's completely unguarded."

Tabea nodded to show Nerissa that she had received the information and concentrated. She left her body and sped across the island. It was harder here than it was in open space. More resistance due to the atmosphere, but not quite as difficult as underwater. Perhaps there was some form of mineral in the ocean here that made it more difficult. Tabea wasn't sure how long she'd be able to keep up. She could already tell her energy was draining. Still, she pressed on. She couldn't afford to fall back now, to give up. She couldn't afford to fail this time. At least the ground was a better conductor than the Penyali buildings were.

She reached the ship, vaguely recognizing the energy signatures of her friends nearby, and entered its data stream. Swiftly, she accessed the ship's computer, analyzing the make and parts at the speed of light and then commanded the parts she wanted to follow her.

She sped back, pulling most of the alien ship behind her, ignoring how much she was weakening, and united with Calliope once more. Her friend was able to bolster her power a little, keeping her up and supporting her as the pieces filed in. Then, together, they shaped a new body for Calliope, though minimalist, more advanced than the old one had been and still aimed to be operated by humans.

She gave Calliope everything she had.

Greeted by black and white dots in her vision and ringing in her ears when returning to her body, she dropped to the ground, her breath heaving.

"Tabea!" Nerissa yelled, crossing over to her. "What's wrong?"

Tabea tried to look up at her, but she couldn't even make out her face. She closed her eyes.

"Too much... power," she whispered, and then she fainted.

She woke up facing Felicitas and Marco.

"Welcome back, sunshine." He grinned.

Tabea pushed herself up. "How long was I out?"

Nerissa sighed, barely disguising the relief in her voice. "Only a few minutes. It's a good thing they're from the med team."

Tabea looked from Felicitas to Marco. "Thank you."

"Are you kidding me?" Marco burst out. "That was freaking awesome! I've never seen anything like it!"

Tabea managed a thin smile and sat up fully. "Thanks. But we've gotta go."

Nerissa nodded and turned to the other two. "You two, go back to the crew and prepare them for the escape. We'll come as soon as we have Besma and Yuri back."

Tabea flinched at Yuri's name, but she bit her tongue. She couldn't bring herself to tell Nerissa what he'd done yet.

"They were captured?" Felicitas' hands flew to cover her mouth.

Tabea nodded grimly.

"We'll fill you in later. Now go!" Nerissa ordered as she put one arm under Tabea's, helping her stand.

Tabea felt wobbly, but she wasn't in danger of falling over. She wanted to speak to Calliope before she left, but she found that she had used up too much of her energy. It would be difficult enough piloting the submarine without her powers, but she would manage, and hopefully, her powers would return in time for the crucial moment.

Nerissa half-carried her to the submarine and they filed in like before. Weakly, Tabea wrapped her hands around the controls and after taking a few deep breaths to gather and focus herself, they set off.

Nerissa gave her an extended sidelong glance but didn't speak.

Within moments, they were back at the larger city dome, now back to the same problem as before of not getting detected by anyone. Instead of heading back to the parking lot, Tabea kept an eye out for docking points higher up in the towers.

"You wouldn't happen to know where they're keeping Besma, would you?" she asked, but Nerissa shook her head.

"I didn't exactly have the chance to track them."

Where would they keep her? Unlike with Tabea, they wouldn't pretend to be on her side—not in the same way, at least, because it couldn't possibly work. Suddenly, she wished she had a way of contacting Sh't'ani. They would know how to find out. The only other person who might have an inclination... would be Yuri. Grinding her teeth with worry, Tabea headed toward the tower where he was kept. She found a docking station—luckily currently not in active use— then pulled up the hood of her space witch robe over her head.

"You should stay and hide around here somewhere," she told Nerissa, but the latter only crossed her arms and lifted one eyebrow.

"And let you go off on your own when you're obviously in suboptimal condition? Yeah, right. You don't always get to be everyone's hero, space cadet."

Truthfully, Tabea was a little relieved. Having the extra hand really could come in handy, and she might not have to explain anything about Yuri. He might take that responsibility over from her.

They peeked their heads around the corner, out of the docking station. Seeing no one, Tabea waved for Nerissa to follow her. They were a few levels too high up to reach Yuri, but that could be remedied quickly. By now, Tabea knew the rough layout of most of these towers—it was more or less the same for all of them. Finding the elevator was no problem, and thanks to Nerissa, operating it wasn't, either. However, the floor they now found themselves on was considerably busier than the other one had been. If Nerissa had a disguise as well, it wouldn't be quite as much of a problem, but this way... trying to think of a solution gave Tabea a headache.

"This is a stealth mission," Nerissa whispered into her ear. "My specialty."

Tabea could practically hear the cocky grin, but she still allowed Nerissa to push past her.

"Follow me, and don't lag behind!"

Tabea knew better than to argue, and she was rushing after Nerissa from shadow to shadow, corner to corner, waiting for good opportunities at each location while she whispered directions to her nemesis.

Before long, they had reached the narrow passage

leading to Yuri's room, miraculously, without incident.

Tabea indicated toward the door, and Nerissa worked on opening it. They entered swiftly, closing it behind them to avoid detection, and turned to find General P'cha'me sitting in a chair beside Yuri.

P'cha'me's tail swung satisfied as she narrowed her eyes at them. "C'ru suggested this might happen, but I didn't fully believe it. I'm glad I listened to him." She casually stood up and sauntered over to Tabea, grasping her chin and forcing her to look at Yuri. "It's remarkable, isn't it?"

Tabea remained silent, her core frozen solid in both fear and shock. She hadn't yet restored her powers— how could she get them out of this?

"It looks so human—acts human, too. Our scientists really outdid themselves with this one."

Yuri, who had been staring at them with an expression of shock, now averted his gaze, guilt and regret drawn on his face.

"It had all of you fooled, didn't it?" P'cha'me continued. "And now you came to save it, how foolish you've been."

Nerissa crossed over to Yuri and threw her arms around him. "Yuri! We'll get out of this, don't worry. I'm so glad to see you!"

Of course. She couldn't understand P'cha'me. Tabea was the only one who had received the translation implant. Except now... perhaps Besma had received one as well.

"I..." Yuri's voice broke, but he recovered. "I'm so sorry."

Nerissa held him at arm's length, confused. "What are you talking about?"

Then, realization dawned on her face, and she whipped around, her eyes meeting Tabea's. In them, she read everything she hadn't known before.

P'cha'me moved her grip to Tabea's shoulder, digging her talons in painfully. Blood trickled down Tabea's arm, but she didn't give P'cha'me the satisfaction of making a sound or even flinching. She had no doubt as to what would be next. The pain that was about to be inflicted on her — nothing compared to this trivial prick.

"Well, we'd better be going. We have work to do, after all." P'cha'me veered Tabea out of the room and turned to Yuri before leaving. "See to it that one doesn't cause trouble."

Yuri nodded almost imperceptibly.

The door shut and Tabea was alone with P'cha'me, pulled along whether she liked it or not. She'd fallen right into their trap. They'd predicted her movements. Had Sh't'ani been involved? Had the Penyales predicted Tabea's stunt on the hangar island as well?

At least they wouldn't find Calliope helpless. Tabea had seen to that.

Chapter 24

She'd guessed right.

P'cha'me brought her into a large hall with the orbital construction already set up. There weren't many Penyales here—only a handful of space witches, including C'ru.

Besma struggled in his grasp when she saw Tabea enter.

"Tabs!" she shouted, wriggling free and running over to her. Her approach was cut short by P'cha'me stepping in the way and grasping Besma's throat with her talons. She squeezed slightly, enough to make Besma make a gurgling, choking sound as she tried to pry the talons away from her neck. P'cha'me didn't even seem to notice the girl's struggle. Her eyes were set on Tabea, watching, as if to see how she would react.

Even though she still felt week and powerless, Tabea glared at the general, suppressing every urge to jump forward and attack her.

"Let her go," she said slowly. "She has nothing to do with this."

P'cha'me didn't respond. Instead, she lifted one

talon and poised it so the sharp tip poked into Besma's throat. Besma flinched, her eyes wide, staring at P'cha'me, still clutching at the general's claws as a drop of blood found its way down Besma's neck. The grasp loosened a little to allow Besma to breathe, but no more. P'cha'me's tail flicked curiously.

Fury was raging in Tabea's stomach at seeing her friend being dangled in front of her like this, but she forced herself to remain calm.

"If you want to use my power, you will *stop* hurting her," Tabea ordered, hoping she was managing to make her voice remain steady and serious.

"You don't seem to understand," P'cha'me said, amused. "You're not in any position to ask for anything. If I need to kill this one, so be it. There's a whole barn full of others."

To underline her threat, she pushed her talon deeper into Besma's neck and pulled it to the side, creating a long, gashing wound, which, though shallow, produced immediate squalls of blood that tainted Besma's T-shirt.

"Stop!"

The terrified screech had left Tabea's mouth before she could even hold a thought. The crimson liquid was still pouring, mixing with tears of fear flowing from Besma's wide eyes. P'cha'me's talon lifted but remained poised in a position where it could be at Besma's throat in a matter of the blink of an eye.

"Stop," Tabea repeated, whispering. Her eyes were glued to Besma's, begging for forgiveness, trying to figure out a way out of this mess. This was Tabea's fault. All of this was her fault. And she had to make it right.

Besma met her gaze, glassy with tears and fear, but her lips were pressed together into a thin line, and her brows furrowed, proving that despite everything, she was determined to get out of this. She trusted Tabea.

Time to prove herself worthy of that trust.

Tabea tore her gaze away from her friend, glanced at C'ru, curiously hovering nearby, and then looked up at P'cha'me.

"I won't resist," she promised. "But promise me you won't harm her any further. You won't harm any of my friends."

P'cha'me's tail weaved slowly from side to side in a calculated manner.

"If from now on you do exactly as we say, I promise your little friends will not be actively harmed by us."

Her phrasing left far too many loopholes, but Tabea could only clench her teeth and accept it.

"Tabs, no, don't!" Besma's cry was cut short by P'cha'me squeezing her throat again.

"I'll do it, so stop!" Tabea shouted, and the general's grip was released once more, leaving Besma coughing and spluttering.

She didn't have a choice. Her power hadn't returned.

Left without options, Tabea allowed herself to be strapped into the orbital machine by C'ru.

How they expected to siphon off her power when she had none, she didn't know, but she suspected that they didn't realize that she was drained. And perhaps she wasn't. After all, her energy had trickled back enough that she could sense the machine in front of her, threatening as it was.

"It'll be quick," C'ru promised. "And once we've unlocked your secrets, you will be able to rest."

A shudder ran through her at his last word. He'd spoken unemotively, and the meaning of his words was not lost on her. They were going to break her. Literally.

She didn't doubt that they had doubled up on the guards for the rest of the crew—maybe even injured some more of them for good measure ahead of time. Only a miracle could help them now. Or complete and utter chaos.

The machine turned on, the ring at first orbiting slowly, then faster and faster until it was only a blur. Tabea closed her eyes, expecting the pain to start. But she still wasn't prepared for it when it came. She screamed her heart out as every part of her body was burning and sliced up while being melted back into her shape. Ashes and embers coursed through her veins, burning at every touch. Her lungs were filled with syrup, drowning and suffocating her without releasing her to death. Her skin and flesh disintegrated, leaving behind only her skeletal, animated remains. At least, that was the reality of pain she felt.

But equally bad to the physical pain was the knowledge that she'd failed—she hadn't been able to save anyone, and before long, all of her friends would be used as test subjects as the Penyales tried to create more space witches to manipulate and use, like they were using her.

She didn't want to think of that, didn't want to think about her enemies. Instead, she wanted her thoughts to dwell on those she cherished, their faces, and their joint memories.

A certain feeling of peace rolled over her, not quite covering up the pain, but dulling it nonetheless.

Suddenly, Tabea felt freer. She remembered flying through space alongside Calliope, practicing tai chi with Callaghan, doing her lessons with Shinay, helping out Hammond and Vincent, and joking around with Besma.

She felt lighter, remembering Callaghan's mantras.

Let the energy flow. Don't resist it.

And Calliope as well.

You need to let it be a part of you, not just a tool you use, you know.

And Tabea let go.

Allowing everything to be taken from her, allowing the machine to blow past her resistance and brush it away, she became one with the universe. The pain dissipated into no more than a meaningless itch as she flew past planets and asteroids. The desolate plains of Viridian, the heat of the sun, the infinite dance of the solar systems and galaxies. She could feel the other one hundred and eleven true space witches in an infinite distance, and she could sense every living creature dying and being born. The pain that brought the first breath, the freedom and release that brought the last. Feeling the energy exchange, she saw the chaos that made it beautiful and perfect.

Time to add a little more chaos to create true balance right here.

She opened her eyes, blazing with silver light, and lifted her head, blasting a beam into outer space. In it, she encoded a very important message, knowing it had been received the moment she sent it. Then she destroyed the machine. It wasn't hard to flip it into overdrive and self-destruction. All she had to do was give it more power than it could handle. Not a difficult task for someone who was made of pure energy.

She noticed C'ru and the other space witches try to stop it, to turn it off in time, but they weren't fast enough. The connectors were already fried, and the machine wasn't going to work again anytime soon. To complete the job, Tabea pushed just a little more energy its way to make it explode.

Even the straps holding Tabea down had burned away.

Enough play time. Now things right here needed to be dealt with.

Most of the space witches had gone for cover to escape the flying debris, but two had stationed themselves on either side of P'cha'me, creating a forcefield as protection.

Tabea got to her feet easily and slowly, deliberately, walked toward them, toward P'cha'me, who, talon still at Besma's throat, stared at her with equal parts wonder and horror.

"Let. Her. Go," Tabea commanded in no unclear terms. Her voice barely sounded like her own. There was more resonance in it, as if someone much older, something much less human, was talking through her. P'cha'me narrowed her eyes, putting pressure on Besma's neck. A new drop of blood emerged. Besma didn't react to it. Her eyes were fixed on Tabea as closely as everyone else's.

Suddenly, a claw reached around Tabea's head, pressing into a specific spot on Tabea's forehead.

Tabea only smiled and turned to C'ru.

"That won't work anymore," she told him. C'ru stepped away, fear finally reaching even him. He understood. He'd read his own scrolls, after all. So he knew exactly what was happening.

Tabea turned her attention back to P'cha'me. She didn't have much time.

Like the machine, her body could not withstand that much power, either, at least not for long. She was already burning up from the inside out. If she kept this up for much longer, she would die.

P'cha'me still didn't release Besma.

Sick of waiting, Tabea took matters into her own hands, and, using technomancy, commanded parts of the machine to come together into something new around the general.

P'cha'me only saw it coming in time to jerk her hand back before it would have been cut off. Besma, now released, grabbed a long metal pole—a part of the destroyed machine—and whacked any Penyales who dared to get in her way as she ran toward Tabea.

As their hands clasped together, Tabea felt a weight drop off her shoulders, as if a mountain were splitting apart in that instance. The blood on Besma's neck was already drying. It really had just been a superficial cut.

"Let's go," Besma whispered, her voice still raw from P'cha'me's choking, and Tabea nodded.

Without further hesitation, they ran for the exit. Using the last of her strength, Tabea jammed the doors so it would take the other space witches a while to open it again. Then she released all of the galactic power she had been holding. Her eyes returned to normal, only to burn and water, and she was able to take no more than three steps before she collapsed—

—directly into Sh't'ani's arms.

Besma flinched back, but Tabea smiled. "Hey Sh't'ani," she said weakly. "I'm glad to see you."

"And I you, T'bea," Sh't'ani responded gently, yet quickly. "We must hurry." They picked her up carefully, ensuring to cradle her head.

"It's okay," Tabea said to Besma, who was preparing to whack Sh't'ani with her metal pole. "They're my friend."

Besma glanced at Sh't'ani uncertainly and, though grasping her pole a little tighter, nodded and followed as the Penyali nurse led the way.

Tabea lost consciousness for a moment during their escape, despite the adrenaline pumping through her veins. From the few glimpses she caught, she gathered that getting outside took a little while, as they needed to duck around corners to avoid detection by some guards who had been alerted by the sounds of Tabea's destruction.

They had barely reached the outside of the hall when Yuri and Nerissa ran toward them.

"There you are!" Nerissa shouted, relief flooding across her features, though they clouded over into uncertainty when she saw Sh't'ani.

Tabea became vaguely aware of tumultuous activity around them. Penyales were running all over the place, not even paying attention to them. And above them... The sunlight was blocked by something and something was consistently disturbing the ocean's surface.

"The planet is under attack," Yuri added. "We've got to go — *now!*"

Tabea nodded, clarity slowly returning to her again. "You can let me down," she told Sh't'ani. "I can walk alone. Thank you for all your help." She threw her arms around their neck and squeezed before letting go again. "You should get somewhere safe."

But Sh't'ani shook their head. "Nowhere is safe for me now."

Tabea understood. In helping her, Sh't'ani had sacrificed everything. The Penyales would never accept them again.

"Then you can come with us," she decided.

"*What?*" Nerissa and Besma shouted in unison. Tabea pointed at Yuri.

"If you can bring the genetically engineered lifeform who got us into this mess, then I can bring a trustworthy friend who is literally incapable of lying and has done nothing but help me since the day *he* betrayed us."

Nerissa's confused gaze flew from Sh't'ani to Yuri and back. Besma looked no less puzzled.

"How about we discuss the details later?" Yuri asked, his gaze focused behind Tabea.

"Get them!"

The shout from the hall's entrance spurred them into action. Tabea glanced back.

C'ru and the other space witches were filing out, hands raised to use their powers.

What are they going to do? Tabea thought frantically, looking around them to take notice of the first moving object. She noticed a generator to their left that was trembling suspiciously, moments before it took off.

"Everybody, down!" Tabea shouted, and they all flattened themselves to the ground, just in time for the large object to fly overhead them and miss. Tabea glanced back again. C'ru's tail was stiff with anger, and his eyes were blazing with fury. Clearly, he'd recovered from the surprise she'd given him. She gulped.

The only reason why they had missed was that it

was harder for multiple people to aim at the same target simultaneously. It was like multiple, blindfolded people operating a single slingshot at the same time.

"Go, go, go!" Yuri urged everyone on. He crouched down next to Tabea, as everyone else kept moving, to help her up.

"I don't know if it means anything to you." He panted as they ran on, pulling her along by the hand. "But I'm really sorry I tricked you all."

Tabea glanced at him. She didn't doubt his sincerity, not this time.

"I'm guessing you didn't have much of a choice," she said, glancing back again. C'ru raised his hands again, along with the other space witches. Before he could give a command, though, one of the towers collapsed in front of them, creating a massive hole in the dome.

Tabea didn't know if this was better or worse for them, but she sped up nonetheless, following her friends to the submarine lots as fast as her tired and aching legs would carry her.

Besma and Nerissa had already filed into one of the small underwater transporters with Sh't'ani when the crashing waves reached them, but Tabea and Yuri were swept off their feet. Their hands were torn apart and Tabea immediately lost all sense of direction as she was pulled under by a strong current. She tumbled wildly through the water, not knowing up from down. Even though her eyes were open, trying to see anything, she could make out nothing in this water. Then, finally, she reached the surface for just a moment, breaking through to the air, with barely time to take a single gasping breath before she was pushed under by another wave. Whether by shock or weakness, she didn't know, but as she was thrown around with neither sense nor purpose, she breathed in the water and it burned its way to down her throat and to her lungs. Thrashing around wildly in a desperate attempt to find air succeeded finally, as she grasped on to a piece of floating debris. Pulling herself up, she coughed, spluttering, to eject the water that had so forcefully entered her body. When she was finally able to take a breath with burning lungs, she looked around.

The city looked completely different than it had only moments before. Two towers had come crashing down on the dome, cracking it, but outside, many more had been scattered around the ocean floor in pieces. Submarines and boomerang hovercrafts were swarming around the dome without order, heading up, mostly, where shadows and light followed one another in a rapid-fire storm. None of her friends were anywhere in sight.

"Yuri!" Tabea yelled, though her voice was weak getting past her aching throat. Her body was tiring too. She really wasn't sure how long she could hold on to her life craft. There were only waves around her, and the water was rising quickly. Before long, she would be pushed against the dome's ceiling, but even if she managed to make it to the hole, she would never be able to make it up to the surface quickly enough. They were too deep down, and she had too little strength left.

Her clothes were heavy in the water, and they seemed intent on pulling her down. Another wave crashed over her head, tearing the debris from her grasp as it pushed her under water once more. She managed to fight her way back up, but only for a moment before her clothes pulled her under again. Her lungs screamed at her with fire and pain while she held her breath, trying to get back to the surface.

Then a hand grasped her wrist and pulled her up and out of the water, pulling her into a dry seat. A hand remained on her back as she coughed out any water she'd swallowed. When she returned to her senses, she realized she was in the cockpit of one of the submarines, with Yuri sitting next to her, grinning impishly.

"Now we're even," he said as he pulled her into the submarine. "You've saved my life, and now I've saved yours."

Tabea shoved Yuri aside after he almost flew them straight into a crumbling tower. She took control of the craft with ease, starting to get comfortable with the controls, and skillfully avoided the falling debris and other submarines around them.

She wondered where C'ru and his underlings were. If they caught so much as a glimpse of her and her friends, it was over. C'ru would command the submarine to return and there was nothing she could do about it in her current state. But right now, he either wasn't in any position to use his powers, or he simply didn't know in which of the thousands of submarines she was. She banked on the latter.

She kept the transporter low in the water, close to the ground, to avoid detection and give them more time to evade falling debris.

Before long, they reached the island, though things were just as chaotic here as they had been at the city. Submarines were whizzing through the waters here, too, and, the water being shallower, the enemy lasers reached all the way to the seabed, creating pillars of boiling water. Tabea weaved through falling transporters, darting behind rocks and through water plants.

Sweat poured in streams from her glands. She felt like she was back in the simulators—the feeling of fear the same, even though it was so much more fatal now.

"Look out!" Yuri warned, pointing at a submarine that had clearly lost all control and was now hurtling toward them at an insane speed.

Tabea narrowly avoided colliding with it by making their craft do a belly roll sideways.

Soon, they reached the facility Nerissa had described to her, and, after docking, Tabea sent Yuri to help the others get the rest of the crew out and ready into submarines set to follow her, hoping that any guards would be more concerned with warding off the attackers than guarding weaponless and injured prisoners.

Some small enemy ships were now diving into the waves as well, heading for the city's center. Unlike the boomerang hovercrafts or the fishlike submarines, these were dark, roundish capsules, with fluttering wings, almost like those of a dragonfly.

You won't find me there, Tabea thought, both satisfied and startled at how well her plan had worked.

Now, she drew forth the last shred of power she had to call for her friend.

"Callie, can you hear me?"

"Loud and clear. By the way, I've engaged camouflage mode and left the island because, let me tell you, it's pandemonium up here!"

Tabea sighed with relief. She'd hoped giving Calliope more autonomy would help her for situations exactly like this, though admittedly, she hadn't expected it to be needed quite so soon.

"Great! When I give you the signal, I need you to come into the water and open the loading bay so we can all enter with our submarines. And then, you need to get us out of here — fast."

"Roger that. And Tabea?"

"Yeah?"

"Good job."

Chapter 25

Weakened as she was, Tabea waited in her submarine, watching everyone else squeeze into the remaining pods by the edge of their dome. The machines held more people than their design really allowed for, but Tabea hoped that with a distance that short, it shouldn't matter too much. Yuri programmed all of them quickly, Sh't'ani helping him to make sure that all of them locked on to the one Tabea commanded.

Meanwhile, the battle still continued. Almost all of the guards had been drawn into the fight, leaving it an easy task for her crew to deal with the few remaining Penyales. They were sitting at the side of the dome, tied together, glaring at everyone, Sh't'ani and Yuri in particular. Tabea was only glad that they were protected from direct blasts from the enemy spaceship above by the island's overhang.

Her heart jumped when she saw Callaghan, unharmed, file into one of the submarines with Hammond and two cadets. Another jump was reserved for Vincent, clutching his left arm in a sling as he followed Marco and Felicitas. His face was purple and bruised—but he wasn't the only one injured. Many of the crew had blemishes on their faces, or a limp to their walk. Muted anger once more flooded through Tabea, but she suppressed it. Now was not the time for that. Instead, she needed to focus, to regain her energy, so that she could get them all out of here.

She closed her eyes and breathed deeply, focusing on her chakras one by one, willing her own energy to flow from one to the next. The steady trickle of returning power grew, but not by much. She opened her eyes again to watch her crew, but kept going with her breathing exercise.

It wasn't long before everyone had boarded one of the machines.

That was her cue.

"Callie — now! We'll be heading away from the island."

Seeing as Yuri had joined Nerissa in one of the other machines, Tabea turned her submarine around and shot forward, all the others falling in behind her at similar speeds.

One look at the radar told her that they'd drawn some of the fire away from the main fight. She grinded her teeth. She'd hoped that they'd be able to avoid detection for a little while longer. But it had been inevitable. After all, what could be more suspicious than a small fleet of ships heading away from the fight?

She raced on until she saw a dark square opening up ahead where before there had only been water. She drove straight into it and braked with full power. The other submarines did the same, some crashing into one another, and the opening closed once again, leaving them in complete darkness.

The world around them trembled as fire hit them,

and Tabea opened her submarine and jumped out before Calliope had even had a chance to fully drain the water.

She sprinted to the new bridge, looking at the screens. Despite their camouflage cloak, they were still in the line of fire. A lot of the shots missed, proving that it was mostly aimless, lucky shots.

Calliope, as the humanoid shape Tabea saw her in her core, appeared on the holo-pad next to her.

"Water drained and Cabins pressurized. Shields at seventy-eight percent. Preparing to leave atmosphere now."

Tabea nodded and rushed to the pilot's seat. "You focus on firing back and blocking their shots. I'll get us out."

It was the first time she'd flown a large spaceship the normal way outside of a simulation, but Tabea *knew* this. This was her element.

She raised Calliope's nuzzle and shot up, breaking through the water planet's atmosphere within seconds. Her heart soared when she saw the planet grow smaller underneath, but they weren't out of the woods yet.

The scanner showed that one ship had been waiting out here, and another was pursuing from Cerulean.

Unbeknownst to her, the ship's senior officers, along with Nerissa, Yuri, and Sh't'ani, had entered the bridge.

"This is... different," Callaghan muttered. Tabea glanced back.

"It's still Calliope," she assured him.

As if to underline her point, the holographic projection of Calliope as Tabea saw her appeared on a circular pad next to the helm. A well-trained figure wearing a space core uniform and sporting a pixie cut smirked at him from the translucent, blue sheen.

The personification of the ship saluted at Callaghan.

"I'll get us out of here in no time. Leave it up to me, captain."

Callaghan looked to Tabea, slightly panicked, but she only smiled and shrugged.

"It's a new feature I installed so I'm not the only one she argues with anymore."

Callaghan cleared his throat. "In that case, it's nice to meet you officially, Calliope. We'll be in your hands." Then he crossed the room to Tabea and studied the screens in front of her. "How is the situation looking?"

Tabea pointed at the dots behind them. "Two pursuers. I think one of them is Penyali and the other the pirates."

Calliope switched the screens to create a rear view. The difference in the ships was clearly visible—one elegant, sleek, yet menacing—the picture-perfect Penyali ship, and the other displaying indications of many fights, looking somewhat dilapidated in its patchwork design but probably nothing but a killing machine.

"The pirates," Yuri said confused. "How did they get here?"

"I called them," Tabea said nonchalantly, though she didn't let the ships out of her sight. To her relief, they were beginning to shoot at one another, fighting out who would get to claim the *Calliope* as their prize. This should give them ample opportunity to escape.

She could feel multiple eyes on her. "They were looking for me the same way the Penyales were, and for the same reason, so I figured, why not let them battle it out?"

Both of the ships trembled and Tabea could feel the crackling energy from here.

"They both have space witches," she whispered to herself. Sh't'ani walked up behind her.

"But none of them as powerful as you," they said, awed.

Akari walked up as well, pushing Tabea gently out of the pilot's seat.

"If that's the case, can't you, you know, make them" — she mimicked sparkles with her hands — "vanish?"

Tabea shook her head, watching Akari take back her controls. She took an inward inventory. Her energy was still returning painfully slowly. It was a miracle she hadn't passed out yet. Only adrenaline kept her standing at this point.

"Right now, I basically have no power left," she said. "It'll take me a few days to recover."

Someone wrapped their arms around Tabea from behind. It was Valeria Shinay.

"Well, I'm just glad you're all right, kiddo." She smiled warmly, squeezing Tabea.

Tabea smiled back, the relief finally catching up to her. She'd done it — she'd managed to leave the planet with all of her friends.

When Shinay released her, Hammond clapped her shoulder.

"Well done, lass," he said. "I like what ye've done with the ship."

It could have been her imagination, but Tabea thought she could make out a little more moisture than normal in the old man's eyes.

She wanted to turn to Callaghan then, but something

on the screen caught her attention.

The pirates' ship veered off, after clearly having taken some vital internal damage, and the Penyali ship was once again hot on their trail.

"High Priest C'ru," Sh't'ani whispered, fear marking their features. Tabea nodded. He was the only space witch on Cerulean who had that kind of power—and he had plenty of underlings to help.

She turned to Calliope's hologram and smirked. "Callie, wanna try out our secret weapon?"

Calliope sighed wistfully. "I thought you'd never ask."

Tabea left it to her friend. Only a moment later, a powerful blast shocked the Penyali ship—a blast imbued with not an insignificant amount of Tabea's own power—a little extra she'd included during her remodel of Calliope's body.

"What was *that*?" Yuri asked, staring, as the other ship momentarily lost power. It regained it after a moment, though only for basic functionality. Tabea had made sure of that.

"A goodbye present," she said. "You could imagine it sort of like an EMP with a little extra spark." She snapped her fingers." Which… should lock their space witch powers as well."

Callaghan looked at her, shocked and awed in equal measure. "When did you learn how to do that?"

Tabea shrugged and her gaze darkened. "It's something you pick up when it's done to you over and over."

She'd been able to break free from it herself, but she doubted that C'ru could figure it out. She wasn't even certain that any of the other space witches on Cerulean were powerful enough to break her lock, but then... He did still have that small amount of her power in a battery. If he were smart, he'd use it to heal Viridian.

Calliope engaged hyper speed, and they leapt away. "I'm making course for terrestrial ground," she announced, and Callaghan nodded.

"Thank goodness that's over," Nerissa sighed, glancing at Tabea. "Now I can go back to hating you."

A small smirk had appeared in the corners of her lips, and Tabea smirked right back at her. But Callaghan shook his head with one concerned look back at Tabea.

"No, I'm afraid it's only just begun."

Callaghan called Tabea, Nerissa, Yuri, and Sh't'ani into his office after he had settled the rest of the crew and left the bridge in Calliope's command.

He looked at them slowly, moving from one pair of eyes to the next and finally resting on Sh't'ani's two pairs.

"We haven't been officially introduced. I'm Jim Callaghan, captain of this ship."

Tabea translated for both of them.

Sh't'ani gave a little bow. "I am Sh't'ani. I was charged with looking after T'bea."

Callaghan's gaze shifted to Tabea for a moment when she translated, and she smiled.

"I vouch for them," she said sincerely. "Their heart is in the right place."

As if to reinforce the point, Sh't'ani knocked on their chest—on the right side.

Callaghan nodded, a smile now coming to his face as well. "In that case, Sh't'ani, I welcome you aboard the Calliope. You're welcome to join us as a crew member, if you wish, but we would also be happy to drop you off at an intergalactic port."

Sh't'ani glanced at Tabea, their tail waving.

"I would like to stay with T'bea. She's my friend."

Their look contained so much warmth that Tabea couldn't help herself. She threw her arms around Sh't'ani's waist insofar as it was possible for her and beamed at Callaghan while repeating Sh't'ani's words for him.

"In that case, what's your skill set or interests?" he asked.

Sh't'ani reflected on this for a moment. "I would like to learn about human food," they decided.

"Then it's settled. I'll have one of the cooks instruct you." Callaghan's gaze wandered over to Yuri, and it hardened. "From what I understand, you betrayed us to the Penyales so they could get their hands on Tabea."

Yuri cast down his eyes. "Yes. That's true."

Nerissa stepped in front of him. "He didn't have a choice," she argued. "They literally *made* him. How in the world was he meant to disobey? Besides, he helped us escape."

"He did save me from drowning," Tabea added.

Callaghan gazed sternly at the two girls, but then he sighed, defeated. "There's nothing I could say that would make you two change your minds on this, is there?"

They both vehemently shook their heads.

"All right then. Yuri, you can stay. But I haven't yet

decided in which capacity, and you can be certain that I'll be keeping an eye on you."

Yuri nodded, intimidated, but clearly relieved at the same time. Nerissa beamed at him and clutched on to his arm.

"You three are dismissed. Nerissa, show Sh't'ani to one of the empty rooms and introduce them to the cook, would you? We'll need to do something about that language barrier at some point, but I suppose that can wait a day. In the meantime, I'm guessing that Yuri can translate."

They left, leaving Tabea alone with Callaghan. Giving a deep sigh, he stood up and crossed around the table before throwing his arms around Tabea, holding her tightly.

"I have a lot of questions, but for now, I'm just really glad you're back with us, kid. For a while there, I thought we'd lost you for good."

Tabea closed her eyes and hugged him back, relishing his familiar scent that always calmed her—a scent that smelled like home.

"Never. You're stuck with me."

THE END

Acknowledgements

There are many people that deserve to be mentioned here for the part they've played in the creation of this book, and I am sure that there are many more who I haven't thought to name. But like any other author, I knew two things: I may have written the story, but the book was created by many.

Let's start with the two people adding visualization to the book and its characters: KimGDesign for the amazing work on the cover, and Alex van Gore for all the fantastic illustrations within the book.

Then there is my editor Amy McNulty, of course who got the book on the right track and helped me deal with issues that I, as not a native anglophone, would not have noticed or considered.

And I could never forget about my beta readers who gave me suggestions as to how the original story could still be improved: Peter Hanrahan, Eimear Bannister, Michaele Johnson, Sara Emrick, Rachel Baker & Natália Virág.

Additionally, there is one person in particular without whom this book would have never been written. This novel is based on a short story I wrote for my anthology "A Touch of Magic", published in 2019.

It was thanks to the enthusiasm one of the other participating authors showed for it that I even considered the possibility of turning it into a book—so thank you, Brenda J. Pierson. Without your encouragement, this book would not exist.

Of course, I also received support from other people during the making of this book, such as John Valentine—who shared his appreciation of my writing with me, Trina Birt—who will enthusiastically absorb anything I write, no matter how bad I may believe it to be, and, finally, Zerah J. Miller—a dear friend who blindly believed in me and cheered me on right up to the day she passed away.

2020 and 2021 have been trying times. I lost a dear friend, my grandmother, and my cat within a few months of one another, never even mind the pandemic, but working on this book (and several others) has helped me stay sane, focused, and hopeful. It gave me something to look forward to, even when isolation made things seem bleak. It meant that there was always something to be excited about; something I could share with those around me and help all of us escape reality for just a little while. So this part of my thanks goes to the story itself and the characters within.

MORE BOOKS BY JANINA FRANCK

Short Stories

The Weight of Time *(A Touch of Magic; 2019)*
A Spark in Space *(A Touch of Magic; 2019)*
Override *(Brave New Girls: Girls who Tech and Tinker; 2020)*
The Wizard's Bride *(Space Bound; 2021)*
Káto Kósmos *(Sing, Goddess!; 2021)*

Chronicles of the Bat

Captain Black Shadow *(2016)*
White Devil *(2018)*
Sand and Snow *(2020)*

ABOUT THE AUTHOR

Growing up in the Black Forest as a hopeless dreamer with an overactive imagination, Janina Franck began writing at a young age to give a voice to the stories living inside her head.

As a teenager, she moved to the emerald isle of legends and myths, Ireland, where she completed her basic education, and went on to study Modern Languages and Multimedia. Since then, she has also lived in Bordeaux, France, and Iporanga, Brazil.

While her surroundings changed, her desire to create stories did not, which she now pursues across various types of media, while travelling to quench her thirst for new impressions and adventures.